Into the Wonder
Book 3

Oak, Ash, and Thorn

Into the Wonder, Book 3:
Oak, Ash, and Thorn

Copyright © 2015 by Darrell J. Pursiful.

All rights reserved.

Published by Puggle Press

ISBN: 978-0692584040

Of all the trees that grow so fair,
Old England to adorn,
Greater are none beneath the Sun,
Than Oak, and Ash, and Thorn.
Sing Oak, and Ash, and Thorn, good Sirs
(All of a Midsummer morn)!
Surely we sing no little thing,
In Oak, and Ash, and Thorn!

—Rudyard Kipling,
Puck of Pook's Hill (1906)

Table of Contents

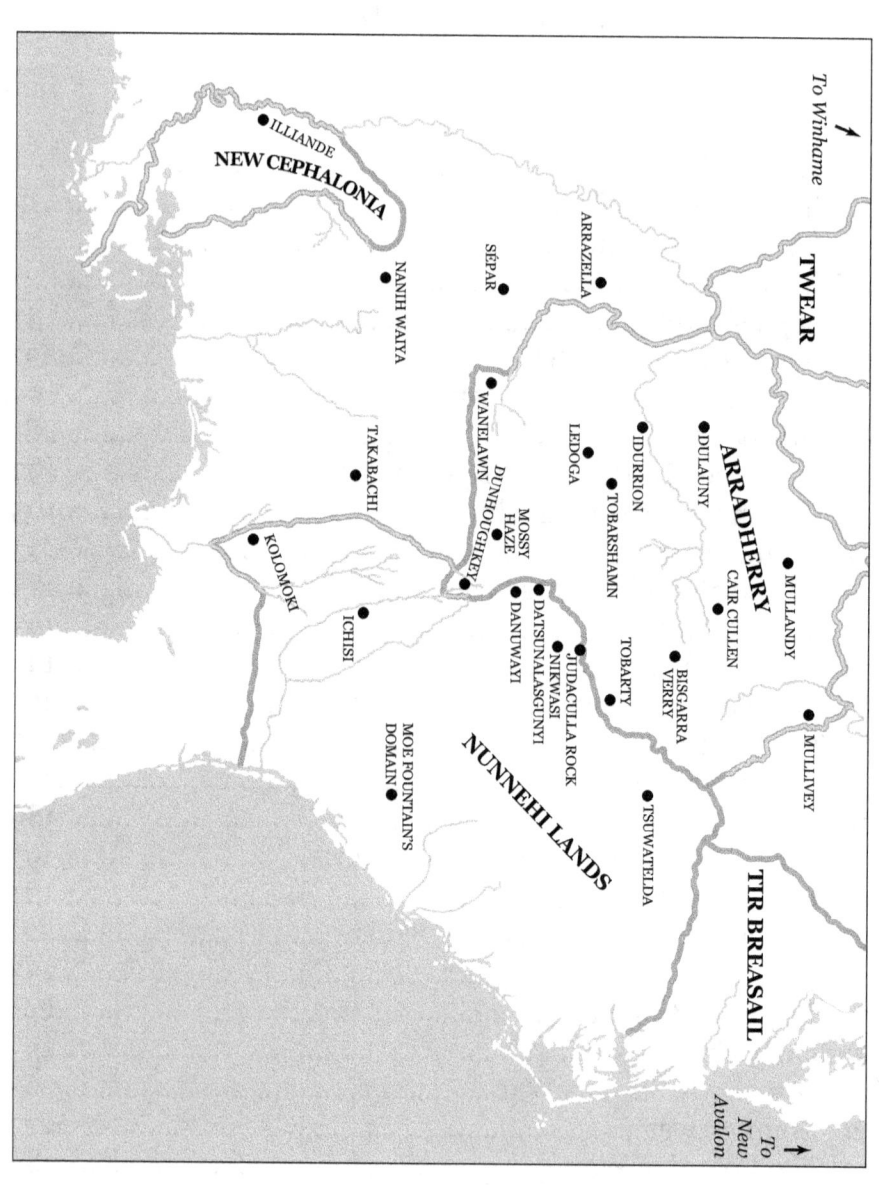

Chapter 1

Combat Magic

Taylor hit the ground half a second before an explosion of smoke and sound would have knocked her off her feet. She scrambled forward on her belly, bare feet propelling worn and calloused knees and elbows over the scorched grass.

"Get up!" her friend Ayoka shouted. "We're almost there!"

Taylor panted. She was dripping with sweat. She had swum through swamp water before, but this was worse. The grimy feel of sweat against her skin brought back unpleasant memories of the Louisiana bayou.

The pain, explosions, and shouting were new, though.

She lunged forward and somehow rose to her feet. Wobbly or not, at least it was something.

In the thick fog, she couldn't see any farther than the end of her outstretched hands. But she didn't have time to worry about visibility. The sounds of marching feet in every direction had her complete attention.

Ayoka was out there somewhere, waiting for her signal.

She cursed under her breath. *Where are you?*

Something caught her attention. It wasn't physical, but that didn't mean it wasn't real. It came in fast at eye level: a subtle pulse of magic she'd have never noticed a month ago. Instinctively, she held up the two-foot-long wooden sticks she wielded in each hand and crossed them in front of her. At the same time, she threw out a magical pulse of her own.

1

The blast ripped through her shield spell like tissue paper. The world spun around. The next thing she knew, she was lying on her back.

The marching stopped.

"Taylor!" Ayoka cried.

She struggled to hear the sounds of approaching footsteps. She knew they were coming, but the Fair Folk can move as silently as cats when they want to.

"Are you okay?" Ayoka asked as she knelt beside her friend. Taylor heard Ayoka's sticks clatter to the ground.

"No."

"Up," a firm masculine voice demanded. The speaker was still hidden in fog.

Ayoka offered Taylor an arm. Taylor clasped it and let herself be pulled to her feet. She wiped her brow. Heavy sweat splashed to the ground.

Taylor wore red gym shorts and a gray tank top, both now smudged with mud and grass stains. Her dark blonde hair was tied back in a grimy ponytail. Her elbows and knees bore bloody scrapes. Ayoka was dressed much as Taylor was, but the look seemed a lot more hardcore on her.

The fae who had blasted her finally appeared: a tall, lean nunnehi—one of the "ghost warriors" of Native American legend. Dressed in denim shorts and war paint, he stalked toward Taylor and grabbed her left wrist.

"Block!" he snarled.

He grabbed her right wrist. "Blast!" he said. He tapped the side of her head. "Focus!"

"I'm trying!" Taylor protested.

"Try harder," the young man said through gritted teeth.

"Be patient, Tsisgwa," Ayoka said. "Taylor didn't grow up playing stickball like we did. It's going to take time."

Tsisgwa grunted and walked away. With an impatient wave of his hand, the fog began to dissipate. The open field where they stood came into view, and beyond it, the houses and ceremonial

2

mounds of Ichisi, the fae city hidden in the heart of Macon, Georgia.

"I asked *you* to teach me how to fight," Taylor told Ayoka. "Not your cousin."

"I am teaching you. This is the same way I learned—the same way all nunnehi learn. Through stickball."

"War's little brother, right?" Taylor sighed.

Ayoka nodded. "There's a reason we call it that. Tsisgwa is very good, and he's a good teacher, too. He taught me. You need to listen to him."

Taylor grunted noncommittally.

"How do you feel?"

"Miserable. Sore."

"Good. You're building muscle tone."

"I'm not trying out for the Olympics. I just want to be able to defend myself from a magical attack—and fight back if I have to."

"Well, part of that is being in good physical shape."

Taylor wanted to say something back, but she thought better of it. She had, after all, been the one asking Ayoka for help. A month ago, she'd found herself in the middle of a magical firefight. She and her best friend, Jill, had barely made it out alive; and her cousin Évastre had been driven into hiding. She didn't even know she had a fae cousin until she was standing beside him in the shadow of his burned-down mansion. Évastre's was just one more life her psycho family had turned upside down.

Taylor swore to herself she would never let anything like that happen to her again. If that meant putting up with Ayoka's drill-sergeant of a brother....

Tsisgwa rejoined the girls. Now, however, another fae was with him. He was shorter than Ayoka's cousin and thickly built, but it was all muscle. His bare chest was covered with tattoos, and his head was shaven bald except for a single scalplock adorned with beads and feathers.

"Ayoka," Tsisgwa said, "this is Athlan Tastanagi."

3

The newcomer regarded both girls with steely eyes. His face was expressionless. He bowed sharply to Ayoka. "My lady," he said.

Ayoka stood tall and returned Athlan Tastanagi's bow with a slight tilt of her head. It was as if the newcomer's address transformed her. Suddenly she was no longer the stickball-playing tomboy Taylor had befriended months ago but a refined, graceful member of the fae nobility. Come to think of it, that was exactly what Ayoka was.

"A pleasure," Ayoka said with a smile. She turned to Taylor and explained, "Tastanagi is a title of rank. But I believe Athlan is actually the Tastanagi Thlakko, isn't he? The Great Tastanagi: Chief Coloma's most senior officer?"

"The Red Chief has seen fit so to honor me, my lady."

Taylor knew a little about how the nunnehi governed themselves. Each town had a White Chief who ruled in times of peace, a Red Chief who conducted warfare, and a Medicine Chief to mediate between them. Ayoka's grandfather was the White Chief of Tsuwatelda, an important nunnehi city in North Carolina.

If Athlan was second in command under the Red Chief of Ichisi, he was a very important fae indeed. That despite the fact that he didn't look much older than Tsisgwa.

"You may tell your grandfather that Tsisgwa Imathla is already distinguishing himself in the Red Chief's service."

"He'll be pleased to hear it," Ayoka said.

Taylor took it that "Imathla" was Tsisgwa's military rank. She had no clue what it meant.

Ayoka had explained that Ichisi was actually Tsisgwa's hometown. Now that he had come of age, he had pledged himself to military service there. As far as Taylor was concerned, what that really meant was that Ayoka could come visit every now and then.

"Athlan Tastanagi," Tsisgwa said, "allow me as well to present Taylor Smart, a friend of Ayoka."

For the first time, Athlan seemed to notice Taylor's presence.

"Taylor Smart, yes," he said. His eyes might have blazed holes in her, as if he were probing her, searching for something. His mouth curled into something approximating a smile. "They say you bloodied the noses of some booger fae last month. Good."

Taylor bristled. "Booger fae" was what the nunnehi called Fair Folk of European ancestry—but never to their faces. "You realize that I'm a booger fae, too. Right?"

Athlan raised his hands defensively and gave her a slight bow. "I mean no offense, Miss Smart. My people have a history with the sídhe—as no doubt you already know."

"Well, you don't have a history with me."

"Indeed," he said. Taylor crossed her arms in front of her as Athlan sized her up. "And you're learning stickball?"

"Slowly," Tsisgwa said. Taylor snapped her head at him and arched an eyebrow.

"Tsisgwa is bound to be a good teacher," Athlan said. "He is certainly a good player."

"We were just finishing for the day," Tsisgwa said.

"Were we?" Taylor asked. Now that she had caught her breath, she was ready to keep going. As much as she hated to admit it, Taylor needed what Tsisgwa could teach her.

Athlan betrayed another subtle smile.

"Are you sure, Taylor?" Ayoka said. "It's been a full morning."

"I'm ready for more," Taylor said. She glared at Tsisgwa and allowed a pulse of presence to tinge her words. "*If you are.*"

Tsisgwa smiled. He smiled easily, Taylor judged, unlike Athlan. "Good," he said. "Why don't we try your exercises again?" He turned to his commander. "Unless you have need of me, Tastanagi?"

"Not at all, Imathla. This looks interesting."

Taylor settled into the fighting stance Tsisgwa had taught her: knees bent, body slightly crouched. She held up her hands, palms out, facing Tsisgwa with about five feet of distance between them.

"Okay," she said.

5

Tsisgwa braced his left hand in front of him. "Show me a blast," he said.

Taylor flexed her right hand and closed her eyes. She reached down deep into herself to draw up feelings of anger, rage. After the workout Tsisgwa had given her, it wasn't that hard.

"Take your time," Tsisgwa said. "Remember your war-formula."

"Right," Taylor said. She hummed the simple war chant Tsisgwa had taught her. Magical energy began to warm her weary body.

She let it settle in the palm of her hand, a point of violent energy that, had she opened her eyes, would have looked like a shimmery, wispy ball. In her imagination, she bathed that ball in the power of her true name.

Neunhirri, she thought. *I am Neunhirri, Laughter in Winter.* She made the words fit the rhythm of her chant.

She opened her eyes and jerked her arm forward, imagining the energy slamming into Tsisgwa's belly with the force of a semi truck. The shimmering bolt launched toward him. Without breaking eye contact, he swept his left arm down and away from his body. The blast struck an invisible barrier inches away from him, sending out ripples of translucent smoke.

But the blast wasn't done. It rebounded toward Taylor.

She threw up both hands and shrieked.

Her own blast slammed into her chest and landed her on her back.

Ayoka let out a sympathetic moan. Athlan chuckled to himself.

"All right," Tsisgwa said. There was no missing the impatience in his voice. "You tell me: what went wrong?"

"Focus?" Taylor said.

"Magic is governed by laws," Tsisgwa said, pumping his hand for emphasis. Taylor did not like being lectured to. "One of those laws says that any spell I direct at you has the potential for creating a bond between us. It may be based on anger or hatred, but it's still a bond. If I'm not careful, my spell can backfire."

"What goes around comes around," Taylor said. Very slowly she rose to her feet, this time waving off Ayoka's help.

"That's what makes combat magic difficult," Tsisgwa said. "You've got to harness those aggressive emotions and turn them toward your enemy. But you've also got to separate yourself from them. Let them pass over you without touching you. Do you understand?"

Taylor sighed. "No, not really."

Tsisgwa grumbled.

"Then maybe that's all for today."

"No!" Taylor said. "Not till I get it right."

"I only have one day off!" Tsisgwa quipped.

"Then you're going to have to do a better job teaching me," Taylor said. She lowered herself once more into her combat stance.

"Taylor, you look beat," Ayoka said.

"*I told you I'm not finished,*" she snapped. Ayoka backed away.

"I'll drill with you," Athlan offered. Taylor, Ayoka, and Tsisgwa all stared at him.

"Call it an apology for that 'booger fae' comment."

Taylor glanced at Ayoka, who merely shrugged.

"Fine by me," Taylor said.

She and Athlan squared off. Athlan raised his left hand.

"Ready?"

Taylor nodded. She settled herself and began once more to meditate on her true name.

"Blast!" Athlan commanded.

It took a couple seconds longer than Taylor wanted, but when she finally jerked her right hand toward Athlan, she could feel the pulse of angry magic coursing from her gut all the way out to her fingertips.

Athlan blocked the attack effortlessly.

At least this time the blast didn't rebound against her.

"Not bad," Athlan judged. "Plenty of raw power, that's for sure. You need focus, however."

"So I've heard."

"Now show me how you block."

Taylor took a breath. She extended her left hand, palm outward, and cringed in anticipation.

Athlan gestured. Taylor was flat on her back—again—before she knew what hit her. Only now, she also suddenly had a splitting headache.

Athlan offered her his hand. Taylor ignored the gesture. She pulled herself up, brushed grass and dirt off her elbows, and resumed her fighting stance.

"Again," she said.

"Taylor," Ayoka said, "you don't have to—"

"*I said, 'Again'.*" All she could think of was how powerless she had felt last month, captured by hostile fae, bargaining for the life of her best friend, Jill. She didn't have a clue how to defend herself back then. It was pure luck they had escaped at all.

As it was, Taylor had ended up in debt to Mara Hellebore. The only way to save Jill was to promise her evil grandmother a favor. Taylor didn't know what Mara would demand of her, or when.

She only knew she didn't like feeling helpless.

Next time will be different, she vowed to herself.

Athlan obliged her by taking his own fighting stance.

"Blast!" Taylor said.

Athlan gestured again. He might have been swatting at a mosquito. Taylor staggered backwards three or four feet but at least managed to stay upright for a second or two before crumpling to her knees.

Ayoka approached once more to offer her a hand. Taylor waved her off. She stumbled to her feet and stalked toward Athlan.

"Had enough?" she spat.

8

Athlan quirked an eyebrow. "You are something, Taylor Smart," he said. "And I do apologize for my remark earlier. I'm afraid I dishonored myself in front of my better." He bowed his head to Ayoka. "But I must be about my duties. By your leave, my lady."

Ayoka nodded. Athlan motioned for Tsisgwa to follow him, and the two walked away.

Taylor didn't move as they veered to the right, out of her field of vision.

"Are they gone?" she asked.

"Yes."

"Then help me walk. Please?"

With Taylor's arm draped over Ayoka's shoulder, the two walked—Taylor mostly limped—to the bank of the Ocmulgee River. The two girls waded out until it was waist-deep and ducked themselves under. Ayoka had explained that running water washed away any ambient magic that might have clung to them. Taylor let the river wash away the sweat, the dirt, and the magical residue of her morning workout.

Once she had put on the dry clothes she'd left at Tsisgwa's house, she said goodbye and headed for home. It was getting on lunchtime, and she was famished.

She strolled up Ichisi's main north-south thoroughfare and through the gate at the north end of town. There, she hiked up the side of a small mound. With an effort of will and an outstretched hand, a swirl of sparkling dust whipped around the top.

Taylor stepped into the vortex. For a second, she plummeted through a whirlwind of sights and sounds—flashing lights, forest streams, massive rocks jutting toward the sky.

Then she materialized out of the chaos and into the center of a ring of mushrooms six feet across. In the Wonder, the whole area was cloaked in deep, old-growth forest. But Taylor had landed Topside, in the mortal realm. There, it was just a few acres of trees and tall grass nestled between residential streets.

9

She slogged home, hopped the back fence (the iron of the chain-link was cold to her touch and sent a momentary shiver up her arms), and walked across the yard to the back door. She still felt worn and sweaty.

Her next-door neighbor was working in her yard. She looked up to give her a suspicious look.

"Good morning, Mrs. Dibney," Taylor called, looking her straight in the eye. Mrs. Dibney pretended she hadn't been staring.

Taylor didn't have time or energy for Mrs. Dibney. She needed a shower—a real shower. She wouldn't object to a few minutes collapsed on her bed, either.

She passed through the kitchen, where her dad was sitting at the table, drinking coffee and reading the newspaper.

"Hey," he said. He set down his coffee cup and pushed his glasses back on his nose. His thinning brown hair was a few shades darker than Taylor's, and his small, paunchy form was nothing like his tall, slim daughter's.

"Hey," Taylor said.

"Good visit?"

"I guess." Taylor still wasn't sure how to talk to her parents about her other life. Which was fine, because they weren't sure how to talk to her, either. Raising a mythological being couldn't be easy. "Just let me clean up, okay?" She edged past him.

"Sure. I didn't mean to.... I'll talk to you later."

Taylor heard her father sigh as she headed toward her bedroom.

She kicked off her tennis shoes and set them in their place on her closet floor. She threw her dirty clothes in the laundry hamper and shut the lid. She rearranged some things on her desk that her mom must have moved when she'd dusted that morning.

A half hour later, she emerged from the bathroom showered and dressed in denim shorts and a tie-dyed tee shirt she liked to wear on lazy Saturdays. Recharged by the warm shower and the fresh clothes, her attention turned to food.

She made herself a peanut butter sandwich and ate it in about four bites. After making and eating another and washing it down with a glass of milk, she decided to practice her piano. It wouldn't be too many weeks until she'd resume her lessons, and Mrs. Phelps, her piano teacher, had given her plenty of things to practice over the summer.

She passed her mom on the way to the living room. Mrs. Smart was carrying a basket of clothes to the laundry room. She smiled at her daughter.

"Good morning, doodle bug," she said.

"Hi, Mom."

"Did you have a good time?"

Taylor wondered how to answer that. She had been knocked around, blasted, scared out of her wits, and baptized in river-water—and all at her own request!

"Okay, I guess." She sat down at the piano and started her warm-up exercises.

Her mom had followed her into the living room, her laundry basket balanced on her hip.

"What did you do?"

What Taylor thought was, *I was practicing how to defend myself from my homicidal grandparents!*

What she said was, "We played some stickball. It's a game they play...there."

"I see," her mom said. "It must be some kind of game. You've never been interested in sports before."

"Well...it's something Ayoka likes."

"Ayoka, your new friend?"

Mrs. Smart really was trying to process everything that Taylor had told her parents ever since she came back from Louisiana. Taylor knew it couldn't be easy. How do you deal with the fact that your adopted daughter is a being straight out of mythology?

"That's right." Taylor transitioned from simple scales to a Chopin piece she had learned by heart last year.

"Your dad and I were wondering..."

11

The tremor in Mrs. Smart's voice made Taylor stop playing and turn to face her.

"Yes?"

"We were wondering if you'd like to have Ayoka over for dinner sometime."

Taylor's heart skipped a beat. She usually felt sad for the kids in her class whose parents didn't take an interest in their lives. She was starting to see the advantages, however.

"Oh, Mom," she said. "I-I don't know if that's a good idea." She pictured Ayoka arriving looking like she did when she first met her last spring: a tall, barefooted Native American fae in blue jeans and a cloak of woven feathers. She'd just materialize out of thin air in the middle of the living room—the nunnehi were experts at invisibility—and give her parents a matching set of heart attacks.

Assuming they survived, they'd start asking her questions. They'd find out that Ayoka was actually twenty-six years old, even though she looked only half that. They'd learn that her idea of a good time involved explosions and other forms of magical mayhem on a stickball field, and that her hundred-year-old cousin commonly ran around half-naked, covered in warpaint, and wailing on people with a flaming war club.

"Ayoka is not...." Taylor was going to say her friend wasn't really a people-person, but that was a lie. In the little time they had known each other, Taylor was impressed—even a little jealous—at how easily Ayoka made friends.

Her mom looked at her, waiting for her to finish her sentence.

"She's not...from around here. She's just visiting her cousin. She'll have to go home pretty soon."

Mrs. Smart frowned, then said, "I guess school's starting back everywhere, huh?"

Taylor wasn't sure the nunnehi even had schools.

"I guess," she said.

"Well, if she visits Macon again, we'd love to have her over."

"Okay," Taylor said.

But she still wasn't sure it was a good idea.

12

Chapter 2

The Summer Court

Belas Wakefire sat on his throne, resplendent in his green and gold robes of office, an oak-leaf circlet of pure gold upon his brow. The Primus of the Summer Court of Arradherry straightened his back and uttered a single command: "Approach."

There was electricity in the air. Two hundred pairs of eyes followed the drama unfolding in the center of the chamber. The heads of all the major houses were arrayed in a circle fanning out from the Primus and the Chief Matron like the wings of a majestic eagle, wrapping the nervous young fae in its embrace. Just as many pisgies, hulderfolk, ellylls, folletti, and other lesser sprites followed the proceedings from the balcony.

The man who stepped forward was a hundred or more years the junior of the man on the throne—who himself was rather young for his position. Claudia sensed he was nervous, but also practically giddy. From her vantage point, she could see his wide grin even as he trembled before his Primus.

Claudia Fountain took in the scene from her seat behind the Primus's wife, Dubessa Fairchild. Dubessa had only been the Chief Matron of the Summer Court for a month, but she had wasted no time acclimating to her role. She sat tall and straight to the Primus's right in her flowing gossamer robes of green and gold. A wreath of columbine adorned her long, black hair. She cradled her ceremonial foxglove wand in her left hand and glanced at the other members of the Summer Triad. Claudia took up her pen and writing tablet, ready to transcribe the official proceedings of the Court.

She couldn't remember the last time this many fae had come to watch the Court's business. There were plenty of more interesting things to do in Bisgarra Verry.

She couldn't blame them. The past month had been anything but ordinary. There was no telling what might happen next.

The younger man stood before Belas. "My Primus," he said, bowing.

"Dollin Seaborn," Belas said. His voice reverberated throughout the chamber. "I thank you for your service to this Court in the administration of the recently acquired rath of Tobarty. With my own eyes I have seen that you have ruled well over the past several weeks. It has not been easy for any of us after the scandalous revelations concerning the former Chief Matron of this Court..."

A wave of hisses and mumblings broke out in the chamber. Sídhe lords and ladies whispered "oath-breaker" and scowled with revulsion.

"As I said," Belas continued, "it has not been easy for any of us. But the Summer Court is now stronger that it has been in many decades. My own brother Primus, the esteemed Crom Cornstack of the Winter Court, has acknowledged this fact by bequeathing to Summer the right to administer the rath of Tobarty."

The crowd murmured warmly.

Belas raised his voice and addressed the crowd. "The Triad and I are in agreement that Lord Seaborn henceforth be granted seisin of Tobarty as its rightful Teyrnus. What say ye?"

The claps, foot stomps, and shouts of "Indeed!" and "Hear, hear!" confirmed the lords and ladies of the daoine sídhe agreed with the Court's decision.

"You have proven yourself worthy, Lord Seaborn. Receive your reward."

Belas's eyes twinkled as he held out his hands, cupped, as if to receive a gift. Seaborn stepped forward, knelt, and folded

14

his own hands together in what Claudia's human mother would have thought a gesture of prayer, and then placed those hands within the Primus's waiting grasp.

The Primus raised his voice again. As he spoke, he infused his words with a rustle of presence, the mysterious power the sídhe used to project an aura of unquestioned authority. "May the Court records show," he said, "that on this, the final day of the Summer Assize in the forty-first year of my Primacy, the Triad and I concur in naming Dollin Seaborn as Teyrnus of Tobarty."

The hall erupted in applause. Claudia jotted notes so she could prepare a proper record of the meeting later for Dubessa.

The newly installed Teyrnus of Tobarty stood and backed away, still bowing to his Primus, until he reached the middle of the open floor. Then he turned and walked back to his seat.

Belas allowed the celebration to continue for a minute or more before quieting the crowd with a raised hand.

"There is one final action this Court must take before rule passes to the Autumn Court tomorrow," he said. He gritted his teeth and continued to project presence. This was going to be the hard one, Claudia knew.

"It is left for us to finalize the composition of the Summer Triad."

Murmuring broke out once again. The make-up of the new Triad had been a contentious topic for more than a month.

Claudia wasn't at all sure Belas Wakefire could resolve the matter in a single day.

The Summer Primus once again raised a hand. Though it took a bit longer this time, the crowd eventually quieted down.

"First, as to the matter of the matronship of Nuala Redmane, the Court agrees with the findings of Chief Matron Fairchild's internal investigation that Matron Redmane had no knowledge or complicity in the crimes of her cousin, the former Chief Matron."

The young blonde fae two seats down on Dubessa's right nodded courteously, if not warmly. Dubessa returned the gesture.

A few people grumbled at the Primus's declaration, but not many. Some even dared to clap their hands.

The reaction didn't surprise Claudia. Even though Anya Redmane had been disgraced, it would have been hard to depose Nuala without it looking like a purge of anyone opposed to Dubessa. If the new Chief Matron had to irritate the conservatives who demanded all honors be stripped from the house of Redmane, she was confident a show of mercy would solidify her reputation as an evenhanded and forgiving leader.

Plus, Dubessa's support for her continued service placed Nuala in her debt.

And the daoine sídhe always kept score.

"Second, as to the matter of elevating a new member to the Triad..."

The murmuring continued. A chant of "Osanda! Osanda!" broke out in the balcony. Some on the main floor grumbled about unruly commoners.

Dubessa whispered something to the woman on her immediate right—a blonde woman about Dubessa's age, give or take a century. The look on the new Chief Matron's face could have soured milk. Claudia steeled herself against the subtle traces of magic that swirled around the room. Waves of presence ebbed and flowed. To someone of lesser abilities, being in the thick of it would have been suffocating, disorienting.

"It is the decision of the Court...," Belas continued. The cries of "Osanda!" only died down when several sídhe nobles furtively gestured for those in the balcony to hold their peace.

"It is the decision of the Court that Gwenllian Birdsong—"

A chorus of boos erupted, mainly from the balcony. On the floor, half the Gentry stood to clap their hands. Claudia hunched over her writing tablet to block out the chaos. Things were only going to get worse. She had to keep her wits.

16

"*Order!*" Belas demanded. He projected a wave of presence that brought the room to attention.

"Primus," Dubessa said. The Chief Matron always referred to her husband by his title at Court proceedings. The uproar from the upper gallery had given her time to compose herself. Whatever she was feeling—and Claudia had no doubt she was furious—none of it escaped onto her face or into her voice. "If it please the Court, perhaps I could speak to this matter?"

Belas gestured for her to proceed.

The Chief Matron stood to speak. "The Court is well aware that Acting Matron Birdsong has served with distinction since the unfortunate events of June," she said. "Her loyalty to the Court is unquestioned, her honor is irreproachable, and her obvious intelligence and skills are already a proven asset—"

"And the fact she's the Primus's cousin is just a happy coincidence, is it?"

Sídhe lords and ladies gasped as all eyes turned toward a brunette woman clothed in green and brown.

This woman stood and gazed intently in the direction of the Chief Matron. She displayed not a trace of fear.

Her name was Osanda Morning.

Dubessa regarded her for several tense seconds.

"Cousins by marriage, not by blood," Gwenllian Birdsong said through clenched teeth. "Though I don't see why that matters, Ms. Morning."

The brunette fae smiled broadly. "Of course you don't," she said. "I'm sure it doesn't matter at all that we are giving our new Chief Matron not one but two Triad members beholden to her."

More murmuring and grumbling broke out all around the chamber. Gwenllian Birdsong nearly sprung from her seat, only held back by Dubessa's hand on her arm.

"The first should be grateful she hasn't been banished along with her oath-breaking cousin," she continued, "and the second is already bound to the house of Fairchild by her marriage to Aemeron Wakefire." She planted her hands on her hips.

17

"How could that *possibly* interfere with the fair and unbiased operations of the Summer Court?"

The balcony once again erupted in shouts of "Osanda!"

"Gwenllian Birdsong's reputation is beyond reproach," Dubessa insisted. "She comes from a distinguished house of the tylwyth teg and offers this Triad a measure of much-needed diversity."

"I thank you, Chief Matron," Acting Matron Birdsong said.

Osanda Morning merely scoffed.

"You've had your say, Osanda," Dubessa said. "It's time we moved forward."

"Despite the obvious divisions among the Gentry?"

There was more grumbling and whispering.

"We must provide a united front," Dubessa said. "We dare not lose our advantage over Winter just as their lieutenants in the Autumn Court begin their Assize. You know that."

"I find it questionable whether we have yet an advantage to lose, Chief Matron," Ms. Morning said. "And I fail to see the wisdom of unity at the price of our principles."

At this, the balcony erupted in applause—as did many among the Gentry.

"The era of the former Chief Matron is behind us," Ms. Morning said. "We dare not continue to skulk and scheme like a brood of unseelie nightwalkers."

"Hear, hear!" an older sídhe interjected. Claudia recognized him as one of the more conservative members of a well-regarded family. She glanced at the balcony. If Osanda Morning commanded support not only from the commoners but also from the likes of Tellus Forge....

"Summer is meant for better things than that," Ms. Morning continued. "We are the brightest and best of fae society. It behooves us to act like it."

"Be that as it may," Belas said. "It is the decision of the Court that Gwenllian Birdsong be elevated—" The chambers practically shook. Belas shouted, "...to a permanent seat on the Summer Triad!"

18

"Osanda! Osanda!" the balcony thundered. Arguments broke out among the Gentry on the main floor.

Belas looked at the ceiling and pinched the bridge of his nose. He glanced across to his wife, who subtly shook her head.

"The Court will come to order!" he called.

Claudia got her tablet ready. She had known what was coming was a possibility. She also knew it was something Belas and Dubessa had hoped to avoid.

"*Order!*" Belas repeated. Gradually, the crowd settled down.

"Well," he said. "It is obvious that the Gentry are divided." Claudia could see he was choosing his words carefully. He held his head up, though, both confident and defiant. No one would have known from his expression that he had just lost a round to a powerful rival.

"May it never be said that your Primus refuses to listen to the wisdom of his peers," he said. "We have a difference of opinion about who would best serve the Summer Court as the newest member of its Triad. It seems unlikely we will be able to reach a consensus before the Assize concludes at sundown tonight. I propose we table the matter for now."

More murmuring, but this time more appreciative, bubbled through the chamber.

"The Court..." He hesitated, but only for a second. "The Court rescinds its recommendation for the elevation of Acting Matron Birdsong subject to further review. Let the two Gentrywomen each make her case to the ruling houses."

"And then?" Gwenllian challenged. The color had drained from her face, just as her hopes of an easy confirmation drained from the room.

"Technically, we have until the Eve of Beltane to decide," Belas said. He swallowed. "At that time, after both candidates have been given a fair hearing, I will abide by the decision of the Gentry."

Claudia bit her lip. Nine months. How much mischief could Gwenllian and Osanda wage in nine months?

The suggestion seemed to satisfy the crowd, though. That is, except for Belas Wakefire, Dubessa Fairchild, and Gwenllian Birdsong.

"Does anyone else have business to bring before this Court?" the Primus asked. The crowd was mercifully silent.

"Hearing none, let the Summer Court stand adjourned."

Chapter 3

Merely Mortal Enemies

In Macon, Georgia, school started the first week of August, with Taylor knocking on Jill Matthews's door first thing in the morning.

Jill's twin brother, William, met her and breezed passed with a nod and a goofy smile. "See you later," he said.

It must have been hard on William seeing his sister...the way she was.

She sat in the living room with her backpack at her feet. Her hands clenched the armrests of a big, comfy chair, but she didn't look comfortable.

Her mom was doing something in the kitchen. Finding any excuse not to be in the room while Taylor was busy trying to keep her daughter from going insane.

"Morning," Taylor said.

Jill nodded.

"Ready?"

Jill sighed. "Gonna have to be." She sat up straight. Taylor pulled over a footstool and sat facing her friend.

"All those people...," Jill muttered.

"It'll be okay," Taylor said. She took a couple of deep breaths, calling on the power of her true name. Almost instantly, she felt the tickle of magical energy dancing up and down her body like static electricity.

"Last night was rough," Jill volunteered. "Last-minute school shopping."

"Uh huh."

"Crowds are the worst."

"That's what you've said."

"I just...can't handle seeing, well, *everything*."

"I bet a bunch of frantic parents and kids the night before school starts would be rough." Taylor imagined the magic she had gathered wafting across the space between her and Jill. She tried to will her magic to touch Jill's eyes.

"That's not the half of it," Jill said. "It's not just emotions. When I look at somebody, I see...I don't know...who they really are. What they're all about."

"Yeah?"

"There was this mom at Walmart. She looked fine on the surface, but..." Jill shuddered. "She wasn't right. Something was wrong with her. I don't know what, but it was like she was being crushed under a thousand-pound weight."

"That's intense."

"There's more people like that than you'd think. And you know the worst part?" Her voice broke. "There's nothing I can do to help them."

Taylor didn't say anything. She tried not to show it, but she was boiling mad inside. Mara Hellebore had done this, opening up Jill's Second Sight so far she couldn't shut it down even when she wanted to.

She just sighed and kept pouring magic into her friend's eyes.

"But it's not all bad, right? I bet babies are fun to look at."

"Sometimes I almost think I can guess what they're going to be when they grow up." Jill grinned, but only for a second. "It's hard to explain. I'll imagine somebody dressed in a fancy suit. Or they'll be holding something—a tool or a book, maybe."

"So, it's kind of symbolic?"

"Yeah."

Taylor bit her lip. There was something she hadn't yet dared to ask.

"What do you see...when you look at me?"

Jill hesitated. Taylor looked at her.

"Nothing."

"Nothing?"

Jill shook her head. "It's like you're not even there."

"Whoa."

"But I don't think that's a bad thing," Jill quickly added. "At least, it's not to me. Taylor, you're the one person who's not going to freak me out if I...if I really see them."

"It must mean I'm the one person in the world who's exactly what she appears to be," Taylor said, grinning.

A half-hour later, Taylor sat stewing through first period.

It wasn't enough that for the first time in middle school she and Jill were not in the same cluster group.

It wasn't enough that she was still worn out from trying to pump as much magic as possible into Jill to keep her from freaking out around other people.

What really got to her was that Principal McFarland, in his infinite wisdom, had decided to move Mrs. Markowitz from seventh grade to eighth.

Mrs. Markowitz was starting her thirty-fifth—and last, she declared with a sigh—year of teaching English at Archibald Bulloch Middle School. The projection equipment, though standard in every classroom, hung unused from the ceiling as she waddled back and forth writing on the board, explaining the topics they would be covering that year—and her expectations as far as discipline. Mrs. Markowitz was what you'd call "old school."

Rules weren't really Taylor's thing, however, and she'd heard all Mrs. Markowitz's speech before. It's not that she was bad. She didn't get sent to the principal's office nearly as often as some kids. She understood right from wrong. She didn't bother anybody—and she wished everybody else would just leave her alone. But school rules didn't always make sense to her, and she had never been afraid to say so.

23

Mrs. Markowitz droned on and on about her classroom rules. Her tiny, round body was full of vigor despite her years. Her short hair was fiery red—bordering on orange. She never managed to buy the same kind of hair color twice in a row. Taylor had thought about starting a betting pool on what color it would be next month.

She glanced across the room to where William Matthews was taking copious notes. What, she wondered, was Mrs. Markowitz saying that was worth writing down?

William and Jill were both a lot better at rule-following than she was. She figured that was one reason her parents encouraged her friendship with Jill, hoping sooner or later some of that general agreeableness would rub off on her.

Stranger things have happened.

On the other side of the room, Shelby Crowthers pretended to pay attention to the board while checking out the cute boys. The pickings were pretty slim, Taylor thought. Middle-school boys seemed to suffer their own unique form of brain damage that only got worse in the presence of girls like Shelby.

Jared McCaughey sat behind William—but Shelby would rather be seen in public without her makeup than admit Jared McCaughey was cute. He had committed the unpardonable sin of continually failing to recognize how cool and pretty Shelby was.

He seemed to take his rejection in stride. To be honest, Taylor wasn't sure he'd ever realized he was in Shelby's doghouse.

And he *was* pretty cute.

At long last, the bell rang, and Taylor and her classmates headed for science with Mrs. Cline, a so-so teacher about her parents' age. Then it was off to lunch and—hopefully—a few minutes with Jill.

Jill's class was already in the cafeteria when Taylor arrived, but she had managed to save her friend a seat. Taylor set her tray on the table and sat down.

24

"So, what's Mr. Appletree like?" Taylor asked. Jill's schedule put her one period ahead of Taylor as they rotated through their core classes.

"Not too bad," Jill said with a frown. "His eyebrows are a little distracting. And it looks like a lot more geometry this year."

"You made it through Barfield's class last year."

"Thanks to you." Jill forked a chicken nugget into her mouth.

"How are you feeling? Are you keeping it together?"

"I'm okay," Jill said. Taylor noticed she'd been keeping her head down. "Let's not talk about that here."

"Whatever. Just asking."

Taylor rearranged the orangey-brown lump on her plate. The cafeteria lady had said it was sweet potato, but she wasn't entirely convinced.

A loud crash interrupted the conversation.

Tommy Morgan had spilled his lunch tray. A couple of kids started clapping and cheering—standard procedure at Bulloch Middle School. Tommy turned red as he scrambled to clean up his mess as best he could.

"Way to go, Tommy!" Shelby Crowthers cackled one table over. She and her best friend, Jasmine Brown, giggled to themselves—but not so quietly that everybody couldn't hear them.

"That boy is hopeless," Shelby chuckled.

"Two left feet," Jasmine chimed in.

"Give it a rest, will you?" Taylor blurted. "Like you've never done anything klutzy?"

Shelby whipped around in her chair. She flipped her long blonde hair out of her face with the practiced ease of a super-model in training.

"Tommy is beyond klutzy," she said with a smirk. Then she affected an attitude of concern. "Oh, did I hurt your feelings? Is he your new boyfriend?"

Taylor twisted around. "Nobody deserves to be laughed at, Shelby. Didn't they teach you that in kindergarten? Or were you absent that day?"

Shelby sniffed. "Yep, he's your boyfriend all right."

25

Taylor felt her body tingle: an electric shiver creeping up her spine. She was instinctively gathering magic, drawing it from the Wonder. She suppressed the urge to give it form.

"Now you listen here," Taylor started.

"Taylor," Jill said. Taylor knew that tone: Keep cool. Walk away.

"You know," Taylor said. "I just realized you're not worth arguing with." She hazarded a bite of chicken. A bit too salty, but not bad as far as school food goes.

Shelby just sputtered. She said something impolite and sort of obscene, but Taylor pretended not to hear it.

The magic drained off her and back to wherever it went when she didn't need it. Jill watched her compose herself. She probably couldn't see the magic swirling around without opening her Second Sight—and she'd been working hard not to to that. Just as well, Taylor thought. No need to freak her out using magic at school.

"One of these days," Taylor whispered, "Shelby is going to do something that makes her look stupid. And if there is justice in the universe, I'll be there to watch."

"Amen," Jill said.

Taylor spent most of Mr. Appletree's math class wondering how soon they would get their elective class assignments. She always signed up for chorus as her first choice.

She hadn't had a lot of luck with her second choices. Her parents insisted she do phys-ed last fall. With her asthma, they always worried about her overall health and thought some structured exercise would do her good. It was a disaster. On the days she even felt like dressing, she always got picked last, she got worn out halfway through the period, and she ended up going to her next class red-faced, sweaty, and out of breath.

She spent the spring semester of seventh grade in art. It wasn't bad, but Mr. Kirby was fresh out of college and let the kids walk all over him. The class was a complete joke, and Taylor put her foot down and refused to sign up for it again. She heard a rumor that Mr. Kirby quit at the end of the year for "health

26

reasons." She figured that was grown-up for he'd gotten sick of teaching.

She doodled in her notebook as Mr. Appletree explained about the textbook and how students could go to a website at home and get extra help with their homework.

Mr. Appletree was almost as old as Mrs. Markowitz and almost as short. His bushy eyebrows popped up from behind his horn-rimmed glasses. (Jill was right: they were very distracting.) He spoke in a monotone that didn't mix well with a full stomach and a warm, summer afternoon.

Shelby propped her head in her hands and struggled to stay awake.

Jared McCaughey noticed and winked at Taylor. Taylor smiled in spite of herself.

William took notes. Lots and lots of notes.

And then it was off to social studies.

Mr. Ramos was Taylor's homeroom teacher. She had reported to his room first thing for attendance and morning announcements, then headed off to Mrs. Markowitz to have the life sucked out of her.

Mr. Ramos was new. He looked as young as the artful Mr. Kirby, but he wore a broad smile and almost bounced with enthusiasm as the students filed into his classroom. He called most of them by name.

"Good afternoon, Jared!" he said. He had the slightest trace of a Spanish accent. "Good to see you, Shelby! Tommy, what's up?"

He wants to be our friend, Taylor realized. *This is going to be a disaster.*

His thick, black hair was a little longer than most teachers', and he wore blue jeans with his dress shirt and tie. He had rolled his sleeves up, and his sport coat was draped over his desk chair as if he hadn't had time to hang it up.

He waited for everyone to find their seat.

"Now, I know you've been dying to find out what we'll be doing in social studies this year," he began. He was grinning ear to ear.

It should be a crime to be that excited about social studies, Taylor thought.

He rattled on for a while. Geography. States and capitals. Georgia history. Whatever. But Taylor perked up when he said, "...and we'll talk a little about Creek and Cherokee mythology."

"You mean like the nunnehi?" she said.

Mr. Ramos gave her a curious look. "That's right, Taylor. Among other things. I'm surprised you've heard of them."

"Taylor's into all that geeky mythology stuff," Shelby offered. For once, Taylor didn't mind Shelby's interruption. She wasn't sure how to explain that she had been spending her weekends with the nunnehi!

"Well, that's very interesting," Mr. Ramos continued, smiling. "Though we prefer the word 'nerd.'"

The class giggled at that.

He continued, "And there's nothing wrong with being nerdy, Shelby. Anybody can be cool. There are entire industries dedicated to telling you what's cool and what's not. TV, movies, music.... Coolness is the path of least resistance. But being a nerd? Well, that takes courage! It means you stand out from the crowd—but you're okay with that. It means you're comfortable just being yourself, even if other people laugh at you. Am I right?"

A few kids—mostly the type that Shelby liked to crack on— nodded or murmured things like "That's right" and "Yeah." William actually clapped his hands—but stopped when nobody else joined in.

Taylor flashed her sweetest smile toward Shelby, who just sat there seething.

"So, here's the rule in my class," Mr. Ramos continued. "Everybody is free to be themselves, and everybody is entitled to the same level of respect that you would expect from others. Are we clear?"

"Yes, Mr. Ramos," the class agreed.

"Now, I have some paperwork to give you. Your parents need to fill this all out and you can bring it back to me tomorrow. All right?"

When the final bell rang, Taylor sprang from her seat and maneuvered through the crowd to her locker. By the time she was ready to go, Jill had arrived.

"Mrs. Markowitz really needs to retire," she said with a sigh.

"Tell me about it," Taylor said. Then she grinned. "What did you think of Mr. Ramos?"

Jill smiled.

"Mr. Ramos won't last two months at this school," Shelby said from behind them.

"Is that so?" Jill said, spinning to face her.

"Oh, give me a break! With all that touchy-feely crap? 'Coolness is the path of least resistance,'" she said, mocking his accent. She shook her head. "This place is going to eat him alive."

Once again, Taylor felt a tingle of magical energy swirling around her.

"It must be tough being the center of the universe, Shelby," Taylor said. "Does everything revolving around you ever make you seasick?"

"You think you're so smart," Shelby scoffed. "You're just a freak, you know that? Is that why you ran away from home? Because you finally figured out what a loser you are and you couldn't take it any more?"

Taylor whipped around. If anybody was going to say something about her making the news over the summer for supposedly running away from home, it would have been Shelby.

The frustrating part was, there was no other way to explain it—not without getting locked up in some institution. *That's right, officer. I only ran away to escape from the evil faeries who were trying to kill me. But we've got that all sorted out now, so no problem!*

It didn't make hearing it any easier.

29

Jill came to Taylor's defense. "Shelby, just be quiet about things you don't understand," she said.

"Oh, I understand," Shelby nodded. "You may not want to admit it, but your friend is cuckoo for Cocoa Puffs."

"*That's enough,*" Taylor said. She spoke barely above a whisper, but she intentionally threw enough presence into the words to force Shelby to pay attention.

Shelby gasped, and her face went blank, as if she had forgotten what she was about to say.

"*Now leave.*"

Shelby took a deep breath and tried to compose herself. As she turned away, she muttered, "Freak." She sashayed off, finding the nearest cute guy to smile at on her way down the hall.

And then she walked straight into the boys' bathroom.

"Hey!" some boy shouted.

"Get outta here!" another demanded.

Shelby practically bounded out of the boys' room. She kept her head down, but Taylor could see her pink, blushing face beneath a veil of blonde hair. She shuffled down the hall without looking up and quickly vanished.

Kids clapped and cheered.

Boy, it felt good to see Shelby make a fool of herself.

William Matthews emerged from the boys' room, wide-eyed. He approached his sister.

"Somebody want to tell me what just happened? Was that Shelby Crowthers in the...in the..."

"That was her," Jill said. "As to what happened..." She glanced at Taylor, who only smiled innocently.

"I...I guess she got confused," Taylor said. Try as she might, she couldn't keep the grin off her face. "It could happen to anybody."

Jill arched an eyebrow and crossed her arms. "Uh huh," she said.

30

Chapter 4

The Rules of Magic

Friday night after the second week of school, the Matthews's houseguest arrived. William was out the door as soon as the old burgundy Buick LeSabre rolled into the driveway. His mom wasn't far behind.

His sister, Jill, watched from the front window.

The driver's door slowly swung open. An older lady eased herself out—short, round, and draped in a loose-fitting dress of yellow, brown, and red. Atop her head was a mass of gray hair twists, tied in a knot in the back and trailing halfway down her back.

Behind her turtle-shell glasses, her bright, brown eyes twinkled.

She was exhausted, William judged, but she didn't want to show it.

"Maymay!" he shouted.

William's grandmother smiled her big, infectious smile and raised an arm that barely reached high enough to hug his neck. He had gotten taller over the past few months. He had to keep pulling down the tail of his favorite Superman tee shirt to keep from showing his belly button. And (to his great relief!) his voice had finally stopped cracking every other sentence.

His mom smiled.

"Good trip, Momma?"

"Good," she said. She leaned on her walking stick. "But too darned long! William, help me with my things, will you?"

31

She ambled to the trunk and popped it open. Her orange tabby cat, Merle, hopped out of the car and began to inspect the front lawn.

William hefted a suitcase in each arm and started for the house.

"I wish you'd have let us buy you a plane ticket," Jill's mom said.

"Then I'd have had to ship my things. Really, Sophie, you worry too much."

William's mom pulled a third suitcase out of Maymay's trunk. For her part, Maymay shouldered a huge green canvas bag and took her time reaching the front porch. She limped a little, but she had her old, hand-carved walking stick to lean on. Who knows how many hours she had logged in the car the past few days? But more than that, she acted like whatever she was carrying was super heavy.

She stopped in the doorway, closed her eyes, and breathed deeply. "Good," she said. "Very good."

A second later, she noticed Jill off to her left in the living room.

"There's my girl!" she said.

The two drifted easily and quickly into a warm embrace.

William approached, not wanting to interrupt. "Maymay," he said at last, "your room is this way."

The Matthews's guest room was small but comfortable. The three suitcases were already out on the double bed. A chest of drawers and a small writing desk completed the room's furnishings.

"Jill, help me clear off some space on the desk, won't you?"

"Yes, ma'am."

Maymay took stock of the room, nodding with approval. Merle leaped onto the bed and stared back and forth between Jill and William.

"This will do just fine." Maymay smiled. "Oh, William?"

"Yes, Maymay?"

32

She set her canvas bag on the desk and was already pulling out a plastic shopping bag filled with a rainbow of tiny Tupperware containers. As William approached, she handed him four horseshoes.

"William, I want you to find a hammer and some nails in your daddy's tool chest and put these up."

He was sure his jaw dropped onto his chest.

Maymay chose not to notice. "Front door, back door, Jill's room, and your room, I think. Just to be on the safe side."

"Uh..."

"And if your momma asks, tell her to come talk to me."

"Yes, ma'am." William took the horseshoes and ducked into the hall. But not before he heard his grandmother giving instructions to her cat.

"Give the place a good once-over, will you, Merle?"

The cat mewed and scooted out the door.

William found a hammer and some nails easily enough. He carried them in one hand and the four horseshoes in the other to the front door.

He looked up, decided he would need a chair to stand on, and left everything in the entryway while he went to get one. He met his mother on his way back from the kitchen.

"William, what are you doing?" his mom asked.

"Maymay wanted me to...uh...hang some horseshoes..." It sounded stupid when he said it out loud like that.

"What?"

"She said they go over the doors..."

His mom rolled her eyes, sighed, and took off toward the guest room. William figured he might as well follow her.

He entered the room two steps behind his mom. Maymay was deep in conversation with Jill.

"Now, as soon as I get these suitcases off my bed," she was saying, "I'm going to take a nap. Don't forget to practice your breathing exercises before you go to bed. We talked about that in New Orleans. We'll get started tomorrow. And unless your

33

momma has other plans, I'll make us some red beans and rice tomorrow night for supper."

Maymay had finished emptying her canvas bag onto the writing desk. In addition to the little containers of who-knows-what, there was something that looked for all the world like a magic wand, ancient and decorated with intricate carvings. And there were some books. William read the cover of the one on top.

"Grimms' Fairy Tales?" he asked.

"Knowledge is power," Maymay said. "It's mostly accurate, at least in my experience."

"Momma," William's mom interrupted. There was a note of confusion in her voice. "Did you ask William to nail horseshoes to the walls?"

"That's right," Maymay said. "Better safe than sorry."

William hovered behind his mom, still mystified by his assignment—and a little bit freaked out by the fact that his grandmother owned a magic wand! Merle weaved between his legs.

"B-but...?"

"Y'all have a good, strong threshold, Sophie, but you can never be too careful. I'll add some wards as soon as I get my things sorted. The horseshoes will help, too." She nodded toward Jill. "Iron, you know."

"Iron," Mom repeated.

"It wouldn't hurt if we had a couple more—for your room and mine."

"Fine. I'll just look up blacksmiths in the phone book."

"Your best bet's Ebay," Maymay said. "Just make sure they're good, old-fashioned wrought-iron horseshoes. Aluminum won't do a lick of good. Understand?"

Mom closed her eyes and expelled a long, slow breath.

"Listen, Sophie," Maymay said. "I tried to protect you from all of this when you were little. Maybe that was a mistake; I don't know. But things have changed. The Good Neighbors went after my grandbaby. I'm not going to take that lying down."

34

"The Good Neighbors?" Jill said.

"That's what the French called them. *Les bons voisins.* You don't want to be badmouthing them—even if you want to. They're very touchy."

She turned back to Mom. "Now, I can help if you'll let me. I can make sure the house is safe. And I can help Jill, too. She has a gift, but she can't control it yet."

"Control it?" Mom said. "Can't you just...make it go away?"

"I'm sorry, Sophie," Maymay said. "It's just who she is. The Good Neighbors did something to her, true, but she had her gift before they ever came into the picture. We'd be having this conversation sooner or later."

It didn't take Jill's Second Sight to realize Mom was struggling with all of this. Mrs. Matthews bit her lower lip and looked first at Jill, then at Maymay. William tried, unsuccessfully, to nudge Merle away.

"I don't understand this," she said. "But I want Jill safe." She let out a long sigh. "What do I have to do?"

"Let William nail up those horseshoes," Maymay said. "Start buying milk in half-gallons instead of gallons. You can keep one in the fridge and the other in the freezer until we need it. Two witches in the house means milk is liable to start curdling. There's not much to be done about it till Jill gets her gift under control."

"Milk curdling?" William said with a grin. "My sister makes milk go bad? Oh, I cannot wait to tell—"

"Nobody," Jill said with fire in her eyes. "You're telling nobody. Got it, bro?"

William knew enough to be quiet, but he couldn't help giggling a little.

"And Jill and I will need someplace we can work undisturbed. What's in your basement?"

"Other than the laundry room? Not much. We mostly use it for storage."

35

"That's perfect. We'll work every weekend. School nights if you don't have too much homework. And Sophie, I'll want to work with William, too."

"Me?" William gasped. This wasn't as amusing as it was a minute ago.

"What?" Jill and her mom sputtered together.

"Jill tells me you've got at least a little bit of Second Sight," Maymay said. "What do you think, Merle?"

The cat mewed. Only then did it leave William's side and jump back onto the bed.

"Well, there you have it," Maymay said. She looked lovingly at William. "If you'll work with me now, we can head off any problems like your sister is having."

William wouldn't have thought he could be any more bewildered than he already was. As it turned out, he was wrong.

The next morning, William threw on a pair of shorts and a plain black tee shirt. He wasn't sure exactly what to expect, so he just dressed as he normally would for a Saturday at home. He did, however, salvage a spiral notebook from last year's supply. He took a pen and crossed out "English." He wasn't sure what he should write instead.

He padded downstairs. His dad was in the kitchen reading the newspaper and drinking coffee. He wore nice shorts and his white polo shirt with "Riverview High School Athletic Department" over his heart. He had a whistle around his neck on a nylon cord.

"How's the football team shaping up?" William asked.

"Huh?" His dad looked up from his paper. "Oh. Fine. A lot of good kids this year."

"That's good," William said.

Mr. Matthews folded his newspaper. "So.... Horseshoes, huh?"

William gulped. "Maymay told me to—"

"I know. You're not in trouble."

36

"Is Mom mad?"

"Oh, yes. But she'll get over it. She's gone to get her hair done. That should give her a little time to cool off. She's not too keen on all this...whatever you want to call it."

Maymay called it magic. William wasn't sure what to call it, but whatever it was, he knew it was for real. Jill came back different after running away with Taylor. It was like part of her had shut down—or rather, she was trying to shut down something inside her that she didn't like.

He couldn't explain it any better than that, but he and Jill could always tell when something was up with one another. Something was definitely heavy on Jill's heart.

"Maymay says she can help Jill," William said.

Mr. Matthews grunted.

"D-do you think she can?"

William's dad put down his coffee cup and folded his hands in front of him.

"My grandma used to talk about folks going to see the root doctor to get curses lifted off of them. She thought it was the dumbest thing there ever was. I can hear her now, laughing at the whole idea...."

He leaned forward. "But there's no denying something has got hold of your sister. And my mother-in-law is about the wisest woman I've ever known."

The Matthews men sat in silence for the longest time. At last, Mr. Matthews said, "Take care of your sister, William."

"D-dad?"

"I'm going to hope and pray that Maymay can help her. I'm willing to believe she can. But either way, she can't follow her to school. To church youth meetings. You two have always leaned on each other.... I don't want that to stop."

"I know."

"If you wanted to pick back up with your tae kwan do lessons...we could find the money somewhere."

37

William was suddenly awake. He'd given up martial arts a couple years ago. His parents didn't want the after-school lessons to interfere with his grades.

"I'll think about it."

"I've tried to prepare you kids, William." Mr. Matthews's hands balled into fists. "Peer pressure, bullies, profiling. It can be a dangerous world."

"You've done great, Dad." William wiped dust or something from his eyes. Because he was totally not about to cry.

"The last few weeks, it looks like the world got a whole lot bigger. A whole lot scarier. Magic? Evil faeries?" He laughed, but there was no humor in it. "So, if your sister needs you...if your mother or I can't be there for her..."

"I'll take care of her."

"Good."

"Has Maymay gotten up yet?"

Mr. Matthews smiled. "She's been up for a couple hours. Last I saw her, she was asking if we had any gardening tools."

William quirked an eyebrow.

"Go look for her if you want," Mr. Matthews said. "I've got to get to work."

William found his grandmother at the corner of the front lawn, digging in the grass with a garden trowel. She'd laid her walking stick on the ground. She reached past it to a brown paper bag from which she drew a small object: some kind of statue as best William could tell.

She dropped the thing in the hole, talking to herself the whole time.

William stepped off the front porch and approached her.

Maymay gestured with her hands, and William realized she wasn't talking to herself. She was talking to whatever it was she was burying in the yard.

By the time William came up beside her, she had finished her conversation and begun packing the dirt back into the hole.

"Good morning, William!" She said. "Help me up, will you?"

"Maymay, what—?"

"Just a little extra protection, sweetheart. Is Jill up yet?"

"I think so."

"Good. Then it's time we got started."

By the time Jill joined them in the basement, William had stacked most of the boxes and random junk along the far wall and rolled up the big area rug to expose the black and white tile floor. Maymay sat on a folding chair, unpacking a hodgepodge of equipment from her canvas bag onto a card table.

William sat across from her.

"Morning," Maymay said jovially. "Sleep well?"

"Yes, ma'am."

"Then let's get to work." She pulled out a couple of black stones from her bag.

William lifted one to inspect it more closely. It was about as wide across as a watch face, but lighter in his hand than he'd expected. Etched on both sides were jagged lines with no discernible pattern. They might have been criss-crossing lightning bolts. Maybe ancient runes.

"What is this?" William asked.

"Think of it as a spell-jamming device. It's made of jet. Keep it in your pocket. If you're afraid somebody's trying to put the whammy on you, give it a squeeze."

William and Jill both looked at their charms, dumbfounded.

"Really?" Jill said. "Just squeeze it?"

Maymay nodded. "If that doesn't work, this is what you say: 'No fairy takes, nor witch hath power to charm.' Try it."

The twins repeated the words.

"Is that some kind of spell?" William said.

"That's right," Maymay said. "*Hamlet*. Act One."

"You got a magic spell...from Shakespeare?" William scratched his head.

"In ancient times, folks used Homer for all kinds of magic," Maymay explained. "You'll learn soon enough that you don't want to trifle with words. You've got to be careful; on the lips

39

of a powerful witch, they can have a life of their own. That's why it's always best to twist them a little: sing your magic word, or say it in poetry, or in a different language. Heck, make something up if you have to."

"Or quote Shakespeare?"

"Any poetry will do in a pinch." Maymay winked. "You should see what I can do with Maya Angelou."

"What's the deal with the carvings?" William asked.

"Crooked lines," Maymay said. "Magic likes to travel in straight lines. Crooked lines mess it up."

William looked again at the little piece of jet in his hand. "But...it's a rock."

"And that reminds me. You two need to be sure to clean your rooms every day."

"I-I beg your pardon?" William said.

"A messy room will interfere with your own magic. But a tidy room will settle your mind and give your magic room to grow.

Maymay sat up straight. "But I'm getting ahead of myself. Let's get started."

William reached for his notebook and flipped it open.

"First lesson," she said. "Things look like what they are."

He wrote what Maymay had said before he realized he didn't know what it meant.

"Uh...what?"

"It means there's a correspondence between things," Maymay said. "Certain objects have certain magical properties. If it looks right—or smells right, or blooms in the right season, or in some other way reminds you of what you're trying to make happen... Well, it probably helps."

"Probably?" Jill said.

"Most of the time. Folks have a lot of different opinions about what does what. You've got to figure out what works for you."

William eagerly wrote this all down.

Merle slipped down the stairs and found his spot by Maymay's feet.

"But some things are pretty much universal," Maymay said. She stood up and snatched a few items from the pile the table. "Come over here, you two. William, be a dear and scoot that card table back. We need a big space in the middle of the room."

William did as his grandmother asked. Merle jumped out of the way. Maymay led Jill by the elbow into the center of the room.

"Here you go, Jill," Maymay said, handing her a grease pencil. She set the rest of the items at her feet: a lighter, a bag of potpourri, and four votive candles. "William, you stand over here with me."

"M-maymay?"

"Like I said, some things are universal. This is one of them, and it brings us to rule two: symbols have power."

William scribbled away. Maymay stood back from Jill and spoke to her very deliberately.

"Now, honey, I want you to draw a circle on the floor. Make it good and big. It doesn't have to be perfect. Just make sure your lines meet up with each other. No gaps. Understand?"

Jill stooped down and traced a thin, red circle six feet across.

"All right," Maymay said. She gestured toward the floor. "What is that?"

Jill gave Maymay a deer-in-the-headlights look. She hated pop quizzes! At last, she said, "It's a circle."

"Uh huh." Maymay smiled. "And?"

Inspiration refused to come.

William said, "It's a boundary."

"Exactly!"

"It's a symbol, right?" he continued. "How many kids' games are there where you stand or sit in a circle? Things look like what they are. A circle marks off the inside from the outside. That's...that's what it is. I think."

"Very good," Maymay said. "Now, Jill, I don't want you to cross the circle until I say. You've drawn it, but you're not done casting it."

"O-okay?"

41

"So next I want you to take those candles and put them at the four cardinal points—north, south, east, and west." She pointed to the appropriate spots on the circle. "Then sit down in the center and strew some of those flower petals around. Gardenia," she said in an aside to William, "good for positive mental vibrations."

William took everything down as Jill followed her grandmother's instructions.

"Eventually, you'll be able to cast a circle with just a little bit of willpower, but we've got to walk before we can run."

Jill nodded, obviously perplexed. She lit the candles and sat down cross-legged.

"Now concentrate," Maymay said. "Do your relaxation exercise."

Jill closed her eyes. She took in a slow, shallow breath, held it for a second, then released it even more slowly. She repeated the process three or four times.

William watched, wondering what was supposed to happen. At first, he wasn't sure anything was. Then he noticed the candles. In each one, the flame had shifted from yellow to an unnatural yellow-green.

"Whoa," he whispered.

Jill opened her eyes. She gasped when she figured out what William was looking at.

Merle paced around the edge of the circle, never coming close enough to touch it.

"Why'd the flames turn green?" William asked.

"Strong magic will do that," Maymay said. "A witch puts off a kind of magical field when she—or he—is conjuring. Flames changing color is one of the signs."

Jill looked at her grandmother. She was getting scared.

"Now, that's a good, strong circle of power," Maymay said. "I could break it in a snap just by stepping over the line, but no magic can get in or out.

"Jill, what do you see?"

Jill looked at Maymay and then at William. She squinted. She scrunched her eyes like they were tired.

"Nothing," she said, bewildered. "I mean...You look...like you," she said. "No...auras...or whatever you call them." A grin spread across her face. "It's just the way it used to be."

Maymay smiled. "Honey, I know you've been struggling these past few weeks. If things get to be too much, you just cast yourself a circle. Understand?"

"Yes, ma'am." Jill exhaled.

Maymay suddenly became alert.

"William, someone's coming," she said. There was no doubt in her voice.

"That'll be Taylor," Jill said. "She's been helping me with... uh..."

"With your Second Sight," Maymay said. "I see. William, go invite Taylor in."

William opened the door. Taylor stood at the edge of the grass, edging away from a ghostly presence, a cat that seemed to be made of smoke stalked toward her. William realized it looked like the statue Maymay had buried in the yard.

"Come on in," William called. He eyed the ghostly cat. "It's all right." The cat seemed to evaporate.

Taylor strode forward.

"Jill around?"

"Y-yeah," William said. He backed away from the door. "Come on in."

One step inside and she stopped cold.

"What was that?" she said.

William glanced up. Above him was the horseshoe he had nailed over the door.

"Hello, Taylor," Maymay said, coming up behind William. "It's good to see you again."

"M-Mrs. Blay?"

"Please call me 'Maymay.' Are you all right?"

43

"Y-yeah. But for a second there..." She noticed William was looking over her head. She turned around and saw the horseshoe for the first time.

"That's new."

"I hope you don't mind," Maymay said. "It's nothing personal, dear, but given all that's happened..."

"That's for me, isn't it?" Taylor said. "An iron horseshoe to keep the Fair Folk away?"

"Not you," Maymay said, her voice calm and kind. "But you've got to admit, some of your relatives can be a bit...pushy. Do you feel all right?"

Taylor stopped to think. "Okay, I guess. For a second, I felt really cold."

"A little bit of iron isn't going to hurt you," Maymay said. "Or your relatives either, for that matter. It's more of a 'No Trespassing' sign. It tells them we know our rights and we're not going to put up with any nonsense."

Maymay leaned on her walking stick. "Jill is in the basement," she announced. "She tells me you've been trying to help her with her Second Sight."

"Trying," Taylor said. "I don't know how much good it's doing."

Maymay gestured for Taylor to continue as they headed for the basement.

"I can pretty much call up magic whenever I want now. I just...imagine sending some Jill's way. She says it helps."

"Hmm," Maymay said. She opened the basement door and gestured for Taylor to go first.

"Why don't you go visit with Jill. I need to speak with William for a minute."

Taylor descended the stairs. Maymay gestured for William to sit at the kitchen table.

"William," she began, taking the seat where William's dad had sat earlier. "I need to ask you a question, and I want you to tell me the truth."

"Yes, ma'am?"

44

She regarded her grandson, sizing him up. William wasn't sure what to expect.

"Do you have any feelings for Taylor?"

"Maymay?" William felt his face warming.

"Do you think she's pretty? Would you like to ask her out?"

"I-I know what you mean," William sputtered. "That's kind of personal, don't you think?"

"Uh huh," Maymay said, crossing her arms. "Well?"

"I don't know," William protested. "She's Jill's best friend. Doesn't that make her almost like another sister?"

"You tell me."

I am not discussing my love life with my grandmother! William thought. *Even if I had one!*

"Honey, I don't mean to embarrass you," Maymay said.

Too late!

"I just wanted to say...I'd look for another girl if I were you."

This got William's attention, and he wasn't sure why.

"Maymay...," William began. He felt a headache coming on. "I'm only thirteen years old," he said.

"Then I expect your father has talked to you about girls."

"Maymay!" This conversation was quickly drifting into the Twilight Zone.

"I just don't know if you should be thinking about Taylor in that way."

What was that supposed to mean?

"O-o-kay?"

"Now, don't get me wrong. She seems like a fine young lady."

"Just not for me? I mean, *if* I were going to ask her out— which I really don't think... That is, when I'm old enough to date..."

"Calm down, William. All I mean is that she's...not like us."

"Maymay, I thought your grandpa was French Creole."

She nodded. "And part Houma Indian. So?"

"So...I don't see why Taylor's race should matter."

"Now, William, do you honestly think I'd have a problem with Taylor because she's white?"

"No!" As soon as Maymay said it out loud, he realized it was silly. There wasn't a prejudiced bone in Maymay's body.

"I'm sorry, Maymay."

"If I had a problem with Taylor," she explained, "it would be because she isn't human."

Chapter 5

Shape-shifting

It was well after dark. Taylor still wore the clothes she had put on that morning: tee shirt, jeans, and flip-flops. She sat by her bedroom window looking out on the back yard.

Birds chirped. It was a windy night, but still pretty warm. August in Macon was like that.

She stroked the smooth face of her Seeing Stone—a teardrop of reddish-brown stone with a hole in the middle. Ayoka had given it to her to replace the one she lost in a fire in Louisiana. Another five minutes, and she'd use it to find out what the holdup was.

A whirlwind of gold- and silver-sparkled dust arose beyond the back fence—a sure sign someone was coming through the mushroom ring that had appeared there in June. No Topsider would have seen the disturbance except maybe somebody like Jill.

Taylor exhaled. *Finally!* She set down her Seeing Stone. She wouldn't need it, after all.

She rose from her desk chair even before she saw the signal: a tiny ball of amber light floating above the fence. She knew instinctively it was held in the hand of the person she'd been trying to reach.

She closed her eyes and willed her own ball of faery fire into existence. With the signal given, she slipped out of her bedroom, down the hall, out the back door, and across the yard.

"Taylor!" Danny called.

"Shh! Not so loud!" she whispered back. But she couldn't keep the grin off her face. She hadn't seen her pooka friend in over a month. In the dim, flickering light of his faery fire, his unearthly features took on a sinister mien—tapered ears, long nose, eerie amber-colored eyes that seemed to glow with their own internal fires. He was Taylor's height and dressed in a hodgepodge of European and Native American gear including moccasins, woolen trousers, and an old-fashioned cotton trade shirt. Over his shoulder, he wore a canvas bag decorated with exquisite nunnehi beadwork.

"What's the matter?" Danny said. "You said you needed me. Something important."

Taylor nodded. "Help me up."

Danny helped her jump the chain-link fence and land safely on the other side. She held on to Danny's hand and dragged him deeper into the patch of woods behind her house.

"It's been a while," Danny said. "You doing okay?"

"I guess. You?"

"Can't complain.... Now, what was it you was scrying me about?"

Taylor took a breath. "I need to ask a favor."

Danny looked this way and that. "Something you can't ask during the daytime?"

"My folks are still a little touchy about...everything. They're cool about me hanging out with Ayoka, but I don't want to worry them any more than I have to."

"I dunno. The way you're talking is making me plenty worried."

"It's nothing bad, Danny. I promise."

The pooka looked at her. "Okay. Shoot."

"I want you to teach me how to shape-shift."

Danny's eyes flashed amber fire. He stood with his mouth open.

"Well?"

48

"I don't know, Taylor... There's a lot to learn. And it'll take time. A lot of time. Shape-shifting ain't as easy as it looks, you know."

"It doesn't look easy at all," Taylor confessed. "So, how about it?"

Danny shrugged. "If you want to learn magic, I could teach you a little pishoguery."

She shook her head. "Your specialty is shape-shifting."

"Yeah, well..."

"Come on, Danny. You know what the Winter Court has put me through. I need every edge I can get."

"Listen, Taylor, you don't want to be going up against your folks—your fae folks, that is."

"I'm not going up against them," Taylor insisted. "But sooner or later, they're going to come to me. You know that, right?"

Danny grimaced. He swiped his foot back and forth on the damp grass.

"I just don't think—"

"Okay," Taylor said. "If you can't do it, you can't do it. I understand."

"Now, it ain't that I *can't* do it..."

"I found a book about Our Kind in the library. It said there was something called a leshy that's supposed to be a pretty good shape-shifter. Maybe I could find one of those..."

"A leshy? Gimme a break! You don't want to be messing with them types, Taylor."

"Danny, you *know* I'm going to learn how to shape-shift. I'd rather learn from you. If you'd rather not—"

"Aw, Taylor. A leshy?" Danny shook his head.

"It's your call, Danny. If you don't think you can do it..."

"I can do it!" Danny said. His eyes blazed. "There ain't a leshy in the woods that can out-shape-shift me!"

"You are pretty much the best at what you do," Taylor conceded, grinning.

"Darn right," Danny sniffed. "But it still ain't going to be easy."

"I understand," Taylor pressed on. "But if I get cornered again like I did last time, I want a way to fight back."

Danny sighed. "You ain't gonna let this go, are you?"

"Not on your life."

"Okay," he said. "Let me take care of some stuff. I'll come back in a couple weeks, and we'll get started."

"Thanks, Danny."

"Don't thank me just yet," the pooka said. "Once you see how hard this is gonna be, if you still want to thank me, you're welcome to."

"I can't wait," Taylor said. "Two weeks?"

"Three, tops."

Those three weeks were worse than waiting for Christmas.

She visited Ichisi nearly every weekend for stickball, even though she still wasn't any good at it. She did make progress, however, in messing with Sheby Crowthers, which she practiced at least once a day. She summoned glamour, slowly and carefully, and sent it in a subtle wave in Shelby's direction, willing her to have what her dad might have called a "brain hiccup."

It didn't always work. If she was too forceful, it would just make Shelby trip or walk into a wall or something—and that got boring after the first couple of times. Too gentle, and it had no effect at all.

When it did work, though, it was fabulous. The first week of school, Taylor managed twice to send Shelby on a detour into the boy's bathroom. In the second week, she experimented with making her forget what she was about to say when she raised her hand in class.

One day in late August, she even managed to send her into the boy's locker room instead of the chorus room. Between the shouts of protest, the catcalls, and the shrieks of embarrassed teenage boys, pretty much everybody on that end of the building heard about Shelby's latest escapade.

It was a deliciously gratifying way to practice magic. William, who was suiting up for gym class at the time, saw things differently.

Not that she ever admitted to what she was doing to William or Jill. Jill figured out Taylor's game right away, of course, and probably told William as soon as she could. That's why William gave her the stink-eye all through computer science class that day. As she put the finishing touches on her PowerPoint, William helped Mr. Dreyer fix some kind of bug with one of the printers—all the while intentionally turning his back on Taylor or, if he had to pass her way, giving her an angry stare.

She didn't really care. Shelby had been a thorn in her side since grade school, and it felt good to finally see her taken down a couple of notches.

Plus, it gave her a way to practice magic every day. The way Danny had described it, a little magical weight training wouldn't be a bad idea. She got the impression shape-shifting would be a whole lot harder than anything she had tried so far.

Finally, in early September, Danny contacted her on her Seeing Stone to tell her he'd pay her another visit in two nights' time.

When the night finally came, she pretended to get ready for bed, then waited by her window for Danny to arrive.

"You really want to do this, huh?" Danny stepped through the ring behind Taylor with his fire orb blazing in his hand. It gave off no heat at all, but it still bathed the wood in a warm, golden glow.

Taylor nodded. "You're not backing out on me."

"I said I'd teach you," Danny fussed. "I keep my promises." The pooka glanced around—right, left, even up into the trees— taking stock of his surroundings.

They were in the Wonder, where the little patch of woods behind Taylor's house stretched out for miles in every direction.

51

Danny drifted slowly in a circle, preoccupied. He'd been munching on a carrot. He finished the last bite just as Taylor spoke up.

"A wolf would be cool," she offered. "Or a mountain lion. Something you'd think twice about messing with. Or does it have to be a shape the teacher can do?"

"Huh?" Danny said. He kept looking around. "No, it don't work like that."

"What's the matter?"

"Nothing.... Here, this'll do." He led Taylor to an overturned pine log and had her sit on it like a bench.

Taylor found herself shivering—and it had nothing to do with the cold. She was actually going to learn how to shape-shift. Things were about to get real.

Her mind begin to wander in some not-so-happy directions, though. She imagined herself turning into an animal and then getting stuck. Shape-shifting really did look hard, now that she thought about it.

"Wait. Should I...I don't know...do warm-up exercises or anything? Just like that?"

"You ain't getting cold feet, are you?"

"What? No! It's just..."

"Look, this ain't like glamour, Taylor. I been working on a new shape myself. Even for me, it ain't easy. If you really want to learn, you're gonna have to put in a lot of time."

"A new shape? What is it? And how much time?"

"I'll show you when I'm ready. And a couple years maybe."

"Oh."

"A little pishogue would be lots easier. You could look like anything you want."

"No!" Taylor definitely wanted "real" shape-shifting in her bag of tricks. Illusions weren't good enough. "Just tell me what to do."

Danny sat cross-legged in front of her on the grass. He let his fire orb vanish, but neither of them said anything. They sat there and waited for their eyes to readjust to the darkness.

52

In the Wonder, the stars were brighter than they would have been Topside, and there were more of them. Taylor could make out the shape of Danny's face, the soft glow of his eyes, but not much else.

"Okay. Close your eyes."

"I can barely see as it is!"

"Do you want me to teach you or not?"

"Okay, okay. Eyes closed."

"Good. Now, listen. Smell. Feel the breeze on your skin. Take it all in. Every bit of what your body is telling you. Understand?"

"I-I think so."

"It won't happen all at once, leastways not until you've had more practice. Just...ease into it."

Taylor tried to settle herself down. Before long, she became aware of the sounds of crickets, the sweet aroma of the grass, the gentle breeze in her hair.

"Now, keep your eyes closed. Remember how you call up a magic mist?" Danny said. "This is the same thing only different. Instead of pulling the magic over you, I want you to push it out. It ain't a veil or a blanket, it's whiskers reaching out, feeling around for what's there."

Taylor nodded. This was one of the things Ayoka and Tsisgwa had been teaching her, too.

Instinctively, she started to meditate on her true name. Her body became leaden, still. A sense of lightheadedness welled up. She tried to imagine magic gently pulsing outward from her into the darkness.

It felt like half an hour before Danny said anything else.

"Okay," he whispered. "Tell me what's out here with us."

Taylor thought about it. She took a few slow, shallow breaths.

"Crickets," she said. That one was easy; she'd been hearing them all night. And she thought she had heard the flapping of wings earlier. "Some kind of bird. An owl?"

"Are you asking me or telling me?"

"An owl...and...some frogs, I think."

Danny held his peace.

53

"Anything else?" he finally said.

Taylor thought hard. She shook her head.

"How'd I do?"

"Not too bad I guess—for your first try."

"Well...good."

"You missed a couple of 'possums. And a rabbit."

"Well, you have to admit, I didn't really—"

"Some mice. A lizard."

"Hey, like you said: it's my first try."

"A deer came through about ten feet behind you. I got no clue how you missed that..."

"I get it, okay? I need more practice."

"Oh, and that wasn't an owl. It was a nightjar—you were guessing on that one."

Taylor shrugged her shoulders. "You got me."

"How do you feel?"

Taylor's body tingled, like an arm or a foot falling asleep except from head to toe.

"Weird," she said. "Like...I don't know. Kind of good. Refreshed."

"Sitting outside like this always makes me feel better," Danny said.

"Now what?"

"Keep practicing. Different animals are active at different times of day or night, so you've got to practice at different times, too. And tonight I was just showing you what to do. When you do it for real, you've got to spend more than five minutes on it."

"Five minutes? I feel like I've been out here forever!"

"Topsiders used to be better at this," Danny said. "Now you've got too many lights. Too many reasons not to go outside and look up at the stars, you know? But it'll come natural before too long."

Danny stood up and started to walk away. Taylor followed him.

"But...but that wasn't shape-shifting. That was just... meditating."

"Uh huh," Danny said. He trudged to the ring from which he had emerged and called it to life with a gesture. "Call me when you figure it out."

"Figure what out?"

Danny simply smiled and vanished into the sparkling whirlwind.

Chapter 6

There's Always a Catch

As usual, it was a warm September in Macon. That was fine with William, though, because it meant Mr. Smart would pay him to keep his lawn mowed for at least a few more weeks.

He tried to get the job done early, both to avoid the heat of the day and to keep the rest of his Saturday free for the things he wanted to do. He had an essay to write for English class. He wanted to review some of the things Maymay had been teaching him and Jill. Plus, he heard a trip to the mall might be in the works—the perfect chance to see what new video games were out.

He circled the big apple tree in the Smarts' back yard with the mower, then traced a long, straight row to the opposite fence.

William actually liked yard work because it gave him time to be alone and think. Lately he had a lot to think about.

Maymay had said Taylor wasn't human. Was that true? Sure, he'd heard Jill's story about elves and faeries and swamp monsters—but this was Taylor Smart! She spent nearly as much time at his house as her own. She went to the same school he did, complained about her teachers, and did everything else a normal teenager did.

At the fence, he pulled the mower around and headed back toward the apple tree.

Jill teased William that he had a crush on Taylor. He really wished she'd give that a rest. He appreciated her quick wit, that's all. Nobody could burn Shelby Crowthers like Taylor could! And the girl was completely without fear: you never knew what she'd do next. But that was actually pretty cool.

Scary, but cool.

He smiled as he rounded the apple tree again.

It was definitely not a crush. Appreciation, that's all.

William wiped the sweat from his brow and pressed on toward the fence. He swung the mower around once more.

He scratched his head. He looked over his shoulder. Something wasn't right, but he wasn't sure what.

He pushed on.

Anyway, even if he did think of Taylor *that way*, why was that any of Maymay's business?

William glanced toward Taylor's bedroom window. He didn't think she was home. Even if she was, he wasn't sure what he would say to her. *Hey, I was just wondering what species you were?* Nope, not the best conversation starter.

At the apple tree, William stopped. He shut off the mower. Something was definitely wrong. Hadn't he already mowed that line?

He shook his head. The engine cranked on the first pull, and off he went again. This time, he paid close attention to the line he was tracing: mowed grass to his right and the back fence, unmowed grass to his left and the house.

Straight ahead was the side fence and Mrs. Dibney's yard. He walked slowly, deliberately, holding as straight a course as he could. He swung the mower around one more time.

He half-moaned, half-gasped when he saw he hadn't made any progress.

There was nothing to do but press on. Another march toward the apple tree. Around the apple tree and...

"What the...?"

The line he had just mowed—that he *knew* he had just mowed—didn't look mowed at all!

His hands dropped away from the mower, releasing the safety lever and shutting it off once more.

William wandered into the middle of the yard and knelt on the grass. He brushed his hand over it, leaned down to study it from a closer angle.

The grass was growing before his very eyes.

What's more, tiny mushrooms started to pop up. They began as little creamy white pinpricks against the lush, green grass but gradually blossomed to full size.

William rubbed his eyes.

He stood back up and self-consciously looked around. Nobody was there.

By now, that single stripe of lawn was a two-foot-wide jungle of grass, weeds, mushrooms, and thistle.

He tried to turn around, but his left foot was entwined with quickly growing ivy. He cursed and kicked his foot free.

Another snake of ivy started to wrap around his right ankle. "Gah!"

He jumped away, jerked to a stop when he reached the end of the ivy's slack, and slammed into the grass. A sharp kick set him free, and he scrambled away on his hands and knees.

He rolled over and sat up, breathing hard.

There was movement in the woods behind the back fence.

William sprang to his feet. All he had with him was the jet amulet in the pocket of his shorts. Something magical was happening, and he was unarmed!

He took a deep breath and tried to open his Second Sight.

Was that laughter he heard? Coming from...somewhere?

Taylor appeared at the back fence and clambered over. Rather than acknowledge William, her eyes were fixed on the lower branches of the apple tree.

She didn't look happy.

"Danny Underhill!" she shouted.

"There you are!" The voice came from above. William backed away as someone dropped from the lowest branch of the tree.

It couldn't have been the Danny Underhill from school last year. This guy was older, with pointy ears, bushy eyebrows, and

59

a ridiculously big nose. He smiled really big. "I been waiting for—"

"What are you doing?" Taylor interrupted, gesturing to the long strip of high grass and then to William—grass-stained, wide-eyed, and jumpy.

"Just having a little fun," Danny said with a chuckle. He turned to William. "I remember you from last year," he said. "You're Jill's brother, right?" He extended his hand.

William backed away. His face was hot, and not just from the sun.

"*Not okay!*" Taylor said. Danny flinched and raised his hands in surrender.

"Aw, I didn't mean nothing," Danny said.

"Y-you...?" William managed.

"Did you figure it out, then?" Danny said. He eased toward Taylor, grinning.

"We're not talking about...that," Taylor said. "Honestly, Danny, do you always just... I mean, look at him!" She pointed to William. "You scared him half to death!"

"I'm not scared!" William protested.

"It was just some harmless fun," Danny said. "I got bored waiting for you."

"Well...next time you're bored, pick on somebody who deserves it."

"All right, all right! By oak, ash, and thorn, cut a pooka a little slack, will you? It ain't easy holding back all the time, I'll have you know."

"Hey," William interrupted, "when you two finish talking about me like I'm not even here..."

"I'm sorry, William," Taylor said. She sighed. "Danny's been trying to teach me something. I told him to meet me here, but I guess I'm running late."

"What's he teaching you?" William said. "Practical jokes?"

"Now, that would be awesome," Danny said as a mischievous grin spread across his face.

"*No,*" Taylor said.

"No, seriously," Danny pressed on. "Is Shelby Crowthers still as big a pain as I remember? 'Cause there's a couple of things—"

"*No, Danny.*" Danny flinched again.

"Taylor's taking care of Shelby on her own," William said with a smirk.

Taylor shot him an evil glare. "Is that what Jill told you?"

"She says you've been putting the whammy on her since August."

"Well, she's free to believe whatever she wants."

William looked her in the eye. As usual, he got absolutely nothing from her—no emotion, nothing. But he did realize something. It wasn't so much what Taylor said but what she didn't say.

"Are you telling me Jill's wrong?"

Taylor didn't break off eye contact. She bored into William with her icy blue eyes, daring him to look away.

He didn't.

"Just tell me you're not doing anything, Taylor. I'll believe you."

She sighed. "I don't have time for this. Don't you have a lawn to mow?"

"If I can." He gave Danny an ugly look.

"Sure," Danny said. "Sorry about before. Like I said—"

"You got bored. Right." He started up the mower and finished up in just a few minutes while Taylor and Danny talked under the apple tree.

When he finished, Taylor looked unhappy.

Danny said, "Just keep working on it. It'll come to you."

"Why can't you just tell me?" Taylor said. "I want to know now!"

"And *that's* why I can't just tell you," Danny said. "You gotta work it out for yourself. But you're not far off, I promise."

"A lot of good that does me."

Danny shuffled his feet nervously. "I'm gonna be busy the next couple months. I got me a job on a farm up north, and

61

the boss is gonna need me for a while. Oh, but hey: I ran into Shanna up that way."

"Really?" Taylor perked up immediately. "Shanna's my birth mom," she explained to William. "How's she doing?"

"Fine, I guess," Danny said. "We didn't really have time to talk. But I know she misses you."

"I miss her, too. Tell her that if you see her again, okay?"

"Sure thing, Taylor. And about that other thing...soon as I can get back down here, we'll get together."

"Yeah, fine," Taylor said without much enthusiasm.

Danny patted Taylor's shoulder. A second later, he vanished in a flash of light.

William jumped backward, and his eyes grew big as saucers. "Whoa!"

Later that night, Jill sat in the center of the circle of power. An unlit candle rested on the floor three feet in front of her, just inside the circle. Maymay sat on her folding chair stirring a big ceramic bowl with a long, silver spoon.

The basement didn't even look the same anymore. Sure, there were still stacks of boxes along one wall and the area rug rolled up and propped against another. Beside that, the room was taking on the feel of what could only be called a wizard's lair.

The conjuring circle where Jill sat had been traced and re-traced so often it was the next thing to a permanent fixture on the floor. Every week, Maymay had William and Jill scrub it clean so they could start over. First they'd trace the boundary before every lesson with something temporary like salt or sand. After a few days, Maymay would relent and let them just draw the circle with a grease pencil and leave it for a while. Then she'd make them scrub the pencil lines and start over again. Maymay admitted it would save time to leave the circle intact, but she insisted both twins know how to quickly and accurately draw their own.

Most of the supplies Maymay had brought from New Orleans had found a new home in the basement. One Saturday in August, she drove the twins to Walmart for a plastic folding table and some storage crates from which she fashioned a makeshift work desk with shelves full of cigar boxes, Tupperware containers, and stoppered glass bottles.

It was these supplies that most captured William's attention. They were all labeled in Maymay's spidery handwriting. Some of them were exotic: essence of lemongrass, frankincense, hemlock. Others were just odd: graveyard dirt, spider webs, owl feathers. William didn't have a clue what to think about the dusty top-shelf jars of baby's giggles, moonbeams, and gumption.

"This is silly," Jill said. "Don't you have any Shakespeare for this? Maya Angelou? Beyoncé?"

"The more powerful the spell, the more precautions we have to take," Maymay said. "You don't want it to burn the house down."

"But..."

"No buts. We've been over this."

"She's right, sis," William said. As usual, he had his notebook open. "Words can take on a life of their own. You can't just use ordinary language."

"Your brother is right," Maymay said. "You've been doing your visualization work, haven't you?"

"I guess," Jill said.

"You guess?"

"I mean, sure. Sure, Maymay. What do I do?"

"And you remember the incantation?"

"Here, sis," William said. He handed her an index card.

"You made flash cards?" Jill cocked her head and set her hand on her hip.

"You *didn't*?"

"Settle down, you two," Maymay said. "Whenever you're ready, Jill."

With a sidewise glance at William, Jill set the flash card with the spell Maymay had taught them in front of her.

63

"Just take your time," Maymay said. "Make a strong mental image of what you want to happen and hold it tight."

"Yes, Maymay."

"And remember your breathing."

She took a deep breath. She extended her trembling right hand toward the candle. Merle watched from underneath Maymay's seat. His tail swayed lazily back and forth, but his eyes never left Jill. The cat was as interested in her performance as Maymay was.

She slowly intoned the line her grandmother had taught them:

Sharba pesharba flammante fayah pyripeganyx.

William realized he was holding his breath.

The basement was utterly, painfully quiet.

"It isn't working!" Jill sighed.

"Then try again, baby," Maymay said. "Four times through is the rule for this spell. And remember to focus. You need to have a clear picture in your mind of what you want to see. That matters even more than the words."

Jill closed her eyes and collected her thoughts.

She intoned the words again. Again. Three times. Four.

On the final syllable, the candle shot to life.

William gasped, grinning and wide-eyed.

Jill stared in turns at her hand, her grandmother, and the burning candle.

"Very nice," Maymay said. "Now, how about blowing it out?"

"The same way?"

"That's right. Imagine it in your mind, then direct that image onto the candle. Do you remember the wind spell?" Maymay flashed a mischievous grin. "Or would you like one of William's flash cards?"

Jill's face reddened. "Uh...I'll take the flash card."

William triumphantly slid the second card toward the circle but without crossing it.

64

Jill closed her eyes yet again and took several slow breaths. She held out her hand and began to intone:

Amou aneme phthaneme pneuma ventibus thoou.

On the fourth repetition, a wind swept through the basement and snuffed out the candle. More than that: it knocked it completely over!

Jill squeaked.

Maymay sucked in a breath. "Child, that is some impressive spellwork!" she said.

William's turn wasn't nearly as interesting. He returned the candle to its place, took his seat on the floor, reactivated the circle, and went through the same breathing and relaxation exercises his sister had. When he felt ready, he intoned the four-fold incantation from memory.

Nothing happened.

After three tries, he wanted to give up.

After five tries, Maymay let him.

"I don't get it," he said. "I did everything exactly the same as Jill."

"Apparently not," Maymay said.

Jill smiled the way only a twin sister can when showing up her brother.

"I know that incantation by heart," William muttered. "I don't understand a word of it, but I know it. I can practically say it backwards."

"Then maybe that's what you should do," Maymay said.

"Come again?"

"Like I told you, the words aren't magic. They're just a safety feature. A container you put the magic in."

"Right," William said. Then he hazarded a question. "Maymay?"

"Yes, William?"

William pondered how he wanted to start.

"Words have power, right?"

65

"That's right."

"And witches have to be careful how they use words so the power doesn't get loose?"

Maymay nodded.

"Well..." He took a breath, the decided to go for broke. "What if somebody magical—I mean really magical—ever told a lie?"

Maymay stirred the mixture in her bowl while she considered how to answer.

"William, have you ever told a lie?"

"Ask him about Taylor," Jill said with a giggle.

William's ears grew hot.

"I'll take that as a yes," Maymay said, trying not to smile. She gave the bowl another stir. William discerned a pattern: three stirs clockwise, three counterclockwise. "You said it before," she continued. "Words can take on a life of their own. The more magical someone is, the more that's true. That's why the Good Neighbors take oaths and promises so seriously."

"You don't want to swear an oath unless you really, really mean it," Jill offered.

"Exactly."

"But could they actually lie?"

"I suppose they could—if they were willing to deal with the consequences."

"What consequences?"

"Do I look like a Good Neighbor?" Maymay scoffed. "I can't say for sure, but I bet it would cause them problems if they did. If you want to be 100 percent sure, you've got to make them tell you something three times."

"Why three times?"

"How should I know?" Maymay said. "That's what I was taught. Near as I can tell, it works."

William pondered this.

"But you've got to remember this," Maymay continued. "And Jill, you need to hear this, too. The Good Neighbors might not be able to flat-out lie, but they've got plenty of workarounds."

"Workarounds?" Jill said.

"They won't lie to your face, but they don't have to tell you the whole truth, either. They might tell you half the truth. And if they ever do tell you the whole truth, there's always a catch."

Maymay finished stirring. "That feels about right," she said. "Now, who remembers what I put in this bowl?"

"Salt," Jill said.

"That's pretty obvious," William said.

"Okay," Maymay said, "then what else?"

"Uh... Black pepper?"

"And garlic," Jill added.

"Angelica root," William said. "Red brick dust. And ashes from that piece of paper you burned last week—the one with the funny writing on it."

"Those are the main things," Maymay said. "So do you have any guesses what this is supposed to be?"

"I was going to guess a spice rub till William mentioned the dust," Jill confessed.

"I should know this!" William said.

"Take your best guess."

"Okay...salt. Angelica. Red brick dust...." William had grabbed his notebook from where he'd left it on the floor. He flipped through the pages and finally said, "Some kind of banishing spell?"

"Exactly," Maymay said. "To be specific, it's a charm against pests." She handed the bowl to Jill and pulled herself to her feet. "Your daddy says you've got a mole in the back yard. We're going to get rid of it.

William looked at the gray-white mixture.

"The easiest kind of magic is waking up the magical properties that something already has."

"I remember," William said. "Salt for purity. Silver for protection. That's why you used a silver spoon, right?"

"That's right," Maymay said. "So let's go outside and see what we can do." She scooped handfuls of the mixture into three plastic cups. She led the twins upstairs and into the back yard. It didn't take them long to find a mole hole.

67

"Now, all we've got to do is sprinkle the mixture around the hole and say the activation word."

"What's that?" Jill asked.

Maymay shook about half of one cup of the mixture onto the ground. She closed her eyes in concentration, took a breath, and hissed, "*Hexiphore.*"

There was a shimmer of light around the hole.

Maymay flashed a satisfied smile.

"That's it?" William said.

"It doesn't have to be fancy to work," Maymay said. "We made a pretty good batch, I'd say. We won't have any problems with moles for a while."

"How long?" William asked.

"For normal garden pests, probably till the next full moon if the weather stays clear. For pestier pests—say, a door-to-door salesman—I wouldn't give it much past sunrise."

"Cool," Jill said.

"Now, you two each take a cup and look for more holes. If you find one, you do just like I did."

"Yes, ma'am," they both said.

"And then go take showers: both of you. You've been working a lot of magic today. It'll stick to you if you're not careful, and you two go through enough milk every week as it is. Running water will take care of it."

They nodded again and headed off.

William meandered through the back yard, looking for holes. But his mind was on Taylor. He had confronted her about Shelby, and she acted like she hadn't done anything—but she never denied it. He tried to remember if he had ever heard Taylor tell an outright lie. More often, she was brutally honest with everyone, whether they liked it or not. (Usually not.)

He wondered what would happen if she ever did tell a lie—or even tried. Would it hurt her? Could she even do it?

Taylor Smart might not be the girl he thought she was.

68

Chapter 7

The World's Worst Baby-Sitters

Taylor visited Ichisi nearly every weekend to play stickball. Even when Ayoka wasn't there, she worked up the courage to join the other children in their pick-up games.

It got on her nerves that kids who looked a lot younger than her were so much better at it. She had to keep reminding herself that, despite appearances, she was probably one of the youngest kids on the field.

Tsisgwa was always ready to give helpful pointers. He had taken it upon himself to hang out with the children on his days off. He was something of a local celebrity, it turned out. The kids' parents remembered when Tsisgwa was a youngster. Now that he had returned to Ichisi, they couldn't wait to see him playing stickball again.

Athlan Tastanagi had also taken an interest in the children's games. At first, that seemed odd to Taylor. But when she remembered that stickball was a kind of warrior training, it made sense that the Red Chief's right-hand man would want to know if any of the children showed talent.

Taylor did not show much talent—and that ticked her off. She was used to things coming easily to her; she didn't appreciate having to work for them. But work she did—and listened to Tsisgwa's instructions, even when she didn't want to.

A time or two, Athlan himself joined the game. He was a terror on the field, often taking on five or six the older kids single-handed. He made it look easy, leaping and spinning about, changing direction in mid-air, throwing glamours and blasts and other kinds of attacks one after another and seemingly never wearing out.

If Taylor could only be a tenth as good....

Athlan seemed genuinely pleased when Taylor made progress. Her blasts were still a joke, but at least she finally got the hang of using her magical senses and conjuring a proper shield spell at least occasionally. Though she was far from his best student, it wasn't long until at least she wasn't his worst.

And after nearly every game, the kids would gather around and sing. Music was one thing Taylor definitely shared with other Fair Folk. They could go on for hours, belting out one song after another, in the most beautiful harmonies Taylor had ever heard. And they were as interested in her music as she was in theirs.

Taylor would put up with a lot of abuse if it meant she could sing afterward.

Whenever she could, she stole away to the Wonder to practice whatever it was Danny had been trying to teach her.

She hoped all that sitting in the woods was Danny's kooky way of teaching her some important shape-shifting technique. Either that, or this was just one of his pranks—and not a very good one. A month into her lessons, she didn't feel any closer to shape-shifting than when she started.

But she pressed on. It was all she could do.

One sleepless night in late September, she sneaked out of the house after midnight to take a walk in the woods beyond her back yard.

She had become familiar with the maze of narrow paths weaving through the trees of the Wonder. On a clear, moonlit night like this one, she could see almost as well with her night vision as she could in the light of day. She walked at least a mile before she found a favorite clearing and sat down at the base of a huge magnolia tree.

She closed her eyes and, just as Danny had taught her, drew magic from the Wonder and sent it gently wafting outward like ripples on the surface of a pond.

She took several deep breaths.

She opened not only her magical senses but her hearing as well. She made out the scurrying feet of small forest creatures—opossums and squirrels and such. Her consciousness brushed past a barn owl on the hunt. She never heard it, but she was sure it was there, somewhere high above her.

A lizard skittered across a fallen tree branch.

Then she became aware of something else. A predator of some sort—at least, that was the vibe it gave off. But it moved out of range before Taylor caught a clear mental image of what she was sensing.

It refreshed her to sit in the silence. A lot of folklore said that Her Kind were most active at dawn and at dusk. The mythology didn't always get it right, but that one had the ring of truth. The starry sky and the quiet breeze were invigorating in a way she couldn't put into words.

She sat for another ten or twenty minutes—probably longer than she had ever sat still in her life! She made a mental inventory of the animals she sensed. It was getting easier to work out their location just by feeling the way they crossed her magical field.

Then something disrupted that field: a big, loud presence was heading her way. Several presences were out there in the woods.

And they were laughing.

She sensed it before she heard it: lightness and joy and wonder. Then she heard a child's squeal of delight echoing more in her mind than in her ears. This was followed by good-natured chuckling from deeper voices.

Taylor shifted gears. Rather than send magic outward, she drew it in, allowing it to surround her, to wrap around her. She disappeared from sight in a blanket of magical mist and headed off in the direction of the sounds.

71

She slipped through the old-growth forest with ease, following her intuition as much as her ears for a good ten minutes.

She was in the Shallows, a bit of the Wonder where the boundary with the Topside world was thinner and more easily crossed. As she gazed ahead, she could see both worlds superimposed over one another, the untamed forest and the mundane city. With a little concentration, she could shift from one to the other.

She came at last to a small neighborhood cemetery (there were a few of those sprinkled throughout Macon). It seemed to be as "real" in the Wonder as it did Topside. Cemeteries, ancient ruins, mountain streams, mushroom rings—these were the kinds of places where a person could cross over from one world to the other if they knew what they were doing, and maybe even if they didn't.

A haze settled over the place. Pinpricks of gold and silver light sparked like fireflies.

A bright blue light flashed among the gravestones. A child broke out in uncontrollable giggles.

Still cloaked in mist, she tiptoed out of the woods, through the haze, and into the cemetery.

"Do another one, Haggler," a man's voice said.

This time, the light was vivid green. As Taylor approached, she saw it took the form of a unicorn that pranced about and flicked its tufted tail.

The little girl at the center of the action laughed so hard she nearly fell over. She couldn't have been more than two. She wore pink footie Disney princess pajamas and clutched both a threadbare blanket and a one-eyed teddy bear, and she practically jumped for joy as the unicorn leaped and danced above her head.

Three little folk gathered around her. One, the shortest of the three, couldn't have been three feet tall. He had curly white hair and pale features—an albino by the looks of him. He gestured with both hands and made the unicorn roll and tumble and waggle and snort.

As he put his illusion through its paces, he grinned at his buddies. The tallest one (relatively speaking) was gray and bat-eared. He reminded Taylor of Silas Bludgitt, the church grim who haunted the cemetery at her church. This one, however, looked like he didn't miss too many meals.

The third one was short, though still taller than Haggler the albino. He wore a bowler hat with a long, tapering turkey feather in it and a braided pigtail that fell down down his back and almost to his ankles. He held a walking stick with a ball of faery fire at its tip, bathing the entire scene in warm, golden light. All three wore simple clothes. They had propped their traveler's packs against a gravestone.

Taylor drew closer until she was almost in their circle. She watched her breathing. As long as she didn't draw attention to herself, she was effectively invisible, but any sound might break the illusion.

The unicorn faded away, and Haggler conjured something else: a majestic pink swan. Then a purple monkey.

Taylor was enthralled.

The husky, bat-eared creature reached into his pack and produced a wooden recorder. He piped a happy tune. Haggler slapped his hands on his knees. His conjured monkey faded away.

Bowler hat began to sing:

Of all the trees that grow so fair,
The woodland to adorn,
Greater are none beneath the sun,
Than oak and ash and thorn.

Haggler joined in, adding a bass harmony line to the chorus:

Sing oak and ash and thorn, my friends,
All of a Midsummer's morn!

73

Surely we sing of no little thing,
In oak and ash and thorn!

Hidden behind her glamour, Taylor smiled even though what she was seeing bewildered her.

The little girl cackled with delight. Bowler hat and Haggler continued to sing and slap out the rhythm on their knees.

Mighty oak was e'er bespoke
Through many a far-off land;
Ash of worth, the hub of the earth,
Turns the vision of every man;
Thorn will sting, but still doth bring
Her sweets to base and well-born;
Thus do we see the nobility
Of oak and ash and thorn!

Bat-ears swayed back and forth as he played. Bowler hat picked the little girl up and danced her around the circle. She squealed and babbled along as they repeated the chorus.

Sing oak and ash and thorn, my friends,
All of a Midsummer's morn!
Surely we sing of no little thing,
In oak and ash and thorn!

All four fell to the ground and rolled and laughed themselves silly.

"Again!" the little girl begged.

"We should make a verse that rhymes 'green corn,'" bowler hat said. "It'd be a big hit in Ichisi."

"There's too many verses already," bat-ears said with a dismissive gesture. "I can't keep 'em straight."

"The way I hear it," Haggler said, "about a hundred years ago, a Topsider made up some verses of his own."

74

Bowler hat scoffed. "That's all we need: some know-nothing Jack trying to rewrite the Fair Folk's music!"

They all laughed.

The little girl squealed and wiggled and pleaded, "Again!"

"Let me try," the bat-eared creature said. "Look at this, sweetie."

He cracked his knuckles and gestured ostentatiously. Then he crossed his eyes, puffed out his cheeks, and blew a world-class raspberry that dropped the girl to her bottom in a fit of giggles.

His whole body expanded and transformed: big, floppy shoes; blazing red hair; an even bigger pot belly; and a colorful, mismatched outfit that would have been the envy of any clown in the circus.

"Good one, Pete," the albino said with a chuckle.

The bat-eared clown resumed his original form, and the laughter eventually settled down. The little girl yawned. Her eyes were starting to droop.

The three little folk glanced at one another. The albino tapped his knees nervously.

"What do you think, Wasko?" he said.

The little person in the bowler hat frowned.

"I don't see as we have much choice," he said. He smiled at the little girl and reached into his pocket.

"Hey, sweetie," he said. "Would you like some candy?"

Taylor sucked in a breath. All at once, this was no longer fun.

The little girl reached forward. Taylor was suddenly shaking and sweaty.

"*No!*" she shouted. As quickly as that, her glamour failed. The little folk and the girl jerked their whole bodies around to see where she was standing behind a gravestone.

The bat-eared little person was closest to her, Pete. He rolled onto his back and crab-walked away. Bowler hat let fly a curse Taylor hoped the little girl didn't understand.

75

"W-what! Where'd you come from?" he said as he regained his feet. Haggler picked up the girl and shielded her from Taylor with his body.

"Where did *she* come from?" Taylor said, pointing to the girl. "And what do you think you're doing, tricking her into buying in? She's just a little kid!"

Bowler hat thrust his walking stick forward.

"*Did I say you could move?*" Taylor said. The weight of her presence bowled him over. He dropped the stick to the ground, and its light snuffed out.

Taylor took a breath and summoned blue-white faery fire into both her hands. She flooded the graveyard in a cold, severe light.

"N-no, ma'am," bowler hat squeaked. "B-but you don't understand..."

Taylor glared at him. "You've taken a little girl from Topside. You're about to give her some faery food and bind her to the Wonder. Once she's bought in, she might not be able to go back to her parents." She was breathing heavy. She extended both arms, hands up, and willed her faery fire to glow even brighter. "What don't I understand?"

Pete, the bat-eared creature, softly blubbered. "I told you we shoulda left her, Wasko," he muttered. "I told you."

Wasko, the one in the bowler hat, composed himself. He moved very slowly, deliberately. "Now, Miss," he began. He swallowed and cleared his throat. Taylor had his full attention.

"Well?"

"See... It ain't what you think. The fact is, well, she don't have much of a family to go back to." He frowned. Taylor judged he was probably sincere.

"Wasko's right," Haggler offered. He patted and rocked the child in his arms. "We were about to make camp here, you see, and then we heard the little one crying."

"We just wanted to help," Pete added, flinching as if terrified that Taylor would unleash divine fury against him. "We found her right quick." He gestured into the distance. With a little effort, Taylor could make out the ghostly outline of a Topside house. "She was sittin' up in her crib, bawlin' her little eyes out."

"Saddest thing you ever seen," Haggler said.

"That doesn't give you any right to take her from her parents," Taylor stated. Once again, the three little folk shuddered.

"Th-that's what you don't understand, miss," Wasko said. "You see...her mom...she...." He pantomimed upending a bottle.

"She musta had a rough night of it," Pete offered with a shrug.

"She was sleeping it off," Haggler said, still swaying with the girl in his arms. "We tried to wake her up. But to tell you the truth, she ain't gonna be up to much even when she does."

Taylor said nothing.

"If you don't mind my asking, miss," Wasko said, "I'm thinking you've got the look of the Gentry about you. Don't you think maybe you could find a place for this sweet thing among your people?" He reached over to rub the little girl's back. She was nearly asleep—Taylor wondered if Haggler had put some kind of sleeping spell on her to keep her calm.

"She don't look like she'd cause nobody no trouble."

Taylor looked at each of the little folk in turn, last of all to Haggler and the child he was rocking.

"My people...," she began, "...aren't really good with children."

"Then maybe the tall folk at Ichisi?" Wasko said.

"The tall folk?"

"The isti chapchagi," he explained. "That's what we call the folks that live in the mounds."

"You mean the nunnehi," Taylor said.

"Yeah, they'll answer to that, too. You just say the word, Miss, and we'll—"

"By oak, ash, and thorn," Haggler interrupted. "You're her, ain't you?"

"Her who?" Pete said.

"The Hellebore kid."

77

Pete and Wasko fixed their eyes on her with renewed awe—or terror.

"Well, it makes sense, don't it?" Haggler continued, a tremor in his voice. "Th-they say she lives around Ichisi, and she'd be about your age."

"Wait, how do you know about me?"

"Then it's true!" Pete said. "They were right!"

"They? Who's they?" Taylor said.

"Everybody," Wasko said. "Leastways, all the little folk. If you don't mind me sayin', Miss Hellebore, you're...kind of a big deal these days."

"B-but in a good way!" Haggler added. "Your grandma, well, she ain't the most popular fae in the Wonder—"

"Do tell."

"...so a lot of us little folk liked the idea of somebody getting one over on her for a change. And not just little folk, either. There's field folk and forest folk and such that feel the same way."

"They say you poked Mara Hellebore's eyes out," Pete said, his own yellow eyes wide with wonder.

"I heard you turned her into a chicken," Wasko said with a sly grin.

"I don't know who you've been talking to," Taylor said, "but I never turned anybody into a chicken—or anything else."

"Well, be that as it may," Wasko said, "and not to change the subject...but don't you think we should do something for little Mabel here?"

"Mabel?"

"We was thinking of calling her Mabel," Haggler said. "Seeing as we don't rightly know her real name, and she don't seem all that interested in telling it."

"So, what do you say, Miss Hellebore?" Pete said. "You don't want a sweetie like this going back to a mom who can't take care of her."

Taylor studied the child's sleeping form. She couldn't help but imagine what it was like when her own grandparents

78

snatched her away from her mother thirteen years ago. Did they do it while Shanna was asleep? Did she wake up and find her baby girl was gone?

She couldn't bring herself to put any mother through that. Even one who would never win the mother-of-the-year award.

"Everybody deserves a second chance," she said at last.

"So...?" Wasko asked.

"Take her home," Taylor said, sighing. "But write down the address for me. If I find out she's in trouble, I'll let the Topside police take care of it."

"Promise?" Haggler said.

Taylor nodded.

"You three don't live around here, do you?"

"We're from Mossy Haze," Wasko said. He answered Taylor's confused expression by adding, "That's in Arradherry Land. Up north."

"But things been getting a little dicey lately up that way," Haggler said. "Put us in mind for a change of scenery, if you take my meaning."

"I think so," Taylor said. Her friend Danny moved around a lot, too, and probably for the same reasons.

"Take Mabel home," Taylor said. "If it doesn't work out... There's a man in Ichisi called Tsisgwa. He'll know how to find me."

"Yes, Miss Hellebore," Wasko said.

"But if Mabel is in trouble, I want the Topsiders to take care of it. Do you understand?"

"Absolutely, Miss Hellebore."

"All right, then. Take her back, and bring me that address," she said. The first smudges of pink light were fighting to break over the treetops. She sighed. "And please try to hurry: I have to get ready for school."

79

Chapter 8

Oath-bound

Claudia stood patiently, waiting to be summoned in. The bright, professional furnishings and décor of the Chief Matron's outer office were familiar, but that didn't put her at ease in the slightest. Ever since June, she had been living in unfamiliar territory.

She studied the ceiling while Belas Wakefire finished his tirade. The door to the inner office was open, and Claudia could see him pacing back and forth within.

"The gall!" he thundered. "I don't know what she expects to accomplish with this stunt, but by Danu—"

"Obviously, she's sending a message to her supporters," Dubessa Fairchild said, her voice composed—but only barely. Claudia listened carefully while pretending to go over some notes in her writing tablet.

"Visiting the nunnehi, apologizing for the supposed failures of the Seasonal Courts of Arradherry…. It's theater, Belas. Pure theater. The savages know Osanda can't establish policy for the Chiefdom."

Claudia knew Osanda Morning had been making overtures to the nunnehi, of course. It was a topic of heated conversation throughout the Chiefdom. She was perfectly within her rights to travel wherever she pleased, but it still made Belas and Dubessa bristle. Whatever Osanda said or did would reflect on the Summer Court—and perhaps sway members of the Court in her direction.

"But she isn't doing it for them," Belas said. "It's all for the rabble who back her, isn't it? They fear war is coming—and they want no part of it. They take this little apology tour of hers as a signal she'll work for peace."

Claudia bowed her head lest either of them notice her smirk. The "rabble" backing Osanda Morning included members of some of the most prestigious houses in the Summer Court.

"I'm sure that's her plan," Dubessa said. "Remind everyone of how bad things were under the former Chief Matron."

Belas scoffed. "I bet she won't even have to mention the fact that I was the Summer Primus for over forty years—or that you've been a member of the Triad even longer."

"Guilt by association," Dubessa agreed. "We get saddled with all the faults of the former Chief Matron, and Gwenllian is made to look like our hand-picked crony. Meanwhile, Osanda positions herself as a voice for change: a return to the old ways before...*she* came to power."

"I don't like it at all."

"We shall have to see what becomes of this little stunt of hers," Dubessa said. "If you'll excuse me, darling, I have an appointment." She glanced toward the doorway.

Belas looked at the ceiling and expelled a breath. "As do I."

"Not Seaborn again?"

"I honestly thought he was ready to be made a Teyrnus." The Primus shook his head.

"If the job is too much for him...," Dubessa began.

"I can't pull him out now. Osanda would just say it's evidence of my own incompetence in appointing him. As if I only gave him Tobarty because of his connections."

"Didn't you?" Dubessa said.

"Dubessa!"

"I'm only joking, darling. I swear, some days you have to laugh to keep from crying."

That seemed to mollify the Primus. "He'll grow into it—in time," he said. "At least, he'd better. I'll leave you to your meeting." Belas stood and marched through the anteroom, nodding in Claudia's direction on the way out.

"Chief Matron," Claudia said. She stood in the doorway to the inner office, waiting to be invited in.

Instead, Dubessa rose from her mahogany desk. "Walk with me," she said. Rather than the professional attire she preferred for official audiences, she wore a simple green skirt and loose cream-colored peasant blouse. Claudia felt overdressed in her customary business suit.

Dubessa breezed into the hallway without a word. Claudia followed, sidestepping a curly-haired fae in work clothes rushing past with a flower pot.

"You served the former Chief Matron for many years."

"Thirty-seven years next Beltane," Claudia said.

"I remember," Dubessa said. "You became her assistant shortly after my husband was elevated to the Primacy."

They walked the stony corridors of the rath of Bisgarra Verry, shaded in the fading sun. Little folk and lesser sprites scurried about, either cleaning the walls and floors or carrying papers and packages. The Chief Matron nodded and smiled as they passed.

They exited the keep itself and strode through the inner court. The sky was warm and clear.

"Do you hear from your father often, Claudia?"

Claudia swallowed.

"From time to time," she said. "Cymbees can be somewhat... distant."

"Indeed," Dubessa said. "And has he always lived in the Nunnehi Lands?"

This was a touchy subject, Claudia knew. The former Chief Matron, Anya Redmane, never suspected her true loyalty was to Tewa, the White Chief of Tsuwatelda in the Nunnehi Lands. But in the past few months, Claudia had come to realize that very little got past Dubessa Fairchild.

"Only the past three or four hundred years, Chief Matron. He was born in the Congo—as I'm sure you know."

"I know as much about Mwalilwa Fountain as is in my predecessor's records," Dubessa said. "Which is to say: quite little."

83

Claudia debated mentioning that her father's friends called him "Moe." It didn't seem relevant, all things considered.

The two women skirted around a couple of young men angrily protesting their love for a young woman—a pretty, dark-haired fae who seemed mortified to be the subject of their attention.

"I'm not surprised," Claudia said, suppressing a smile. She wasn't at all surprised that Anya Redmane had kept information about her father. Nor was she surprised Dubessa found Mrs. Redmane's records lacking. In fact, it filled her with great satisfaction.

As they reached the outer courtyard, craftsmen plied their wares in countless tents and outbuildings. A wandering minstrel fiddled a happy tune, but had to duck aside when a gang of workmen sped past. He had no sooner resumed his song when another man—this one with the head of a donkey—lumbered through.

But Claudia stayed focused on the Chief Matron. Frankly, she'd lived in Bisgarra Verry too long to be distracted by such foolishness.

"He keeps to himself," she said at last. "And, I might add, he is decidedly neutral to politics, Chief Matron."

"So you say," Dubessa said. She stopped to admire the work of a weaver trading his wares with strangers who'd come to town. "But what about his half-human daughter, hmm?" She didn't give Claudia time to respond, but added, "You were present at Dunhoughkey this past spring when Shanna Hellebore went missing."

"Mrs. Redmane required my presence. Yours as well, as I recall." She kept her voice steady as she, too, ran her hands over the selection of fabrics.

"I, however, was not the Hellebore whelp's jailer," Dubessa snapped—a little too loudly. The weaver stopped to listen. Others glanced fleetingly in the Chief Matron's direction. "When she vanished from the belly of the Dunhoughkey dungeons, I wasn't there."

84

"My understanding...," Claudia began, choosing her words carefully, "is that the Dunhoughkey garrison have yet to account for Mrs. Hellebore's escape."

She struggled to keep the edge off her voice. It pleased her that she had managed to cover her and Danny Underhill's tracks so well. But it wouldn't do to look pleased under Dubessa Fairchild's interrogation.

Dubessa gave her a piercing stare. Claudia couldn't tell what it meant, but she was sure it meant something.

In the distance, people clapped as the minstrel finished his tune. The donkey-headed man ambled back the way he had come, now arm-in-arm with an elegant fae lady.

"Chief Matron," Claudia said, "I have sworn an oath of allegiance to the Summer Court. I am no oath-breaker."

It was true: What she did at Dunhoughkey, she did to preserve the Court, not to undermine it.

Dubessa glared at her. She must have felt Claudia's presence, but it only annoyed her.

"And yet, the former Chief Matron was, in fact, an oath-breaker."

"No one is more surprised at that than I am, Chief Matron. But she broke her oath long before I came into her service. I am just as upset about recent events as you are."

Dubessa said nothing. They exited the outer courtyard through the southern gate.

"If I may ask, Chief Matron, where are we going?"

"To your new assignment."

"New.... Am I no longer to be your assistant?"

"Your oath is to the Summer Court. I feel you can offer the greatest service to the Court elsewhere."

And there it was. *She doesn't trust me*, Claudia thought. Or at least, Dubessa didn't know if she could trust Claudia. A new assignment might well be a test of loyalty.

Past the southern gate, before the rolling fields began and at some distance from the humble homes that dotted the road leading into the rath, was a ring of standing stones—the main

85

terminal of the Fair Folk's rapid-transportation network for people coming or going from Bisgarra Verry.

The ring sprang to life with a swirling vortex of sparkling dust. Out of the whirlwind stepped a sídhe aristocrat. Claudia recognized him as one of the conservatives who quietly favored Osanda Morning. He had with him a young boy, dark-skinned and wide-eyed—a changeling fresh from the Topside world by the look of him.

The two sídhe exchanged perfunctory greetings before the Gentryman and his charge headed for the rath.

Claudia turned to Dubessa.

"Chief Matron," she said. "My father and I... If we have offended—"

"Not at all, Claudia," Dubessa said. "Not at all. Don't think of this reassignment as a demotion. Think of it as...an opportunity to prove your worth."

Claudia swallowed.

"If you please," Dubessa said, offering her arm. Claudia took it.

Dubessa gestured with the other arm, and the ring of standing stones once more sprang to life.

She nodded, and both women stepped into the ring.

They appeared seconds later beside a lake. Waves lapped lazily on the shore under the purple light of the setting sun. There was no one else in sight. Beyond a narrow beach, a dark forest loomed.

Claudia watched as a pinprick of light at the center of the lake expanded, waxing and waning with the waves.

The glow moved directly toward Claudia and Dubessa and took golden shape beneath the water.

"You have a reputation for impeccable attention to detail, Claudia," Dubessa said. "To be honest, I doubt my predecessor would have lasted as long as she did without your administrative skills."

"Thank you, Chief Matron."

86

The water churned and parted. Waves piled up on either side of a narrow causeway that widened and brightened as a single figure strode toward them: golden-haired, bright-eyed, dressed in a gown so white it glowed.

"That is why I am lending you to Mrs. Birdsong."

Claudia's stomach rumbled unhappily. She felt like she had swallowed a hornet's nest—or maybe the hornet's nest was about to swallow her!

Gwenllian Birdsong stepped onto the beach. Without a word, the twin walls of water collapsed behind her as soon as she was clear of the surf.

She looked every bit as formidable as the most powerful sídhe Claudia had ever met: tall, graceful, unnervingly beautiful. Her white gown whipped around her in the breeze giving the impression she might take flight at any moment.

"Chief Matron," she said with a graceful nod and a smile.

"Gwenllian," Dubessa answered. "I believe you've met Claudia?"

"Indeed." She smiled. "I'm sure we will get along swimmingly."

Claudia nodded.

"You're part cymbee, is that right?"

"Yes, ma'am."

"So you won't be easily intimidated, am I right?" She strolled around Claudia, sizing her up. Claudia remained stock-still. "And your mother? She was a deathling?"

"As you say, ma'am."

"By custom, that would make you a changeling. Not truly a fae."

Claudia said nothing.

"Have you ever considered binding yourself by the *padam*'s oath?"

"No, ma'am," Claudia said. "Knighthood isn't for me. I prefer to serve the entire Court rather than any house."

"Yes, that would tend to make things less...complicated," Mrs. Birdsong said. "Still, Dubessa says you're quite talented.

If things work out, perhaps I'll persuade you to change your mind."

"Ma'am?"

"Claudia," Dubessa said, "I'm lending you to Mrs. Birdsong until Beltane. I expect you to render her your most devoted service."

"As you wish, Chief Matron."

"I don't have to tell you that it is crucial that she prevail in this...unseemly spat with Osanda Morning. Her success will reflect upon you as well."

Or her failure.

"I shall serve her as I have served you, Chief Matron," Claudia said.

Dubessa offered a wry smile. "I'm sure you will."

"How soon can you be ready to travel?" Mrs. Birdsong asked.

"It...it depends, I suppose."

"I'll meet you in Bisgarra Verry tomorrow at sunrise. I'll need you to be my secretary, seer, and general assistant. Pack accordingly."

"Yes, ma'am."

"You and I are going on a little trip, Claudia," Mrs. Birdsong said. Her eyes gleamed with barely constrained fury. "There are things I need to know. I expect you to help me learn them."

A few days later, Claudia sat in Dollin Seaborn's outer office, arms folded over the writing tablet on her lap. Gwenllian paced the floor.

The Acting Matron was a bit too excitable for Claudia's taste. In other words, she was about average for Matrons of the Summer Court.

Let her fume over being kept waiting. The delay gave Claudia time to take the measure of the Teyrnus of Tobarty.

The office décor was a jumble. There were pieces of dark wooden furniture, large and blocky and adorned with spidery knotwork patterns. Silver knobs and fixtures graced the doors and windows. All this was a leftover from the previous Teyrnus, when Tobarty was a rath of the Winter Court. Maybe Seaborn had ordered new furniture that hadn't arrived yet. At least, Claudia could hope.

It was evident that Seaborn had tried to brighten things up with colorful tapestries and floral arrangements. The result was a room with an identity crisis, bright and cheerful and grim and functional all at the same time.

But Claudia was more interested in the conversation unfolding on the other side of the great oak door.

"...your presence at the rede next weekend. Apparently it's traditional."

The Teyrnus's assistant—Claudia's counterpart—was a tall, blond sídhe. As they had only just arrived in Tobarty, she hadn't yet learned his name. There was something thin and nasal about his voice.

"No," the Teyrnus said. "These people have to learn that Tobarty is now a rath of the Summer Court. Let them have their rede if they want. I won't lead it."

The closed door muffled his voice, but Claudia sensed impatience. She guessed this wasn't the first such conversation between the Teyrnus and his assistant.

"Teyrnus," the assistant said. Claudia could imagine the strained look on his face. "It would be wise to reconsider." Something indecipherable followed. He must have turned his head.

The assistant's voice resumed. "But disrespecting their festivals might cause them to form an opinion...and not a favorable one."

"I've made my decision, Aerd. It would be unbecoming for a Teyrnus of the Summer Court to welcome the start of the Winter Assize."

"For them, it's only Samhain, Mr. Seaborn. A harvest festival, nothing more."

Claudia imagined what the assistant's body language might have told her.

89

"Then let them bring in their harvest without me."

"As you wish, Teyrnus. Shall I send in Matron Birdsong?"

Seaborn said something under his breath.

The door swung open, and the blond assistant stepped into the outer office. His gray-green suit had been pressed to within an inch of its life. He anticipated Gwenllian's pacing and positioned himself in front of her, standing at attention.

"The Teyrnus will see you now," he announced with something approximating a smile.

"Indeed," Gwenllian muttered. She marched past him and into the office before he could show her the way.

Claudia followed, nodding thanks.

Dollin Seaborn's mahogany desk was much smaller than Dubessa Fairchild's and stacked with papers and parchments, inkwells—common black, myrrhed, and dragon's blood— as well as quill pens, a reading lamp, an incense burner (currently unused), and three or four golden trinkets of some sort. The desk was actually one of the few pieces of furniture in Tobarty that wasn't hideous.

Seaborn stood upon Gwenllian's arrival. For all their faults, the sídhe had impeccable manners, the Summers especially so. Even when they were trying to kill you.

"Matron." He bowed deeply and put on a smile at least a little more convincing that his assistant's. But there was no mistaking the frustration in his voice.

"Mr. Seaborn," Gwenllian said. "I trust I have not come at a bad time." She said the proper words, but the acid in her voice said she didn't give a whit if her visit inconvenienced the Teyrnus.

Of course, he chose not to notice the slight. Instead, he gestured for Gwenllian and Claudia to sit.

"Can I bring you something to drink?"

"Coffee. Black," Gwenllian said. Claudia waved off the question.

Seaborn glanced at his assistant, who nodded and bowed out of the office.

90

"I won't waste your time, Mr. Seaborn," Gwenllian said. "I take it you know why I'm here?"

He leaned forward in his chair.

"The Primus has complete confidence in my leadership, Mrs. Birdsong," he said. His eyes darted back and forth as he fiddled with his hands. He took a breath and lowered his voice an octave. "Complete and utter confidence."

"Teyrnus," Gwenllian began, "we do not..."

"If you think anyone else could handle the job better than me, you're wrong. Now, I'll admit—"

"Teyrnus, please—"

"—it isn't easy. The change in political alignment will take the locals some getting used to, but most of them couldn't care less about such matters, so I really don't see—"

"*Teyrnus.*" Gwenllian projected the slightest trace of presence. "We are here to discuss Osanda Morning."

That finally got Seaborn's attention. He sat back in his chair. "Oh."

"Mr. Seaborn," Claudia said, "the Matron and I fear Ms. Morning's recent ill-advised...excursion...has undermined the Chiefdom's standing with the nunnehi."

Gwenllian added, "If they believe she speaks for the Summer Court...."

Seaborn leaned forward. His hands gripped the armrests of his chair. "They can't," he said. "Everybody knows you're in. The election next spring is just a formality. Even the nunnehi know that. They'd have to."

"Forgive me, Teyrnus," Gwenllian said, "but I seem to detect a note of doubt in your voice."

"You'll never find anyone more loyal to the Summer Court, you understand?"

"Of course."

Claudia studied the Teyrnus's wearied expression.

"Mr. Seaborn," she said, sneaking a fleeting glimpse toward Gwenllian. The Acting Matron didn't cut her off. "No one questions your loyalty—or your competence..."

91

"Nor should they!"

"...It's simply that, positioned as you are, so close to the border...."

"We hoped you might have heard some things," Gwenllian explained. "My assistant and I are headed to the Nunnehi Lands. We've already made our arrangements. But anything you could tell us about the mood on the other side of the border...."

"The border?"

"The Nunnehi lands," Claudia said. "If you could help us us...."

"Of course," Seaborn said. "Though, if you want my opinion, you're wasting your time. Let Osanda have her fun; it won't change anything. Not really."

He leaned back, once again at ease. "Tell me what you need. I'll have Aerd get right on it."

Chapter 9

The Three-Headed Chicken of Doom

Friday night was Halloween. Taylor had decided a couple years ago she was too old for trick-or-treating, but Jill enjoyed it, and it was hard to say no to free candy, so right after dinner she threw on the costume she had come up with and headed across the street to Jill's house.

Jill opened the door decked out in a white smock and chef's hat. She carried a black plastic witch's cauldron that just about worked as a cooking pot.

"Ready?"

"One minute. William is having trouble with his cape."

Before Taylor could ask, William appeared in a Batman outfit. The cape didn't hang quite right on his shoulders, and Taylor could see where it was tied in the front. Not quite authentic, but definitely handmade—and the custom black goody bag with the bat-emblem was a dead giveaway. She suspected Maymay's handiwork.

"What are you supposed to be?" William asked, wide-eyed.

Taylor wore a short blue dress over black leggings. She'd put a streak of blue in her hair and put a stick-on sequin on one nostril like a diamond nose stud. She wore dangly earrings and her purple pendant shaped like a hellebore flower. She topped the whole thing off with the black leather jacket Shanna, her birth mother, had given her.

"I'm a fae princess," she said.

93

"That would not have been my first guess," William said.

"And how many fae princesses have you ever seen?"

He shrugged. "Whatever. Let's go."

Taylor gestured with her jack-o'-lantern-shaped pail, and off they went.

The best houses for candy were a couple of blocks over. The sun had nearly set by the time the three reached the right street. They had timed it almost perfectly. Most of the little kids had already gone home, but most of the bigger kids wouldn't be out until later. They didn't quite have the neighborhood to themselves, but it wasn't too crowded, either.

Jill leaned into Taylor before they reached the first house. She sighed.

"I need to say something," she whispered. "Don't be mad."

"What?"

"You've got to quit giving Shelby such a hard time."

Taylor scoffed.

"Enough is enough," Jill said. "What you're doing to her... messing with her head...."

William had already reached the doorbell. A kindly mom opened the door, and a couple of costumed preschoolers dropped candy in each of their bags.

"Oh, look, Billy! It's Batman," the mom gushed. "And a chef! How cute!"

Taylor came to the doorway.

"Mommy, who's she supposed to be?" Billy asked. The mom looked nervously first at her children, then at Taylor.

"I'm a fae princess," Taylor said flatly.

From her expression, that was not the answer Mom was expecting.

"Where I come from, this is what fae princesses look like, all right? Trick or treat."

"Uh...right. Billy, give some candy to the...uh...fae princess."

The three kids said thank you and moved on.

Taylor let William pass in front of them.

94

"Are you saying Shelby hasn't been a royal pain ever since we've known her?"

"No," Jill said. She paused, choosing her words, as they strolled to the next house.

"I'd have thought you'd enjoy her getting a taste of her own medicine."

"That's just it, Taylor. She's not getting anything like what she's ever done to us. Sure, she's obnoxious. She's so full of herself it isn't funny."

"And you don't think she deserves to be taken down a couple of notches?"

"Not like this," Jill said. "Not when she doesn't even know what's happening. Not when she can't even defend herself."

"*Now listen*," Taylor started. Instinctively, she threw some presence into her voice.

Jill flinched, but only for an instant.

"Just...chill, okay?"

Taylor bit her lip. She hated people telling her what to do, but Jill was one of the few who could get away with it. And maybe tormenting Shelby Crowthers had become a bit too enjoyable lately.

"If she doesn't bother me, I won't bother her," she said.

"Hey, guys," William called. He had stopped at the end of the next driveway, waiting for the girls to catch up. He was looking upwards.

"Is that some kind of toy airplane?"

"Where?" Jill said.

William pointed.

Taylor followed his finger. High in the sky, a shadow darted across the darkening sky.

"Is it a plane? Or is it a bird?" Taylor said.

"It's... Oh no!" Jill gasped.

Taylor looked again. It was a bird: a huge copper-red vulture. It was swooping out of the sky right toward them.

And it had three heads.

"Y-you guys see it too, right?" Jill said.

William's mouth dropped open. "Holy...three-headed...."

"I'll take that as a yes," Taylor said.

Taylor screamed and hit the deck—hard. The concrete scraped the heels of her hands, provoking another scream, this one more angry than frightened.

The creature zoomed over her. If she hadn't ducked, at least one of its fierce beaks would have torn into her. Instead, it swooped upward, screeching angrily.

Other kids saw it, too. An elementary school age Cinderella shrieked and barreled into her dad's arms. A couple of preteen Ninja Turtles panicked and froze in the middle of the street.

"I thought vultures only ate dead stuff!" William shouted.

"*I* thought they only had one head!" Taylor quipped. She scrambled back to her feet. Her left hand was bloody. She wiped it against her leg.

The vulture circled around, preparing for another attack.

"Move, kids!" Taylor bounded toward the two Ninja Turtles.

William watched the three-headed vulture begin its second dive.

"It's aiming for Taylor!" he called to Jill. He tore off his Batman cowl and slipped his cape from around his neck. At the same time, he ran into the street after Taylor, trying to put himself between the monster and its target.

It was too fast. It leveled off at about shoulder height and plowed toward Taylor like a torpedo. It was even bigger up close: a wingspan of at least eight feet, with three fierce beaks as big as pickaxes.

"Taylor!" William called. She spun around and made an upward slashing motion with her left hand.

There was a momentary flash or distortion—something William didn't recognize—and the monster veered off with a grunt. It had run into some kind of invisible barrier. Once again, it gained altitude and started circling above their heads.

Taylor shepherded the Ninja Turtles to the curb. A lot of the other trick-or-treaters had taken refuge inside homes or behind parked cars. Dracula ran screaming around the corner followed by Hello Kitty and Spider-Man.

The monster screeched and began another dive.

William mentally worked through his list of resources: a few spell ingredients in the pouches of his utility belt (because seriously, how could he resist?), his protective amulet, and his sister, the magical powerhouse. A few yards away, one of the Ninja Turtles had dropped his quarterstaff: a wooden mop handle painted dark brown. *Why not?* William thought, and scooped it up.

Frantically, he wrapped his cape around his left arm. The monster was closing in on Taylor again. This time he was ready.

He wished Maymay were there.

He dived in front of the creature, shielding Taylor with his cape-wrapped arm. One of the monster's heads latched on.

"Ow!" Even through layers of fabric, that sucker's beak was sharp! And it burned: William choked back the bilious scent of acid. Smoke arose from his cape.

The second head aimed higher up his arm. Before it could strike, William let loose with his improvised club.

The beast hissed and slashed with its talons. William danced around in a circle—anything to keep it from making contact with his unprotected thighs. He got in three or four solid blows with his stick, but it didn't even faze the thing.

Then there was another flash. The monster squealed and let go, flapping clumsily to regain altitude.

William exhaled.

Jill was breathing heavy. "What...what was that—?"

"Not now," William said. "It's coming back." He glanced toward where Taylor had been standing, but she must have taken cover.

It didn't matter; the creature was coming after him now.

He pondered his options.

What would Batman do?

He'd be the goshdang Batman, you moron! He began to form a plan.

"Jill! How about some wind!" he called.

"What?"

"Amou aneme..."

"Oh, right!" Jill began to chant.

Amou aneme phthaneme pneuma ventibus thoou!

As soon as Jill started, William switched his mop handle to his left hand and pulled a plastic snack bag from his utility belt. Then he realized he needed both hands for what he was planning. He dropped his stick and opened the zip-top seal.

Amou aneme phthaneme pneuma ventibus thoou!

A gentle breeze began to blow.

"It's coming in!" William called. He positioned himself to intercept. "Try to blow it down!"

Jill nodded and kept on chanting. She extended her hands toward the monster.

Williams hands were shaking and clumsy. Stupid bat-gloves! He finally just upended the bag, filling his right hand with a scoop of a grayish, grainy mixture. He silently practiced the activation word.

Amou aneme phthaneme pneuma ventibus thoou!
Amou aneme phthaneme pneuma ventibus thoou!

The wind picked up strength.

The monster swooped toward William, hissing angrily.

Jill mimicked pushing something to the ground with both hands.

The wind concentrated in a powerful downdraft, smashing the monster into the pavement.

It was now or never.

William leaped as close to the vulture as he dared, slammed the handful of mixture against its back, and shouted "*Hexiphore!*"

The vulture grunted and tried to nip at William's legs with all three beaks. This time, it came up short. In fact, after a moment's fury, it recoiled from William's presence completely.

William emptied the rest of the bag into his hand and raised it over his head.

Six beady eyes trained on him, blinked, and turned away. The vulture hissed something in three-part harmony. It took off with a running start, climbed into the air, and flew away.

Jill ran to her brother's side. She leaned into his shoulder and breathed hard for what seemed like an eternity.

Frightened faces started to appear in windows and doors all around.

"Dang fool kids and their drones!" a man shouted to his neighbor.

"Oughta be a law against them things!" the neighbor agreed.

Jill stumbled toward William. "Banishing spell?"

William nodded.

"That was not a mole."

"Nope."

"How did you know it would work?"

"I didn't," William admitted. "We're lucky it did, but I don't know for how long. We need to—" He cut himself off. He suddenly remembered something.

He pushed himself away from Jill and looked around.

"Jill?" he said. "W-where's Taylor?"

Taylor tried to blast the vulture, but nothing happened. Then it flapped away, stunned. Maybe Jill or William had done something to it. She wasn't sure.

But that's when things started getting weird. The creature's wing beats slowed to an impossible rate. It hung still in the air in precisely the way that vultures don't.

Jill and William had also slowed down. William was in mid-jump, recoiling from the monster's powerful wings. Jill was a frozen statue of panic.

99

Children ran for cover in slow motion.

Somebody hit the mute button on the world.

"What the—?"

A will-o'-the-wisp flitted by.

Taylor followed it with her eyes. It zipped among the parked cars and down the block at a leisurely pace.

At the end of the block was a shimmering pillar of light. It wasn't super bright—more like the way heat distorts the air rising off of hot concrete—but concentrated into a narrow line, like the world itself had a perfectly straight crease in it.

The orb of faery fire circled around, then plunged into the pillar and vanished. A second later, it reappeared, blinked two or three times, then disappeared again.

"Okay, I'll bite," Taylor said.

She gave her frozen friends another backward glance, then trotted down the street and into the portal.

It took her into woods, and Taylor realized she was still only a few blocks from her house. Since the mushroom ring in back of her house connected to a faery woodland, it stood to reason she was still in the same general area.

She started to summon an orb of faery fire to light her way, then thought better of it. Instead, she drew the glamour around her into a magical mist, concealing her from any prying eyes. It arose from between her shoulder blades and enveloped her like a warm blanket. A lot of things in the Wonder could see through glamour, she knew, but she still took comfort in being practically invisible—as long as she didn't sneeze or step on a twig or something equally stupid.

The fire orb she had followed into the Wonder zipped ahead of her. She tried to keep it in sight while moving as silently as she could.

Above her, something fluttered in the trees. She could see in the dark better than most normal humans, but whatever it was moved so fast she never got a clear look at it.

Then she heard a thin, raspy chuckle.

She resisted the urge to call out "Who's there?" Has anybody in real life ever been stupid enough to do that? Instead, she took a slow breath and tried to remember Danny's lessons. She allowed her magical senses to flow outward from her body, probing the darkness, searching for living things.

A raccoon in a tree behind her.

A couple of frogs in a nearby stream.

An owl circling above—must have been what she heard before.

Then she felt it. It wasn't precisely human but close enough. It was trying to flank her, coming up on her right.

She stood perfectly still.

It hesitated. Could it see her despite her glamour? Was it waiting for her to make the first move?

It chuckled again.

"I know you're out there," a male voice taunted.

It inched forward. She couldn't see it, but she *felt* it with her extended senses.

She lowered her body into a defensive stance and silently began to repeat to herself the war formula Tsisgwa had taught her.

She flexed the stinging fingers of her blood-streaked hand, gathering magic for a blast.

The wind shifted. A flock of dead leaves migrated across her path, kicking up dust. They skittered in front of and behind her. Some slammed harmlessly into her before continuing on their way.

"There you are!" the voice said.

Then she figured it out: the blowing leaves betrayed her location.

Rats!

There was nothing for it but to face him.

A long, lean figure emerged from the woods. He was dressed in all in black. Ugly did not begin to describe his warty, skeletal face. In his hand he carried a burlap sack.

101

"Have I met your cousin?" she said. In fact, the first faery creature she had ever seen in all its glory was a bag-man she and Jill had nicknamed Uncle Waldo.

He crept closer.

Taylor tried to remember everything she knew about bag-men. They were like other kinds of bogeymen: not super-powerful—but powerful enough.

"You know what happens to bad little girls," he taunted, waving his sack.

She thrust her right hand forward, pushing the magic of her blast toward the bag-man's chest.

It passed over him like a harmless puff of smoke.

Taylor swore under her breath.

The bag-man saw his opportunity and sprung toward Taylor. Taylor dodged and tried to block his advance with a shield spell. It caused him to stumble, but only for an instant. Then he was charging her again, hollering at the top of his lungs.

Taylor dove for the trees.

The bag-man caught her by the collar of her jacket. She wriggled out of it and sped away. He cackled with glee and continued the chase.

Taylor knew he was right, but what could she do about it? If he had beaten her magic mist, if her combat magic had failed, she would have to try something else.

She realized Shelby Crowthers might have the answer.

She skidded to a stop and spun around, hands in a defensive stance. She summoned glamour and poured it into a single syllable.

"*Boo!*" she said.

The bag-man's eyes glazed over, as if he had suddenly forgotten what he was supposed to do. He teetered a bit, like he was drunk or drugged. The expression on his face suggested Tommy Morgan being asked to solve an algebra problem.

"*She went that way!*" Taylor said, pointing, and she threw as much presence into it as she knew how.

The bag-man grunted and stumbled into the woods.

Taylor retrieved her jacket.

"All right!" she called. "The vulture, the faery fire, the time-stop...thingy. That's not the work of a bogeyman, so who else is out there?"

Frogs and crickets, apparently.

Taylor slowly turned, taking in her environment.

Then a familiar female voice pierced the night.

"Only me."

The voice came from behind Taylor. She spun around. In the distance was an aura of pale blue light that hadn't been there before.

She bit her lip and walked toward it.

A woman sat in a white chair. Her sky-blue gown was sleeveless, exposing the pale skin of her arms. Her luxuriant black hair was tied back from her face in a complicated network of silver threads.

But the most arresting thing about her was her sunglasses—and the red welts behind them.

"Mara," Taylor said.

Mara Hellebore nodded.

An owl descended from the trees, took its place beside the Chief Matron of the Winter Court, and expanded into a human shape: a Native American man in jeans and a Grateful Dead tee shirt.

Taylor jumped back and conjured a shield spell.

"There's no need for that," Mara said. "Mr. Hook won't hurt you...without my permission."

Taylor lowered her guard, but only slightly.

Mara looked her over and arched an eyebrow. "I see you've inherited your mother's fashion sense. Pity."

Taylor's birth mother—Mara's daughter—was a sore spot and a potentially dangerous one, so she left the comment to hang in the air. She took a breath and said, "So, just passing through, I take it?"

"Just keeping an eye on my investment," Mara said. "Or have you forgotten our agreement from this past summer?"

"I haven't forgotten," Taylor said.

"You owe me a favor," Mara said. "The price for sparing your deathling friend."

"And...?"

"And I was curious what you could do. I see you've become passably competent at the art of addlement. That's impressive."

"I've been practicing."

"You'll find it is a glamour that only works on the weak or the distracted."

"I can see that."

"You'll find that I am neither."

"I can see that, too."

"The bogeyman was merely intended to collect you and bring you to me. I was hoping to see what you'd do against Ellen. One on one, without your little friends to help you."

"Ellen? You named a three-headed vulture Ellen?"

Mara shrugged.

"In any event, I don't believe you're quite ready to pay your debt. Another year or two, perhaps."

"Oh, joy."

"Have no fear. I will not forget about you."

That was exactly what Taylor was afraid of. But she wasn't going to let her grandmother know that.

"How're those eyes doing?" she said.

Mara winced. Her cheeks reddened. Taylor suppressed a smirk.

"Mending," Mara growled.

Taylor cocked her head. "Pity."

Mara straightened the folds of her gown. "I believe we're through here. For now. Should you see Anya Redmane, be sure to tell her she is missed."

She waved her arm, and Taylor vanished in a swirl of sparkling lights.

Chapter 10

Dinner with the Nunnehi

Seaborn had provided a servant to help Claudia and Gwenllian with their things. Blue was roughly eleven feet tall, maybe eleven-six, with brown skin and straight black hair in a bowl cut. He had high cheekbones and heavy eyelids.

He wore woolen trousers, a single leg of which would have provided ample material for a new suit for Claudia, and a simple buckskin vest. He wore no shoes, and something about his flat, stubby feet reminded Claudia of an elephant's.

"Blue, we're grateful you can come with us," Claudia said. "I hope it isn't an inconvenience."

The giant uttered a satisfied grunt. "Travel," he said with a smile, as if that explained everything.

Other than being twice as tall as he should have been and nearly ten times as massive, his most striking feature was the heavy, sloping brow ridge that seemed to push his eyes downward toward his earlobes. It gave him a sad puppy-dog face even when he smiled.

Blue was smiling as he picked up Claudia's suitcase between his thumb and fingers and slid it deftly into a humongous canvas backpack. Gwenllian's things had already been packed. With Claudia's added, there might have still been room for a Great Dane or two.

"Is that everything, Blue?" Gwenllian said.

"Everything," he repeated with a nod. His voice was soft and flat, though unspeakably deep.

"Then go put on some nicer clothes. We don't want the nunnehi to think you're being mistreated."

Blue fingered the hem of his vest and gave Gwenllian a forlorn look. Claudia guessed he would rather be comfortable than meet someone else's idea of presentable. But he nodded and excused himself.

Gwenllian turned to Claudia. "I assume you've had dealings with these people?"

Claudia chose her words carefully. "My father lives in the Depths," she said. "There weren't many nunnehi in my neighborhood growing up."

"They're worthy opponents," Gwenllian said. Then she grinned and added, "but manageable."

"I take it you've dealt with the nunnehi before?"

"Long ago. The last time the Summer and Winter Courts were trying to kill each other, the nunnehi sent a scouting party to test our defenses."

"Trying to capitalize on the disorder," Claudia said.

"Precisely. My husband was Teyrnus of Dunhoughkey in those days, and that is where they tried to enter Arradherry."

"Unsuccessfully, I take it?"

"We suspected the nunnehi would try something like that." She smiled. "My husband's men were ready for them."

Blue returned wearing a clean pair of trousers and a white cotton long-sleeve shirt. He was still barefooted.

"Much better," Gwenllian said.

To Claudia, she said, "We let them go, of course—no need to bring foreigners in to a situation that was already messy enough as it was."

"You just...let them go?" That didn't sound like the sídhe.

Gwenllian nodded. "Let's just say the nunnehi leader was... motivated to bargain for his men's freedom."

Ah. So Gwenllian at least got something out of the incident.

"Ready?" Blue said.

"You're quite right," Gwenllian said. "We'll be late if we keep yammering like this. Blue?"

106

Blue lifted the oversized pack to his back—over 200 pounds of clothing, papers, supplies, and provisions—without even a sigh. The three entered the ring of standing stones outside the rath of Tobarty and disappeared.

They entered Tsuwatelda shortly after noon. Claudia shivered from the crisp mountain breeze. Even with the sun shining in the clear turquoise sky, it was bound to be chilly at this altitude.

An escort of warriors in buckskins and scarlet ribbons met them at the standing stones outside the town's wooden palisade, offered perfunctory words of greeting, and then marched them into town with a dozen or so warriors leading the way and an equal number taking up the rear. They had introduced themselves as an honor guard, but Claudia suspected they were more of a subtle warning: Don't try anything.

Tsuwatelda was one of the largest fae settlements on the continent, very nearly the rival of Bisgarra Verry itself. Claudia took in the sights, careful not to appear overly familiar with one of the leading towns of Arradherry's traditional enemy.

Fifteen thousand pairs of eyes marked their passing. Blue in particular seemed to be quite a spectacle. The giant ambled along behind, smiling and even waving in embarrassment as if everyone had come out to see him and not the sídhe noblewoman who had come to confer with their Chiefs. Some, especially the young, stopped to gawk. Their parents called them to their chores, however, and they reluctantly turned away.

Older fae and little folk snatched furtive glances as a Matron of Arradherry's Summer Court processed down the main thoroughfare toward the town square. Claudia judged a mixture of curiosity, wariness, and outright anger at their passing.

A swarthy little person smirked at them and shook his head as he took a draw on his pipe.

A dapper Native American fae in a nineteenth-century topcoat bowed deeply as they passed, the feathers adorning his braided hair falling forward. Something about his phony smile told Claudia his gesture was more than a little sarcastic.

Tsuwatelda's Council House stood atop a massive artificial mound at the center of town overlooking the vast stickball field. The Council House wasn't their goal, however. In fact, the mount itself was the highest of Tsuwatelda's high-class neighborhoods. Circling the Council House were a dozen impressive townhouses, the homes of the Chiefs and their extended families.

Standing beside the Council House, a detachment of the honor guard directed Blue toward the guesthouse where Claudia and Gwenllian would stay.

The remainder of the guard led the two women through a broad avenue to the largest of the mound's townhouses.

Claudia held her breath. Gwenllian knew she had grown up in the Nunnehi Lands, and it stood to reason she'd have visited Tsuwatelda at some point. Now, though, she would have to give the impression that she was meeting the important men they had come to see for the first time.

An imposing figure met them at the door: a warrior in full regalia—not the simple buckskins of their escort. A half-dozen earrings circled the lobes of both his ears, and his head was shaven except for a single topknot festooned with beads and red and black feathers.

The warrior gestured for them to enter. They did, along with only four members of their escort. The rest were dismissed with a crisp gesture.

Their remaining escort ushered them to a dining room where sat the men they had come to meet.

At the head of the table sat a man dressed in white. His steel-gray hair was carefully braided and topped with a cap banded with white leather, from which jutted a spray of long, white feathers. The same sort of feathers spread from the tip of the scepter in his hands.

"Chief Tewa." Gwenllian bowed. The action shook Claudia out of her fascination with the nunnehi Chief, and she followed suit.

"Matron Birdsong," Chief Tewa said, returning the salute. He didn't make any gesture toward Claudia or even acknowledge her presence.

On either side of the long, low table sat the other Chiefs, whom Chief Tewa introduced. Chief Inali was the Red Chief of Tsuwatelda, the town's war leader. His ceremonial garb was much like Chief Tewa's but in red and black. He wore a red bandana and a multitude of beads, bangles, and feathers on the fringe of his cloak.

Across from him sat Chief Kalahu, the Medicine Chief. He, Claudia knew, was the likely peacemaker, revered for his mystical insight and his magical prowess. His clothing seemed simpler than that of the other chiefs in some ways, but he had countless charms and amulets draped around his neck.

Gwenllian took her seat opposite Chief Tewa, with Claudia immediately to her right. Claudia set her writing tablet on her lap and pulled a pen from her jacket pocket.

"Gentlemen," Gwenllian said, "shall we begin?"

The meeting went pretty much as Claudia expected. Without ever mentioning her name, Gwenllian advised the Chiefs that Osanda Morning didn't speak for the Summer Court, and nothing was likely to come of any promises she may have made.

The Chiefs were respectful but guarded. They said very little, actually, other than to state—numerous times and in various ways—that they hoped the state of peace that had prevailed between the Nunnehi lands and Arradherry for the past seventy years would continue. Chief Inali suggested, not entirely subtly, that this would be easier if the sídhe would simply keep their distance.

There were no fireworks, no shocking revelations. The Chiefs said nothing about Osanda's recent visit.

But the mood was tense. The Chiefs knew Anya Redmane's ouster had thrown all Arradherry into chaos. Who would come out on top—and what would be their intentions toward the Nunnehi Lands?

The past seventy years weren't so much peaceful as lacking any good reason to go back to war. Nobody on either side was sure how much longer that situation would last.

They talked all afternoon. After a brief adjournment, the meeting resumed with a formal dinner later that evening. It was a model of cool but polite formality. The Chiefs' wives joined them at the table along with some of the other leading citizens of Tsuwatelda.

None of this surprised Claudia. Everything was going exactly as Gwenllian had planned. Diplomatic talks would continue as long as they needed to.

And that would give Claudia plenty of time to spy on the nunnehi Chiefs.

"We must know how much damage Osanda has done," Gwenllian had told her back in Tobarty. "Do they believe she has a chance at winning my seat on the Triad? Will they actively try to help her?"

"They're not stupid, Mrs. Birdsong," Claudia said. "They won't risk war by openly interfering in sídhe politics."

"Not openly," Gwenllian agreed, "but these savages are cleverer than we give them credit for. If they decide they like that woman, I'll wager they've got tricks that would put the daoine sídhe to shame."

And so they met the Chiefs and spouted platitudes about improved relations between "our two great peoples" and the value of non-interference. Gwenllian made subtle comments about Osanda's credibility—or lack thereof. Claudia pretended she was nothing but Gwenllian's administrative assistant.

Then they bade their hosts goodnight and returned to their guesthouse. Claudia changed out of her business suit and put on a simpler outfit: a woolen skirt and loose-fitting cotton shirt girded with a wide leather belt. She slipped on a pair of moccasins and wrapped a voluminous shawl over her shoulders.

Her real work was about to begin.

It was a foregone conclusion that the nunnehi would watch the guesthouse for any signs of magic. Claudia needed a place where she could work without arousing suspicion.

So she sneaked outside and trotted down from the mound and wove her way through the streets of the lower town. She soon found the house she was looking for.

She furtively knocked at the door.

Thankfully, the street was clear. Even so, as soon as Shanna Hellebore opened the door, Claudia pushed past her into her modest home.

"Claudia?" Shanna said. "What are you—?"

"I don't mean to impose," Claudia said, "but I need to ask you a favor."

"Uh. Come in?" Shanna said.

Claudia was already three steps past the door. She gave the room a quick glance. It was a large but modestly appointed combination living and dining room with a stove and kitchen tucked away in one corner and a single bedroom straight ahead.

Shanna looked much as she had the last time Claudia saw her. Her wild black hair was trimmed extra short on the sides and with a shock of electric blue above her left temple that brought out the color of her eyes. She wore a diamond nose stud, black jeans, and a sleeveless top in neon pink tiger stripes.

"What's the matter?" she said.

"Shanna, I assume you know about Gwenllian Birdsong's arrival?"

She rolled her eyes. "Chief Tewa doesn't want me within a hundred yards of the Council House until she's gone. It was the same when Osanda Morning came."

It couldn't have been easy on Shanna. After fourteen years locked in her parents' dungeon, Tsuwatelda was her chance at freedom—as long as she kept her head down. With the constant parade of sídhe noblewomen passing through town lately, even that threatened to disappear.

111

"The White Chief is rightly concerned," Claudia said at last. "I won't say it hasn't been hard on you to stay cooped up here. I'm sorry."

"It can't be helped," Shanna shrugged. "I can't imagine what my parents would trade for information about where I am—or what they'd do to anyone found helping me. But Claudia? What are you doing here?"

"It's complicated, Shanna, and unfortunately the less you know, the better."

"Y-yes?"

"I've got some conjuring to do. I need a safe place to work."

Shanna's eyes met hers.

"You can use my bedroom."

Chapter 11

Faring Forth

Claudia sat cross-legged in a circle she had drawn. With her eyes closed, she reached outward with her magical senses: past the modest furnishings of Shanna's bedroom, past the main room where Shana sat sipping coffee, into the lower town of Tsuwatelda. It was harder indoors, in a populated area, than if she had been alone in the wilderness, but the circle helped her focus.

This was delicate work—not just the magic but the reason she was doing it. If anyone found out, things could get complicated. She was sworn to aid Gwenllian in her bid to secure her seat on the Triad. She was also a spy sent by the nunnehi to keep an eye on the Summer Court.

She never imagined her work for the Summer Court would involve spying on Tewa himself!

While Shanna waited in the outer room, Claudia sat in the dark, gathering her magic. She allowed her breathing to become shallow, measured. Before long, she became aware of creatures lurking in the night. Rodents and snakes and insects would never do, though. She needed...

Aha! A bat.

With an effort of will, Claudia zeroed in on a red bat resting in a tree south of the stickball field.

She settled her senses upon the creature, sidling up to it ever so slowly lest it sense something was wrong.

A few more seconds, she thought. *Easy does it.*

She let her mind enter the bat's body. She allowed herself to hear with the bat's ears and see with its eyes.

113

She shuddered with a slight rush of revulsion—and so did her host.

At first, she only rested beneath the creature's consciousness, getting used to the feel of a bat's body: the lightness of the skin stretched out to form its wings, the span of its peripheral vision, the acuteness of its hearing. When it darted into the sky to hunt for flying insects, Claudia didn't object. Sharing the bat's sensation of snatching a moth on the wing and downing it in one gulp was another matter.

Faring forth took great concentration, and it was tempting to rush the process. But Claudia knew she'd get better results by taking her time.

And so she did nothing but flit around the nunnehi city and the woods beyond for a half hour or more, dining on whatever tiny tidbits the bat could catch.

At last, she felt the time was ripe. She exerted her will and, with another shudder of resistance from her host, took control of the bat's body.

She soared high over the woods beyond the palisade. It took her a few seconds to get her bearings before skirting across the black sky toward the center of Tsuwatelda.

The city was settling down for the night. The autumn sun had set, and children's mothers were calling them home. Claudia flitted over the winding streets of the lower town. She spied Shanna's house, and Shanna herself drawing her curtains for the night. She seemed uneasy, and Claudia couldn't blame her. She'd been careful not to explain what she was up to, but that wouldn't likely matter if the sídhe woman were found harboring a spy.

Down the street, some of Shanna's neighbors were having some sort of get-together. The jumbled sounds of music and conversation filled the air and nearly overwhelmed Claudia's newly heightened hearing.

Convinced that Shanna was all right, she flitted away. Her destination was the central mound, and it was time she got there.

114

She came in from the south, across the stickball field. Blue sat at the foot of the mound, where the older children of Tsuwatelda ringed around him. They were in awe of the giant and delighted that he didn't mind their attention. He smiled broadly as he stretched out his arms and let them feel his rock-hard muscles. In her borrowed bat's form, Claudia thought he was even more enormous that usual.

Guards stood watch at the White Chief's door, which was not unexpected. But Claudia had no intention of going in through the front door. Rather, she landed on the roof. As near as she could tell, her presence didn't set off any magical alarms. As far as the house was concerned, she was just an ordinary bat.

Once again, she wondered of the repercussions if she were discovered. Tewa would have to understand she can't refuse Gwenllian's orders, right? Her value to the nunnehi hinged upon the quality of her service to the Summer Court.

And yet, Tewa was bound to object to any agent of Arradherry spying on him. Honor would demand satisfaction. Claudia didn't want to think about what it would take to satisfy the honor of the White Chief of Tsuwatelda.

She scrambled across the roof, listening for signs of activity below. Finding a sliver of an opening under the eaves of the house, she crawled in. Once inside, she followed the sound of muffled voices.

The space above the ceiling was dark and dusty, but it gave her access to much of the house's floor plan. She pivoted her bat-ears, easily picking up the direction of the conversation. Sliding into a tiny crevasse, she found herself inside an air vent that opened into Tewa's private office.

The White Chief sat on a cushion with the other chiefs around him in a semicircle: Inali, the Red Chief, grim and menacing even in repose; Kalahu, the Medicine Chief, fiddling with one of the many amulets he wore around his neck.

Before them, standing at attention, was a younger nunnehi Claudia had never seen before.

115

"I don't know, Chief Tewa," he was saying. "She is sincere… but more than that, I couldn't say."

"Sincere or not," Chief Inali said, "how much influence does she *really* have? Hmm? Before we decide what to do about her, don't you think we should ask ourselves that question?"

Claudia's tiny heart raced. She ducked back from the grate. No point risking being seen when her superlative hearing could tell her everything she wanted to know.

"She may have more influence than you think, Inali." This was Chief Kalahu speaking. "She has become something of a symbol, especially among the little folk and the lesser sprites."

"I agree," Chief Tewa said. "She is only now coming to the attention of many. But she represents a challenge to the status quo."

That much, Claudia already knew. Osanda had been shaking things up for months. But what would the nunnehi do about her?

"I urge caution, Tewa," Chief Inali said. "We have been optimistic about winds of change in Arradherry before."

"We trusted Vergosus Bright once," Chief Kalahu added.

"Indeed," Chief Inali said. There was a moment of restless silence before he continued. "I find it hard to trust any sídhe— no matter how young or idealistic."

"Is this the same Inali who once pledged his warriors to support her cause?"

When Claudia heard this, she let out a squeak in spite of herself. When did this happen? They weren't considering an invasion, were they? What were the nunnehi up to?

She dared to creep closer to the grate. She wanted to see the expressions on their faces.

"If it would undermine the seasonal Courts, I would lend my war club to a brood of tie snakes," Inali answered.

Claudia saw the fire in the Red Chief's eyes and knew he was telling the truth.

"I'm inclined to trust her sincerity," Chief Tewa said. He started to say more, then folded his hands on his lap and sighed.

"But?" Chief Kalahu said.

"But how far can any sídhe be trusted?"

There were murmurs of agreement around the table.

"She is, at the very least, a variable in a highly volatile situation," Chief Kalahu said.

Chief Inali agreed. "Perhaps a key variable, if you believe the dwarves."

"The dwarves?" the young man Claudia didn't know puzzled.

"You weren't present when I enlisted the dwarves to help her find her birth mother," Tewa said.

And Claudia felt sick to her stomach.

They hadn't been talking about Osanda Morning at all. They had been talking about Taylor Smart. The surprise was almost enough to break Claudia's connection and send her consciousness back to Shanna's bedroom.

"...said she could be the most dangerous fae alive," Tewa was saying. "Don't ask me what that means, but after her recent run-in with the Winter Court...."

Claudia gritted her fangs. Her connection was, indeed, breaking up. She had simply been absent from her body for too long.

"You may trust her sincerity," Chief Inali said, his voice now muffled, distant. "But I'm not sure I trust *her*. Not until she's older. Not until she becomes more the person she is destined to be. Our other spy in Ichisi says she is volatile. Unpredictable. Do you agree, Tsisgwa?"

The young man nodded. "She lacks focus," he said. "She's impulsive. She's used to getting her way. But there's no doubt...." Claudia missed the last part. She tried to focus, to remain in the bat's consciousness just a little bit longer.

"All the more reason to keep an eye on her," Chief Inali said. He shifted in his seat. "Tewa, are you sure you want your granddaughter befriending this sídhe?"

"Ayoka knows nothing of my concerns, Inali, and I intend to keep it that way."

"That doesn't answer my question," Chief Inali said.

Chief Tewa bowed his head. He said something that Claudia couldn't catch, then: "It can only help our cause for Taylor to have fond feelings for the nunnehi."

"And if Ayoka learns to have fond feelings for Taylor?"

"Ayoka is a sensible girl. She knows where her loyalties lie."

The table fell silent.

"Tsisgwa," Chief Tewa said, "continue to train Taylor. If in the end she proves an ally, we'll want her able to defend herself. If not...I'll expect you to report..." his voice became garbled again. The room began to blur.

The man named Tsisgwa nodded.

"Keep her safe. Coordinate with...." Again, Chief Tewa's words became a jumble. Claudia nearly groaned in frustration. "...if the situation changes."

"Yes, Chief."

There were further words, but Claudia couldn't hear them. Her vision blurred completely, and with a shiver she departed the body of her bat host. She felt lightheaded. She had fared forth for longer than she had ever tried before.

She opened her eyes to find herself sprawled on Shanna's floor.

She felt weak and disoriented—another reason Claudia didn't like faring forth. She was vulnerable enough while she was away from her body. Even when she returned, though, she was so sapped she wasn't much use to anybody.

She heard voices, but garbled as if she were listening from underwater.

There were two people in the outer room, whispering to each other. Tewa? No, that was before, while she was a bat. This voice was younger. He was talking to Shanna and pacing back and forth.

"...seize pittance cough more than she can chew," Shanna said. At least, that's what it sounded like as Claudia's brain started to unfuzz. She rubbed her eyes. When she opened them again, she caught a glimpse of movement in the open doorway. She saw black curly hair above a ruddy pink face with an

118

over-large nose. She smiled as she recognized her old friend. Shanna continued, "You've got to help her understand that, Danny."

"Danny," Claudia said, stumbling forward.

"Claudia," Danny said, grinning. "I didn't mean to interrupt you. To tell the truth, I didn't even know you was in town. I just came by to—"

Claudia cut him off with a hug, but pulled away just as quickly. Rising to her feet so fast made her lightheaded. Danny and Shanna steadied her and guided her to a chair.

"Claudia is traveling with Gwenllian Birdsong," Shanna said.

Danny sucked in a breath.

"I might have figured you'd be in the middle of that," he said. "Summer's keeping you busy."

"You don't know the half of it," Claudia said. She started to say more but stopped herself. The less people like Danny knew about what she was doing, the less someone else—either Tewa or Gwenllian, take your pick—could get out of them.

It was coming back to her now. The nunnehi Chiefs had been talking about Taylor Smart, wondering if she could be trusted. Wondering if they could use her.

She eyed Shanna and pursed her lips. Time to change the subject.

"Help who understand what?"

Now it was Shanna's turn to look nervously at the others in the room. She started to say something, but Danny interrupted.

"I sorta been...teaching Taylor some magic."

Oh.

"Danny's been living in these parts," Shanna said. "But he's also keeping an eye on Taylor...at my request."

"She lives somewhere Topside of Ichisi, doesn't she?"

Shanna nodded. "Danny has been a dear, popping down there." She gave him a smile, which made Danny blush. "It's just so frustrating not to be able to see her in person!"

"We been over this before, Mrs. Hellebore," Danny said.

"And I've told you, it's Shanna."

119

"Well, Shanna then. And the fact is, Chief Tewa has a point: You ain't got no business leaving Pilot Knob. Or Tsuwatelda, as the folks here call it."

"I know, I know," she said. "If I keep my head down, my parents can still pretend I didn't escape from them." She spoke as if rehearsing an argument she had heard too many times. "If I start showing up outside Tsuwatelda, it could be difficult for everyone. Honor would need to be satisfied."

"That's right," Danny said.

"Well, it doesn't mean I have to like it. Oh, Claudia, I'm afraid Taylor is in trouble!"

Do tell. "What's the matter?"

She sighed. "Danny tells me... He says Taylor is very angry with my mother. She tried to hurt one of Taylor's Topside friends."

Danny jumped in. "It's like she's on a mission or something. She's got me teaching her about shape-shifting—which a thirteen-year-old ain't got no business messing with!—and I hear Chief Tewa's granddaughter's been teaching her how to fight."

Under Tsisgwa's watchful eye, no doubt, Claudia surmised.

"I'm just afraid...." Shanna choked back a sob.

"What is it, honey?" Claudia said.

"I'm afraid she's going to end up like Aulberic."

Claudia had never met Aulberic Redmane. Everyone knew the story of how he and Shanna ran away together.

"He was hotheaded, too." Shanna said. She clenched her fists. She was still a Winter fae, after all. She wouldn't let her emotions get the better of her, even among friends. "All the Redmanes are, really. It was his idea for us to elope. No planning whatsoever. When my father caught up with us...he and his men...Aulberic thought he could stand up to him. He... He..." Shanna took a long, slow breath.

"Now, don't be thinking about that," Danny said. He placed a hand on Shanna's shoulder. She looked at him fondly.

"Danny's right, Shanna." Claudia stood back up. She put both her hands on Shanna's shoulders and looked her in the eye. "There's nothing to be gained from living in the past. Certainly not from letting it color your present."

"Taylor ain't like Aulberic," Danny added. "She ain't gonna go off half-cocked just 'cause she's got a mind to get one over on Mara—your ma, that is."

"B-but the shape-shifting, the combat magic..." Shanna protested.

"Maybe she's just being cautious," Claudia said. "There's no denying Taylor has made some mighty impressive enemies this past year."

"Claudia's right," Danny said. "She just wants to be able to protect herself. That's all."

"Are y-you sure?"

"Darn right I'm sure. She was the one that figured out how to spring you from Mrs. Redmane *and* your folks, wasn't she?"

Shanna nodded.

"That just goes to show you." He tapped the side of his head. "She thinks ahead. She takes after you that way, I expect. And she's too smart to get roped into doing something stupid—even if she wants to."

"I hope you're right, Danny."

"I'm pretty much always right." He gave her a sly grin. "Trust me. The last thing on Taylor Smart's mind is picking a fight with Mara Hellebore."

Chapter 12

A Special-Delivery Message

Taylor spent Saturday morning planning how to fight Mara Hellebore.

She crouched in her combat stance, squared off against Athlan Tastanagi himself. Tsisgwa was away on some kind of official business, but for some reason the Great Tastanagi had taken an interest in her training. The two of them faced each other at the edge of the stickball field while Ayoka and a dozen other kids played.

"Now," he said.

Taylor flexed her right hand, then thrust it forward, propelling a concentrated ball of magical force into Athlan's stomach.

"Excellent!" he said. And Taylor could feel it, too. She had finally managed to conjure a decent blast. True, the Great Tastanagi brushed it away with a casual gesture. But she wasn't going to let that discourage her. She was finally making some progress.

And she felt awful.

As soon as the blast left her body, so did her energy. She was sapped. She wasn't about to give up, though. Her run-in with Mara on Halloween only made her more determined to learn how to defend herself.

She wobbled on her bare feet as Athlan prepared to blast her in return. He moved slowly, exaggerating his gestures so Taylor knew exactly what was coming. Still, it barely gave her time to raise her left hand, concentrate on her true name, and throw up a magical shield.

Athlan's blast popped it like a soap bubble.

Taylor was stunned to realize, however, that she hadn't been thrown to the ground.

"You're learning," Athlan said. "Now, come at me again. At once!"

"I can't." Taylor may have still been on her feet, but her magic was spent.

"You must," Athlan said. "The booger fae won't wait for you. You must come back fast and h—"

Athlan took a step back. He shook his head as if waking up from a deep sleep.

"Hard."

Taylor grinned.

"Very good," Athlan said. "For a second I lost my train of thought. Some kind of glamour trick?"

Taylor nodded. "And I heard that word again."

"My apologies," Athlan said. "I've devoted my life to defending my people against...." His face darkened, as if he was remembering something unpleasant from long ago. "Against the sídhe and their allies. I know how devious they can be. How important it is to stop them."

"I guess I understand," Taylor said. "But try to remember I'm one, too, okay?"

"Of course."

"So, my glamour trick almost worked?"

Athlan nodded. "Almost. Against someone your own level, it might have worked perfectly."

"Well, I had to do *something*," Taylor said.

"A blast is your most basic attack," Athlan said. "But you already know it takes a lot out of you. Even the strongest warriors need time to recharge."

"Right."

"The mark of a true warrior is how he or she fights in the meantime. We nunnehi prefer to use elf-shot or to confuse the enemy with our invisibility. Others shape-shift. Some use

124

illusion or other talents. The key is to be resourceful. Know your strengths."

Taylor wiped her sweaty hands on her gym shorts.

"My friend Silas said something like that once," she said. "It's more than just lobbing fireballs around."

"Indeed. Our Kind fight with illusion and misdirection at least as much as with blasts or elf-shot. When the fae go to war, things are rarely as they seem."

"I'll try to remember that."

"What do you think? Can you blast me again?"

She shook her head.

"Not to worry," Athlan said. "Speed will come with practice."

"Fast is last," Taylor said with a huff.

"What?"

"Something my piano teacher says. Don't mess yourself up trying to play a new piece of music *a tempo* before you've really learned it."

Athlan grunted appreciatively. Then he looked at Taylor as if he'd just remembered something.

"Cedar," he said.

"What?"

"The aroma of cedar will help you focus."

"Cedar," Taylor repeated.

"Yes. Essential oil of cedar. Mix it with a base oil like safflower or sweet almond. Put the mixture in a bottle with narrow neck along with reeds or bamboo skewers."

Taylor looked at him like he was crazy. He continued, "If that sounds too complicated, the Topsiders sell kits with everything you need. Try a candle shop."

"And that will help me focus?"

Athlan nodded. "Absolutely. Try it."

Taylor wasn't convinced, but it wasn't the weirdest thing she'd heard in the past year.

Just then, Ayoka sprinted up to Taylor. "We're starting a game," she announced. "Want to play?"

Athlan nodded that he had finished his lesson. Taylor was sore all over, but the thought of Mara Hellebore's smirking face left her no choice. She reached out her hands for the sticks Ayoka was offering her.

After a couple of hours, Taylor was completely beat. She went home exhausted and plopped onto her bed without even bothering to shower.

She laid motionless on her belly as the fire in her muscles gradually cooled.

She had nearly fallen asleep when she heard a gentle tapping on her window.

What now? she thought.

She forced herself up and lurched toward the window on her sore legs. She pulled open the blinds and gasped. A brown, bulbous head topped with a feathered bowler peered over the window sill.

"Miss Hellebore?" the little person said.

Taylor slid the window open.

"Miss Hellebore? It's me, Wasko. Remember?"

She leaned over the window sill and looked down. Wasko was standing on Pete's shoulders. Haggler was holding Wasko steady with his hands against his legs.

"I remember," Taylor said. "But keep it down, okay?" She glanced toward her bedroom door. Thankfully, it was shut. "What are you doing here?"

"We're on a mission," Wasko said, his eyes darting left and right.

"A mission? How did you even find me?" Taylor said.

"It wasn't easy. Took the better part of three days—oof!" He caught himself on the window sill as Pete grunted and shifted his weight. "Can we come in?"

"I guess," Taylor said.

Wasko flopped into the room, then gave Pete a hand up—but not without bumping into Taylor's bookshelf and knocking half a dozen books to the floor.

"I said keep it down!" Taylor whispered.

126

"Sorry," Pete said. The two little folk hoisted Haggler up last of all.

Her mom called from the living room. "Taylor, are you okay?"

"Fine, mom!" she said. "Everything's...just fine!" She was trying to take things slow with her parents. A trio of uninvited magical houseguests? Not the best idea.

"So this is a Topside house, huh?" Pete said. With Wasko off his shoulders, he had started munching on something from a paper sack. Taylor was pretty sure she saw tiny, black legs. "I figured it'd be...I dunno. Bigger."

"It's big enough," Taylor said. "Now, what do you want?"

"Oh, right," Wasko said. "We been sent on a mission."

"You said that already."

"I did? Good."

"Get on with it, Wasko," Haggler said.

"In my own time!" Wasko snapped. "You don't just barge in with news like this."

"Actually, that's exactly what you did," Taylor said. "Are you going to tell me or not?"

"What Wasko is struggling to say," Pete said, "is that we've got a message for you. Very important."

"Y-yes?"

Wasko elbowed Pete back and took over. He whispered, "It's from...Osanda Morning."

"Who?"

"Aw, crud," Wasko said. "You don't know who Osanda Morning is?"

"Never heard of her."

"Well, she's heard of you," Pete said. "That's why she wants to meet you."

"I was getting to that!" Wasko snapped.

"Taylor, who are you talking to?" her mom called. The little folk went wide-eyed. They ducked and dodged and made shushing motions at each other.

127

"N-nobody, Mom!" Taylor called. She felt a sudden twinge in her belly, as if what little magic she had left in her had drained away.

"Well, turn the volume down on your tablet!"

"Sorry!"

Taylor rubbed her eyes. She felt light-headed.

"Look," she said. "My folks are not quite ready for...well.... Just try to keep it down, okay? Who is Osanda Morning?"

"A Gentrywoman from up in Arradherry Land," Wasko whispered. "She's trying to finagle herself a seat on the Summer Triad, now that Mrs. Redmane's out."

"A sídhe?" Taylor said, apprehensive. "What would she want with me?"

"She don't like the way Summer's been going the past hundred years or so," Pete said. "She's been reaching out to others that might think the same. Others that don't have much of a say in things—dwarves and little folk and the like. Even the nunnehi and other fae who might have a bone to pick with the Summer Court. She says folks like that deserve to be heard."

"And she wants to make sure they are," Taylor guessed.

"That's what she says," Wasko said.

There was a knock at the door. "Taylor?" Taylor's mom said.

The look of terror on Taylor's face told the little folk all they needed to know. Wasko dropped to the floor and rolled under the bed. Haggler dove for the closet.

Pete froze—but at least he remembered to cloak himself with magic mist. As obvious as he was to Taylor, someone who wasn't looking for him would never know he was there.

Taylor's mom pushed the door open just as Haggler shut the closet door behind him.

Pete stood stock still, holding his breath.

"Mom?"

"Honey, here's your laundry." She brought in a stack of clothes and laid them on Taylor's bed. Pete leaned backward to keep her from brushing into him.

"You said you wanted your good jeans for the party tonight."

128

"R-right. Thanks, Mom."

"Do you have Jill's present wrapped?"

"Sure do, Mom. Well, bye—"

"Taylor," her mom laid her hand on Taylor's shoulder. "I wish you'd tell us more about...about what's going on in your life."

"It's still pretty new to me," Taylor said. She suddenly realized Pete had set his bag of snacks on the edge of her bed. She grabbed it while pretending to inspect her laundry and turned her body so it was shielded from her mother's view.

"Fair Folk...," Taylor said. "Magic.... I-I'm not sure what to say. Well, I'd better get dressed—"

"It's just that you've gotten so secretive."

"I-I know," she said. "And I'm sorry." She really was, in fact, but this was definitely not the time for this conversation! "Maybe we can talk about it later. Bye, Mom—"

Under the bed, Wasko sneezed.

"What was that?" Taylor's mom asked.

"Uh..."

A chuffing noise came from outside Taylor's window. Out of the corner of her eye, she caught a glimpse of Haggler in the crack of the closet door, gesturing as if casting a spell.

Thank you, Haggler! Taylor thought.

"I bet...." She came up with a plausible lie, but choked when she tried to say it. The words just wouldn't come out.

"Do you think Mrs. Dibney's dog got out again?" *There. Let Mom come to her own conclusions.*

There was more scratching and sniffing from outside.

Taylor's mom turned toward the window. "I'd better give her a call," she said.

"You better hurry," Taylor said. "And I better start getting ready."

"All right, honey. But please let's talk more later. Okay?"

"I promise."

Taylor's mom left. Taylor shut the door behind her and leaned against it.

129

Pete exhaled.

"Glamour?" Taylor asked. "Dog sounds?"

Haggler crept out of the closet and grinned.

"Thanks, Haggler."

"If you please, Miss Hellebore," Wasko said as he climbed out from under the bed. "Just give us your answer, and we'll get out of your hair."

It took Taylor a second to remember the question. "Right. This Morning person."

Wasko nodded. "If you're willing to meet with her, we'll get word to her."

Taylor sat on the bed.

"And you all know her how?"

"She found us in Dunhoughkey a few days back," Wasko said. "When she found out we knew you, she offered us some work as couriers."

"I hope you don't mind if we name-dropped," Pete said. "Work's hard to come by and...."

Taylor had stopped paying attention. Her mind was filled with other thoughts.

"How much will this hurt Mara?"

"You mean your grandma? The Winter Court?" Wasko said. "That's hard to say. Fellas?"

Pete cleared his throat. "If I may, Miss Hellebore," he said, "I don't rightly know what the Winters think about this business with Ms. Morning. If they think she's causing trouble for the Summer Court, I bet they're all for her."

"On the other hand," Wasko jumped in, "they can't be happy with what she's trying to do: make Summer get back to being more seelie and all."

"Seelie? What's that?"

"Well, you know about the Eldritch Law, right?" Wasko said.

Taylor nodded. "Hospitality. Paying your debts. Keeping your promises. That sort of thing."

"Right," Wasko continued. "Well, one of the things the Courts don't see eye-to-eye on is whether Topsiders have rights

130

under the Eldritch Law. The Summer Court has always been 'seelie,' meaning they say they do."

"And, of course," Pete added, "the Winters have always said they don't. What they call 'unseelie.'"

Taylor sifted all this in her mind.

"So, if Morning gets on the Triad, the Summers might remember what they're supposed to be about? They might actually start treating Topsiders with a little respect?" She didn't mention Jill by name, but that was who was on her mind.

"Most likely," Pete said.

"And that might limit what the Winters could do to a Topsider they didn't like?"

"Six months of the year," Pete said, "somebody might could count on Summer's help if Winter tried to do anything to them. The rest of the year...." He shrugged.

"Six months is better than nothing," Taylor muttered. "And what exactly does this Morning woman want from me?"

"She just wants to meet you," Wasko said. "Like we told you, she's been meeting with nunnehi and other Fair Folk outside the borders of Arradherry, trying to build goodwill, let them know she's on their side."

"Mr. Wakefire's calling it an 'apology tour,'" Pete added.

"Whatever you call it," Wasko said, "folks are impressed. They'd like to think she's on the level."

"So why does she want to meet with me?"

"Everybody knows about Selena Hellebore," Wasko said. "You're the only fae ever to cut both Anya Redmane *and* Mara Hellebore down a notch."

"You're kind of a symbol, Miss Hellebore," Pete said. "They see how you've been treated—and by your own family, no less. It reminds them how power-hungry all the Courts have gotten. Makes them think things should be better. Otherwise...."

"Otherwise what?"

"Nobody likes to say it out loud," Pete said, "but things don't look too good. They say the nunnehi and the sídhe are both

131

itching for a fight. There's been too many old grudges yet to be settled."

"Too many insults to each other's honor," Haggler added.

"You may not realize it, living on human earth like you do," Wasko said, "but Pete's right. You give folks hope. You've faced the worst and come out ahead. So far, at least."

Haggler grinned. "Folks do love to root for the underdog."

Taylor took all this in. Could Osanda Morning be legit? If she was, it might give her an ally—an actual ally—in the Summer Court. She tried to wrap her mind around the concept. It wasn't easy.

"I tell you what," she said at last. "Go find Ms. Morning. Tell her I'll meet with her if she wants. Just...not in my bedroom, okay?"

"Sure thing, Miss Hellebore," Wasko said. "We'll go find her right away. Come on, boys."

Wasko, Pete, and Haggler bowed to Taylor in turn and slipped out the window.

Taylor took a deep breath.

She stretched her still-sore muscles one last time, laid out her clothes, and headed to the bathroom for a long, relaxing shower.

Before she left her room, however, she noticed Pete's snack bag on her bedside table. She must have set it down without thinking.

She picked it up and thought about opening it.

No, she decided. She really wasn't interested in knowing what was in it.

Chapter 13

Osanda Morning

William mostly tried to stay out of the way during Jill's birthday party. When they were little, the twins' parents threw one big party for both of them, but that came to a screeching halt after the Great Birthday Schism when they turned five. Neither of the Matthews twins remembered all the details, but there was general consensus that princesses and superheroes did not belong at the same party.

For some reason, an image of a batarang sticking out of a pastel pink-and-blue birthday cake stuck in William's memory.

Jill, Taylor, and a few of Jill's church friends were out back on the deck as Mr. Matthews grilled hamburgers and Mrs. Matthews fixed lemonade. William found a nice quiet corner in the living room with his Nintendo. Next weekend, he'd have his own get-together with some of his friends (he'd put in an early request for a trip to the movies and pizza afterward).

As he sent LEGO Spider-Man into battle against the Green Goblin, he felt something like a breeze brush across his face. He looked up. The front door was shut, as were all the windows. His next guess was a stray cobweb had landed on him, but that wasn't likely even if his mom hadn't run the whole family ragged cleaning up for the party.

Maymay strode toward the door, walking stick in hand. She looked out the front window, sucked in a breath, then stepped onto the stoop.

William put down his game and looked outside. Nothing.

Maymay walked slowly—even warily—toward the edge of the yard. Sometimes when she was distracted, William's grandmother forgot to actually use her cane; she just carried it in her hand. This was one of those times. What's more, she looked angry about something.

Okay, he thought.

He cracked the door and slipped outside as quietly as he could. He heard his grandmother say, "Well?"

He took a deep breath and tried to open up his Second Sight. He gazed into the street where Maymay was standing, right at the edge of the driveway.

There was some kind of shimmer: a mist rising out of the ground. But nothing more.

"I haven't got all day," Maymay said. "You got something to say, say it."

The mist congealed, took on a shape: a feminine shape in a flowing green gown, with fair skin and long brown hair garlanded with oak leaves.

As soon as the woman came into focus, he also noticed the ghostly cat-form pacing in front of her: Maymay's warding charm had activated again. That's how Maymay knew someone had come calling.

"Holy crap," he muttered.

Maymay gestured for him to stay put but didn't take her eyes off the woman on the street. For her part, the stranger seemed surprised his grandmother stood up to her. She wore a subtle smile, almost like she admired Maymay's pluck.

"Good afternoon," the woman said. "I'm looking for Selena Hellebore. She is expecting me."

William tried to get a read on her emotions. Just as he expected, he got nothing. It was as if she wasn't even there.

"There's no Selena Hellebore here," Maymay said. She tapped the knob of her walking stick against her palm. To William's Second Sight, it began to glow with golden light.

"You'd best be on your way."

134

"I mean no disrespect," the woman said, "but *are you sure Miss Hellebore isn't inside?*"

Something seemed to ripple outward from the woman. William sucked in a breath, but the sensation quickly passed. It didn't seem to have affected Maymay at all.

"If you think your little glamour tricks are going to get past my wards, chère, you are sadly mistaken." Maymay took a step backward. The woman studied the distance between them but didn't step forward.

A grin crept across William's face as he realized how powerful his grandmother's magic must be.

At the same time, he felt a hand on his shoulder, someone nudging him out of the way.

Taylor appeared on the stoop next to him. There was no telling how long she'd been there. She marched across the lawn before William could hold her back. She stood up straight and practically oozed confidence. Whatever was going on, she was ready for it.

"I'm Selena Hellebore," she said. She traded glances with Maymay. "Mrs. Blay wasn't lying to you. She only knows me... by another name."

"I take no offense," the woman said with a stately bow toward Maymay. It wasn't what you'd call humble. "Cordial" was probably the best word for it.

"I take it you're Osanda Morning?" Taylor said.

"Thank you for agreeing to meet me," the woman said. Once she turned to Taylor, it was as if Maymay wasn't even there.

"I'm actually kind of busy. Could we do this later?"

"Unfortunately, I have other places to be. I have a meeting with some leprechauns at six." She glanced at Maymay and at William back on the stoop. "Perhaps we should find a more suitable place to chat."

Maymay started to say something, but Taylor raised a hand to stop her.

135

"It's all right, Mrs. Blay. I was expecting her. Just...not quite so soon. Tell Jill.... Tell her something came up. I'm sorry I have to miss the rest of her party."

Maymay nodded.

"Oh, and Mrs. Matthews wants you to know the burgers are ready."

Maymay patted Taylor on both shoulders, then stepped away. "You just be careful," she said with a sidewise glance toward the woman in green.

The woman addressed Taylor. "I'd offer the hospitality of my apartments in Dunhoughkey—"

"I'm not going to break my oath," Taylor interrupted. "I swore never to set foot in any rath of Arradherry."

"Precisely," the woman said. "If you had let me finish, I'd have said I'm aware of your oath." She seemed only mildly put out by Taylor's interruption. "I admire your resolve. There's a suitable place not too far from here. Shall we?"

"How kind of you to extend me hospitality," Taylor said. She put a little extra emphasis on the last word.

Osanda smirked. "You needn't fear me, Miss Hellebore," she said. "I fully intend to treat you as my honored guest."

"Just checking," Taylor said, with not a trace of guilt. "There's a ring behind my house, over there." She pointed.

The woman smiled. She might have been suppressing a chuckle. "Rings are for children," she said. With a sweeping gesture, a disturbance split the air in the middle of the street.

Then William's Second Sight collapsed, and the disturbance with it.

He knew it was still there, though, because a second later Taylor and the woman stepped through and vanished.

Taylor recognized Osanda Morning's portal (or gate or whatever you called it) as the same kind of thing Mara had conjured at Halloween. It was a shimmering pillar eight or nine feet high

136

and less than an inch in diameter. It throbbed with magical power.

Passing through it felt something like being squeezed through a giant tube of toothpaste. It wasn't as disorienting as ring-travel, but it took Taylor's breath away. When she landed an instant later on the other side, it took her a few seconds to remember she was supposed to breathe.

Her head cleared, and she took a look around.

A heavy fog had settled in—odd for the middle of the afternoon.

"Somebody order a fog?"

"Yes, actually," Osanda said. "Not everyone in the Wonder is, ah, appreciative of my aims. Best to keep them guessing."

That confirmed Taylor's suspicion: the fog was some kind of glamour.

Despite the haze, however, she could tell she and her visitor stood in an old but well kept graveyard. With a start, she realized she knew exactly where she was. She turned around, knowing full well what she was going to see before she did: a quaint, white country church house.

Oak Hill Baptist Church.

Perched on the tallest gravestone was a gray-skinned goblin. He wore a rumpled cotton shirt with the sleeves rolled up and work pants held up with suspenders. He was hunched over with his long, spindly arms spread out—maybe for balance, maybe to let loose a magical attack if necessary.

"Silas!" Taylor called. She would have stepped toward him, but the two redtick coonhounds circling beneath his feet snarled silently. (One of the weirdest things about faery dogs was their barks and growls got fainter the closer they got. It gave Taylor the willies even with dogs she knew.)

She realized Silas and his dogs were eyeing her traveling companion.

"Mr. Bludgitt," Osanda Morning said with a slight bow.

The goblin said nothing, but he perked up his pointed, bat-like ears.

"Thank you for permitting me the use of your...facility."

"Thirty minutes," he said. His eyes never left hers.

"As we agreed."

"Be careful, Taylor," Silas said, finally acknowledging her presence. "I don't know about this."

"It's okay," Taylor said.

"We'll see." Silas hopped down from his perch. One of the dogs sidled up beside him, and he scratched its back. "I hope you don't mind if Goodness and Mercy hang around." His voice said he really didn't care what Osanda Morning thought.

He turned back to Taylor. "If you need me, I'll be in the bell tower." He put emphasis on those last two words and turned his eyes back toward Ms. Morning.

"I'm in your debt, Mr. Bludgitt," she said. Silas grumbled something inarticulate as he headed toward the church house.

"You arranged to meet me...at my church?" Taylor said.

"Consider it a show of good faith. I'm told you...frequent... this establishment." The sídhe woman seemed mildly uncomfortable, out of her element. Taylor watched as she strode forward. Silas's dogs followed.

"At any rate, you trust the church grim." She nodded in the direction of Silas, who was now scaling the bell tower like a grotesque humanoid spider.

Taylor didn't know what to say, so she remained silent as they strolled passed the gravestones.

"I've known some hulderfolk who are Christians," she commented. "They sometimes switch out their children when they're born just long enough to have them baptized."

Taylor wasn't sure where this conversation was going. She was pretty sure Osanda Morning hadn't come to talk theology.

"Hulderfolk. But not the daoine sídhe?"

"We have our own ways. I doubt the deathlings would even recognize it as...what is the word? Religion." She turned to Taylor. "Your ways are your own business, of course."

"Of course."

138

"It's just...those blasted *bells*...." She eyed the bell tower with a look of disapproval. Silas grinned down at her with an expression that said *Give me a reason to ring this sucker*.

"Airsick pills help," Taylor said. "Plus, we don't really come every week. Listen, Mrs...Miss..."

"You may call me Osanda."

"Okay. Osanda. I'm actually missing my friend's birthday party right now, and—"

"And I should get to the point." She smiled down at Taylor. "Very well. I take it you're aware that your grandmother is no longer the Chief Matron of the Summer Court?"

Aware? Taylor, Jill, and Silas were pretty much responsible for it! Not that they knew what they were doing, though. Mara had tricked them into exposing the scandal that led to Anya Redmane's downfall.

"Seems I heard about that."

"Then perhaps you've also heard that the new Chief Matron wants to fill the empty seat on the Triad with someone of her own choosing."

That was pretty much what Wasko, Pete, and Haggler had told Taylor that morning. Dubessa Fairchild was wasting no time asserting her new authority.

"You'd rather have the seat yourself."

Osanda stopped to admire the workmanship on one of the gravestones. "I would rather the Summer Court come to its senses."

Taylor gave her a quizzical look.

Osanda shook her head. "You're too young to remember when the Summer Court stood for something: hope, compassion, vitality. The past hundred years or so, things have gotten out of hand. Our leaders have been so preoccupied with gaining and keeping power that we've forgotten the things that made us great."

"You want to change that," Taylor said.

"Young as you are, Selena, you've seen firsthand what the Summer Court is like."

139

Taylor stopped. "If you don't mind my asking," she began, "why are you telling all this to me? Shouldn't you be, I don't know, making speeches somewhere?"

Osanda smiled and moved to place her hand on Taylor's shoulder. Taylor flinched, and Osanda quickly withdrew it. "First, I'm telling you because you have a right to know. It is part of your heritage, after all."

"I'm a Hellebore," Taylor said, shuddering. "Winter Court."

"By law," Osanda conceded. "But by birth you're also the daughter of Aulberic Redmane. I knew him, you know."

"You knew my father?" Suddenly, Taylor was invested in this conversation more than she had expected to be.

"Things might have been different if he were alive," Osanda said. "He wasn't one to put up with the sort of nonsense his mother indulged in."

"He was a rebel."

"He had a keen sense of right and wrong. People admired him for that, even if he was a bit...unmanageable."

"Yeah, apparently sídhe kids can be a handful," Taylor said.

"By now he'd probably have been the leader of a war band, likely in line to become a Teyrnus—that's what we call the lord of a rath."

"And you think he'd support what you're trying to do?"

"He married outside his Court," Osanda said. "He treated those of lesser birth as if they were his equals. His best friend was a pisgy, by Danu."

"Why is that a problem?"

"Precisely!"

Taylor made a mental note to find out what a pisgy was later. Right now, she had other things on her mind. "You said my father was the first reason you're telling me this," she said. "What else?"

"You could help me, Selena," Osanda said.

"Me?"

"Selena Hellebore, the girl who stood up to both of the leading Courts and won."

140

And *lived* was more like it, Taylor thought. She stared at Osanda.

"Those who are most itching for the old ways see you as a sign of hope," Osanda said. "A friend of pookas and little folk. A sídhe child rejected by her family, exiled to the Topside world—"

"That's not really the way it—"

"...but still willing and able to stand up for herself, as limited as her abilities are."

"I'm practicing," Taylor grumbled.

"Lend me your support, Selena, and help me convince Dubessa Fairchild that the Summer Court is ready for a breath of fresh air."

"What? What can I...?" Taylor was at a loss for words.

"I'm in negotiations to visit Ichisi next year, as soon after Yule as can be arranged," Osanda said. "It wouldn't be prudent for the nunnehi to openly support me. Too many at Court still consider them the enemy. To be frank, some of our people are looking for an excuse to invade."

Taylor found herself shaking at that.

Osanda continued, "But I have spoken to the White Chief of Tsuwatelda, who is second in power only to the Great Falcon at Nikwasi."

"I've met Chief Tewa."

"So I hear. At any rate, they are willing to hear me out—and that gives me a forum."

"And...?"

"All you would have to do is meet with me once more—in Ichisi. Let the world see the two of us together. Let the Summer Court know where you stand."

Taylor gulped.

"Uh... I still don't see how—"

"And one more thing," Osanda said. "It goes without saying that I would be in your debt for such a show of support."

Okay, Taylor thought. *Here comes the bargaining part. Took her long enough.*

141

"You swore you would never again set foot in any rath of Arradherry."

"I thought we'd already covered that."

"Hear me out. If it were simply a matter of having sworn this oath before the former Chief Matron, one might argue that her subsequent dishonor rendered the entire transaction invalid."

Taylor's heart began to pound.

"Unfortunately, the oath was sworn in the presence of the entire Triad, meaning only the Triad could absolve you of your obligation."

Taylor gasped. "You think you can cancel my oath?"

"A sympathetic voice on the Triad could ease the way."

"You're assuming I *want* to go back to Arradherry," Taylor scoffed.

"I'm assuming that you're a duine sídhe," Osanda said, "and that you don't like anyone telling you what you can do or where you can go."

Taylor stood still and looked into Osanda's deep, brown eyes. She hadn't expected that answer. As soon as Osanda said it, Taylor knew she had a point.

One of Silas's dogs approached her to sniff her hand.

"I'll...I'll think about it," she said.

"I'll await your answer," Osanda said.

Chapter 14

Taylor Freaks Out

Thursday afternoon, Taylor sat in the choir room with thirty other seventh- and eight-graders. With the annual winter concert less than a month away, Mrs. Peterson was on a mission, getting her choir members ready.

The week before, Taylor had auditioned for the solo part in the big finale. Now, she was so impatient to hear she'd gotten the part she could barely concentrate on the other music she and her classmates were trying to learn. The school was mostly empty an hour after the last bell. Only the Bel Canto Choir and some of the sports teams were still hanging around.

Tommy Morgan seemed lost, as usual. The poor guy wasn't unintelligent, just clumsy and easily flustered. Apparently, something about "Hanukkah O Hanukkah" wasn't clicking with him.

And, of course, this gave Shelby a chance to whisper snide remarks to her best friend, Jasmine. The two giggled together beside Taylor until she had had enough.

"Hey," she hissed, "some of us are trying to pay attention."

Shelby just shot her an evil glare and went back to her usual nastiness.

"Settle down, you all," Mrs. Peterson said. "We've still got a lot of work to do before the concert."

Shelby and Jasmine sat up straight and smiled. Taylor couldn't believe so many of her teachers were blind to what a wretched person Shelby was.

"I sent all your parents an email about uniforms and call time," she continued. "Here's a hard copy for you to take home as well." She started to distribute the green half-sheets of paper.

"It's almost time to go. Before we do, I wanted to announce the soloist for 'In the Bleak Midwinter.'"

Taylor shushed a couple of tenors who'd been talking about football or something equally lame.

"We had four girls try out," Mrs. Peterson continued, "and you all did a super job. This was a really hard decision."

Get on with it, Taylor thought.

"But I had to make a decision...so the part goes to...Shelby Crowthers!"

Everybody clapped, some more enthusiastically than others. Taylor sat stunned. Had she heard right?

There's no way Shelby sings as good as me!

She felt her face flush. More than that, she felt magic course through her body.

Mrs. Peterson went to take a sip from her water bottle and then put it down, confused. The surface of the water had frozen into a thin disk.

"Now, over Thanksgiving break, I want everybody to work on all the pieces we've practiced. We'll only have two more rehearsals once we get back, and we've got a lot to do to before the concert. Good night, everybody!"

Almost before she'd finished speaking, kids leaped to their feet and stormed toward the door.

Taylor was in a daze that only Shelby's haughty tone could break through.

"Too bad about not getting the solo," she said. She didn't sound sorry at all. "I guess you just weren't good enough."

Taylor glowered. *I'm plenty good enough!*

"Things like this build character," Shelby said. "It's not good to overestimate your abilities." She and Jasmine smiled and giggled.

Taylor wondered if she could freeze Shelby's mouth shut without causing any permanent damage. By the time she decided she didn't care if she did permanent damage, Shelby had already sashayed out of the choir room.

Mrs. Peterson was arranging music folders, getting ready for Friday morning classes.

"Good night, Taylor!" she called cheerfully.

"Yeah," Taylor said. She didn't trust herself to say anything more. She always thought Mrs. Peterson liked her more than this.

Taylor opened her locker long enough to grab her backpack and then slammed the door shut. She heard a startled yelp and leaned into Mr. Appletree's classroom. The math teacher was at his desk grading papers. Taylor hadn't noticed he was in there.

"Sorry," she said. "I didn't mean to scare you."

"It's all right," he said. He adjusted his horn rim glasses. "Is something the matter?"

Shelby Crowthers beat me! That is not supposed to happen!

"Just...school stuff."

"Well, between the two of us, I've just finished grading today's quizzes. You've got nothing to worry about in my class."

"Thanks."

He shuffled toward the door, pulling on his jacket as he did. His bushy eyebrows seemed to dance above his glasses as he smiled at Taylor. He was pretty sprightly for an almost senior citizen.

"Have you thought about a career in mathematics? Oh, I know it's probably too early for you to think about such things, but you've got a quick mind for numbers and patterns." He chuckled. "You grasp the concepts almost as soon as I explain them."

Taylor heaved her backpack onto her shoulder and headed toward the exit. To her horror, Mr. Appletree was going the same direction.

"I hadn't really thought about it." *Please let this conversation be over!*

"Well, whatever you do, I've got a feeling you'll go far. You've got more people in your corner than you realize, Taylor."

145

He smiled. If Taylor wasn't ready to explode with anger over Shelby Crowthers, she might have returned it.

"Yes, sir," she said.

It was a crisp autumn afternoon: cold enough for a light jacket but not so cold to call home for a ride. Her house was only a mile or so from school. Even though the days were shorter, there was still plenty of daylight for a brisk walk home.

Plus, that would give her a chance to let off some steam before facing her parents. Or anybody, really.

She marched home in record time, stewing over Shelby and her stupid solo. She'd promised Jill she'd leave Shelby alone if she did the same. As far as Taylor was concerned, that "don't aim too high" remark crossed the line.

In her mind, she pondered what she might have done. What she might still do tomorrow. And as she pondered, her magic welled up within her.

Agitated birds took flight as she passed by their trees.

When she walked across grass, it frosted beneath her feet.

She was not having a good day.

As soon as she turned onto her street, she saw William outside raking leaves. Taylor set her face on her own house two doors down and across the street. She might have stopped to grouse with Jill, but William was another matter.

He stopped to wipe the sweat from his forehead.

"Hey, Taylor!"

"Yeah. Hi, Will—what's that?" Something was wrong. Off. Taylor's mind raced to figure out what it was. Whatever it was, it made her jumpy. Her magical senses leaped into overdrive but found...nothing. No glamoured enemies waiting to attack. No strange sounds or smells in the air that might signal approaching danger.

She took a half-step backward and instinctively began to draw magic to herself.

All the while, William just stood there in his old, ratty tee shirt.

That was it.

146

"What's wrong with your shirt?" Taylor demanded. Her voice sounded more frantic than it should have.

"What?" William said, looking down. "Nothing."

"No!" Taylor said. "It's...it's...."

Again, William looked down at his shirt, dumbfounded.

"It's inside-out!" Taylor blurted at last.

William didn't see the problem. "So? I'm just raking leaves. It's not like—"

"I said it's inside-out!"

"And that's a big deal because...?"

Taylor wanted to scream. She found herself backing away from William, which she didn't understand at all. He wasn't doing anything threatening. She couldn't even imagine him doing anything threatening.

"Fine," William said, pulling his shirt off. "Just...settle down, okay?"

Taylor started to blush. She threw her hands in front of her eyes.

"Now what are you doing?"

"Nothing," he said. "What's the big deal?" William turned the shirt out and put it back on the right way.

"I don't know! I just didn't need to see... It was inside-out, that's all!"

"Okay, I fixed it. See? No biggie." He looked scared, though. His chest was heaving.

Taylor didn't feel much better. But with William finally properly dressed, her heart rate began to slow. She felt a trickle of sweat on her forehead.

Something caught Taylor's eye. William's grandmother was standing in the window, peering through the blinds. She suddenly felt as if her little fit had been a mistake.

What in the world had gotten into her?

"Okay," she said at last, barely louder than a whisper. "Thanks."

"D-don't mention it," William said.

147

Get a grip, Taylor! she told herself. She didn't get the solo she'd been counting on. She freaked out her best friend's brother. Heck, she'd done a pretty good job of freaking herself out! And she might have offended her best friend's grandma in the process.

She arrived on the front step breathing heavy. A year ago, that much exertion might have set off an asthma attack, but she hadn't had one of those since summer.

Unleashing her fae magic seemed to improve her general health—even if it was making her crazy!

She went inside, plopped her backpack by the door, and headed to the kitchen. Her mom had put a pot roast in the slow cooker that morning. Taylor checked it, gave it a stir, and turned down the heat.

It was 4:45. In half an hour, her mom would be home from work.

In the meantime, Taylor retreated to her room.

"Ugh!" Only then, she remembered she hadn't made her bed that morning. She'd been out back meditating on a raccoon and lost track of time.

She heaved a sigh and started to put her room in order. She couldn't control everything, but at least she could sleep in a room where everything was in its place.

She dropped her backpack underneath her desk, slipped off her shoes and set them side-by-side at the foot of her bed. She got to work making her bed.

Her parents always praised her for being such a good helper around the house. The truth was, it just made her jumpy when things were out of place.

It seemed to have gotten worse over the past few months.

She wondered if that had anything to do with her blow-up with William.

She shook her head. *Magical powers: now with OCD at no extra charge!*

Taylor stayed in her room doing homework until her dad came home and her mom called her to supper.

148

"So, how was *your* day?" her mom asked when they all finally sat down to eat.

"Okay," Taylor said without much conviction.

Her mom dropped the subject. She and her dad had both gotten pretty good at navigating the surly teenager thing.

Taylor separated her onions from her carrots and potatoes while her parents talked about other things. Bills. Thanksgiving plans. Crazy clients at work.

There was a lull in the conversation.

Taylor looked up. Her dad gave her mom a "go-ahead" nod.

"Taylor," Mrs. Smart said, "have you given any more thought to when we might, uh, meet some of your friends?"

Taylor swallowed the bite of potatoes she'd been chewing. *Not now!* she thought. "Uh...."

"It seems like you spend practically every weekend with that Ayoka girl," her mom continued. "Your dad and I just think it's time we met some of the...people...you've been hanging out with."

"Mom, I don't know if—" Something caught Taylor's eye. A single majestic turkey feather danced in front of the window over the sink. She was the only one who saw it.

"It doesn't have to be anything big," her dad said. "I could take you both for ice cream if you like."

"They do like ice cream, right?" her mom added.

"Mom, everybody likes ice cream," Taylor said. She tried to look at anything but the feather—and the bowler hat to which it was attached.

"Then it's settled," her dad said. "You talk to Ayoka and clear it with her parents and.... What's wrong, honey?"

"Nothing!" Taylor blurted—and felt a twinge in the pit of her stomach. Wasko's face popped up, his face scrunched in concentration. He fell backward with a thud.

"I...I'm just not sure that's a good idea."

Her dad sighed. "We promise we won't embarrass you."

149

"It's not that," Taylor said. *I just don't want you to get freaked out.* Wasko's feathered hat didn't reappear. That made Taylor nervous.

Her dad got up for seconds.

And, of course, that was when somebody knocked at the kitchen door.

"Who could that be?" Mr. Smart puzzled.

"Dad!" Taylor called, scooting back from the table. "No really, I'll—"

Too late.

Mr. Smart opened the door.

"SWEET MOTHER OF PEARL!"

Wasko stumbled into the kitchen—all three and a half feet of him. His bowler had went sailing across the tile floor.

Pete sauntered in, grinning from ear to ear. Haggler stood in the doorway.

"Miss Hellebore!" Pete called. "Good news!"

Mrs. Smart whimpered.

Wasko regained his feet. He threw his braid back over his shoulder and wiped his hands on his shirt. He clasped Mr. Smart's right hand with both of his and gave it a vigorous shake. "You must be Miss Hellebore's pa!" he called. "It's an honor, sir. A genuine honor!"

Mr. Smart tried to put his eyes back in his head. "Miss Hellebore?"

"He means me, Dad," Taylor said. "I'll explain later."

"Suppertime, huh?" Pete said, licking his lips. "You don't mind if I, uh..."

"Help yourself," Mrs. Smart said in a daze.

"Nice place you got here," Haggler said as he finally entered the kitchen. He also offered Mr. Smart his hand. Mr. Smart took it automatically and listlessly.

Pete stood up on his tiptoes to investigate the slow cooker. "Bread?"

"Behind you," Taylor said. "Second drawer. Guys, what are you...?"

"Where are my manners!" Wasko interrupted. He grabbed Mr. Smart's hand again. "Wasko's the name. And these are my associates: Haggler and Pete."

Haggler gave a polite bow, smiling up at Taylor's dad with his creepy silver eyes. Pete waved while poking his head in the fridge.

"Don't let us interrupt," Wasko said. "We just wanted to tell your daughter..."

"You got any crickets?" Pete said.

All three Smarts stared at him open-mouthed.

"What?"

Wasko slapped the back of his head. "Is that any way to treat your host?" he said. "You eat what they give you, understand?"

"Sorry," Pete said. "I didn't mean no offense."

"I need a drink of water," Mr. Smart mumbled. He edged back toward his seat on wobbly legs.

"Guys!" Taylor shouted. "You said you had something to tell me?"

"What?" Wasko said. "Oh, yeah!"

"It's about Mabel," Haggler said.

"I was gonna tell her!" Wasko said.

"Okay if I put some mustard on this?" Pete said. He hoisted his roast beef sandwich.

"*Guys!*" Taylor said again.

The three little folk shut up immediately.

"Mabel?"

"The little girl from the night we met each other," Wasko said.

"I remember. Is she okay?"

"She's great!" Pete said—and belched.

"A sweet-looking old lady took her off not half an hour ago," Haggler explained. "Her grandma, from what we heard."

"And her mom?"

"We...uh...kinda encouraged the deathling police to get involved," Wasko said, beaming.

"You..."

151

"Did you know they'll send the police to break up a loud party?" Wasko said.

"I don't underst—"

All three little folk snapped their fingers, and the kitchen was suddenly awash in the loudest, most obnoxious music Taylor had ever heard. It sounded like asthmatic punk rockers belting out Broadway hits accompanied by an out-of-tune electric walrus.

Her mom covered her ears. Her dad, just making it back to his seat, missed and landed on the floor.

"*I get the picture!*" Taylor screamed.

Wasko motioned for the others to cut it out. The room returned to relative quiet.

Mrs. Smart sat with her hands folded in her lap. She couldn't seem to take her eyes off of Haggler. Taylor couldn't blame her; it's not every day a three-foot-tall albino shows up in your kitchen.

Mr. Smart found his way to his seat.

"S-so...," Mrs. Smart said. The color was returning to her face. "You're friends of Taylor?"

"Aw, she's the greatest!" Pete said. Somehow, his entire sandwich was already gone.

"All the seelie fae are really countin' on her," Wasko said.

"Guys," Taylor said. She tried to gesture for them not to go there.

"Counting on her?" her dad said. "I don't understand."

Taylor tried to shout "Nothing!" again but the words caught in her throat. Instead, she gurgled and then said, "Did I tell you Ayoka and I are on a stickball team?"

"Really?" her dad said. "You've never been interested in sports before."

"Yeah," Pete said, "but what does that have to do with—"

Taylor shot him a glare that said *Shut up!*

"You must be pretty good if everybody's counting on you," her mom said. She tried to smile. She really did.

"Yeah, well...."

152

"But Ms. Morning—" Pete began. Haggler blew yellow sparks in his face—causing Mrs. Smart to squeak—and gave him an evil look.

"We better be going," Haggler said. "Don't you think, Wasko?"

"Sure," Wasko said. "We're sorry to take up your time." He nodded toward Taylor's parents.

"We've got some business in town," Haggler added.

"And maybe get a bite to eat," Pete said.

"See ya later, Miss Hellebore," Wasko said. "If you ever need us, you just say the word." He smiled and stuck out his chest. "It's been a pleasure. A genuine pleasure." He bowed again.

"We'll see ourselves out," Haggler said. The three trudged out the door as suddenly as they had come in.

Taylor and her parents sat at the table, staring at their food.

Except her dad. He had left his plate on the counter. He did take a sip of water, though.

Her mom rearranged her potatoes.

Taylor cleared her throat.

"So..." Mrs. Smart said. She didn't look up from her plate. "About Ayoka?"

Taylor swallowed.

"Yes, mom?"

"We... We don't have to have meet her until you think it's time."

Taylor swallowed again.

"Whatever you say, Mom."

Chapter 15

Unwelcome Guests

"All right," Danny said. "You said you figured it out."

Taylor and Danny were in a patch of faery woods that aligned with an empty lot across the street from her Grandma Miller's house on the outskirts of Gray, Georgia. Taylor and her parents had spent the last few days there enjoying Thanksgiving vacation.

"You've got to understand how animals work," Taylor said. "The more time you spend out in the woods, touching them with your magical senses, the better you get. Eventually, how to turn into an animal sort of...comes to you."

Danny listened without comment.

"Am I right?"

"Almost," Danny said. "Just keep thinking about it and—"

"No!" Taylor blurted. "I've been trying to figure this out since August. Why can't you just tell me?"

"I told you it takes time," Danny said. "Like you said, you've only been at this for a few months. Nobody figures out their first shape-shift that quick. Not even a pooka."

Taylor's face darkened. She summoned an orb of faery fire—one of the few bits of magic she was actually good at.

"That's just gonna scare everything off!" Danny protested.

"What's the point? I can't do this. And the next time—" She stopped herself, but too late. Danny's ears perked up.

"What do you mean, 'next time'?" he said.

Taylor bit her lip. She hadn't meant to bring that up.

"Mara...sort of...attacked me."

155

"*What?*"

"Last month. At Halloween. She sent some kind of three-headed vulture after Jill and William and me."

"Three—you mean an ellén trechend? Oh, this is bad!" Danny groaned. "By oak, ash, and thorn, Shanna's gonna have a fit!"

"Yeah," Taylor agreed. A moment later she added, "Promise me you won't tell her."

"Are you nuts? How can I not tell her?"

"I just don't want her to worry, okay?"

"Worry? Taylor, she's already worried to death! You don't know what it's like, cooped up at Pilot Knob like she is."

"*Look, Danny, I—*" She stopped herself when she saw Danny shrink away from her. "Okay. Just forget about it." She turned to walk away.

"News from you is what keeps her going," Danny said.

Taylor stopped and slumped her shoulders.

"She never answers when I try to scry her."

"Chief Tewa's orders," Danny said. "Somebody could be listening in.... At least, somebody who knows her true name."

"Somebody like Mara," Taylor said. "Or Crom."

Danny nodded.

"Sounds like she traded in one jail cell for a different one."

"Maybe," Danny conceded. "But at least folks like her at this one. And she likes them."

"I guess."

"D'you hear anything from up north? It looks like the Summer Court's getting all shook up."

"Osanda Morning?" she asked.

"You've heard of her, then?"

"You might say that."

"Did you hear she was at Pilot Knob a while back?"

"No," Taylor said. "Meeting with Chief Tewa?"

"Him and the other Chiefs," Danny said.

"Do you think she's for real?"

"How should I know? Folks like what she's got to say, that's for sure. Leastways, some of 'em. Is she on the up and up?" Danny shrugged.

"By oak, ash, and thorn, I'd really love it if someone like her could make the jerks in the Summer Court act like grown-ups."

"Oak, ash, and thorn?" Danny chuckled. "You been hanging out with me too much."

Taylor laughed, too. "Be careful or I'll ruin your reputation. But I've heard other folks from the Wonder say that. Nobody's ever explained to me what it means."

"It's just an expression," Danny said. "I guess a Topsider would say, 'By all that's holy' or some such."

"But why oak, ash, and thorn?"

Danny leaned against a tree.

"The way my mom explained it, it's kind of a shorthand for the things you can count on when the going gets rough."

Taylor nodded. "Yes?"

"Well, oak means strength, right? You want something that'll last, you build it out of oak. People gotta be like that, too. Strong. Solid."

"Able to take what people throw at you without breaking," Taylor offered.

"Exactly. And ash... We say the Great World Tree was an ash. The center of the universe. It's like the hub at the middle of a wheel. Everything else turns around it."

"So the ash is a symbol of...grounding? Purpose?"

"Sounds about right. It's kind of like your true name. If you know who you are, what you're all about, that's its own kind of strength. That's what ash is like."

"What about thorn?

Danny grinned. "That's my specialty," he said. "See, the thorn has two sides, don't it? You can get some awfully sweet berries off a thorn bush—but first you gotta get past the thorns."

Taylor scrunched her face, trying to understand.

"Think of it this way," Danny continued. "If you didn't know no better, you'd see the berries and grab 'em. But that's when

157

the thorn gets you! You gotta be careful of a thorn bush, 'cause it'll stick you when you ain't expecting it."

"It's tricky to mess with a thorn bush," Taylor said.

Danny nodded. "You gotta treat it with respect or you're gonna get poked. And you probably won't see it coming!"

Taylor pondered this. She let her fire orb burn down to nothing.

"So... Be strong. Know who you are..."

"And always have a trick up your sleeve!"

Taylor sat back down on the cold ground and pulled her black leather jacket more closely around her. When she remembered why she was out there, she slumped forward. Maybe she'd been too optimistic about learning to shape-shift. She couldn't see that she'd made any progress at all, and Danny's teaching methods didn't inspire a whole lot of confidence.

She stretched and took a deep breath.

"Danny, can't you just give me a hint? Please?"

The pooka smiled and sat down in front of her. They both took a couple of slow, shallow breaths.

"Okay," Danny began, "I reckon I've made you suffer long enough." He cleared his throat. "The thing about shape-shifting is that you don't really know what it means to have your whole body rearranged."

"I don't understand."

"Exactly. You don't know what it's like to walk on all fours. You don't know what it's like to have wings or a tail. You don't know what it's like to see colors different, or be able to tell which animals have peed in your yard just by the smell."

"Okay, that's gross."

"Comes with the territory." Danny shrugged his shoulders. "But think about it. Say you did turn into a wolf—right now. You'd be weak as a newborn. You wouldn't even know how to walk. You wouldn't understand half of what your senses were telling you. It would all be this big jumble, you know? You'd be worse than helpless."

158

"I see." Taylor realized she wouldn't be turning into anything for a good long time. "So, how do I learn all that?"

"You got to fare forth."

Now Taylor really started shaking. She knew a little about faring forth, and most of what she knew gave her the creeps.

"You mean getting inside the head of an animal, seeing what it sees."

"That ain't all there is to it, but it'll do for now. So, are you ready to try again?"

Taylor nodded and closed her eyes. It was well past midnight, but she figured she might as well give it one more try. She focused on her breathing, slowing it down as much as she could. At the same time, she tried to reach out with all of her other senses.

She shivered in the cold.

It wasn't working at all. There had to be animals all around, but she couldn't find them.

Danny sniffed and let out a confused grunt. Taylor shut her eyes tight, trying to concentrate.

He touched her shoulder, and she opened her eyes.

"Come on," Danny said. He looked agitated. "We gotta get moving."

Danny's pointed ears perked up. "D'you hear that?"

"What?" Taylor took a breath. She tried to extend her magical senses. Something was wrong.

"Something's coming. I don't know what."

Danny looked around, sniffing the air.

"Let's go!"

He grabbed Taylor by the arm and pulled her forward. They weaved through the trees as quickly as Taylor's legs could go.

A loud, bellowing bark rang through the woods. The sound drove Taylor to her knees.

"Come on!" Danny shouted.

A second bark joined the first, just as loud.

She let Danny haul her to her feet. They hurried on.

The path they had taken opened onto an empty field strewn with corn flax and stubble. It may not have been a full mile across, but it felt like it with an unknown beastie hot on their trail.

Danny cursed.

"I'm thinking being out in the open would be a bad thing, right?" Taylor said.

"Other way!" Danny said. They spun around and ran three steps back the way they had come before he thrust out his arm to stop her in Taylor in her tracks.

Someone—or some*thing*—was creeping toward them, cloaked in shadow. Dogs still barked in the distance, but more quietly.

Taylor shuddered. Faery dogs were heading their way, and it was impossible to tell from which direction.

"Please tell me you've learned out how to blink," Danny whispered.

"Uh..."

"Okay. New plan. You up for a horseback ride?" His eyes started to glow.

"Say the word."

The shadow took another step forward.

Taylor and Danny backed away.

"Stick around," the shadow said with a cackle. "The more the merrier."

They bolted into the field—it was the only direction that didn't come with a warning sign.

Danny grabbed Taylor's arm and pulled it around his neck. He had just started taking on his horse form when he doubled over in pain. Taylor flew over his broadening shoulders and landed in a heap.

He fell spread-eagle on the ground, his transformation cut short. A wisp of magical energy rose from his back. He had been blasted.

Taylor got to her feet. She crouched sideways to the oncoming shadow with her left hand extended. She flexed the fingers of both hands, bringing magic to bear.

Danny grunted.

His attacker emerged from the woods. He was about Taylor's size and dressed in dark leather. His long, gray hair matched the fur trim of his collar and gave him the look of a shaggy, broad-shouldered beast-man.

He passed a bullwhip from his left hand to his right.

Taylor braced herself.

"Don't you want to play?" whip-guy said.

When he grinned, Taylor saw white teeth and a flicking pink tongue.

"No!" she commanded. *"Go away!"*

He stepped back, but he showed no fear. At best, he was mildly aggravated.

The dogs were becoming indistinct. Taylor could barely hear them over the sounds of wind and tramping feet. Her eyes darted. Wherever they were—and they had to be close—there was no sign of them.

She felt rather than heard a weird buzzing in the air. It set her heart racing even faster.

The creature with the whip advanced.

Taylor's fingers tingled with magical energy. She licked her lips.

Wait.

Tramping feet?

Who—?

The first dog would have bowled her over, but she sensed it coming behind her just in time to turn and release the blast she had been about to use on whip-guy. It yelped silently as it slammed into the ground.

Behind it were two more: lean black hunting dogs with blazing red eyes. The man who held their leashes was over eight feet tall and bare-chested despite the cold. His head and shoulders were home to a matted tangle of moss, and his nose looked

161

as big and bulbous as a gourd. In the moonlight, his color seemed off: neither white nor brown but ashy gray.

Taylor backed away, nearly tripping over Danny as she did. The pooka was struggling to his feet, still dazed.

She wasn't afraid, which surprised her. In fact, her whole body felt turbo-charged. She was ready to fight something. Anything.

A wry smile spread across her face. Anticipation of combat— of killing or being killed—drove every other thought from her mind.

The thrill of the hunt was exhilarating.

She started gathering magic for another blast as she took stock of the new arrivals in the cornfield.

Following the dogs and their gigantic handler was a man on horseback and another half a dozen on foot. A blood-red will-o'-the-wisp circled above the rider's head.

The rider was young and not bad looking, with long black hair and a bronze-barreled shotgun resting on his lap. His horse was dull gray, almost invisible in the low light.

The ones on foot—well, nobody would call them good looking. They all looked wrong. All of them looked deranged: hungry, ready for violence, but also somehow distant, like they weren't entirely aware of what they were doing. They might have been extras from a zombie movie.

Taylor tried not to think too hard about that.

In addition to the moss-man was another who seemed human enough, but his face had been ruined by vicious claw marks. He held a club crowned with a dozen bronze spikes.

"Does your mommy know where you're at, little girl?" the moss-man wheezed. His voice was high-pitched and nasal, totally not what Taylor would have expected. "Does she know about your ugly boyfriend?"

"Who are you calling ugly?" Danny blurted as he got to his feet.

The rest of the newcomers were a ragtag jumble in shabby clothes. One of them was a goblin barely three feet all.

162

It didn't matter what they were, though. Taylor was itching for a fight.

"Or is he just your pet?" the moss-man jeered. "Does he know any tricks?"

Danny came up beside her, yellow fire in his eyes. "Taylor, we gotta go. Now!"

Danny grabbed her arm. She shook him off.

He growled at her.

"Any sign of her, Rudy?" The rider addressed the gray-haired creature with the whip. He didn't seem interested in Taylor at all any more.

"Just these two," Rudy said, shaking his head. "Figure we go find the rest of the gang?"

The rider considered Taylor and Danny. "What do you say? Are you up for a hunt?"

"No!" Danny barked. He flung his right hand forward. Jets of flashing light sparked from his fingers while the pop-pop-pop of firecrackers burst in the air.

The chaos shook Taylor to her senses. She finally realized she was outgunned, outnumbered, and probably only had seconds to live. How had she missed all that before?

"D-Danny?"

The moss-man let loose the dogs. Danny surged forward. At the same time, his body shifted and compacted. In his own dog form, he bounded into the nearest rival. Two dogs wrestled on the ground while two others nipped at them, waiting for their turn.

"Danny!" Taylor screamed.

The rider leveled his shotgun at her.

"Join us or die," he said.

Chapter 16

The Wild Hunt

Before Taylor could answer, an arrow appeared out of nowhere and buried itself in the rider's bicep. He howled in agony and dropped the shotgun. Before it hit the ground, a second arrow took out the dog on top of Danny, and a third landed in the moss-man's chest—to no effect.

"Leave her!"

Taylor turned in the direction of the newcomer's voice.

A blurry distortion of the air resolved itself into the form of a lone man. He was dressed in buckskins, with a war club strapped to his belt. He already had another arrow nocked in his bow, with three more ready in his shooting hand.

Taylor gasped.

"Tsisgwa?"

"Ah, a proud nunnehi warrior," the rider snarled. The arrow had vanished—elf shot could stun or even kill, but it rarely inflicted ordinary physical damage. The rider clutched his injured arm, but seemed more angry than frightened. "Have you come to join the Hunt? You'd be a natural."

Taylor watched the exchange with cold detachment as she tried to push the buzzing out of her head. It made her muscles tense and amplified her senses to the point that every subtle sound or flash of movement nearly overwhelmed her.

She glanced from Tsisgwa to the rider.

There was going to be a fight, she knew it.

She couldn't wait.

165

"I said to leave her alone," Tsisgwa repeated. "This Hunt of yours has nothing to do with her."

"Oh, doesn't it?" the rider smirked. "I'll bet she'd find the experience...intoxicating."

Tsisgwa let fly another arrow. This one landed squarely in the face of the giant who had been handling the dogs. He fell backward with a thud.

The man with the bullwhip advanced on Tsisgwa. As he did, his face changed. High, arching ram's horns sprouted from his temples, his brow thickened, his eyes grew wide and red, and his mouth stretched open to reveal hideous fangs.

Taylor had seen some pretty gruesome-looking faery beings over the past year, but nothing like him. Looking at him sent a shudder through her whole body. His appearance was just plain disturbing, a mashup of every monster in every nightmare that every little kid had ever had.

Whoever or whatever he was, he knew how to scare the pants off somebody.

Tsisgwa fired at the creature, which raised a shield spell and deflected the arrow. He never stopped advancing, so a second later he plowed into Tsisgwa, snarling and cursing, flattening him on his back.

Three of the zombie-things sprang forward to join whip-man stomping on Tsisgwa. It was four against one.

It made sense, Taylor thought. Use overwhelming force against your prey.

Bring him down. Kill him.

She took a step toward the scuffle, balling her fists.

"Oh, no you don't!" someone shouted, and yanked her by the collar of her jacket, flinging her to the ground.

"Let go of m—*Mr. Ramos!?*"

It was, indeed, Taylor's social studies teacher. He was dressed in jeans and an aviator jacket etched with geometric symbols. The four-foot long staff in his left hand glowed with golden light as he offered his right hand to Taylor.

"Come with me, Taylor. Now!"

He didn't give her a chance to think about it. He grabbed her collar once more and started hauling her across the field. The sounds of combat began to fade. The angry barks of the faery dogs got louder.

"Mr. Ramos? What...?"

"Later!" he yelled. "Keep running!"

"B-but Danny... Tsisgwa..."

"I'll help them once you're safe!"

"But..." Taylor looked over her shoulder. She yanked herself free.

One of the larger zombies had Danny in a wrestling hold. His hind legs dangled in the air. Meanwhile, Tsisgwa was somehow holding his own against four attackers, whaling away with his flaming war club.

Moss-man had shaken off the effects of the elf shot and lumbered into the melee.

Danny howled and snapped. His eyes glowed so brightly they looked like fire was spilling out of them onto his black cheeks.

Tsisgwa's war club met an attacker's shoulder with a thunk.

"Taylor, hurry up!"

She shook her head. "We've got to help him! *Now!*"

Mr. Ramos backed off.

"You can't go back," he said. His voice was urgent but controlled. "They almost got you."

Taylor watched as Danny was slammed to the ground.

"It's the Wild Hunt," Mr. Ramos explained. "Get too close for too long, and you'll be forced to join them. Get in their way..."

She took another look back. Tsisgwa was managing; two of his attackers lay unconscious at his feet. Danny, however, could have used some help.

"Then Danny needs us."

Mr. Ramos shook his head. "My orders are clear: I'm keeping you safe."

Orders?

167

She shook off Mr. Ramos's hold. There was no way she was leaving Danny behind. "Okay," she said, "then try to keep up." She sprinted back toward the fray, gathering magic as she went.

Mr. Ramos yelled and ran after her. "Taylor, you don't know what you're doing!"

"What was your first clue?"

"You're smarter than this."

"Look, either help me or get the heck out of my way!"

Taylor marched toward Danny. She flung a blast at the rider. A magical distortion exploded against his face. He leaned backwards in his saddle, more startled than hurt.

"Don't cross me, girl," he said. "You have no idea who you're dealing with."

The buzzing came back. This time, Taylor expected it. More than that, she embraced it. It flooded her body with adrenaline, wiping away the fear, supercharging her strength.

She had a plan. It wasn't completely stupid, but it would take some serious magic.

A grin crossed her face. Her icy blue eyes were wide with anticipation.

Danny stumbled forward on his front paws. He met Taylor's gaze and growled. Mr. Ramos stepped forward, leveling his staff parallel to the ground.

Taylor nudged him aside. "*Danny, come here, boy,*" she said, projecting as much presence as she could.

He let out a doggy whine of confusion. He fell into a crouch, ready to lash out at someone but not sure who. Taylor maintained eye contact. It didn't look like Danny recognized her. It dawned on her that losing to the hunters might not mean death. It might mean something a lot worse.

"He belongs to us now," the rider said.

"*Not if I have anything to say about it,*" Taylor snarled.

The last of Tsisgwa's opponents fell. The nunnehi stalked forward to join Taylor and Mr. Ramos. His war club burst into flames as he took stock of the remaining hunters.

"I'm afraid you don't," the rider said.

The zombie-men lunged forward. Mr. Ramos and Tsisgwa took up positions to her left and her right, fending them off. It had to be now, while everyone was busy.

She took half a second to brace herself. Mara had said addlement only worked on the weak-willed. Well, given his current state, that described Danny pretty well.

She kept her eyes trained on Danny while she slipped into a pitcher's stance and pantomimed throwing a ball back the way she and Mr. Ramos had come.

At the same time, she threw as much glamour as she could muster and shouted, "*Go get it, boy! Get the ball!*"

Danny barked and wagged his tail.

"*Get it, Danny! Good dog!*"

He bolted forward before anyone could stop him. Taylor took off behind him at a run, egging him to find the nonexistent ball.

She put her head down and ran even faster. Danny barked and zigzagged across the field ahead of her.

"To the right!" Mr. Ramos called.

"What?"

"More to the right!"

Taylor looked back. Now Mr. Ramos and Tsisgwa were barreling toward her. Mr. Ramos pointed to a spot in the woods on the far side of the field.

Behind them, the rider was steadying his horse while the rest shambled forward. The dogs were now running loose. They crossed the field, five and ten yards at a single bound. Tsisgwa had retrieved his bow and arrows, though, and took all three of them down in a matter of seconds.

Taylor adjusted her course toward the spot Mr. Ramos had pointed out.

By now, Danny had realized there wasn't a ball to fetch. He shook himself, resumed his two-legged shape, and backtracked to Taylor's side.

"Taylor?"

"Keep running!"

169

"Where?"

"How should I know?"

"There!" Mr. Ramos called. Then he vanished, appearing in a flash of light ahead of them as he ran into the woods.

Tsisgwa fired another volley of arrows at the approaching Hunt.

"Get in!" Mr. Ramos yelled.

The line of trees turned out to be only a few yards deep. On the other end of a narrow footpath Taylor and Danny found a dirt road. Parked on the shoulder was Mr. Ramos's gray SUV.

Danny skidded to a stop. "You want me to get in *that*?"

Mr. Ramos had already slid behind the wheel to start the engine.

"We better do what he says," Taylor said.

A fireball erupted behind.

"A car. You want me to get in a car."

"Yes!" Tsisgwa said. He grabbed Danny by the arm and hauled him toward the car. "And now, if you please."

"B-but..."

"Come on, Danny," Taylor opened the back passenger door and shoved him inside. She felt her magic draining away—par for the course so close to a ton of steel—but scrambled around to get in behind Mr. Ramos. He had laid his staff along the armrest with the end sticking into the back seat and separating Danny from Taylor.

"But we won't have any magic!" Danny said.

"Neither will they," Mr. Ramos said.

Tsisgwa dove into the front passenger seat, and Mr. Ramos sped away before he even shut the door.

"Sorry I'm late," Mr. Ramos said. "Had to stop for gas."

Tsisgwa ignored him. He simply said, "They're coming.... *All* of them."

"All of them?" Mr. Ramos repeated. He cursed in Spanish and floored the gas pedal. The SUV whipped along the dirt road, tossing up pebbles and mud.

"What?" Taylor said.

"...It just ain't natural...," Danny mumbled. His eyes darted back and forth. He looked like he was about to cry.

A blast of light struck the back window but did nothing more than bump the car forward.

"You see?" Mr. Ramos said. "The steel underbody is grounding out their magic, too. If we can just—"

"What do you mean, 'All of them'?" Taylor asked.

Danny whimpered.

"The Wild Hunt," Tsisgwa said. "You only ran into a small scouting party." He sighed. "They've joined up with the main body."

"But if we can outrun them—" Mr. Ramos began.

"They're on foot!" Taylor said. "Or else on horseback. How can we not—"

A bolt of lightning crashed into a tree with a thunderous *crack!* Half the tree tumbled into the road in front of them. Mr. Ramos swerved into another corn field.

"Lemme out of here!" Danny cried. "I can't even blink inside this infernal contraption!"

"Not wise," Tsisgwa said. "I don't like automobiles either, but given the circumstances..."

"I only saw one troll," Mr. Ramos interrupted.

"There were about a dozen more with the main body," Tsisgwa said. "Three big ones. The rest were smaller."

"I hate the small ones," Mr. Ramos said. He peered out the window. "Still another hour at least until sunrise."

"What are the chances the iron will stop them?" Tsisgwa said.

"You never know with trolls. At least my magic is mostly unaffected."

"That's another thing," Taylor said. "*What is my social studies teacher doing here*?"

The car spun out of a tight turn and returned to the road with a lurch.

"Somebody has to drive," Mr. Ramos said. He adjusted the rearview mirror. Taylor looked out the back window.

It shouldn't have been possible, but the Wild Hunt was gaining on them. The one rider who had first accosted them had been joined by six or seven others, and the ranks of people on foot had swelled to more than Taylor could count. Three hulking brutes lumbered behind a small army of others, some of them with spears, shotguns, torches, or even pitchforks.

"You've been spying on me!" Taylor shouted. All this time, and her social studies teacher knew exactly what she was. She wouldn't have thought it possible, but she suddenly felt even more vulnerable and confused than she was before.

"I'm afraid so," Mr. Ramos said. "I'll explain later."

Ahead of Hunt ran half a dozen faery dogs, their eyes ablaze, their snarls and barks drowned out by the rumble of the engine and the crunch of the tires on gravel and dirt.

Danny tried—and failed—to summon a ball of faery fire. He slumped in his seat, shivering and blubbering like a baby.

"Wait a minute! Who's side are you on? Not Summer..."

"Miguel is with me," Tsisgwa interrupted. "But this really isn't the time—"

A shotgun blast thundered in the distance.

"Can't this thing go any faster?" Taylor asked.

"As soon as we get to the main road," Mr. Ramos said. "We're not far from a cemetery. We can cross over to Topside and—"

CRUNCH!

The roof of the SUV dented inward as something heavy landed on it. A tree branch fell off the side.

Danny yelped.

Mr. Ramos cursed again. "How am I supposed to fix that on a teacher's salary?" he growled. He gunned the engine.

"Left up ahead," Tsisgwa said.

Mr. Ramos nodded. The road ended in a T a quarter mile up the road. They barreled to the left at full speed. The nearest of the dogs didn't make the turn and smashed into a wooden fence. Two more dogs piled into the first, but the rest of the pack was able to change course in time.

172

Taylor knew they were barking their lungs out, but she couldn't hear a peep from them.

"Faster!" she cried.

A dog launched itself at the car. It scraped the roof with its claws before falling to the ground, rolling to a stop, and just as quickly bolting after them again.

"Don't they ever give up?" Taylor said.

"They'll break off at dawn," Mr. Ramos said. "We just have to survive that long."

"And be far away from here before sunset," Tsisgwa added.

"Wonderful," Taylor said.

Mr. Ramos swerved to dodge a flaming spear that fell from the sky onto the road in front of them.

The car lurched to one side and started shaking and thumping violently.

"Blew a tire!" Mr. Ramos said.

A dog landed on the roof of the SUV. It might have been the same one as before. Either way, it slashed and scraped against the metal for two or three seconds before being shaken off.

With a flat tire, the car was sluggish. Mr. Ramos fought with the steering wheel to stay on the road.

"There!" Tsisgwa called.

In the headlights, Taylor could see the cemetery Mr. Ramos had mentioned. They were almost there. Her heart skipped a beat.

"Come on, Danny," she said. "We're almost there. Just hang on a little long—"

The car spun completely around on a patch of ice that hadn't been there a second ago. Mr. Ramos fought to keep the car from rolling. They flew backwards into a tree beside the road. The tailgate folded around the cargo area, sending shards of glass in every direction.

Taylor and Danny hit the deck as best they could.

Before they had come to a stop, Tsisgwa was out of the car with an arrow nocked.

Mr. Ramos leaned around. "Stay put!" he ordered. He gathered magic for a blast.

The dogs were on them before Taylor knew it. The first one fell to one of Tsisgwa's arrows, but there were too many of them. He vanished beneath a flood of fangs and claws.

The next thing Taylor knew, someone had ripped the top of the SUV completely off. A nine-foot tall giant, whom she took now to be one of the trolls Tsisgwa had mentioned, had pulled the car apart like it was made of cardboard, leaving the three remaining passengers exposed.

Mr. Ramos thrust forward his hand, blasting the troll. It grunted and staggered backward.

Then he leaped to his feet, grabbing his staff. It began at once to blaze with golden light. He swung it around his body in some impressive martial-arts moves.

"Okay," he snarled. "Which of you *payasos* is next?"

Chapter 17

Unwanted Help

A mass of people surged forward, howling into the night.

Mr. Ramos leaped into what was left of the exposed cargo bed, fighting over Danny and Taylor's heads. He slammed an onrushing fae with the butt of his staff, sending him flying. Then he spun it around, taking out two more. He lifted it high over his head, summoning a shield spell to deflect the force of someone's silvery bolt of magical energy.

"Oooh!" a broad-shouldered man called. He had a huge nose, and his skin was ashy gray. His mouth spread into a taunting grin. "Looky there, Frank. Chico over there's gonna whack us with his stick!"

Another gray man chuckled. "Ain't that cute. It's like a baby toy!"

Mr. Ramos glowered at him as he swept another attacker off his feet.

"Some of us don't need no baby toys, Chico!" the first man snarled. He let loose a blast, which Mr. Ramos barely deflected. He stumbled backward, but managed to keep his footing and not stomp on Danny's head.

"Is it true what they say about magic wands?" the second man, Frank, said. "Are you really just compens—"

Frank fell flat on his back, leveled by a crimson blast from Mr. Ramos's staff. He was about to take aim at the first gray man when when a whip wrapped around his leg and pulled him down. It was Rudy, the demon-faced creature this whole ordeal started with. He cackled as he fell on Mr. Ramos.

175

Rough hands pulled Taylor and Danny from the wreckage of the SUV. A gray-skinned troll, this one barely six feet tall, wrapped Danny in a headlock. Two wild-eyed fae grabbed Taylor by the arms.

She fought back, but they were too strong. Even as the blood-lust rose in her, she knew she had no chance against them.

"Hold it right there!" a voice bellowed.

The mounted Hunters rode forward. The bells around their horses' necks quietly jingled. Orbs of faery fire zipped to and fro above them, pinpricks of silver-white light.

Whatever had been setting Taylor on edge faded without entirely going away. The mob settled down, too.

The leader was a broad-shouldered man astride a gleaming white horse.

Taylor's heart climbed up into her throat when she recognized him, but her brain leaped three steps ahead, considering possibilities. Maybe, just maybe...

The leader smiled beneath his white-blond beard, making the geometric tattoos that adorned his face subtly contort. He turned to the dark-haired rider who had first accosted Taylor.

"Why, Mold," he drawled, "it looks as if you've found a celebrity."

"C-cousin?"

Tsisgwa struggled to his feet. He had a bloody gash across his back and another that tore the left leg of his buckskin trousers to ribbons. Mr. Ramos had lost his staff, and Rudy's whip was wrapped around his throat.

Another mounted man spoke. "No, you're joking." This man was draped in a scarlet cloak that fell over his horse's flanks. From his head sprung not only wild brown hair but also a pair of three-pronged antlers. He gazed at Taylor with enormous brown eyes.

He gestured, and the nearest fire orb descended to shine on Taylor's face.

"It must be her. She has your eyes." He spoke calmly. If Taylor's presence was a surprise, he hid it well.

"It's her, Kern," Crom Cornstack said.

The first rider's eyes opened wide. "*This* is Shanna's whelp?" He could barely contain his wonder.

"It seems introductions are in order." Crom gazed at Taylor with his icy blue eyes and gestured toward the man with the antlers. "May I present Kern Barrows, Primus of the Autumn Court. And it seems you've already met Mold Cornstack, my cousin's boy."

"Charmed," Mold said. He sized her up and glanced over to Crom. "Can we kill her now?"

Tsisgwa surged forward but was held back by the troll who had ripped the roof off the car.

"Mold, huh?" Taylor glared defiantly. "You got a sister named Mildew?"

Mold stared daggers at her. He pushed his horse a step toward her, clenching his fists, then stopped himself as he caught sight of his older cousin's frown.

"Don't be so hasty, Mold," Crom said. "She may be able to help us."

As if!

"We're looking for Anya Redmane," Kern Barrows said. "There's a rumor she's been seen in these parts."

"And?"

"She doesn't deserve your protection," he continued. "She is an oath-breaker, an enemy of all Fair Folk."

"You actually want me to help you?" She nearly laughed in their faces. That itchy feeling of pent-up aggressiveness continued to fade, but it was still there. She had to keep it under control.

"Think carefully how you respond, my dear," Crom said. "Anya is our quarry, not you. Help us, and we *might* let you live."

Taylor's mind went into overdrive. They thought she knew something about Anya's whereabouts. She couldn't let them think otherwise.

"Are you prepared to bargain?" she said.

177

"Taylor, no!" Mr. Ramos called. He struggled futilely against Rudy's whip.

Crom regarded the social studies teacher, then Taylor. Her offer seemed to intrigue him.

That was good, because Taylor already knew she was safe.

Now, all she needed to do was convince Crom to let the others go free.

"You love to bargain as much as the next sídhe, don't you, Gramps?" she said.

"You are no more my granddaughter than Shanna is my child," Crom said. "If you think differently, then you are grievously mistaken."

He turned to Kern Barrows. The antlered man shrugged. If Crom wanted to bargain, it didn't matter to him.

Crom addressed Taylor. "You may go if you tell us what you know."

"But cousin—" Mold protested.

"Not good enough," Taylor interrupted.

There was a collective gasp from the mob.

Taylor swallowed and then pressed on. "You might have heard: I owe your wife a favor. Seems to me I need to be alive for her to collect."

"Your point?"

"Once you knew who I was, *my* life was never in danger. That's why you stopped your flunkies."

"Hey!" Mold interrupted, insulted. Crom rolled his eyes as if to say "Tell me we're not related."

Taylor said, "The point is, I'm walking out of this no matter what. Either that, or you're spending the next hundred years sleeping on the couch."

An uneasy chuckle spread through the Hunt. It confirmed Taylor's hunch that whatever magic was making everybody lose control earlier had been suspended.

"So how about this: I tell you everything I know about Anya's location, and *all* of us go free?"

178

"Unacceptable!" Mold Cornstack said. "The Wild Hunt has rules—"

Crom raised a hand to silence him. He permitted a wry smile to cross his face, shifting his geometric tattoos like a living mosaic.

"Fine," Taylor said. "Then good luck finding Anya without my help." She projected presence enough to seem confident of her position. Maybe that would be enough. It pretty much had to be, because she didn't have a backup plan if they turned her down.

Crom nudged his horse closer.

"If you're trying to trick me..."

"No trick," Taylor said. "Everything I know about Anya's whereabouts. Everything. I swear."

Crom peered down at her.

Taylor looked up at her grandfather. "Your turn."

"Cousin, don't," Mold said. "It's bad enough we have to set *her* free..."

"These three are nothing compared to Anya," Crom said. Then to Taylor he said, "Tell us everything, and you and your friends are free to go."

"I think you're forgetting something," Taylor said.

Crom heaved an exasperated sigh. Taylor could almost hear him thinking, *Teenagers!* "I swear," he said.

She looked around. The antlered Autumn Primus sat rigid in his saddle. The rest of the Hunters, mounted and on foot alike, shifted restlessly, waiting for what Taylor had to say.

"Well?" Crom prompted.

"Everything I know about Anya Redmane's whereabouts."

"Yes. Sometime tonight, if you please."

"Sure," Taylor said. She swallowed.

"The absolute truth, *Gramps*, is...." She threw up her hands. "I got nothing."

"I beg your pardon?" Crom said, leaning forward.

"Not a clue," Taylor continued. "I haven't seen or heard of her since June. She could be anywhere."

179

Mold seethed. "You lying little..."

"*I'm not lying*," Taylor said. Her ripple of presence caused many in the mob to shudder. "I promised I'd tell you everything I knew." She folded her arms. "That's what I just did."

"Insolent, double-dealing..."

"Enough, Mold," Crom said. "I believe her."

"B-but—!"

"I've kept my part of the bargain," Taylor said. She looked her grandfather directly in the eyes. "What about you?"

"As you wish," Crom said. He raised his voice and shouted, "The girl is not to be harmed!"

Wait, what?

"What about my friends?" Taylor demanded. "You promised they'd be free to go!"

"And so they are," Crom said. He gestured to the various Hunters restraining Tsisgwa, Danny, and Mr. Ramos. They all backed away. Mr. Ramos snatched his staff from the ground; Tsisgwa his bow.

"I would suggest they leave before the Hunt resumes. Say, twenty seconds or so."

Taylor felt a tickle at the back of her mind, a welling up of primal anger. The magic of the Wild Hunt was coming back to life.

"They will, of course, be granted the usual courtesies," Crom said.

"They're allowed to either join us or die," Kern Barrows explained.

"But which they choose is completely up to them," Crom said. "They are, after all, *free*."

"If they survive," Kern dead-panned, "they do get a tee shirt."

Danny struggled to stay on his feet. He felt the urge to become a dog, to growl and snap at the mob of trolls, elves, woodwoses, and other members of the Wild Hunt.

He had to think fast, before the frenzy took over.

Tsisgwa looked awful. The trolls had really worked him over. The other guy looked a little better. He'd been throwing around a lot of magic, though. He was bound to more drained than he was letting on.

Danny ached all over. A dog's bite to his shoulder burned like fire and left his whole arm numb. Another bite on his left flank stabbed him with pain with every breath.

He took less than a second to survey the situation. Taylor was accusing Mr. Cornstack of cheating. He was surprised she hadn't figured out yet there's no such thing as the spirit of the law when it comes to the Fair Folk. The only thing that counted was a person's exact words.

He had to do something. Too much longer, and they'd be so overwhelmed by the draw of the Hunt they'd have no choice but to join it.

Then he caught the eye of one of the trolls standing behind Ramos. He was one of the little ones—no taller than Danny himself.

Perfect.

"If somebody's gonna kill me, at least don't let it be a troll!" he shouted. His nerves were on edge. He was ready to let someone have it, but if he could hang on a little longer...

"I'd start running if I were you!" the troll shouted back.

Danny backed off, edging away from the car.

"You got something against trolls?" someone said. It was another troll, a seven-foot-tall female with splotchy green skin and a single horn growing off-center out of her forehead.

Kern Barrows grinned savagely and elbowed Crom Cornstack as if to say, *This is going to be good.*

"Big 'uns are okay, I guess," Danny said. "At least you know where you stand with them. But dinky little tussers..."

"Hey!" the smaller troll shouted.

"He has a point," Ramos said. "Everybody knows the little ones are a poxy waste of skin."

There were scattered titters from the crowd.

181

Danny suppressed the urge to smile. *Good*, he thought, *he's caught on*. The thing about trolls was they loved starting fights. They knew how to push your buttons—but it wasn't hard to get them riled up, either.

Ramos sidled up to Tsisgwa and offered him his shoulder.

The smaller troll advanced. Ramos pivoted to place Tsisgwa behind him.

"You think you're better than us?"

"I think on a scale from one to ten, you're a sack of puke."

"You stinking faery!" the troll roared, springing forward.

"Who are you calling a faery?" Rudy shouted. He cracked his whip.

Danny subtly brushed his hand against Taylor's. Just another couple of seconds...

"I oughta—"

"Who's stopping you?"

Just as the troll took a swing at Rudy, Danny threw Taylor onto his back, became a horse, and blinked away. He reappeared outside the circle of Hunters.

Tsisgwa and Ramos appeared half a second later.

The Wild Hunt had devolved into anarchy as trolls and fae fell on each other with animalistic glee. Crom and his mounted henchmen and shouted orders to no avail. It wouldn't be long, though, before they restored order.

Danny bolted toward the cemetery with Taylor clinging to his shaggy black mane. The others sprinted behind.

Another blink brought everyone within the boundaries of the graveyard.

Taylor slipped off Danny's back, and he resumed his two-legged shape.

"We gotta get out of here!" he called. "As soon as those guys figure out we're gone—"

"Agreed," Ramos said. He gestured, and a swirling vortex of sparkling dust arose from the earth. "We'll regroup at Ichisi."

"Tsisgwa," Taylor said. "Mr. Ramos. What are you doing here?" She looked angry.

182

"Taylor, we gotta go," Danny said. "The Hunt—"

"You've been spying on me?" With the danger passed, she started to shake. She was about to do something stupid and give the Wild Hunt a chance to catch up. "Does Ayoka know about this?"

"No," Tsisgwa said. "But your friend is right. We're not safe here. We should go."

"Fine!" Taylor barked. She raised her hands and opened a portal through the Wonder. "I'm leaving!"

She stomped into the swirling vortex and vanished.

Taylor didn't settle on a destination until she set foot in the portal. All she knew was she wanted to be alone.

They were spying on me! she fumed to herself as she spun through the darkness. Hills and valleys, graveyards and standing stones, flashed before her eyes, a chaotic spectacle that would have left her dazed and nauseated a few short months ago.

She felt sick at her stomach anyway, but it had nothing to do with ring-travel. Above the thunderous rush of wind, she heard Danny calling her name.

Why were they spying on me?

Taylor leaped out of the chaos into the patch of woods behind her house in Macon. The first gray light of dawn was breaking over the trees to the east.

Rather than heading home, she marched through the woods, hopped over the tiny stream at the bottom of the hill, and trudged up the other side. She exited the woods a block over from her street and took off, half running, half walking.

"Taylor!" Danny called.

"Go away!"

"Taylor, we need to talk!"

He was gaining on her. Taylor didn't look back, but she could hear more than one set of footsteps as well as Tsisgwa's labored breathing.

"Taylor, hold up!" Danny said.

She spun around. "Did you know about this?" she roared.

"Nobody knew," Mr. Ramos said. With Taylor stopped to challenge Danny, all three caught up to her. Mr. Ramos hobbled forward, supporting Tsisgwa.

"You need to calm down," her teacher said. "You'll wake the neighbors."

"Not until I know why Ayoka's cousin and my freaking social studies teacher have been following me!" It felt good to let off some steam. After the adrenaline rush of the Wild Hunt, she was ready to collapse. If she didn't scream, she would cry—and there was no way on human earth she was going to let them see her cry!

"You're not doing this on your own!" she accused. "Who sent you two? Athlan?"

"Taylor, you have to believe we only want to protect you," Mr. Ramos said.

"*Who sent you?*" she repeated. Mr. Ramos took a step back. Danny let out a defeated squeak. Then she had a terrible thought. "Did Shanna send you?"

"No," Tsisgwa said. He sounded tired but alert. "Your mother has no idea we're here."

"*Answers,*" Taylor said. "*Now!*"

"Tewa sent us," Mr. Ramos said.

Tsisgwa nodded. "My people were concerned your family might try something. After what happened last summer...." He broke off with a coughing fit.

"Tewa asked Tsisgwa to keep an eye on you," Mr. Ramos said. "And Tsisgwa thought it would be good to have someone at your school."

Taylor just stared at him.

At last, she threw the heel of her hand against his chest.

"All this time, and you never bothered to mention you're a fae?"

"It never came up," he said with a halfhearted smile. "And for the record, I'm a changeling."

184

Taylor studied his kind face...and the staff in his hand. It no longer glowed, but it was covered with geometric designs and smears of what might have been troll's blood.

"Y-you're human?"

"We couldn't take the risk of you or your friend Jill seeing through anyone's glamour," Tsisgwa said.

"So... what?" Taylor said. "We just go back to school next week and pretend none of this happened?"

"That would be best," Mr. Ramos said.

"Well, forget it!" Taylor said. "I don't like being spied on. Understand? If I need anybody's help I'll freaking ask for it!"

She spun around and marched down the street. Tsisgwa tried to call after her, but she wasn't hearing it. She had to keep moving, to blow off steam, to be in control for a change. It might not have been smart, but it was all she could think to do.

She charged on, soon leaving the residential street for a major thoroughfare. Amid the darkened storefronts only the corner Red-E-Mart had its lights on.

Taylor headed that way. She needed chocolate.

"Taylor!" Danny called. He had been shadowing her but keeping his distance.

"I don't want to talk to you!"

"Then just listen," the pooka pleaded.

Taylor marched up to the door. It was locked. The lights were just for security.

"Look, I understand you're riled up about Mr. Tsisgwa and Mr. Miguel..."

"Hah! You think?"

"...but there's something you're forgetting."

Taylor spun around and glared at Danny. He flinched. Taylor didn't say anything. It wasn't an invitation for Danny to continue. It was more of a dare.

The pooka took it.

"They saved our lives."

Yeah. There was that.

185

Taylor took a breath. She looked around. "Where are they, anyway?"

"Headed for Ichisi."

That made sense. Tsisgwa needed to see a doctor. Thinking about what he'd done for her took a little of the edge off her anger.

"They could have told me what was going on," she said.

"I know."

"They *should* have told me. I deserve to know. If Tewa thinks I might be in danger, then I really deserve to know!"

"I ain't arguing with you," Danny said. He threw his arms wide. "But it is what it is. You can't change what's already happened."

Taylor realized she was pacing and stopped suddenly in front of Danny. He took a step back to avoid her slamming into him.

"I feel like..." She clenched her fists. *Get a grip, Taylor!*

"Y-yeah?" Danny said.

"I feel like everybody's just sitting around watching me. Trying to figure me out. They don't care about me, Danny. They just care about what I can do for them."

"Aw, c'mon, Taylor. That ain't exactly fair. Chief Tewa—"

Taylor jabbed a finger into Danny's chest. "Chief Tewa. Osanda. Mara. They're all the same, and you know it."

"No," Danny said.

"*I beg your pardon?*" She sent a wave of presence. Danny steeled himself and started again.

"No, Taylor. Yeah, some of Our Kind can be pretty brutal, but not all of them. You gotta take the good with the bad."

"So when do I get to meet the good ones?" she spat. As soon as the words left her mouth, she regretted them.

Danny shrunk from her. He bit his lips and bowed his head.

"Oh, Danny," she said. "I'm sorry. I—"

"Shanna asks about you all the time," Danny said.

Taylor started to shake. A tear rolled down her cheek.

186

"All the time," he said again. "I figure she'll find out soon enough that Chief Tewa's sent Tsisgwa and Miguel—Mr. Ramos."

Taylor turned her back on Danny. There are just some things you don't want to do in front of a pooka. She sniffled and wiped away a tear.

"You know what I bet?" Danny continued. "I bet she'll thank him for looking out for you."

"Fine," Taylor said. She started back toward home. She breathed deeply the crisp morning air. She had to clear her head. She had to make things right with Danny, just...not right now. Not when her nerves were this frazzled. And besides, Mom and Dad and Grandma Miller would be waking up before long. She didn't want them to worry.

"Taylor?" Danny said. He was following her.

Taylor didn't turn back, but she answered him. "Okay. I get it."

She crossed the street with Danny loping after her, still keeping a respectful distance.

"But I'm still mad. D'you understand?"

"Sure. Got it."

"And you can tell Chief Tewa I'm mad at him, too."

"Next time I see him."

"And Shanna?" She dared to look over her shoulder.

"Yeah?"

She sighed. "Tell her I'm all right. Please?"

"You bet."

They had made it almost to the Matthewses' house.

"I've got to get going," she said. She jogged to her own house and swung around to the back yard.

Danny watched her the whole way.

Chapter 18

Seeds of Distrust

Claudia spent the next few days taking notes at Gwenllian's meetings with the nunnehi chiefs. She spent the next few nights faring forth to see what else she could discover about Chief Tewa's dealings with Osanda Morning.

She didn't bother to tell Gwenllian that Chief Tewa had been keeping an eye on Taylor. The Acting Matron had never even mentioned the girl, and Claudia certainly wasn't going to bring her up.

Nor did she tell Danny—though that omission bothered her.

Danny was serving as Shanna's go-between, passing messages to Taylor in Ichisi (or Macon, or whatever the Topsiders called it) and bringing word back.

Sure, she could have let Danny know the nunnehi chiefs had an interest in Taylor. But as soon as Taylor found out, she'd want to know how Danny knew it, and if she wasn't careful, she could end up exposing Claudia as a double agent.

She had to hope Taylor would find out soon enough in ways that didn't involve her.

Claudia wasn't nearly as successful after her first night. Faring forth wasn't always fruitful because she couldn't always find a suitable host small enough to pass without notice and maneuverable enough to sneak into the places where Chief Tewa and his comrades held their private meetings. The one time she did ride a mouse into the walls of Chief Tewa's private office, she learned nothing she didn't already know.

189

She tried scrying. Second Sight was usually limited to the here and now, but there were techniques to perceive people and events at a distance or even in the past or future. Claudia had never been especially adept at such methods. She found to her frustration that she still wasn't.

She and Gwenllian took most of their meals in the guest house, though occasionally another member of Tsuwatelda's nobility hosted a banquet in their honor.

All was going, if not well, at least acceptably until one morning in late November. Gwenllian and Claudia were to have breakfast with Chief Tewa—a private, unofficial meeting to hash out some of the issues between them.

They arrived at Tewa's house to find it under heavy guard. The warriors forced them to wait outside for twenty minutes with no explanation. Other warriors milled about, their faces stern. The guards at Chief Tewa's door barked orders in the nunnehi language. The whole place was alive with activity—far more than might have been expected so early in the morning.

At last, the guards ushered Claudia and Gwenllian into Chief Tewa's house. Rather than proceeding to the dining room, however, they were left to wait another twenty minutes in the great room.

Gwenllian demanded an explanation, of course, but no one told her anything.

Claudia feared the worst, that somehow her nightly forays had come to someone's attention. She'd been found out, and Chief Tewa would be forced to confront Gwenllian.

When the White Chief finally appeared, it was obvious he wasn't there for a social call. He was flanked by two of the biggest, meanest-looking warriors Claudia had ever seen. His expression was one of barely controlled rage.

"I was awakened before sunrise this morning by an urgent message from my counterpart in Ichisi," he began. "It seems the sídhe have seen fit to unleash the Wild Hunt in the Nunnehi Lands."

Claudia swallowed. What was Crom Cornstack thinking?

190

Gwenllian gasped. "Chief Tewa, if the Winter Court has been so foolish as to—"

"There are reports of property damage as well as some minor injuries," Chief Tewa continued. "Be grateful nothing worse happened." He glowered at her with barely controlled fury.

Gwenllian hesitated before saying, "This is precisely why it is incumbent upon the Summer Court to offer a strong counterbalance to the power of the Winter Court. It is in your best interest, in the best interest of all your people, to—"

The White Chief raised a hand.

"I will not tolerate Arradherrian interference in the Nunnehi Lands. Of that, you may be certain."

Gwenllian tried again. "Chief Tewa, I'm sure when all the facts are known, you'll see that this was all some sort of misunderstanding."

"We shall see," Chief Tewa said.

Gwenllian and Claudia ate breakfast in the guest house. They had barely sat down, though, when a scry came from Belas Wakefire. Gwenllian invited Claudia to listen in as he brought them up to speed.

"There's been an incident," he said.

"So we've heard," Gwenllian said with a sigh. "What was Cornstack thinking, leading the Wild Hunt across the border?"

"He says he was on the trail of the former Chief Matron."

"Nonsense!" Gwenllian blurted. "What would she possibly be doing in the Nunnehi Lands? She has no friends here."

"Could he be testing the nunnehi?" Claudia said. "He may want to spy out their defenses—though I shudder to imagine why."

"You never know with Cornstack," the Summer Primus said. "But whatever he thinks he's doing, it's bound to cause us trouble."

"It already has, Primus." Gwenllian filled in Wakefire about the mood in Tsuwatelda.

He listened intently and punctuated Gwenllian's report with curses of his own.

"Do what you can there to calm the savages' nerves. I'll try to do the same here." He rolled his eyes upward and shook his head.

Claudia bit her lips to keep from saying something she'd regret about who the real savages were in this situation.

"Primus?" Gwenllian said.

He collected himself and continued. "Cornstack's little escapade has the raths along the border up in arms. Seaborn has already scried me twice from Tobarty."

Claudia's stomach churned.

"Primus," Gwenllian said. She struggled to put words together. "This...this is terrible!"

"That's why it's a good thing you're in Tsuwatelda," the Primus said. "Assure the White Chief the Summer Court had nothing to do with this."

He ended the scry without another word.

The next few days were nerve-wracking. And, despite everything Gwenllian did to assure the Chiefs of Arradherry's goodwill, no one seemed convinced.

By the end of the week, all parties agreed it would be best if the Summer Court's diplomatic visit were cut short.

Claudia was in the guest house, busy pretending not to listen as Gwenllian peered into her Seeing Stone and explained the most recent developments to Dubessa Fairchild.

"I couldn't say, Chief Matron," she said as she paced about the guest house's main room. "Even if Cornstack tells the truth, the nunnehi won't accept it..."

Claudia focused on packing. She'd already gathered her own things. Now she was working on the papers, books, and magical supplies she and Gwenllian had brought.

Neither of them was having a pleasant morning. The entire city was up in arms as news spread about the border incident. Crom Cornstack insisted he was within his rights to track a fugitive from Arradherrian justice wherever she might go. It seemed few in Tsuwatelda bought that excuse. Some seemed positive a full-scale invasion was imminent.

Gwenllian had already been in contact with the Chief Matron the night before, and with the Primus three times before that. Another scry so soon could not be good news.

"Yes, Chief Matron," Gwenllian said. "I agree that's not likely.... No, Chief Matron, I didn't realize.... Already?"

Claudia carefully wrapped her scrying bowl in its velvet bag. It gave her an excuse to stay in one spot and eavesdrop.

The Acting Matron let out an exasperated sigh. "People will believe anything the birds tweet, I suppose.... She what?"

Gwenllian's outburst took Claudia by surprise.

"Osanda is flirting with disaster," she said.

Claudia hadn't considered how this mess would affect Osanda. As she thought about it, though, it seemed more and more like a gift ready-made for her.

She would no doubt begin speechifying about the scandal of sídhe interference in the Nunnehi lands. That was what Gwenllian and Dubessa would fear. A pointed statement against the violence would win Osanda friends among the conservatives on the Summer Court, who were notorious isolationists. At the same time, it would position her as someone who could smooth the nunnehi's ruffled feathers.

"We'll soon leave for Tobarty," Gwenllian said. "Yes, Chief Matron.... I'll see you there."

Claudia packed the last of the equipment: a cauldron, a silver mirror, and a collection of potion ingredients. She put away the hemlock root and the unicorn tears. The sunbeams had gone a bit stale, though, and she wondered if it wouldn't be best just to leave them. At this point, a little more sunshine in Tsuwatelda couldn't hurt.

Gwenllian let out a frustrated grunt. "This is a complete disaster," she spat.

"Trouble, Mrs. Birdsong?" Claudia asked innocently.

"I'd have thought that was obvious."

Claudia chose to let Gwenllian talk. She snapped shut the case of magical ingredients and slid it into its spot in a steamer trunk.

"Osanda will have a field day with this!" the Acting Matron said at last. She paced back and forth, hardly paying attention to Claudia. She was venting for her own sake.

"Surely she can't blame you for the actions of the Winter Court," Claudia said. She tried her best to keep her tone even, professional.

"She doesn't have to blame me!" Gwenllian said. "The nunnehi already believe Arradherry is itching for war. She just has to repeat the rumors that are already being tweeted." She stalked from the room only to return half a minute later with her own packed suitcase.

"People will draw their own conclusions."

Claudia said nothing.

"Curse Crom Cornstack!" Gwenllian said. "He's going to get me removed from the Triad without even trying!"

"To say nothing of provoking a war," Claudia said—but Gwenllian wasn't listening.

"I will not stand for this!"

"No, Mrs. Birdsong."

Gwenllian rubbed her hands together. "I will not give my seat to Osanda Morning, do you hear?"

"Of course not, Mrs. Birdsong."

"And if I have to take drastic action...." She let the possibility hang in the air. Claudia caught herself shuddering.

"I believe we're ready," Claudia said.

"One moment," Gwenllian said. She raised her Seeing Stone to her lips and breathed across it to answer an incoming scry.

"Yes?"

She waited, listening. As soon as she recognized the voice, she rolled her eyes. She motioned for Claudia to join her.

Claudia placed a hand on Gwenllian's shoulder. At once, another room was overlaid upon the nunnehi guest house, a vibrant lime-green hologram of an office with mismatched décor

194

and an agitated Dollin Seaborn seated at his great mahogany desk.

"...getting out of hand," he was saying. "What are you going to do about it?"

"I am not the Teyrnus of Tobarty, Mr. Seaborn," Gwenllian said. "I hardly see how it's any of my business how you—"

"Talk to Wakefire!" Seaborn interrupted. There was something wild, manic in his eyes. He swayed back and forth as he spoke. "I need more men. The locals are out of control. My men can't contain them—to say nothing of reprisals from the nunnehi!"

"The nunnehi are not planning an invasion, Mr. Seaborn," Claudia interjected. "I'm sure of that much." At least, not yet.

"My assistant is correct," Gwenllian said. "And at any rate, I was under the impression Tobarty was already as fortified as any rath of Arradherry."

"They don't trust me!" Seaborn blurted.

"Who doesn't trust you?"

"My men!" Seaborn leaned forward. His eyes darted back and forth, and he continued in hushed tones. Claudia thought he'd seemed nervous before. Now he was beside himself.

"They don't know it, but I hear them," he continued. "The things they say about me when they think I can't hear. They think I'm weak. They don't respect me. And now the nunnehi are riled up—and blaming us! If there's trouble, I don't know if I can count on them. They're liable to desert."

"Mr. Seaborn," Gwenllian said, her voice calm, "let me assure you—"

"They're plotting something, by Danu!"

"Mr. Seaborn—"

"They expect trouble from the locals. The unseelie oafs have resented the Summer Court taking over from the start. Now they see their chance to bring the Winters back."

"Teyrnus, with all due respect, you're not making sense. Why would warriors loyal to the Summer Court help—"

"Talk to Wakefire!" Seaborn shouted. "He'll listen to you. He won't listen to me. He thinks I've gone mad! Mad!" He giggled a little.

"We're leaving for Tobarty within the hour," Gwenllian said. "We can discuss this further once we arrive."

"Talk to Wakefire!"

"Goodbye, Teyrnus." Gwenllian said. She ended the scry with a wave of her hand.

"That...was not encouraging," Claudia said.

"I knew Seaborn was young, but I thought he was at least competent," Gwenllian said.

"Perhaps he was...before."

Gwenllian turned toward Claudia and arched an eyebrow.

"I was just thinking about something else, Mrs. Birdsong. Pay me no mind." By all accounts, Seaborn *was* a capable leader, but something had changed. Or more to the point, something had changed *him*. Claudia wondered why Crom Cornstack had turned over the rath of Tobarty so easily.

Gwenllian sighed, and her whole body seemed to slump under the weight of the past few days. "As much as I dread it, we should be going."

"Yes, Mrs. Birdsong."

Claudia went to call Blue.

She knew Seaborn's reputation. She knew he was a competent leader despite his youth.

Something had changed. And it couldn't have happened at a worse time.

Chapter 19

Three Questions and Some Bad News

The nearest laundromat to Taylor's house was in a strip mall not too far from their street. It was wedged between a convenience store and a Chinese take-out place. Taylor had hoped to come home from Grandma Miller's and spend Sunday night hanging out at Jill's house. Instead, she helped Jill carry laundry in from Mrs. Matthews's car. The little bell over the door tinkled as they stepped in from the darkened parking lot. The harsh glow of the flickering fluorescent lights made Taylor squint.

Washing machines went four rows deep down the middle of the room, with banks of dryers along the right wall and a service counter, vending machines, and bathrooms on the left.

They were the only people there apart from a teenage attendant behind the counter, playing video games on his phone.

Jill's mom got change from the machine.

"Thanks," Jill whispered. "Mom's been a little edgy ever since Maymay came." She started separating the clothes into neat piles. "I think the washing machine was the last straw."

"No problem," Taylor said. When she went to Jill's house, she and her mom were carrying out overflowing baskets of laundry. Jill was apologizing for something, and her mom was trying—not too convincingly—to pretend that everything was fine.

"And...you did what, exactly?"

Jill started loading the first washer.

197

"William and I...had an accident."

Taylor nodded for Jill to continue.

"See...Maymay and William and me...we kind of have an aura."

"Okay?" Taylor was mystified—but curious.

"That's why witches always used to curdle milk, blight crops, stuff like that. They didn't mean to. It just..."

"I'm not—"

"Apparently it works on washing machines, too."

"Oh."

Mrs. Matthews returned and jammed a row of quarters into two machines.

Nobody said anything. Jill and her mom didn't even look at each other. As soon as the machines were loaded and running, Mrs. Matthews retreated to a row of chairs across the front of the building. She pulled a paperback novel from her purse.

Taylor and Jill stayed with the laundry.

For a while, they stole glances at Mrs. Matthews without saying anything.

"I think she's kind of in shock," Jill finally said. Her voice was barely above a whisper.

"When I look at her...you know...with my Second Sight, it's like she's wrapped up in a storm cloud."

"She's sad?"

"She's mad. She doesn't like that Maymay never told her about—" She made a spooky hand gesture, apparently the international symbol for magic.

"I'm sure she had a good reason," Taylor said.

"I guess."

They let the conversation drop. Before long, the washers stopped, and Jill and Taylor moved the clothes into the dryers. Mrs. Matthews kept reading.

Taylor didn't know what to say. It was hard enough to talk about things with her own parents. They were getting used to the idea—slowly—that their daughter was a mythological being. Pop-in visitors like Wasko, Haggler, and Pete didn't help matters, but they were coming around.

Mrs. Matthews was different, though. She had strong opinions about how things were done. Those opinions didn't leave her much room for children who could do magic.

The kid behind the counter cursed. Apparently he lost his game.

Eventually, the dryers stopped.

"Almost finished," Jill announced to her mom.

Taylor started folding the clothes and putting them back in the laundry baskets.

As they worked, another customer came in: a woman in green with a heaping basket of bed sheets. It struck Taylor as awfully late at night to start doing laundry, but she figured maybe the person had just gotten off work or something.

She was humming a tune Taylor had never heard before. It was slow and mournful, like something from another world.

Jill grabbed Taylor's arm and gestured for her to look at her mom.

Mrs. Matthews had a glassy, distant expression.

"Something's up," Jill said. Her eyes were suddenly alert. She pulled a black stone from her pocket. Before she closed her fist around it, Taylor noticed its surface was carved with angular grooves.

"What's the matter?" Taylor said.

Mrs. Matthews set down her book.

The other customer was still humming. She had gotten to work on the back row, in the far corner of the laundromat.

"This isn't right," Jill whispered.

Mrs. Matthews stood up. She walked past Taylor and Jill with the same vacant expression on her face, She headed for the back row. Was that other customer somebody Jill's mom knew?

"Can I help you?" the woman said.

As soon as Taylor heard her speak, her heart started to race.

"Oh, no," Taylor said. "That's impossible!"

"It's not impossible," Jill said. She squeezed her stone tightly.

199

"Stay here!" Taylor said. But Jill had already turned toward the end of the row.

Taylor followed. She rounded the corner and sprinted to the back row just as Mrs. Matthews said, "D-do I know you?"

She stood transfixed ten feet from the woman in green. Her arms hung limp at her sides. Her voice was weak and slurred, like someone just coming out of a deep sleep.

Jill stood next to her mom in a half-crouch.

Taylor started to sweat.

"Mrs. Matthews," Taylor whispered. "Y-you need to move away."

Taylor approached slowly, quietly, giving herself time to gather magic. It was her, all right. But what was she doing at a laundromat?

Jill held forward the stone in her still-clenched fist. Her voice broke as she whispered, "No fairy takes, nor witch hath power to charm." At the same time, she tried to pull her mom away.

Mrs. Matthews held her ground. Her eyes were heavy.

"I'm afraid it doesn't work like that," the woman in green said. She turned to Jill's mom. "Isn't that right, Mrs. Matthews?"

The woman wore a simple peasant skirt of forest green, a green and beige sweater, and white tennis shoes also trimmed in green. Her long, stringy hair, now dusted with traces of white, had once been fiery red.

Both she and Taylor stiffened.

"Selena Hellebore," the woman said.

"Mrs. Redmane."

"I'll deal with you momentarily," Anya Redmane said. "First, it seems I have a customer."

Mrs. Matthews looked frightened, but she couldn't turn away, no matter how hard Jill tried to move her.

Mrs. Redmane held up a sheet from her laundry basket. She went back to singing her mournful tune. As she did, the sheet changed. Splotches of red emerged from out of nowhere, oozing, spreading, growing into a crimson stain.

A bloodstain.

"I-I don't understand," Mrs. Matthews said. Her voice trembled.

"Of course you don't." Mrs. Redmane held the sheet away from her body to keep from getting blood on her clothes. "Sophie, isn't it? May I call you Sophie?" She leaned forward as if sharing a secret. "You've never even heard of the washer at the ford, have you?"

"Ford?" Taylor said. She planted her hands on her hips. "This is a coin laundry!"

"Times change," Mrs. Redmane said. "People don't wash their clothes in rivers anymore, do they? But I respect the ancient customs—no matter what my detractors say."

"M-mom?" Jill said. As much as she pulled on her mom's arm, she just wouldn't budge.

"So, what will it be? The basic package or the deluxe?"

"B-basic package?" Mrs. Matthews said. "W-what are you talking about?" She was waking up—but that only made it worse. Fear overran confusion, leaving her shaking like a leaf in a summer storm.

"You need to leave," Taylor said. "These are my friends."

Mrs. Redmane paid no attention to her. "With the deluxe, I will truthfully answer any three questions you care to ask." She still hadn't put the bloody sheet in the washer. What was she waiting for? "In return, you must answer three questions for me."

Jill started mumbling something. Praying, most likely.

"I must warn you, however, that my questions can be quite pointed."

"*I told you to go!*" Taylor said. She knew her presence would have no effect on her grandmother, but maybe it would do something for Mrs. Matthews.

"The basic package is free, of course," Mrs. Redmane said. She held the sheet aloft. "I simply tell you who is next to die in your family."

201

That's when Taylor figured it out. That wasn't a bloodstained bed sheet her grandmother was holding, it was a shroud—a cloth like they used to wrap dead bodies in.

And it was meant for somebody in Jill's family.

Taylor dropped into a crouch and started to conjure a blast. Before she could, though, a fierce wind blew through the laundromat, pushing Mrs. Redmane back two steps.

It was Jill. The words she'd been mumbling must have been some kind of spell. Now she was gesturing with her right hand, directing the wind where she wanted it to go.

Taylor seized the moment and dragged Mrs. Matthews away. "Come on, Mrs. Matthews!" she said. "Let's get to the car and—"

A second later, Jill came flying over one row of washers and slammed into the next with a thump.

"No pounding on the machines!" The attendant said without looking up from his video game.

Mrs. Redmane rounded the corner.

It was a clear shot to the door. Taylor debated making a run for it, but she would have to drag Mrs. Matthews to the exit, and that would give Mrs. Redmane as much time as she needed to do...practically anything she wanted.

Nobody moved. Mrs. Redmane folded her arms in front of her.

Taylor concentrated on her true name.

"Jill, get your mom out of here," Taylor whispered, never taking her eyes off her grandmother.

She pushed Mrs. Matthews toward Jill, who took her by the arm.

In the same motion, she swung her right arm forward. She reached deep inside her for all the magic she could find and concentrated it in a single burst of energy.

When the blast hit her, Mrs. Redmane barely flinched.

Taylor cursed.

Jill and her mom scrambled to the car.

202

Taylor could do nothing but block the way with her body. If her grandmother was going to do something, at least she wouldn't get a clean shot.

"Do you *have* to keep ruining my life?" she growled.

Mrs. Redmane gave her a condescending look. "*Your* life? I hardly see how *your* life enters into it. I was simply proposing a bargain with a deathling. I do it all the time."

"That 'deathling' is my best friend's mom!"

Mrs. Redmane tossed the bloody shroud into the washing machine and reached for another from her basket.

"She's...kind of frazzled right now," Taylor went on. "If you've done anything to her—"

"Nothing at all, child. Nothing at all. My job, such as it is, is to prepare people for grief, not to inflict it. The loss of a loved one can be such a traumatic time."

Mrs. Redmane lowered her head. She was no stranger to grief. She had already lost her husband. She'd watched her son, Taylor's father, murdered before her eyes. She'd given up her elder son to save his life, only to be rewarded with his rejection.

If her job now was to help mortals grieve...she could probably tell them a few things.

"I just wish you'd have left her alone," Taylor said.

"I suppose you want me to make her forget about this little encounter?"

"If you can...it would be nice."

"I am a Summer fae," Mrs. Redmane said. "I'm always nice."

Taylor and her grandmother stood there for a few seconds, neither knowing what to do or what to say.

"I'm out of quarters," Mrs. Redmane said at last. She stretched a couple of crumpled bills toward Taylor. "Why don't you make yourself useful and see if the change machine works?"

Taylor couldn't quite manage to move. Locking eyes with Mrs. Redmane had paralyzed her. It wasn't anything her grandmother was doing, though. She was certain of that. It was just the shock of seeing her again—and here of all places!

203

"Have you gone deaf, child? Or simply stupid?" Mrs. Redmane thrust the bills toward her again.

"Uh..."

Taylor accepted the bills and backed toward the change machine. She caught a furtive glance of Jill outside loading the laundry into the trunk. Her mom was sitting in the driver's seat with her head back and her eyes closed.

She inserted the bills and returned with a handful of quarters.

"What are you doing here, anyway?" she managed to say.

"Adjusting." There was bitterness in her voice.

"Oh."

For the first time, Taylor paid close attention to all the ways her grandmother had changed since last summer. There was some gray in her hair, though she still didn't look any older than her adoptive parents. She was paler. She had always been fair-skinned, but now Taylor could see hints of blue veins criss-crossing her bare forearms and neck.

Her hands seemed almost transparent as she loaded the quarters into the washer.

"There," she said.

The kid at the counter answered a call on his phone. It distracted them both for just a second.

"You ask what I'm doing here?" Mrs. Redmane said. "I'm fading."

The Fair Folk didn't die of old age. When they got tired of the world, they simply "faded." At least, that was how it had been explained to Taylor. She didn't really understand it.

"...And until I do, I am keeping my distance from your grandfather."

"Crom," Taylor said.

"He has summoned the Wild Hunt, as you might know."

"I may have heard something to that effect."

She scoffed. "I'd rather fade than give him the satisfaction of taking me alive."

"You're...hiding from him?"

204

"Can you think of a better place to hide from the Wild Hunt?" Mrs. Redmane asked. "Let them tromp about in the Wonder for a hundred years. They'll never find me. Even from the Shallows, this place—" she looked about with disgust "—is practically invisible."

Taylor looked around. The fluorescent lights were brutal. The whole place smelled of cigarettes. There was a dead cockroach in one corner.

Her grandmother was right: It would be hard to imagine a less magical place.

She met her grandmother's gaze. She was used to seeing anger and pride in those bright, green eyes. Now she saw something else, something she couldn't quite put a name to.

It made her feel sad.

It almost made her feel sorry for Anya Redmane.

"I'll erase your friends' memory of our confrontation if that is what you wish."

"Thank you."

She shook her head. "I'm not offering you a favor, Miss Hellebore. I'm offering to grant you a wish. I expect to be paid for my services."

Taylor bit her lip.

"We'll just write it up as the deluxe package, shall we?"

"Three questions," Taylor said.

"Or I can simply do nothing, and your friends can cope with tonight's events as they will."

Jill had already been through worse, but not her mom. Taylor worried about the toll all this magic stuff was taking on her. She didn't look good at all.

If anything happened to her, it would be one more thing for Taylor to feel guilty about.

"Deal."

"Very well," Mrs. Redmane said. She smiled, and that made Taylor more nervous than when she frowned. "Where do you hope to be in a hundred years?"

"What?"

"I'm speaking in round figures, obviously. Among Our Kind, one is generally thought to reach adulthood at one hundred years, give or take. So tell me, Miss Hellebore, what hopes do you have for your future? Or, as your Topside parents might phrase it, what do you want to be when you grow up?"

Taylor bit her lip. She'd known the Fair Folk live for centuries. Somehow she'd never applied that fact to herself. A hundred years? A hundred freaking *years*?

She imagined her parents long dead in their graves. Okay, in her head, she understood her parents would eventually die. Grandpa Miller died. It's sad, but it's part of life.

But what about Jill? Or even William? Would she show up at their funerals, young and full of energy, and stand next to their grandkids as her best friends' bodies were lowered into the ground?

"Miss Hellebore?"

Mrs. Redmane's voice jolted her. She looked her in the eyes, stunned. At last, she answered, "I...I don't know."

Mrs. Redmane quirked a wry smile. "An honest answer, albeit a disappointing one. Let's move on. Who understands you?"

Oh, you're good, Taylor thought.

She weakly answered, "Jill." She pushed back the image of the preacher, the graveside, the weeping grandchildren who won't be born for decades.

"I sense some hesitation," Mrs. Redmane said.

Taylor searched her heart. Jill understood her better than anyone. At least, she did until last summer. Sure, Jill knew the truth about Taylor, but did that mean she understood her?

She thought about what Jill had said about looking at her with her Second Sight: It was like she wasn't even there.

She wondered if anyone truly understood her.

Did she even understand herself?

"Jill's the best I've got," she whispered.

"For now," Mrs. Redmane said. "Are you ready for number three?"

206

Taylor was still reeling from number one! She'd spent the past seven months hoping she could lead a normal human life—or at least figure a way to deal with the magical world on her own terms. Her grandmother was stripping that hope away one question at a time.

"I don't want to do this anymore."

"I'm afraid the time to back out was two questions ago."

Taylor studied the floor.

"Where do you belong?"

Taylor began to shake. "Where do I belong?"

"Was I not speaking English?"

It was English, all right. And it was the question Taylor had been asking herself her whole life. Was there anywhere she fit in—really fit in? Was there anywhere she could be herself, where she didn't have to hold back, or pretend, or watch what she said or did?

She looked at Mrs. Redmane in icy silence.

"I need an answer, Miss Hellebore."

"I know!"

They stared at each other for another thirty seconds.

"Miss Hellebore?"

"I know!" Taylor said. She took a breath. "I belong... wherever I can protect people from the likes of you," she said. Her eyes brightened. The temperature in the laundromat fell five degrees. "And in a hundred years, I'll be able to do it, too. So you—and whoever comes after you—had better be ready, because I am sick and tired of all this mess-with-people's-lives, nobody-matters-but-you, faery bullcrap!"

"I see," Mrs. Redmane said. "Is that all?"

"No!" Taylor said. She swallowed. "It doesn't matter if nobody understands me. I'll do it anyway, because..."

"Yes?"

"Because I can." She folded her arms.

"Well, then," Mrs. Redmane said. "I accept your answers. Your friends will have no memory of my presence here."

"Good."

"The only thing left for me to do is tell you who is next to die."

"Wait, what?"

"The basic package is free, as I already explained. Whatever I once was, Selena Hellebore, I am now a portent of death." She spread her arms. "It's what I do."

Taylor swallowed.

"But whose death? That is an interesting question, isn't it?" She had pulled another shroud from her basket. Like the first one, bloodstains began to swirl and grow across the fabric.

"Y-you're trying to scare me," Taylor said. It was working.

"I'm trying to prepare you," Mrs. Redmane said. "Watching a loved one die is hard, but I'm afraid it's on your horizon. Within the year, I'd say. Two at most."

"I don't want to know!" Taylor shouted.

Mrs. Redmane chuckled. "Forewarned is forearmed. Isn't that what the deathlings say? Let me tell you and you'll be ready—"

"*Shut up!*" Taylor said. Her presence commanded her grandmother's attention. She took a second to collect herself. She had to distract her. She was about to tell her that someone she loved was going to die. Whatever it took, she did not want to hear that.

"I will fulfill my destiny, Selena Hellebore," Mrs. Redmane said.

Then it came to her: something that might throw Mrs. Redmane off balance.

"What about Évastre?" Taylor said.

Mrs. Redmane stopped.

Évastre du Marais was her other grandchild, whom Taylor had only recently learned about. He was the son of Mrs. Redmane's firstborn, Lorcan.

"And Lorcan. He might still be alive, right?" Taylor continued. "D-do you know where he is?"

Mrs. Redmane glowered. "*No*," she said, eyebrows raised.

208

"B-but you still care about him. After all you did to protect him..."

"That is quite enough," Mrs. Redmane said.

"W-wouldn't you like to meet Évastre? I mean, without the explosions and everything? Just sit down and talk to him? Learn about his life?"

"I am not obliged to answer *your* questions, Miss Hellebore."

"No," Taylor agreed. "B-but...don't you think it would be good to have a real family again?"

Mrs. Redmane flushed. "*We are through here,*" she said. This time, the presence thrummed through Taylor's body like a bass note you felt rather than heard. She closed her eyes and gritted her teeth.

When she opened her eyes, her grandmother had vanished along with her basket and her bloody shroud.

Taylor exhaled.

Woozy, she made it to the Matthewses' car and melted into the back seat.

"Let's go," she said.

Mrs. Matthews smiled and cranked the engine.

Chapter 20

In the Bleak Midwinter

Taylor was doing fine until she passed Shelby Crowthers in the choir room. She gave her a withering glare, but didn't try to addle her anymore.

She wanted to, though. Ever since Mrs. Peterson passed her up and gave the big solo to Shelby, it was all she could do to contain herself.

For her part, Shelby accepted the honor with her usual degree of humility and decorum. In other words, she couldn't shut up about it.

Every day.

For three weeks.

If it weren't for her promise to Jill—or Anya's little lesson about interfering in the lives of Topsiders—there was a decent chance Shelby would have been sent off for brain scans by now.

At least then she wouldn't be primping in front of the full-length mirror in the choir room as the Bulloch Middle School Bel Canto Choir waited for their turn on stage.

The girls were arranging their long, black skirts and cream-colored tops. The boys fiddled with their bowties—or waited for Mrs. Peterson to help straighten them out.

Somewhere in the auditorium, Taylor's parents and the Matthews family were waiting, probably impatiently, for the winter concert to be over. The younger choir sang first, so at least they got off to a good start. Taylor knew from experience things would go downhill from there.

211

The sixth-grade concert band would be the worst. She knew. She had heard them at last night's dress rehearsal.

The Bel Canto Choir was last on the program. Shelby would sing her solo, everyone would clap, and then Taylor could finally go home.

Christmas break couldn't come soon enough.

Taylor spied Shelby laughing with her friends and decided she had had enough. She got up to go to the restroom.

She thought about staying there till the concert was over.

The corridor rang with the sounds, mostly in tune, of something from *Polar Express*. That meant the seventh- and eight-grade band was halfway through their set.

As she stalked to the girls' room, something tickled her senses. Someone approaching from behind.

No, she thought. There was no way the Wild Hunt had caught up with her after all these weeks. Or that Mara or one of her minions would show up?

She spun around, already gathering magic. Then she saw who it was and, just as quickly, let it ebb.

It was Mr. Ramos.

He actually looked pretty good in his suit and his red Santa Claus tie. Good for a social studies teacher, anyway. He offered Taylor an easy smile that Taylor did not return.

"Shouldn't you be getting ready?" he said. "The band is almost finished. That means you're next."

"Shouldn't you be reporting my position to headquarters?" she scoffed.

They stared at each other for a minute, Mr. Ramos compassionately, Taylor...less so.

At last, Mr. Ramos spoke. "We haven't talked since your run-in with Mrs. Redmane."

"You knew about that?" She planted her hands on her hips. "Of course you knew about that! You just didn't do anything to stop it."

"I wasn't there," Mr. Ramos protested. "Tsisgwa was about to do something, but he says you had the situation under control. He thought it best to let you work things out with your grandmother by yourself."

"And teach me a lesson, maybe? Remind me how much I could use a bodyguard?"

He shrugged. "You seemed to indicate you wanted some space."

Taylor gritted her teeth. She turned to head back to the choir room.

Mr. Ramos said, "Shelby has a pretty voice."

Taylor stopped in her tracks.

"Just saying."

She turned back around. She looked into Mr. Ramos's deep, brown eyes. She had never understood the expression 'laughter in their eyes' until she met him.

"She may not always look it, Taylor, but Shelby has been going through a lot the past couple years."

"Poor baby," she spat. "What could that *possibly* be like?"

"I know, I know," Mr. Ramos said. "Listen, it's not for me to say any more than that. Just know that this solo means a lot to her. I'm happy she's getting the chance."

"And you want me to be happy about it, too? Even though I'm better than her?"

"*Because* you're better than her," Mr. Ramos said. That got Taylor's attention. Teachers weren't supposed to admit that all their little darlings weren't equal. Then again, her other teachers didn't know Taylor had supernatural powers. "Trust me, Taylor. Your time will come."

In the distance, the audience started to clap.

"I'd better go," Mr. Ramos said. "Two more songs, then I'm supposed to introduce you guys. Break a leg!"

He was gone as quickly as he had appeared.

Taylor sighed.

"Maybe," she said to the empty corridor. She thought about her birth mother. Shanna had told her one of the names people gave to the daoine sídhe was "children of pride." She hadn't sounded particularly, well, proud of that.

213

And she knew what pride had done to Anya Redmane.

Just then, the show choir members filed out of the choir room. Mrs. Peterson gave her an impatient, quizzical glare. Taylor shrugged and found her place in line.

William was working the lights with Jared McCaughey. The other boy, all bright eyes and dimples, manned the big flood-light. William operated the panel that controlled the rest of the lights.

He checked the program scotch-taped to the console. The Bel Canto choir was the final act. Three more numbers and he could go home and take something for the headache the sixth-grade band had given him.

William ticked off each song as they finished it. "Hanukkah, O Hanukkah." "Ding Dong Merrily on High."

Mrs. Peterson took a bow and motioned for her choristers to do the same. When she turned back around, she nodded to Shelby Crowthers. Shelby gave a backward glance (and probably a smirk—William couldn't see it for sure) to Taylor and then weaved down through the soprano section to a microphone on the stage floor.

William checked to see that Jared was ready with the spotlight. Jared gave him a thumbs-up.

Mrs. Peterson raised her arms. On the downbeat, the accompanist began to play.

Shelby stood there in the spotlight. She looked startled.

Mrs. Peterson leaned toward her and said something William couldn't hear. It seemed to shake Shelby awake, though. She said something back and grasped the microphone.

Another downbeat. The accompanist played the intro again.

William studied Shelby's face this time. She really did look lost. It wasn't like her to get stage fright. She usually ate it up when she was the center of attention.

But she had missed her cue again. She just stood there like she didn't know she was supposed to be singing. A couple of parents in the back row started to murmur.

Mrs. Peterson started the song for a third time.

It didn't matter. Shelby looked completely bewildered.

But this time, another voice chimed in from the back row of the soprano section. William waved for Jared to aim the spotlight at Taylor. She had started to sing.

In the bleak midwinter, frosty wind made moan,
Earth stood hard as iron, water like a stone;
Snow had fallen, snow on snow, snow on snow,
In the bleak midwinter, long ago.

It was a slow, almost mournful tune. Taylor hadn't gotten more than a couple of lines into the song when William felt his heart racing. Jared was transfixed. One of the alto girls wiped tears from her eyes. A couple of parents uttered rapt gasps of delight.

The song was so wonderful it almost hurt to listen to it.

The rest of the choir joined in on the second stanza. They sang better than he had ever heard them, with Taylor's voice soaring above them, improvising a descant that drew out every harmony and made it ring.

The audience swayed slowly to the rhythm.

Uh oh, William thought. In a flash he new what was happening. Taylor was glamouring the whole auditorium!

In a half-swoon, he squeezed the jet amulet in his pocket and whispered the protective spell Maymay had taught him: "No fairy takes, nor witch hath power to charm." His mind cleared almost instantly. Taylor's voice was still beautiful, even otherworldly. But it wasn't putting him in a trance any more.

There was nothing he could do for the audience, though. They sat enthralled by every note. He found his parents and Jill sitting on the far side of the auditorium. Mom and Dad

215

were deep in reverie. Jill twisted around to shoot him a look of concern, to which all he could do was shrug.

Shelby had somehow found her voice, or at least remembered she was on stage, and joined in despite her dazed expression. It was all Mrs. Peterson could do to carry the beat. She was listing to one side like she was drunk.

William knew from rehearsals that the song was almost over. Taylor—or Shelby or *somebody*—had one more solo part on the final stanza. Then, with any luck, everybody would snap out of whatever spell Taylor had thrown on them.

If Shelby intended to sing the final stanza, she never got the chance. Instead, Taylor's voice rang out over the auditorium:

What shall I give him, poor as I am?
If I were a shepherd I would give a lamb.
If I were a wise man I would do my part.
Yet, what shall I give him? Give him my heart.

The accompanist played the final chord.

The audience sat in stunned silence for what seemed like a full minute, but was probably only a few seconds. Then they erupted in applause. They shouted and whooped and jumped to their feet.

Somebody's grandma shouted "Wow!"

Taylor didn't smile, even as she took her bow. Her expression was more of a satisfied smirk.

But that wasn't all. William couldn't help but note the look of anger slowly spreading across Shelby's face. For that matter, now that the spell was broken, Mrs. Peterson was figuring out that something about that song didn't go like they had rehearsed it. She looked at Taylor with a stern—if confused—expression.

As soon as the stage lights were shut down, William hurried into the hallway outside the auditorium. Parents were congratulating

216

their children. Kids milled about, joking and visiting with each other.

His parents and the Smarts were talking together. Mr. Smart said something to him about his good work on the lights. He nodded, but hurried past. He spied Jill and Taylor by the doors to the lunchroom, and it looked like trouble was brewing. Jill jabbed a finger at Taylor. Taylor, red-faced, held up her hands in a defensive posture.

William was there in a matter of seconds.

"I didn't do anything to Shelby," Taylor was protesting. "I gave you my word, didn't I?"

"I only know what I saw," Jill said flatly.

"Well, maybe you need to get your eyes checked."

"So it just so happened that Shelby's brain checked out right as she was about to sing her solo? The solo you've been mad you didn't get? You're calling that a coincidence? And then you just decided you'd save the day by stepping in and singing it anyway?" Jill tried to keep her voice down, but other kids were starting to notice.

"Keep it down," William whispered.

She backed off and shut her eyes, counting to ten.

"And what's the idea putting the whammy on everybody?"

"What?"

"Oh, come on, Taylor!" Jill said. "You mean you didn't notice?"

"Notice what?"

Jill huffed and stomped away.

Taylor looked at William.

"What?"

"You *were* coming on pretty strong up there," William said.

She asked what he meant with her expression.

"You know," William said. He wiggled his fingers in front of him, pantomiming casting a spell.

"I didn't...," Taylor blurted. William nodded sheepishly that she did.

"Really?"

He nodded again. "Everybody but me and Jill. You might have gotten us too, but.... You know. Magic."

Taylor stood speechless.

Shelby Crowthers appeared. She stared daggers at Taylor as she passed. Taylor met her gaze but said nothing. Shelby looked like she had been crying.

"W-William, I promise you—"

He wasn't listening. Instead, he followed Shelby as she marched up to her parents. They hugged her and said something. William couldn't hear them, of course, but he was almost as good as his sister at reading people's emotions. And he'd only gotten better since Maymay started teaching him about his Second Sight.

Shelby's parents were confused. He bet Shelby had been telling them for weeks about her big solo, and then it didn't happen.

There was something else, too, though. There was something about the distance between Mr. and Mrs. Crowthers as they stood there, talking to their daughter. Something about the exasperated glances Mrs. Crowthers gave Mr. Crowthers as he dominated the conversation, the impatient hand on his arm to tell him it was time to go.

Something wasn't right in Crowthers-land.

"You believe me, don't you?" Taylor said.

"Huh? What?" Suddenly, William was back in the present.

"You've got to believe me. Shelby just got stage fright or something. I didn't have anything to do with it."

William sighed. He also realized that was the second time Taylor had said she was innocent.

"Maymay says...folks like you can't hardly tell a lie. Lying sets up some kind of cosmic feedback or something."

"Well, that settles it, then."

"Just tell me one more time."

"William!"

"Just humor me, okay?"

"Fine!" Taylor huffed. "I didn't addle Shelby. There, satisfied?"

218

He looked into her icy blue eyes and read...nothing. He re-played their conversation, searching for any loophole Taylor might have used. The Fair Folk didn't lie, but that didn't mean they were always honest.

He bit his lip.

"I believe you, Taylor," he said.

He tried with all his heart to mean it.

Chapter 21

Taylor Perfects Her Blasting Skills

Taylor enjoyed a quiet Christmas with her family at Grandma Miller's. It was good to get away from stickball and shape-shifting and magic. But—she hated to admit it even to herself—it was also good to get away from Jill.

Jill still wasn't convinced Taylor had nothing to do with Shelby's mishap at the Winter Concert. It wasn't worth fighting over. It was just disappointing, that's all. Your best friend is supposed to believe you when you tell them something.

She and Jill hadn't really talked since. Part of her wondered if that's why, in the first week of January, Jill invited her to go to the mall and help her and her brother spend their Christmas money. Maybe she thought it was time to make nice. Maybe somebody told her it was time to make nice.

Either way, it felt awkward tagging along. But she figured at least she'd get a trip to the bookstore out of it.

"Maymay, can I go now?" For his part, William had had about all he could take. He stood in front of his grandmother in the department store with the shirt he'd picked out in one hand and his wallet in the other.

Mrs. Blay rolled her eyes, but addressed him sweetly.

"You're sure this is what you want?"

"Yes, ma'am."

Taylor tried not to grin too much. Watching William squirm made it almost worth being dragged along.

221

"The blue one is nice, too," Maymay said. "A young man needs to be able to dress up every now and then."

William took a second to compose his thoughts. "I just like the red one..."

Mrs. Blay looked at him. "And?"

He sighed. "And I'll still have money left over for a new game." Before she could say anything, he added, "Maymay, I've got plenty of clothes, but I was hoping—"

"Do you hear me arguing with you?" Mrs. Blay said. "It's your money, William. Your momma said you need a new dress shirt. I don't see why you can't spend the rest on something you want."

"You're the best, Maymay!" William said. He passed her the shirt and a handful of bills.

"We'll call you when we're ready to go," Mrs. Blay said.

William was already halfway to the exit, but he gave her an appreciative smile.

Jill appeared with a stack of clothes: a pair of jeans, some tops, and some dresses.

"Child, how much Christmas money did you get?"

"I can't decide what I like best," Jill said. "What do you think, Maymay?" She struggled to hold up two of the dresses for her grandmother to see.

"Honey, they both look fine to me. Do you have an opinion, Taylor?"

"Huh? Oh. I dunno. Whichever."

Jill sighed a little too loudly.

"Maymay?"

"Just try them both."

Jill walked toward the fitting rooms.

Taylor clasped her hands behind her back. She pretended to be interested in a display of scarves, then just stared up at the ceiling.

"Taylor, I'm glad you could come with us today," Mrs. Blay said.

"Thanks." She rocked absentmindedly from side to side. She bit her lip. "Mrs. Blay?" she said, "I don't know what Jill told you about the Christmas concert. I promise you I didn't do anything to Shelby."

"Yes?"

"I...just wanted you to know."

Maymay turned to face Taylor head-on.

"Taylor, can you look me in the eye and tell me you didn't do anything to Shelby that night?"

Her eyes went wide. Jill had a way of cutting through the crap with her. Apparently it was hereditary. Taylor thought about it for a second. Did she believe with one hundred percent certainty that she wasn't responsible for Shelby's brain hiccup on the night of the concert?

No.

Could she tell Jill's grandma it wasn't her fault?

"Yes, ma'am."

"Then I believe you. You seem like a good girl, Taylor, all things considered. And you're Jill's friend. That counts for something in my book."

"Thanks." Then it registered. "What do you mean, 'all things considered'?"

Mrs. Blay shook her head in a "bless-your-heart" kind of way.

"Taylor, you and Jill have been friends for a long time. From what I've seen, you're good for each other."

"Yes, ma'am?"

"Jill's more assertive around you than with most of her friends. A sensitive soul like her is liable to be walked all over if she's not careful. You push her—but only so far. It's safe for her to stand up for herself with you. I appreciate that."

"I do what I can," Taylor said. She wasn't entirely sure this was a compliment.

"And—if I may say so—I bet Jill's good for you, too."

Taylor nodded.

223

"A girl like you is not likely to care much for rules and such. I'm glad Jill's around to keep you from doing anything we'd all regret."

Taylor felt her face getting hot. That *really* didn't sound like a compliment.

"A...a girl like me?"

"Oh, I know a lot of...folks like me..." (She looked around to make sure no one was eavesdropping) "...have been burned by... folks like you," she said. "But you can't judge a whole group of people by the actions of a few, am I right?"

"Y-yeah?"

"You're all right, Taylor. If Jill counts you as her friend, then that's good enough for me."

"Thanks."

"It's not your fault where you come from."

Uh. What?

"M-Mrs. Blay, I don't see how—"

"Now, don't get me wrong. There's good and bad among all kinds." She smiled and put her hand on Taylor's shoulder. "You're one of the good ones."

One of the good *ones?* Taylor thought. Her mind jumped to Danny, to Silas, to Ayoka. To Haggler and Pete and Wasko. She pictured Shanna—unflappable Shanna—with her blue-tinted hair and her warm and loving smile.

"Thanks," she said. She tried to keep the tremor out of her voice. With some effort, she held back the wave of presence she wanted to unleash. "But isn't that kind of..."

"Yes?" Mrs. Blay said with a smile.

"Nothing."

"Ah, here she comes now," Mrs. Blay said. Jill emerged from the fitting room and hung most of the clothes she'd picked out on the rack by the entrance.

"Well, sweetie, what did you decide?"

Jill cast an eye at Taylor, like she didn't like the idea of her and her grandma talking. Taylor wasn't entirely happy about it, either.

"I think I'll get these tops. That's all."

"Whatever you want, sweetheart." She smiled. "What do you two say to a treat? Didn't I see a cookie place on the way in?"

"Fine by me," Jill said. "Taylor?"

"Sure," she said. "I'll go find William."

"We can just call him," Jill said. She was already digging in her purse for her phone.

"No," Taylor said, "I'll go get him while you pay. I could use some fresh air."

"Okay," Jill said. "Meet you at the..."

Taylor was already gone.

The Shoppes at River Crossing was an open-air shopping center on the north side of town with just about any kind of store you'd want. It was still fairly new, and the folks in charge kept it in pretty good shape. The sidewalks were clean and the walls were graffiti-free. There were a couple of nice restaurants. They'd even installed a dozen or more life-size bronze statues of children playing, spaced along the main thoroughfares.

William absentmindedly watched the sparse crowds pass by out the window of the video game store as he weighed his options. He only had enough birthday money left for two new games, but there were at least four he needed.

Needed, he thought with a chuckle. His dad would have something to say about whether he "needed" any new games. Whatever. He read the description on the back of the latest *Batman: Arkham* game. He'd been thinking about it for a few months. It was definitely time for that one. And the other?

He meandered through the rows of games. Adventure? First-person shooter?

Then he realized something wasn't right. The only other customers, a little girl and her dad, were hunched over the educational games, oblivious. The music playing on the speaker system kept thumping along. But something had changed.

In an instant William figured it out. He was being watched.

225

He jerked his head to the left. An employee spun away from him a little too quickly and ducked into the next aisle.

William sighed.

Seriously? he thought to himself. *I'm in here like every other month!*

He put down the copy of *Broken Age* he had been looking at and turned to the earbuds, cases, and other accessories on the far wall. Not surprisingly, the same employee was close by, pretending to rearrange a display.

William could hear his dad lecturing him. Some people will never get to know him as the honor student, the loving son, the good-natured church kid. The truth is, they don't even care. All they can see is "young black male"—and they start to get nervous.

He knew the drill. Always say "sir" and "ma'am." When you buy something, carry the receipt where people can see it when you leave. And for heaven's sake, no sagging!

His favorite? Whistle classical music. Apparently a black kid wasn't a threat if he liked Mozart. It was ludicrous, but maybe that was the point. Sometimes you had to laugh to keep from busting heads.

He smiled and nodded at the employee—a new guy. He fought back the urge to say something snarky. It would have made him feel good, but it wouldn't help the situation.

"William!" Taylor said, breezing through the door. "Your grandma is going to buy us cookies. It's time to go."

"Okay," he said.

You see? he imagined telling the new guy. *White girl walks right up to me like she's not afraid or anything!*

Instead, he put his *Batman* game on the counter. He'd save the rest of his money for later.

"I'm ready to check out, sir," he said. He nearly choked on the "sir," but that was part of the drill—and anyway, Mom and Dad expected him to always use his best manners. New guy smiled and met him at the counter as if nothing had happened.

William slid a couple of bills across the counter.

226

New guy slid back his game, his change, and his receipt. William nodded, mumbled "Thank you," and turned toward the entrance.

Taylor seemed impatient or distracted or something. As usual, what was really going on inside Taylor Smart's head was a mystery for the ages.

For a second, they made eye contact. Those icy blue eyes were impossible to read. There had always been something about those eyes for William, even before he found out Taylor's secret. Maymay had made a mistake trying to warn him away from her. It just made her even more interesting.

"Mind if we run in here?" Taylor said. They had made it to the Yankee Candle store.

"You never struck me as the type for candles," William said as he followed her inside. Taylor picked over the collection of essential oils.

"I'm looking for cedar. Do you see any?"

"Uh..." William joined the search. "No. Would lavender do?"

"I don't think so. Somebody told me cedar would help me focus my...um...."

"Really? I haven't heard that one." He wished he had a pen to write it down.

"Yeah, he said I should buy one of these kits. But it has to be cedar." Taylor chuckled. "Like he would know about buying things."

William didn't understand, and his face must have shown it.

"Our Kind don't actually use money," Taylor said as they exited the store.

"No money? How can you have an advanced civilization with no money?"

"Magic. Duh."

Obviously.

"Plus, people trade favors. Like bartering only more intense."

"Sounds complicated."

227

"Somehow it works." Taylor grinned. "I'd like to see what my grandparents would say about a place like this, though. A mall has got to be the most un-faery place there is."

William pondered all this as they passed a bronze statue of a girl balancing on a log. On a whim, he expelled a breath and, with it, allowed his magical senses to reach out toward Taylor. He immediately felt something: an icy, tingly sensation that made his neck-hairs stand up.

Taylor stopped.

"Did you feel that?" she said. "We're being watched." She spun around and shouted to the sky, "Just leave me alone!"

William's face flushed. "Sorry," he said. "That was me."

"What?" She rounded on him, eyes blazing. "Are you trying to spy on me, too?"

"No!" he protested. "Nothing like that. Maymay wants us to work on our magical senses. That's all. I just..." Too late. She was already walking away. "Taylor!"

She spun around and glared at him. He threw up his hands in surrender.

"I'm sorry," he said again.

Taylor bit her lip. "Yeah," she said. The death-glare subsided. "I guess I'm a little edgy. You'd never do anything like that."

"S'okay."

"Just...warn me next time, all right?"

William nodded.

They ambled down the sidewalk together toward the cookie place. Even in the late afternoon, it was nearly dark. A month ago, River Crossing would have been packed with holiday shoppers. Now, they had the place mostly to themselves.

William's nerves mostly settled down, but something still wasn't right. Maybe he hadn't fully shaken off the sensation of Taylor's magic. Maybe he was still upset about the video store.

"I take it your grandma is a tough teacher," Taylor said. Her comment startled William back to earth.

"Jill thinks she goes too fast," William said. "She'll pick it up soon enough."

228

"How about you?"

William shrugged. "I guess I see the patterns better than she can," he said. "She can do more...stuff." He abruptly changed his last word as a clutch of older teenagers shuffled past them. "But I think I'm better at seeing how it all fits together."

"Theory," Taylor offered. "It's like music. There's performance, and then there's theory."

"I'll buy that."

"Look, I'm sorry I snapped at you before," Taylor said. "The last few months have not been what you'd call wonderful."

He placed his hand on her shoulder, let it slide to her elbow, then self-consciously pulled it away.

Taylor looked into his eyes. Her shy smile turned immediately to concern, however, as her gaze fixed on something over William's shoulder.

An angry voice said, "Sweetheart, is this joker bothering you?" Only he didn't say "joker."

William whipped around. It was one of those older kids. They must have turned back while he and Taylor were talking.

There were four of them. Designer clothes. Perfect hair. One of them wore a letter jacket from an exclusive private school. The graduation year on his sleeve said he was a couple years older than William.

Taylor gave them a look of utter contempt. William had to admit, she was pretty good at that.

"Butt out!" she shouted.

"Let's go, Taylor," William said, grabbing her by the elbow.

"Hey! Don't turn your back on me, boy!"

The next thing William knew, there was a hand on his shoulder, spinning him to face a big blond kid, maybe a wrestler or a football player. There was alcohol on his breath.

"Come on, Jimmy, he ain't worth it," the letterman said.

"Wanna bet?" he said.

229

Everything shifted into slow motion as Taylor watched the big blond kid round on William.

William's face betrayed no emotion. As the big kid threw his punch, William sidestepped it. Off-balance, the kid stumbled forward, nearly falling.

"Leave him alone!" she shouted. She was too startled to put any presence behind her words. They ignored her.

Now the blond kid was back on his feet and hopping mad. He charged toward William again.

"I mean it!" Taylor cried.

"Taylor!" William shouted. He reached toward her, but a punch to his gut stopped him cold. He doubled over and fell to one knee.

"Jimmy!" the kid in the letter jacket shouted.

The blond kid kicked William in the gut. One of the other kids laughed.

Without even realizing what she was doing, Taylor gathered magic. It coursed up and down her spine and out into both arms. This time, she had no problem getting their attention.

"*Leave him alone!*" she said again. All four kids reeled backward. One tripped on a crack in the sidewalk and nearly fell over.

"Nobody tells me what to do!" the blond kid slurred, charging now toward Taylor. "D'you understand, girlie?" Only he didn't say "girlie."

He jabbed at her with his finger.

Block, she thought. She brushed him away with her shield spell, throwing him into the kid behind him, the one who had told her to be quiet. It took hardly any effort at all, but they flew back as if they'd been kicked by a mule.

She smiled as the magic continued to course through her.

In a single, easy motion, she pivoted her body, thrusting her right hand, palm outward, toward Jimmy, the leader of the bullies.

Blast, she thought.

The air rippled as a wave of magic arced between her hand and the bully's head. His eyes rolled back into his head and he crumpled to the ground.

He didn't move.

The other three stood there, stunned.

Taylor glared at them with murder in her eyes. Breathing hard, she braced for another attack. She welcomed it.

"W-what did you do to Jimmy?" one of the thugs squealed. He tried to get their leader on his feet, but it wasn't working.

"T-Taylor?" William gasped.

Between coughs he twisted his body around, struggling to get up. There was no mistaking the look of terror on his face.

Two of the bullies were helping Jimmy to his feet. The kid in the letter jacket couldn't decide which way to run.

It was too soon for another blast, but that didn't mean Taylor couldn't scare those kids witless with a little addlement. She began to shout when another voice cut her off.

"*Bazagra!*"

Suddenly, all the magic fell off of her. She spun around, confused.

Mrs. Blay charged forward. She had what could only be called a magic wand in her hand. She slid it into her purse as she addressed the bullies.

"You boys need to move along."

Jill's grandma glared at them. She held her walking stick aloft. A pulse of golden energy swirled around the knob.

Letterman bolted.

The other two dragged Jimmy down the sidewalk as fast as they could. They were shaking so badly they could barely walk. One of them was sobbing.

Taylor looked around. Other shoppers had stopped to see what the commotion was all about. Some stood open-mouthed. A couple had reached for their cell phones.

Jill ran up behind her.

"William!" she called. She helped him to his feet.

"Are you all right, baby?" Mrs. Blay said.

231

William nodded, wobbling on Jill's shoulder. Jill looked wide-eyed at Taylor as she stood there in her combat stance, her chest heaving.

"It wasn't his fault," Taylor offered. "Those kids were looking for a fight. William—"

"You just be quiet," Mrs. Blay cut her off. She looked Taylor square in the eye. There was disappointment there.

And fear.

"We're going home. Now."

Chapter 22

Nobody

The next day, winter break ended, and Taylor walked to school alone.

She planned it that way.

She got up ten minutes early so she could sit on the bench in the park between her house and school and collect her thoughts.

She didn't mean for things to get out of hand at the shopping center. It just happened. But for the first time, everything Ayoka and Tsisgwa had taught her worked exactly as it was supposed to.

For once, she was able to stand up to a bully and protect one of her friends. He may not have been a fae bully, but you have to start somewhere. Thanks to her, William didn't get beaten up.

And there was no getting around the fact that standing up to those jerks was *fun*.

That was what bothered her.

"Where do you belong?" her grandmother had asked her. She wasn't sure then, despite the brave act she put on. Now, after blasting that kid at the shopping center....

She sat on the bench and extended her magical senses. A family of blackbirds were just waking up in their roost deep in the trees. She shivered in the cold, and so did they.

As soon as she saw Jill and William at the edge of the park, she started moving again.

The ride home last night was silent and cold—and not just because Fair Folk like her always got the chills around too much iron. Danny would have thought Mrs. Blay's old Buick was some kind of deathtrap.

But that wasn't the problem. The problem was that something had changed between her and Jill.

The way Jill had looked at her, the way she just sat there in the back seat without saying a word the whole way home, put a knot in Taylor's stomach.

Jill hated that Taylor had used magic against Shelby; that's why she quit doing it. The Winter Concert messed everything up on that front. She knew in her heart she didn't addle Shelby that night. She just got stage fright or something. And Taylor honestly didn't realize the effect her singing had. She didn't even know what had happened was possible!

And then, last night must have been the last straw. Jill finally got to see all that Taylor was capable of, magically.

Or morally.

For her part, Mrs. Blay muttered the whole way home. Taylor couldn't tell if she was casting defensive spells or just talking to herself. But she did catch one word: "soulless."

As soon as she got home, she googled it.

It turns out, in a lot of folk beliefs, faeries didn't have souls. If that was what Mrs. Blay thought....

Taylor wondered what she had been telling Jill and William— either before last night or in the hours since.

Whatever the answer, Taylor wasn't ready to face Jill again. Not yet.

She went through the motions in her morning classes. Mrs. Markowitz was uninspiring, as usual. William kept his head down the whole time, scribbling away in his notebook.

In science class, Mrs. Cline earnestly tried to get the class excited about Isaac Newton's laws of motion. For every action, there is an equal and opposite reaction.

That was precisely Taylor's problem. Action: she brought down the wrath of a hacked-off sídhe on a Topsider bully who seriously deserved it. Reaction: by doing so, she managed to bring down the wrath of her best friend on herself.

That must have been what Tsisgwa was trying to explain months ago. Offensive magic can rebound against you if you aren't careful. That's what was happening, though.

Stupid bullies.

At lunch, Jill sat with some other girls. She hadn't bothered to save Taylor a seat.

Fine.

Taylor scanned the lunchroom. Empty seats were in short supply. The jocks table had a vacancy, as if that were an option. There was an open seat two down from Shelby Crowthers and her posse. Taylor would rather take her chances with the jocks.

As usual, William was sitting with Jalen Harris and the rest of his friends. Also not a great choice, given the current climate in Matthewsville.

Taylor spied a seat one row over—then started.

She did not want to sit there. Shelby would never let her live it down.

But she had to sit somewhere. Her food—which was never exactly warm—was getting cold.

She took a breath and forged ahead.

"Is this seat taken?" she asked.

"Help yourself," Jared McCaughey said, and his voice cracked a little. He smiled as he gestured for Taylor to join him.

Taylor sat down. She didn't say anything or even acknowledge Jared was sitting beside her. She kept her head down and focused on her lunch (her best guess was some kind of pork).

Whispers rippled through the lunchroom. ("Taylor is eating with Jared." "Are they going together?") Taylor ignored them and kept pretending to eat.

"You did great at the concert," Jared said.

Taylor grunted noncommittally and poked at her vegetables.

"No, really," he pressed. "You should sing more solos."

"Thanks," she said, with a twinge of guilt.

235

She wondered what it was like to be completely oblivious to the magical world. At the moment, she'd give nearly anything for that.

She finished her bite. "Jared, can I ask you a question?"

"Sure."

"Do you have a favorite fantasy novel?"

"Uh, that's not really my thing."

Taylor smiled. "We need to hang out more," she said.

In social studies, Taylor followed the same routine she had adopted since Thanksgiving. She sat either with her head down or looking at the board or out the window—anything to avoid eye contact with Mr. Ramos. She never raised her hand when he asked a question, even though she usually knew the answer. She did her work like a good little robot and counted the minutes till chorus.

He didn't press her. Taylor would have made him regret it if he had. That day, however, he held her after class.

"I'm going to be late for chorus," she said flatly.

"It'll wait." Mr. Ramos gestured toward the door. It swung shut and locked itself of its own accord. He spoke to the supply closet. "You can come out now."

The closet door opened, and out popped a little person in a feathered bowler cap.

"Wasko?" Taylor sputtered.

"Pleased to see you again, Miss Hellebore," Wasko said. "Mr. Ramos said I could borrow his classroom. I hope you don't mind the interruption. I know you got important stuff to do."

She looked back and forth between Wasko and Mr. Ramos.

"What are you doing here?"

"Yeah, I'll get right to it. I don't want you to get in trouble with your teachers, after all. That wouldn't be right, so—"

"Can we get on with it?"

"What? Oh! Sure, you bet." He fumbled in his jacket pocket and pulled out a cream-colored envelope.

236

"This is for you," he said.

He passed her the envelope. It bore the name "Miss Selena Hellebore" in a bold, cursive hand.

Taylor tore it open. Inside was a single folded sheet of paper. She read it quickly:

Miss Hellebore,

As per our conversation last November, I have requested of Nocosi, White Chief of Ichisi, for you to be my guest at a reception to be held at his townhouse at sunset on Saturday, the fourteenth day of February. The White Chief has graciously agreed, and I hope to see you there. Please be so kind as to confirm your attendance by means of my messenger, Mr. Wasko Penholloway.

Sincerely,
Osanda Morning

"Nocosi is the White Chief of Ichisi?"

Mr. Ramos nodded. "Nunnehi settlements are somewhat independent of each other, though they all ultimately answer to the Great Falcon."

Taylor knitted her eyebrows.

"Chief Tewa's uncle."

Oh.

"February fourteenth? That's next month," Taylor said. She frowned. Did she really have to deal with this today of all days? She didn't want anything to do with the faery world. She sure didn't want to hobnob with a fae politician who only wanted something from her.

"If you please, Miss Hellebore," Wasko said, "we gotta get going. Do you want me to come back later, or...?"

He was right. It wouldn't be long before kids would try the door and find it locked.

Taylor thought about Jill. Taylor had gotten her friend in trouble once because of who she was. She still felt powerless to keep it from happening again.

Could a shake-up on the Summer Court make things better? Who knows, but Osanda at least seemed willing to help.

The thought gave her hope. Taylor couldn't do much, but if Osanda was right, she could at least send a message. She could remind people of what the Summer Court had become. Maybe she could give people a reason to stand up to them.

"You can tell Osanda I'll go," Taylor said. She felt her stomach twist in knots as soon as she said it.

"Sure thing, Miss Hellebore."

Taylor spent the rest of the day distracted. She went through the motions in chorus and even more so in technology.

The last bell rang, and she sped back to her locker.

Jill was grabbing her math book from her locker across the hall from Taylor's. Taylor wondered if it was safe to say anything.

Her pulse raced. Was she the one Mrs. Redmane was talking about? The one who was going to die in the next year?

She didn't think her grandmother would lie to her. She wasn't sure that was even possible. But she hoped her predictions were less reliable than her word.

Either way, her time with Jill wouldn't last forever. Sixty or seventy years, tops. Then how many hundreds more wishing Jill were there? She wasn't going to waste a single day if she could help it.

"Hey," she said.

Jill didn't respond. Taylor leaned against the lockers, trying to make eye contact.

Jill turned her back.

I'm trying to make nice here, Taylor thought.

"You got a minute?"

Jill slammed her locker shut and started to walk away.

"You're not even going to acknowledge I'm here, are you?"

238

Jill finally faced her. "Did you hear the news this morning?" Her voice was breaking. "They took that boy to the hospital. They say he had a *stroke*, Taylor!"

"Stroke-like symptoms."

"What?" She set her hand on her hip. Not a good sign. But Taylor didn't back down.

"Channel 13 said he had stroke-like symptoms."

"And that makes a difference how? He was fifteen years old! Fifteen-year-olds are not supposed to get 'stroke-like symptoms'!"

The crowd in the hall was starting to notice their argument. They gave the girls some distance but kept their eyes open in case a fight broke out. Or, as they called it at Bulloch Middle School, "free entertainment."

"Keep your voice down, okay?" Taylor said. "They also said he's expected to make a full recovery. Maybe you missed that part."

"No!" Jill said, wagging her finger. "You can't excuse what you did. Don't even try."

Taylor backed away, gathering steam.

A circle was starting to form around them.

"You crossed a line, Taylor. Shelby was one thing. But this?" She threw up her hands in disgust.

"Would you rather I let William get beat up?"

"I'd rather—" she looked around. When she saw how many kids were looking at her, she lowered her voice. "I'd rather not have to deal with any of this...stuff."

"Or me?" It was harsh, but Taylor didn't care. She felt insulted. How dare Jill not understand that she did what she did to help William!

"Maybe...," Jill started. She was shaking. "Maybe that's not a bad idea."

The twisty knot in Taylor stomach returned with about a dozen of its friends.

"Maybe it's not." Having a soulless monster for a best friend was bound to be a drag. Taylor got it.

239

"Hey, guys!" Mr. Appletree, the math teacher, appeared out of nowhere. He wore a genial smile, but both girls knew he was all business. They knew the score. No acts of violence or mayhem when a teacher is watching. The fight, such as it was, was over.

"You know," Taylor said. "I just realized you're not worth arguing with."

She stormed away, elbowing past William.

The worst part was, she had no idea what had happened. She really wanted to make up with Jill, but then she snapped. Jill put her on the defensive—never a good idea!

Jill stood up to her. She always had. The Shelbys of the world would just ignore her. The Tommy Morgans of the world would back down if she even looked at them funny.

She liked that Jill refused to put up with her crap.

She didn't like the idea that Jill had finally had enough. Jill had been through too much. The mess with Mara last summer was just the beginning. Now she had to watch herself or her Second Sight would flare out of control. Her grandmother thought her best friend was a monster. And her mom was not adjusting well to any of it.

What if this was the last straw?

What if this was Taylor's last chance to make things right between them, and she'd blown it?

"Who understands you?" Mrs. Redmane had asked.

Taylor sucked in a breath. The answer was pretty clear.

Nobody.

Chapter 23

The Road to Ichisi

No one in Tsuwatelda believed the Wild Hunt entering the Nunnehi Lands was anything but a provocation of war, no matter what the sídhe said. They took it as a sign the sídhe felt strong enough—or stupid enough—to meddle beyond their borders.

Folks that remembered the last time things got out of hand with their neighbors in Arradherry were getting nervous.

But time passed with no further mischief, though. Danny hoped the one border incident was the end of it, but with the Winter Assize in full swing? Who could tell what Crom Cornstack was up to?

With the winter farm chores finished, Danny spent more time in town. He visited Shanna when he could. She seemed to appreciate having somebody to talk to.

The first week of January, Danny decided to pay her a visit. Dressed in a tan leather duster, he plodded toward her house in the lower city shortly after sunrise.

Shanna was sitting outside her front door drinking a cup of coffee.

"Morning," Danny said. He looked for nunnehi guards on patrol. Of course, he didn't see any. That didn't mean they weren't there.

"Danny," she said. "I was just listening to the news." The birds were indeed chirping away.

"Anything good?"

241

She shook her head. "Chief Inali is still drilling his warriors like crazy. The starlings don't like it, of course."

"Shoot, I don't need the birds to tell me that! You can't hardly blink in the woods without landing on top of them."

"Come in," Shanna said. "We need to talk. In private."

Danny followed her inside.

"Any news from Taylor?" she asked. Danny folded his duster over the chair she offered him at her dining table.

"I ain't seen or heard from her since November," Danny said. He didn't want to push Taylor—she was really steamed at what Tsisgwa and Ramos had been up to.

"This border incident.... You told me Taylor had a run-in with with my father."

"You don't need to worry about that," Danny said. He unconsciously rubbed his shoulder where the dogs of the Wild Hunt had taken a bite out of him. "Chief Tewa's got folks looking out for her."

"He's good at that," Shanna said, frowning.

She continued to pace.

"You okay, Shanna?"

She sighed. "Chief Tewa wants me safe."

"And Taylor, too."

"Does he, Danny?"

"Sure he does!"

"Maybe," Shanna said. "But only because she might give him leverage he can use against the sídhe. What happens when he can't use her anymore?"

"Aw, c'mon, Shanna. Don't talk like that. Chief Tewa's better than that."

Shanna glared at Danny. Her icy blue eyes sent a shiver down his spine.

"You haven't been cooped up here, Danny. You haven't endured his lectures about keeping your head down, not drawing notice."

"No, but—"

242

"He's a little nuts when it comes to the daoine sídhe. Though I suppose he's seen enough over the past thousand years to make him that way. He doesn't trust us. I don't think he trusts *any* of us, not really."

"He acts like he trusts Osanda Morning," Danny said. "I hear he's even planning to meet with her again."

"You heard that? I thought that was a secret."

"Yeah, well..." Danny lowered his eyes.

"You're still full of surprises, I see."

"I notice you knew about this secret meeting, too."

"He's put a tighter guard on me lately," Shanna said. "People talk. And nunnehi aren't the only fae who can escape notice when they want to."

Danny tried not to grin. There was just something about a woman with a tricky streak.

"This meeting is set for Ichisi," Shanna continued. "That's near where Taylor lives."

"That's right."

"You don't think she'll be there, do you?"

Danny's eyes widened. "I never thought of that," he admitted.

"It's all I can think about," Shanna said.

Danny got up. Now it was his turn to pace.

He remembered what the dwarves had said back in April. The one with the eye patch said Taylor might be the most dangerous fae alive. Life and death were in her tongue. He wasn't sure what that meant, but Tewa had heard it, too.

"Having Taylor on her side would sure help Osanda's cause, though," Danny said. "If anybody wants to know what the Summer Court has turned into, all they gotta do is look at her."

"That's what I've been thinking," Shanna said. Then she added, "She's in over her head, Danny. She has been from the day she first learned who she was."

"Probably so," Danny admitted. "If I was her, I'd stay the heck out of this whole mess."

But this was Taylor Smart they were talking about. Her staying out of trouble was about as likely as Shanna joining the Winter Triad.

"As long as Taylor's safety is in the nunnehi's interests, they'll protect her. It's just...."

"Yeah," Danny said. "I get it. Nobody knows what might happen."

The two of them stood there for the longest time.

"I...I could go see her," he said at last. "Keep an eye on her. Just in case."

"Would you, Danny?"

"Sure," he said. He slumped toward his seat. If the nunnehi and the daoine sídhe were going to war, the last place he wanted to be was where the fighting was liable to break out. He felt a hundred pounds heavier than when he came in. "What have I got to lose?"

"I don't believe you understand the situation," Gwenllian said. She and Claudia sprinted to keep up with the long strides of the Teyrnus of Tobarty.

They were outside, on the rath's firing range. Though Gwenllian and Claudia pulled the collars of their overcoats close about their necks, the Teyrnus didn't seem to mind the cold. He was dressed in a simple green tunic and woolen trousers, and his long, brown hair was pulled back into a pony tail. He hefted a bronze-barreled musket on his shoulder.

"Your concern is noted, Matron," he said. "But I am not my predecessor."

He certainly wasn't. Dollin Seaborn was young and inexperienced, flighty, and ultimately unsuited to be the lord of a faery rath. When his men finally mutinied in early December, the Primus yanked him from his post without ceremony.

Gwenllian assumed direct control of the rath until a new Teyrnus could be installed. As of the first of January, that Teyrnus was Coffach Dewberry.

The new Teyrnus towered over Gwenllian. He was supernaturally handsome (of course), dark, broad-shouldered, and obviously no stranger to command. He gestured for an attendant to set up a target 150 yards distant: a pumpkin atop a stack of hay bales.

"The curfew has kept the peace," Gwenllian continued.

"Indeed," the new Teyrnus said. "But don't you think it's time life at Tobarty returned to normal?"

"But Teyrnus," Gwenllian protested. Coffach Dewberry held up his hand to quiet her. He leveled his musket and fired. The distant pumpkin instantly shriveled into a dried-out shell.

"Morale is improving, isn't it?" Coffach said. He set the butt of his musket between his feet and prepared another paper cartridge of elf-shot. He bit off the end, poured the black powder and shot down the muzzle, and packed it tight with the rammer.

Morale might have been improving among the troops, but Claudia didn't feel any better. She wasn't sleeping well, and she didn't think Gwenllian was, either. There was something oppressive about the place, like the Winter Court hadn't entirely let go of it.

The attendant set a new pumpkin in its place. The Teyrnus slid a percussion cap over the hollow metal cone at the rear end of the gun barrel.

Claudia had hoped brightening the Teyrnus's office would help, but the last of the new furnishings had arrived weeks ago to no avail. Everything looked brighter and more cheerful—the new credenza and chairs even set off the old mahogany desk far better than the Winters' dreary things—but the change in décor did nothing to help Claudia's mood.

It was the darkest, coldest part of the year, and Claudia would have preferred to be anywhere but Tobarty. She was sure Gwenllian would agree.

"I simply feel we must proceed with wisdom," Gwenllian said. "You weren't here when your predecessor..."

"Failed?" Coffach said.

Lost it, Claudia thought.

"Overreacted," Gwenllian suggested.

The Teyrnus took aim at his target and fired again: another hit.

"The people are agitated, Teyrnus. Many are still loyal to Winter. Some of them delight in provoking the Summer Court newcomers."

"They'll fall into line." Once again, he paused to reload.

"In time," Gwenllian said. "But people are still fearful of war. The situation has put everyone on edge. Maintaining the curfew until Imbolc—"

"*Do you question the Primus's decision to give me this rath,* Acting *Matron Birdsong?*" His brown eyes flashed. There was just enough presence behind his question to warn Gwenllian away from a direct confrontation.

"I serve at the will of the Primus, no less than you."

"Then we are in agreement."

Another attendant came into view: a freckle-faced pisgy barely a hundred years old. He approached the Teyrnus with a reverential bow.

"News from Dunhoughkey, Teyrnus," he said. He presented an envelope sealed with wax the color of honey.

The Teyrnus ripped open the letter and skimmed its contents. He remained stonefaced.

"Teyrnus?" Gwenllian said.

"Summer Court spies have gotten wind of something," he said. "A meeting has been set for the two weeks after Imbolc."

"A meeting?" Claudia said.

"Apparently Osanda Morning isn't finished stirring things up with the savages," he said. "She means to meet with them again. This time in Ichisi."

"Ichisi?" Gwenllian sputtered. "What is there in Ichisi?"

Claudia held her tongue. She wondered, though, if it weren't so much a matter of *what* as *who*. Taylor Smart lived near Ichisi, and Claudia knew the nunnehi were curious about her loyalties. Did Osanda know something she and Gwenllian didn't?

246

"The savages seem to like Osanda," Coffach said casually. "Perhaps she can do us some good there."

"That isn't funny, Teyrnus," Gwenllian seethed. "Or do you question the Primus's decision to elevate me to the Triad?"

She stormed away before he could answer. Claudia followed.

Gwenllian sputtered curses all the way back to the rath.

"The miserable shrew is going to ruin everything!" she hissed. "Coming in to save the day...giving the nunnehi a reason not to go to war...."

She rounded on Claudia. "She'll be a national hero!" she spat. "And where will that leave me?"

"Matron," Claudia said, "we don't know..."

"Of course we know! She's probably had this planned for months!" Gwenllian balled her fists. "She'll go down to Ichisi, bow and scrape to the savages, probably apologize for every perceived fault of the entire Chiefdom...."

She didn't stop muttering to herself. At last, she arrived at her apartments. She threw open the door and stomped inside.

"I knew it would come to this," Gwenllian said. "I knew it!"

"Matron?"

"She thinks she can get one over on me? She thinks she can play the hero and steal my seat on the Triad?" Gwenllian scoffed. "She'll be sorry she ever made me her enemy. That I swear by my own true name!" The room was suddenly almost unbearably warm.

"Matron, I—"

"Claudia, start packing," the Acting Matron said. "We're going to Ichisi."

William glanced at the clock on the computer science classroom wall. Almost three o'clock. If he hurried, he could finish his graphic design project before the bell rang. His computer wasn't in a mood to cooperate.

"Come on!" he whispered to himself.

"Problem, William?" Mr. Dreyer noticed his frustration.

247

"It keeps freezing up on me."

The computer teacher grumbled. He looked like he wanted to say something inappropriate for children's ears. Instead, he said, "That machine has been acting up lately." Now it was his turn to check the time. "You might as well just shut it down for now. You can finish tomorrow."

"Yes, sir," William said. He shut the computer down.

Get a grip, he thought.

His magical aura wasn't usually strong enough to mess with technology. It usually did other things: spoil milk and butter, make candles burn funny colors. That kind of thing. That's why he was always careful to take a long shower after Maymay's magic lessons. (Maymay said swimming in a creek worked better, but that wasn't really practical.) Running water collapsed the aura, allowed it to refresh. William thought it worth losing his magic for a couple of minutes if it cut down on his parent's grocery bill.

But technology had never been a problem. He could still play his video games or text with his friends.

But when his emotions spiked? Who knew what might happen?

It just so happened he had a lot on his mind today.

He had spent the entire month of January watching Taylor eat lunch with Jared McCaughey. It didn't bother him that they were hanging out together. Well, not much, anyway.

To be honest, he wasn't sure what Taylor saw in Jared. Sure, he had a good sense of humor. Girls were supposed to like that, right? And he was at least kind of good looking. (Most of the eighth-grade girls seemed to agree about that.) And he was pretty smart—maybe not as smart as William, definitely not as smart as Taylor—but smart enough. But take away the looks, brains, and personality, and what have you got?

Okay, he admitted to himself, *the dude's pretty cool.*

And he didn't have that whole freaked-out-by-Taylor's-magic-powers vibe going. That was bound to be a plus.

When he knew he could get away with it, William sneaked glances at Jared with his Second Sight. Maymay said he needed

248

to sharpen his magical senses, after all. With Jared, he always got a sense he was a genuinely good guy: honest, funny, down to earth.

This is getting depressing, he thought.

He and Taylor would sit at lunch and joke with each other. Taylor had even given him the playful shoulder bump. The "accidental" hand brush couldn't be far behind.

But this wasn't about Jared. It wasn't even about Taylor.

The bell was about to ring. He pulled a purple envelope out of his notebook and breathed a silent prayer.

Taylor was near the front of the pack heading out the door. He sprinted to catch up to her.

"Hey, Taylor," he said.

She pretended not to hear him.

"Taylor!"

"What?" She kept walking. She didn't make eye contact.

He poked her arm with the envelope.

"Happy birthday."

Taylor stopped. She stared at the envelope.

"We should have got you something, but...."

"We?" Taylor said. She finally took the envelope from William's hand. "This is from you and Jill both?" Her face said she doubted it.

"Well...not exactly."

She opened the envelope and gave the birthday card a cursory glance.

"She still thinks I'm a freak, doesn't she?"

"She never thought you were a freak," William protested. "She's just scared."

"Well, we can't have that, can we?"

That came out a little loud. Kids turned their way, then kept on heading for their lockers or the exits.

"Come on, Taylor," William said. "It's been a month. Jill really wants you two to be friends again."

Taylor stopped and wheeled around. "Then why isn't *she* having this conversation?"

William didn't know what to say.

Taylor sighed. "I appreciate what you're trying to do," she said. "But Jill's not the only one going through...stuff...right now."

"Yeah," William said. "I understand."

"Do you? Do you have any idea?"

William gulped. He'd just broken one of his dad's rules: Never tell a woman you understand what she's going through. *Okay*, he told himself. *Time to back up.*

"Look...," he started. "All I know is you and Jill make a pretty good team. I never thought I'd see the day you two weren't tight. If I lived to be a hundred—"

"*William.*" She shot him icy daggers that brought him up short.

For some reason, she looked like she was going to cry.

"I'm not like you, William," she said. "And I'm not like Jill. There's no point pretending that I am." She stalked down the corridor.

"Okay," William said. "You're going through stuff, too. Fine."

She kept walking.

"But why can't you let us help?"

She stopped again and waited for William to catch up.

"You can't help."

"I can try."

"You can't help, William." She sighed. "This is...so out of your league."

"Try me," he said defiantly. Just as he said it, a sixth-grader walked past. His backpack fell open, scattering books and papers everywhere.

Stupid magical aura.

"I'm meeting some people," Taylor said. "Next weekend. I'm trying to keep Jill safe. You too."

Keep Jill safe? That was his department. He was the oldest, after all. By only seventeen minutes, but still... "Then let me—"

"William, trust me: there's nothing you or Jill or even your grandmother can do. I don't expect you to understand. It's just... better if you stay out of this. Okay?"

"And you won't even tell me—"

There was no point talking; Taylor had already stormed away.

William felt a chill in the air.

Chapter 24

Party Crashers

What does one wear to hobnob with the fae nobility? Taylor figured she might as well be herself—only a little dressier. Saturday afternoon, she packed her favorite dress—a flower-print in blue and white—along with blue dress shoes, and a white shrug. She put everything in her overnight bag for her "sleepover" with Ayoka.

Her phone chimed with an incoming text.

It was Jared. "hey."

She texted the same greeting back. It was nice to interact with someone who didn't have a magical bone in his body.

"sup?" Jared texted back.

"nm u?"

"did u get math 4 tue?"

Taylor smiled. As if Jared cared about the homework Mr. Appletree gave them! "sure u?"

"not rly. call me?"

She wished she could, but she had made a promise to Osanda Morning. "can't :(gotta go"

"ur fault if I flunk ;)"

"poor baby ;)"

"whatev bye :)"

":)"

She put on comfortable clothes: jeans, tennis shoes, Shanna's black leather jacket, and a purple long-sleeve tee shirt that said, "Never Judge a Book by Its Movie."

She told her parents goodbye and traveled the rings to Ichisi.

253

She appeared outside the wooden palisade. The first time Taylor visited the nunnehi city, security wasn't as tight. She was able to materialize in the heart of town. But since then, things had become more tense.

It wasn't just that the ring on the Great Temple Mound was closed. As she approached the city gate, she noticed a number of warriors standing guard with bows and war clubs.

The city was still full of life, though. As she strolled down the main north-south boulevard, she took in the sights and sounds of thousands of Fair Folk getting on with their lives. Children played in the streets. Men and women went about their daily chores, or congregated on the corners to sing and joke and visit.

Ayoka met Taylor at the edge of the stickball field, and the two girls hurried to Tsisgwa's modest wattle-and-daub house to get ready. It was just two rooms: a small privy in the back and a larger open space with a stove in one corner, a small wooden table, and some river-cane benches along the walls.

"Where's your cousin?" Taylor asked. She hadn't seen Tsisgwa since Thanksgiving but she couldn't shake the feeling he—or somebody—was watching her.

"Busy with security. He's assigned to guard my grandfather."

"Chief Tewa is here?"

Ayoka nodded. "He and Chief Nocosi have been in meetings all day."

"Wow. I guess this really is an important meeting."

Not for the first time, Taylor feared she was in way over her head. "Will you tell me if what I packed for tonight is okay?"

"Of course."

Taylor's outfit passed muster. She put it on along with her necklace and jeweled pendant in the shape of a hellebore flower. For her part, Ayoka dressed in traditional nunnehi costume: a knee-length dress of woven plant fibers in an intricate red and yellow pattern, draped over her left shoulder, with a calfskin cloak to stave off the winter chill.

The formal dinner took place on what Taylor knew as the Great Temple Mound. Topside, it was a vast mound from which

254

you could look across the Ocmulgee River and see the buildings of downtown Macon. In the Wonder, it seemed even bigger and was dotted with the houses of the city's most esteemed nobles: the three Chiefs and their immediate families.

At the top of the mound was the house of Nocosi, the White Chief. In what Taylor decided was his back yard was a pavilion decked out with long, low dining tables and milling with servants, both fae and little folk, putting the final touches on everything.

Ayoka led Taylor to the head table. Inside the pavilion, the temperature was quite comfortable despite the darkening February sky. Taylor guessed magic had something to do with that. Will-o'-the-wisps floated lazily above the tables, providing subdued lighting.

Osanda Morning was already seated next to a white-haired nunnehi in an ornate woolen cloak. She smiled at Taylor but said nothing. Taylor nodded slightly and tried to seem at ease, but her heart was racing.

Ayoka brought Taylor to a steely-eyed fae dressed all in white, from the feathers in his cap to his bleached white moccasins. He gracefully rose from his seat.

"Chief Nocosi," Ayoka said, bowing slightly. "May I present Taylor Smart, also called Selena Hellebore."

The White Chief of Ichisi bowed his head slightly. "My honored guest," he said. "And which name do you prefer?"

"Taylor, I guess."

Ayoka bowed and backed away. Apparently she would be sitting at a different table.

"Taylor, then. Allow me to introduce Coloma, Red Chief of Ichisi." Coloma looked a lot like Inali, his counterpart in Tsuwatelda. They were both imposing men in red and black regalia. Coloma bowed curtly but did not rise from his seat at the far end of the table. This, she realized, was Tsisgwa and Athlan's boss.

Beside him sat Chief Tewa. Taylor felt her face grow warm, but took a breath and got her feelings under control. Now was not the time for snark.

"And Efau, our Medicine Chief." The older fae with snow-white hair next to Osanda smiled brightly. He was wrapped in a cloak covered in intricate designs: whorls, crosses, and stylized eagles and snakes. Behind him stood an attendant holding a four-foot-long staff topped with an arrangement of beads and feathers.

Osanda once more met Taylor's eye.

"I understand you already know Tewa, White Chief of Tsuwatelda," Chief Nocosi said. Chief Tewa was also dressed all in white. He had been seated near Chief Coloma, but he stood to greet Taylor. Behind him, Tsisgwa and another warrior stood at attention. Black streaks of warpaint under their eyes imitated the coloring of a falcon's face.

Taylor bowed politely.

"And, of course, Osanda Morning," Chief Nocosi said. Taylor faced Osanda. She wore a simple honey-colored gown and a wreath of ivy in her golden hair.

"Ms. Morning," Taylor said. She wished Ayoka were there to show her how to act. This was her first diplomatic summit, after all. She stooped awkwardly in what she hoped was an acceptable curtsy.

"Please have a seat," Chief Nocosi said. He guided Taylor to a bench across the table from Osanda and Chief Efau.

Chief Nocosi stood at the head of the table and said some words in his own language. He spread his hands and offered some sort of blessing over the meal, at the end of which everyone began to eat.

The food was as good as Taylor remembered eating in Tsuwatelda. Once again, it was served family style, so everyone filled their plates and passed the dishes around to others.

"Miss Hellebore," Osanda said. "It's a pleasure to meet you again."

"Thanks," Taylor said. "But you can call me Taylor."

"Taylor, then." Osanda smiled. "I look forward to getting to know you better." To Chief Nocosi she added, "I am grateful to

256

the good people of Ichisi for so warmly welcoming one of my kindred."

Chief Nocosi bowed.

"It gives me hope for the future," Osanda continued. "For greater understanding between our peoples."

Chief Tewa said, "*If* the sídhe are interested in fostering such understanding, I welcome the prospect."

Chief Nocosi added, "My brother Chief and I are agreed on this, Ms. Morning—as unlikely as such a development seems."

Taylor followed the conversation like a stickball game, the ball constantly moving back and forth.

Chief Coloma took the offensive. "That is the question, isn't it?" he said. "Are the sídhe prepared to live in peace with those they call 'savages'?"

Taylor scored that as one point for the nunnehi.

"Chief Coloma," Osanda said. There was genuine humility in her voice, and Taylor didn't sense any sort of glamour trick behind it. "You know I am not in a position to speak for the Summer Court of Arradherry."

"And yet, here you are."

"As you say, Chief. Though I cannot speak for the Court, I believe I can speak for the many daoine sídhe—and others—who yearn for change within our Chiefdom. One way or another, their voice shall be heard."

And that tied the score at one point apiece.

They kept talking. One or another of the Chiefs would raise a concern, and Osanda would address it. She was self-assured and she carried herself like a true aristocrat. Even so, she seemed perfectly sincere. She really believed she could turn the Summer Court around.

That gave Taylor hope.

About that time, she heard her name.

"Taylor here is a perfect example of why many of my people are so hungry for change," Osanda said. "They've heard she stood up for herself against power-hungry Gentry who've forgotten

257

they are supposed to rule for the benefit of all." She winked at Taylor. "It gives them hope they might be able to do the same."

"What do you have to say about that, Taylor?" Chief Tewa said.

"I...uh..."

Whatever Taylor might have answered, she didn't get the chance. She had barely opened her mouth when a commotion at the edge of the pavilion got everyone's attention.

"But I'm not here to see the Chiefs," a woman said. Her voice was steady but insistent. Taylor craned her neck to see what was happening. A servant was trying to settle the woman down.

"I'm sorry, madam, but I can't allow you to—"

"Could you perhaps inform Osanda Morning of our arrival?" a different woman suggested. Her voice was familiar. The crowd parted, and Taylor saw her: a tall, brown-skinned fae in a burgundy business suit.

She'd met her before, at Dunhoughkey. It was Claudia, the fae who'd befriended Shanna.

She and another woman, a blonde-haired fae in a flowing white gown and a forest green cloak, were trying to crash the meeting!

As all this was happening, the warriors behind Chief Tewa sprang forward, war clubs ready. Other falcon-painted guards appeared from out of nowhere all around the pavilion.

Athlan Tastanagi was suddenly near the cause of the commotion. His flaming war club crackled and sparked.

"Gwenllian Birdsong!" Osanda sputtered. "Of all people!"

Gwenllian Birdsong? Taylor thought. *The woman whose job Osanda wants?*

"A friend of yours?" Chief Efau said.

Osanda scoffed. "Hardly."

People gasped as a third form appeared over the crest of the mound. He was twice as tall as a man and broader than a doorframe. Taylor thought he looked embarrassed to be there.

258

At the head table, the Chiefs and Osanda stood up. Chief Efau's attendant passed him his staff. Chief Coloma drew a knife from his belt.

Athlan shouted over the commotion. "Come no farther!" He hefted his club toward Gwenllian Birdsong. Taylor couldn't see his face, but his body language said he was itching to take a swipe at the intruder.

The guests had cleared the center of the pavilion, giving everyone (Taylor realized) a clean shot when the blasts started flying. A table and more than a few stools had been overturned. Warriors interposed themselves between the guests and the intruders. At the edge of the pavilion, Ayoka glared, braced for action.

"My lord," Claudia said, her tone conciliatory. She took a half-step forward. "Please forgive our impertinence. We simply desire—"

"Where is Osanda Morning?" the blonde fae thundered.

"Ms. Morning is a guest of Chief Nocosi," Athlan said. "She's no concern of yours."

"Gwenllian Birdsong," Osanda sneered. "What a fine example of the Summer Court! The Law of Hospitality means nothing to you, does it?"

"Osanda Morning," Gwenllian, the blonde fae, answered. "Still wrapping yourself in the Eldritch Law, I see."

"A law some of us still believe in."

Gwenllian moved forward, but Athlan stood in the way. The two glared at each other. The giant let out an agitated moan. He definitely didn't look comfortable being there.

Chief Nocosi crossed his arms. He seemed willing to let events play out, at least for the time being.

Gwenllian glanced at the head table. Her eyes landed on Taylor.

"And you're Selena Hellebore, I take it?" Her eyes, her voice, everything about her said she thought Taylor was beneath her—which wasn't really surprising. She'd gotten used to that attitude from the Gentry.

259

"That's right," Taylor said. *On the weekends, anyway.* She cocked her head and planted her hands on her hips. "Who are you?"

Gwenllian sputtered. "That is no concern of yours, child."

Taylor was starting to hate it when smug, self-important fae called her "child."

"My business is with Osanda," the blonde fae continued.

"We have no business until Beltane," Osanda said. "At which time, we can hope the Summer Court realizes how stupid it would be to make your position on the Triad permanent."

"The stupid one is whoever thinks you will ever speak for the Summer Court," Gwenllian said.

Claudia winced.

"I have my supporters," Osanda said.

"Rabble!"

"Is that your opinion of Tellus Forge, Gwenllian? Shall I tell the Teyrnus of Mullivey that you think of him as rabble? And what of Enya Goldenhead? Murgo Bale?"

"Don't insult them behind their backs, Osanda."

"This has gone far enough," Chief Nocosi said. "Mrs. Birdsong, leave now and I will be inclined to overlook this shameful display of yours."

"I am still a Matron of the Summer Court of Arradherry," she said. "I plead the Law of Hospitality."

A few of the nearest warriors groaned. Chief Coloma sighed and pinched his nose. He leaned toward Chief Tewa, and the two exchanged words in their own language. Taylor figured they were trying to decide what to do: put up with Mrs. Birdsong's impertinence or just kick her out. Taylor hoped for the second.

"Mrs. Birdsong, you have already violated sacred hospitality by your appearance here," Chief Nocosi finally said. He swallowed. "In the name of peace between our peoples, however, Chief Tewa and I are willing to overlook this insult—once."

Mrs. Birdsong grinned.

Taylor groaned inwardly. Keep your friends close and your enemies closer, apparently.

"In any event, it would be inhospitable to send you away in the dead of night. You may remain as my guest until sunrise."

"That's all?" Mrs. Birdsong said. "I demand an opportunity to refute the lies this woman has been telling you!"

"Duly noted," Chief Nocosi said. "Chief Coloma, would you kindly escort Mrs. Birdsong from the premises?"

The Red Chief betrayed the subtlest of smiles and gestured to his senior officer. "Athlan Tastanagi," he said.

Athlan bowed curtly to the Red Chief and slipped his war club, no longer flaming, into his belt. He gestured for Gwenllian to go.

Before she did, though, she turned back. "Do you really think dragging Selena Hellebore into this will help your chances, Osanda?" She sounded like like she was scolding a child.

"At least she's trying to make a difference," Taylor said. Her voice trembled more than she would have liked.

"Search your heart," Gwenllian said. "Tell me if you believe—truly believe—that this woman has any chance at all of being elevated to the Triad."

That brought Taylor up short. Danny seemed to think highly of Osanda. So did Wasko, Pete, and Haggler. They all said she had the support of the lesser fae and even some of the powerful families.

But...could she really be a Summer Court Matron? Would people like Gwenllian—like Dubessa Fairchild—ever let that happen?

Gwenllian and her entourage quietly left.

The guests slowly returned to their seats.

But Taylor had lost her appetite.

Supper was pretty much over at that point. Neither Osanda nor the Chiefs were in any mood to talk, and Chief Coloma was suddenly busy coordinating with his warriors to ensure the rival

261

fae women didn't "accidentally" run into each other in a dark alley.

It had to be close to ten o'clock when Taylor and Ayoka returned to Tsisgwa's place. A big black dog was sleeping near the door. It perked up its ears as the girls approached.

"Is that...?" Taylor mused.

The dog's body shimmered, shifted, and expanded. It stood up on its hind legs, and its glowing yellow eyes twinkled.

"Danny!"

"Hey, Taylor. What d'ya know?"

"Fae politics is stupid."

"I coulda told you that," Danny scoffed. "Is everything okay?"

Taylor sighed. "Hard to tell. Are weapons and insults usually involved at a fae banquet?"

Danny's eyes blazed. "Weapons? What—?"

"The Summer Court was in rare form," Ayoka said. "And it's a pleasure to meet you again, Mr. Underhill. Won't you come in?"

Danny bowed. He and the two girls went inside. "Ayoka, right? I remember you from Pilot Knob." He turned back to Taylor. "I heard Mrs. Birdsong was in town—that she tried to derail your all's meeting."

"She nearly did," Taylor said.

"All she did was confirm my people's appreciation for someone like Osanda," Ayoka said.

"Maybe," Taylor said. "Unfortunately, your people don't get a vote."

"You still think Birdsong will be confirmed?" Ayoka asked.

"She's got connections, that's for sure," Danny said. "A lot of the Gentry'll be afraid to go against her."

"But?" Taylor said. She was looking for any reason at all to be optimistic about Osanda.

"From what I hear, Osanda's got the conservative vote pretty much locked up. And after the Wild Hunt incident a few months back? Well, that's made a lot of folks give Osanda another look."

"Indeed," Ayoka said. "Coffee, Mr. Underhill?"

"That would be great. And it's Danny, if you please." Ayoka snapped her fingers to kindle a fire under Tsisgwa's cook stove and started a pot of water boiling.

"So she could be gaining ground?" Taylor wondered.

"Maybe," Danny said. "Folks that are tired of how Mrs. Redmane and now Mrs. Fairchild have been running things—well, they're pretty much in Osanda's corner. At least for now. I'd give her a fifty-fifty chance."

"A lot can happen between now and the first of May," Ayoka said, frowning.

"But Danny, what are you doing here?"

"Keeping an eye on things," he said. "Shanna wanted me to make sure you're all right."

"You can tell her I'm fine," Taylor said. "Just...frustrated. Worn out. This whole thing is...I can't even. Everybody wants me on their side. They think I'm some kind of symbol. Some kind of good luck charm or something. I wouldn't be surprised to see my face on a tee shirt before this is all over!"

Someone knocked at the door. Ayoka peeked out the window, then swung the door open a crack.

"Is Taylor Smart here?" a woman asked.

Danny gasped. "Claudia?"

Claudia Fountain stepped inside. "Well, well." She smiled. "I can't seem to get away from you, Danny. It's good to see you again."

"You too."

Claudia turned to Taylor. "I'm afraid I'm here on business."

Something churned in Taylor's stomach. "Why does that make me nervous?"

263

Chapter 25

Somebody Starts a War

Mrs. Birdsong was waiting for Taylor in a grove of trees between the Great Temple Mound and the river. She was alone. At least, Taylor didn't see anyone with her. The giant from supper was nowhere to be seen.

Taylor scanned the woods with her magical senses. For all she knew, a whole army of sídhe was out there, ready to strike. Her gut told her that—for once—things were as they appeared. It was just Taylor, Mrs. Birdsong, Claudia, and Danny.

The pooka insisted on coming, and Claudia didn't think her boss would object. Taylor was happy to have his eyes and ears on the situation.

Mrs. Birdsong was still wearing her cloak and gown. A single silver-white will-o'-the-wisp hovered over her head, casting shadows that made her face appear twisted and unearthly.

Taylor was still wearing her blue-and-white dress. She should have been cold, but the night air didn't bother her. If she shivered, it was with anxiety because she didn't know what to expect. Claudia was tight-lipped. Maybe she didn't know anything to tell. Maybe she was forbidden from telling it.

Claudia positioned herself at Mrs. Birdsong's side. Danny tapped Taylor's back to assure her he was still there.

"Apparently you've already met my assistant, Claudia," Mrs. Birdsong said. "When you were a prisoner at Dunhoughkey."

"That's right," Taylor said. Her mouth went dry. She knew Claudia was a spy for the nunnehi. She would have to be careful what she said.

265

"And I don't believe I know your...associate?"

"His name is Danny."

"Danny Underhill?" Mrs. Birdsong arched an eyebrow. "The pooka who humiliated Ambicatus Bright forty years ago?"

"That wasn't my fault," Danny muttered, half to himself.

"Mrs. Birdsong," Taylor said. "You wanted to meet with me?"

She turned her attention to Taylor. "I see you are direct."

"Yeah, well..."

"I don't like that." There was an edge to her voice. She must have still been steamed to be kicked out of Chief Nocosi's banquet. "The deathlings say children should be seen and not heard."

"Neither of us are deathlings," Taylor said.

Mrs. Birdsong gritted her teeth. "No, Miss Hellebore, we are not."

She turned away, and her cloak flared out behind her. Two simple chairs were set in the clearing. Mrs. Birdsong gestured for Taylor to take a seat.

"Let's chat, shall we?"

"That's going to be hard if I'm not supposed to say anything."

"Then listen." Mrs. Birdsong took her seat.

Taylor glanced at Danny, who shrugged and then nodded. Taylor sat down. Danny stood behind her at a respectful distance, just as Claudia stood behind Mrs. Birdsong.

"You simply don't realize what is at stake, so I thought I would do you the honor of explaining it to you."

"You're too kind," Taylor said.

Mrs. Birdsong leaned forward, eyes blazing. She smoldered, but managed to restrain herself. "Hear me out, Miss Hellebore. That is all I ask."

Taylor wanted to keep up the snark. She started to mouth off again when she caught sight of Claudia subtly shaking her head.

She stopped herself. "All right." She crossed her legs and folded her arms in front of her.

266

"I'm not a sídhe, by the way," she began. "Did you know that? I'm of the tylwyth teg. You might say we're cousins of the daoine sídhe—though closer at some times than others."

Mrs. Birdsong sat up straight.

"Osanda thinks I'm hungry for power," she said. "She's right, of course."

"Thank you for being honest."

She shrugged. "Our Kind do not lie easily—as you may have discovered for yourself. But she's wrong to think that would make her a better Matron. The former Chief Matron severely damaged the Summer Court's standing."

"You mean Anya Redmane."

"We do not speak that name, Miss Hellebore." The fire in her eye said Taylor had better not, either. "But my point is that it will take a firm hand to restore our fortunes. We must present a strong face to the Winter Court. Perhaps you heard they attempted some mischief last November."

"I heard," Taylor said.

"Osanda seems to think she is the only member of the Gentry to care about the nunnehi. I assure you, she is not."

Taylor nodded.

"What you need to understand, Miss Hellebore, is that the Winter Court are the real villains here. If you don't feel safe, if you fear for the safety of those you care about, then there's your answer. They are the ones stirring up trouble between us and the nunnehi. They are the ones making mischief in Summer Court raths. They are the ones who used Jill Matthews as a pawn to sow chaos in the Summer Court—yes, I'm quite aware of what happened to your deathling friend last summer. And what does Osanda Morning do? Stir up dissension in the Summer Court and weaken our position."

Mrs. Birdsong crossed her arms and sat back in her chair, defying Taylor to contradict her.

"You'd be a fool to let yourself be used by her," she continued. "You would only be making it harder for the people you care about to lead safe, normal lives."

267

She leaned forward in her chair.

"Osanda's cause doesn't need a symbol," she continued. "For the good of the Summer Court, it needs to be quelled. I intend to quell it—and anyone who stands in my way. By any means at my disposal. Are we clear?"

Mrs. Birdsong's voice and expression betrayed no emotion, but they didn't have to. Taylor's heart raced.

"Are we clear?" she repeated.

Taylor opened her mouth to speak. There was a flutter of movement in the trees behind Claudia.

Athlan Tastanagi emerged, his war club burst into flame, reflecting the fire in his eyes.

Taylor's jaw dropped. She jumped up, kicking over her chair.

Mrs. Birdsong sprung to her feet as well. Claudia whipped around and raised her left hand, preparing a shield spell.

Athlan made a sweeping motion. The air distorted between him and Claudia, and she flew backwards, unconscious.

Danny yelped.

Athlan glared at Mrs. Birdsong. "Are you quite finished?"

Taylor's head swam. She could barely believe her eyes. What did Athlan think he was doing?

Mrs. Birdsong hissed an incantation, and vines began to snake around the nunnehi's ankles. He kicked them away.

By this time, Danny had become a goat. He barreled forward, head down, horns aimed at Athlan's gut.

Taylor wheeled her right arm in a tight circle, gathering magic for a blast.

Athlan swung with his war club. Its weighted knob smashed into the side of Danny's head. The pooka went down with a semi-conscious bleat.

Taylor saw her chance. Whatever Athlan was up to, he was hurting Claudia and Danny. He had to be stopped.

She thrust her hand forward with the strongest blast she could muster.

268

To her surprise, Mrs. Birdsong attacked the exact same time. Not one but two distortions flashed across the clearing from two different angles, both aimed at Athlan's head.

He made another sweeping gesture, leaped back, and whipped his war club over his head.

The blasts hadn't even touched him.

Taylor wobbled to one side, drained by her magical exertion.

"You savage!" Mrs. Birdsong yelled.

"Shut up!" Athlan said. He scrunched his hands into a tight fist while glaring at her with unbridled hatred. Mrs. Birdsong fell to the ground, gasping and clutching her throat.

Taylor backed up against one of the wooden chairs. Desperate, she grabbed it and slammed it toward Athlan's side in a single motion.

Athlan knocked the chair away with his club. It shattered to pieces.

Taylor clutched her arm, now jarred from the force of Athlan's blow. The maneuver left scrapes across the palm of her hand.

Claudia rushed him from behind. With a backhand swing, Athlan buried his war club in her gut with a harsh thunk. She cried out as she fell on her back. Her business suit smoked where the fiery weapon made contact.

Athlan turned back to Taylor. "I never thought you'd defend the likes of her," he said, scowling at Mrs. Birdsong. "I must say, I'm disappointed."

"I never thought *you'd*... Wait. What *are* you doing?"

Athlan sighed. He took a single step toward her.

"My part, to see this 'savage' gets what's coming to her." The Great Tastanagi turned his eyes on Mrs. Birdsong. Taylor's attack with the chair must have broken his concentration, because she no longer looked like she was being choked to death. She was still on her knees, though, and she wasn't in any condition to defend herself.

In the next second, a million things flashed through Taylor's mind. At the top of the list was fear, of course. Athlan was an

269

expert warrior. He could kill Taylor in a heartbeat if the mood struck him. To put it generously, his mood was currently open to question.

Another part of her mind registered Claudia and Danny both struggling to come to. Claudia moaned.

She also considered the meaning of what was going on. A nunnehi attacking one of the Gentry? This was not going to end well.

"M-miss...Hellebore...," Mrs. Birdsong gasped. She looked awfully shaken up. She looked as helpless as Taylor felt.

Taylor cast her eyes on Athlan. He had taken down Claudia and Danny in about three seconds, brushed off blasts from herself and Mrs. Birdsong, and looked like he was going to thoroughly enjoy the murder he was about to commit.

And there wasn't a scratch on him.

"Arrgh!" Danny gasped. He had resumed his two-legged form and, with obvious effort, sprung forward drunkenly. Athlan sidestepped him, and he stumbled to the ground with a moan.

Well, this sucks.

She tried another blast, though she didn't have much magic to put into it. It hit Athlan in the shoulder but only got his attention.

She tried to control her breathing. She was getting lightheaded.

"You still lack focus," Athlan commented. His tone of voice was detached, maybe even sympathetic. He sounded like this was just another combat lesson.

"You should have taken my advice about the cedar oil." He made a fist at Mrs. Birdsong again. She fell face down on the grass, gasping for breath.

"Enough," she whispered. "Please."

Athlan growled at her.

Taylor braced herself and prepared to conjure a blast.

"I have no quarrel with you," Athlan told her. "Walk away, and I'll let you live."

Taylor fired her blast. Once again, Athlan deflected it with barely an effort.

He gestured toward her faster than she could form a shield. Another shaft of distortion arced between the two of them.

Taylor gasped and drew in her left forearm. It was red and blistered, as if she'd brushed against a hot stove, but the sleeve of her shrug was untouched.

Athlan wagged his finger at her. "A blast can do more than stun an opponent, you know. You should have walked away. Consider that a parting lesson."

Taylor fell to her knees.

"Do you honestly think you ever had a chance against the booger fae?" He scoffed. "They would eat you alive."

"Why are you doing this?" she cried.

She forced herself to stand. She had to figure out how to drive him away and get help for the injured—including herself.

Athlan kept taunting her. "The booger fae may be your family, but they aren't your friends. When they're done with you, they'll throw you out with the trash."

She noticed a chair leg at her feet. She scooped it up and lunged at Athlan with a desperate grunt.

He blasted her again. This time, a sharp, shooting pain coursed up and down her right leg.

She crumbled to the ground and pounded the earth to stave off the agony.

"And unlike me," Athlan said, "they won't show restraint."

Taylor called him an ugly name.

"Come along, Mrs. Birdsong," Athlan said. He strode confidently to where she was still writhing on the ground. "We have places to go."

He grabbed her around the middle, lifted her up with ease, and flung her over his shoulder.

He approached Taylor. Her leg felt like it was on fire, and she couldn't bear to move her left arm. She kept it curled up against her body and prayed the pain would go away.

"You should have walked away when I gave you the chance," Athlan said. "I'm truly sorry about this, Taylor."

She said nothing, but she met his eyes. There was no anger there, only grim resolve.

"Then why?"

"I do what I must," he said. He glanced at Mrs. Birdsong with contempt. Then he turned back to Taylor. "Your people won't wait until you're ready to face them. Go home to your Topside life. Stay out of things you're helpless to change."

"And what?" Taylor said. She moved wrong, and fresh pain shot through her blistered arm. "Let you play judge, jury"—she looked at Mrs. Birdsong's limp body—"and executioner?" She shook her head. "You're no better than she is."

They stared at each other for three or four seconds. Something was boiling beneath the surface of Athlan Tastanagi.

Finally, he broke the silence. With a derisive smirk, he said, "Cedar oil." He tapped his forehead with his free hand. "Focus."

He carried Mrs. Birdsong toward the trees. As he walked away, a veil of invisibility fell on both of them, and they vanished from sight.

Taylor felt a hot tear rolling down her cheek.

The whole world was spinning.

Danny moaned and hissed as he struggled to his feet.

She was hurting—bad. She couldn't move her left arm. She was afraid to even try to stand up.

And Athlan Tastanagi had just started a war.

Taylor swore under her breath. Then she collapsed on the grass.

Chapter 26

Boiling Over

Taylor lay on her back in the dark, listening to Danny trying to coax Claudia awake.

Soon, the sound of his voice was joined by earth tremors, slow and measured and coming closer. Something huge was stomping in their direction. Tree limbs snapped nearby.

A minute later, an impossibly deep voice said, "Claudia?"

Danny cursed. Taylor could hear him scrambling away.

The voice spoke again, mixing confusion with anger: "Claudia hurt?"

Taylor opened her eyes. The giant she had seen earlier stood over Claudia's still body. He balled his fists—each as big as a ham—and glared at Danny.

"I didn't do it!" Danny said.

"Claudia!" the giant thundered.

Taylor shouted, "He's telling the truth!" She tried to sit up, but the effort sent fresh daggers of pain down her leg.

"I remember you from Pilot Knob," Danny told the giant. He rubbed his bruised jaw with one hand and kept the other in a defensive position. "Your name is Blue, ain't it? You're friends with Claudia."

The giant growled.

"I'm Claudia's friend, too. So's Taylor over there."

Taylor waved weakly.

"Blue, something bad has happened," Danny continued. "We need to help Claudia."

273

Just then, Claudia mumbled something indistinct. She pushed herself up on her hands.

"B-blue?" she croaked. Her voice was stronger, but she still sounded beat.

"Claudia?"

"Mrs. Bird...?"

"She's gone," Taylor said. "Athlan took her."

"Oh, no," Danny said. "That's bad. By oak, ash, and thorn, that's really bad."

"We've got to tell the Chiefs."

"Tell Chiefs," Blue agreed. "Help Claudia."

He scooped her up and laid her across his forearm with her head in his massive hand and her legs straddling the hollow of his elbow and dangling like a rag doll's.

He stomped away. Taylor lurched to her feet. Her leg was sore and her mind was cloudy. But she offered Danny her shoulder, and both of them stumbled along, trying to keep up. Every step was a struggle. Her lungs burned with the exertion of simply breathing. Danny fell on his face twice, and Taylor hung back to help him up.

Up ahead, Blue ran into some of Chief Coloma's warriors at the edge of the grove. Fortunately, Claudia was awake enough to explain the situation.

As Taylor caught up to him, she kept saying, "It was Athlan." Every time she said it, she got madder.

The warriors didn't seem to pay attention, though. Maybe they couldn't believe he would attack guests of his Chief. Taylor shuddered to think maybe they were in on the whole thing.

In any event, they took Taylor, Claudia, and Danny to the house of Chief Efau. They laid the three of them on pallets in a large circular room, and half a dozen nunnehi healers scrambled to look after their injuries.

A nunnehi offered her a drink for her pain.

The next thing Taylor knew, it was daylight. "Athlan," she whispered.

She clenched her right fist in anger. The Great Tastanagi had mocked her, made a fool of her. All those months, teaching her to fight—and then to attack her like that! Last night he was just toying with her. He could have killed her with a snap of his finger, but instead he taunted her, scolded her. Like she was nobody.

Like she was a booger fae.

She tried to sit up, then decided against it. Her arm was wrapped in bandages treated with the foulest ointment she'd ever had the misfortune to smell. Her leg was uncovered, but smeared with a glowing orange grease that was almost as bad.

Ayoka knelt beside her. Healers zipped back and forth. Somewhere, a woman was chanting. The smell of incense filled the air.

"How do you feel?" Ayoka asked.

"Guess." She stared at the ceiling and bit her lip.

"Danny and Claudia will be fine."

She jerked her head toward Ayoka. She scolded herself for forgetting about them. Heck, she was mad already. What's one more thing to be mad about?

"Claudia?"

"They put her in a private room. She's bleeding internally." Ayoka stared at her with eyes wide. "She took a nasty blast to the gut. She needs to rest. The giant cried like a baby half the night."

Outside, a male voice issued orders in a language Taylor didn't recognize. He sounded pretty mad, himself.

Taylor did catch one word, though: "Coloma."

Her mind went back to the night before. Athlan. Mrs. Birdsong. She shuddered to think what might have happened since then.

"Have they found Athlan?" Taylor said.

Ayoka's forlorn expression was all the answer Taylor needed.

There was more shouting outside. If the first exchange sounded like an officer giving orders to his men, this was clearly two men arguing about something.

"Somebody want to fill me in?" Danny groaned.

Ayoka scooted back so Taylor could see the pooka on his pallet behind her. The left side of his face was packed with a thick plaster. What wasn't under the dressing was so badly bruised Taylor wasn't sure she'd have recognized him if not for the tufts of curly black hair poking through. His prodigious nose was covered with bloody bandages.

"Things are...unsettled," Ayoka said, looking back and forth between Taylor and Danny.

"I think I smell a euphemism," Taylor said.

"Naw, that's just this poultice," Danny said.

Taylor rolled her eyes. She addressed Ayoka. "Unsettled?"

Ayoka took a breath, probably searching for words. "Some don't believe Athlan could have done what you claim."

"But we saw him!"

"I know." Ayoka set her hand on Taylor's shoulder. "But Athlan Tastanagi is a hero. Most people in Ichisi remember his exploits from seventy years ago. He once saved his entire scouting party when they were captured by the sídhe. Ever since, he's been the hometown boy who made good. It's hard for them to accept that he would...do this."

"But you believe us, right?" Taylor said.

Ayoka nodded. "Yes, and many others—even though they don't understand. Some agree he captured the sídhe Matron, but defend his actions even so."

"What? That's crazy!"

"There's little love between our peoples, Taylor. You know that."

"What he's done will only make things worse."

"Many say that as well. They think he may have started another war."

Danny groaned, "Yeah, that's my vote."

276

"Mine, too." Ayoka frowned. "The sídhe aren't going to pretend this attack didn't happen. They'll defend their honor."

Taylor knew a thing or two about the extremes the daoine sídhe would go to defend their honor. Visions of fae armies marching through Macon swirled in her imagination.

She remembered something Silas Bludgitt had told her about the massacre at Bailly Hen when he was young: that Topsiders thought it was a tornado outbreak. A war in the faery world would bleed over to the mortal world, too, she realized. Her parents—and Jill and William—wouldn't be safe.

"The other woman, Osanda, seemed completely stunned. I don't think she understood how deeply the rift runs between the nunnehi and the sídhe. But emotions are running high. Chief Nocosi suggested she go home while she still could."

"Somebody's got to do something!" Taylor shouted.

"Right now, no one can agree what to do. People are taking sides. Some warriors are still loyal to Athlan. They would defend him to the death. Others side with the Chiefs. They want Athlan found—but that doesn't mean they agree about what to do with him when he is."

"Well that's just great," Taylor said. She tried again to sit up, and this time she made it. "Mrs. Birdsong is missing, and the nunnehi are preparing for war."

"That's about the size of it," Ayoka said.

"And nobody knows where Athlan has taken her?"

Ayoka shook her head. "Every ring portal for a hundred miles has been locked down. The whole city is on high alert. Our warriors have combed the countryside for hours. Nothing."

"They'll find 'em," Danny said. "They've got to."

"He could be anywhere," Taylor said. He probably knew the woods around Ichisi as well as anybody. Even carrying Mrs. Birdsong, he could have made pretty good time, gotten to a ring portal before the lock-down. It was hopeless. "He's gone."

"Nunnehi trackers are top notch," Danny insisted. "And they can be as dogged as the Wild Hunt when they put their mind to it. Why, there was a time back a hundred and twenty years ago, me and Claudia was..."

Taylor raised a hand to silence him.

"What?" he said.

"I bet they *are* as dogged as the Wild Hunt," Taylor said. "And just as shortsighted." A weird possibility was coming into focus. It was crazy. Then again, kidnapping Gwenllian Birdsong was crazy!

"What if he's holed up somewhere close by?"

"Why would he do that?" Ayoka asked.

"Maybe he wants to hang around to see what happens next. Maybe he's going to hold Mrs. Birdsong for ransom—force the Summer Court to do something he wants."

"Put Osanda on the Triad?" Danny said. His expression— or what could be seen of it under his bandages—said he wasn't convinced.

"Who knows?" Taylor said. "Maybe he's just nuts. But I'll bet that's it."

"What's it?" Ayoka said.

"It's got to be," Taylor said. She grabbed Ayoka's shoulder and pulled herself up. "He's got a hiding place near here. That's where he's taken her, where not even the Wild Hunt could find him."

"Where?" Danny said.

"The most unmagical place around." Still leaning on Ayoka's shoulder, she said, "We've got to tell your grandfather."

Ayoka led Taylor toward the door.

Danny was up in a flash. "Hey, wait for me!"

Chief Tewa and the Chiefs of Ichisi were meeting in the Council House with the city elders. Getting there and getting in were two different things, however. Not even Ayoka could convince the guards at the door that Taylor had important information to share. In fact, they glared at Taylor and Danny as if they were guilty of something.

The whole city really was on edge, Taylor realized. And when the sídhe came to claim their Triad member—and it was only a

278

matter of time before they did—something bad was bound to happen.

Ayoka finally convinced a guard to pass Chief Tewa a written note. They waited half an hour with no response.

They waited an hour.

The sun kissed the top of the sky and began its slow afternoon descent.

Taylor paced back and forth.

Danny scratched at his bandages.

"This isn't getting us anywhere," Taylor said at last.

"They're trying to figure things out," Ayoka said. "It takes time."

"I've already figured it out!" Taylor snapped. She turned toward the door and shouted, "*All they have to do is listen!*"

The guards stepped forward. Their flaming war clubs crackled to life.

A third warrior emerged from the Council House.

"Tsisgwa!" Ayoka said. She ran forward, but he waved her off.

"I'm to send Taylor home," he said.

"What?" Taylor said.

"For your own safety. The situation in Ichisi is too volatile. You're better off Topside with your parents."

"Fine," Taylor said. It was anything but fine. "But what about Ayoka's note?"

"The Chiefs send assurances they will pursue every possible lead."

"In other words, they don't believe me," Taylor quipped.

"It isn't that they don't believe you, Taylor," Tsisgwa said. "There's just so much going on...they don't know what to believe."

"*I'm telling them what to believe,*" Taylor said. "*They just have to listen.*"

Tsisgwa stepped back.

He shook off the effects of Taylor's presence and said, "Please come with me. And your friend." He nodded toward Danny.

"Come on, Taylor," Danny said. "If there's one thing I know, it's you can't get a politician moving any faster than he wants to move."

"But—"

"Let's go, Taylor," Ayoka said. "You really will be safer. I'll keep pestering them about your note. I promise."

They stopped at Tsisgwa's house long enough for Taylor to collect her bag.

Tsisgwa escorted Taylor, Danny, and Ayoka through town to the north gate, then outside the palisade and up the side of a mound.

Taylor was still limping. Her leg felt warm from the healing lotion. Another couple hours and she'd be good as new. Her left arm was still numb, though. It itched like crazy under her bandages, and she could barely make a fist.

She sighed. All that would just make what she was planning even harder.

Tsisgwa pulled what looked like a powder horn from over his shoulder, unstoppered it, and circled the mound, chanting and sprinkling a fine, green powder behind him.

When he completed the circle, he approached Taylor.

"I've enchanted the ring to open for only a second. Once you're Topside, you're on your own."

"Stay safe, Taylor," Ayoka said.

"Nobody's safe," she answered. "The Summer Court is going to come looking for Mrs. Birdsong, and they are not going to wait patiently for your grandfather and the others to finish their stupid meeting."

As if on cue, a cold wind blew across the mound.

She said out loud what she had been thinking for the last hour. "I've got to go there."

"Taylor, don't—"

"When the nunnehi finally figure out I'm right, they'll need a guide. No one in Ichisi knows the Topside world like I do. I'll go on ahead. Poke around a little, see what I can see."

Danny shook his head—then winced and placed a hand against his jaw. "That ain't smart," he said.

"I'm not stupid," Taylor said. "I know I can't fight Athlan. I don't intend to. I'm just going to see if I can give the nunnehi an advantage...assuming they come around."

"It's time," Tsisgwa said.

"Danny, I'd feel better if you'd come with me."

"Me, too," Ayoka said. "I'll help."

Tsisgwa started to object, but Ayoka shot daggers at him. He sighed. He knew when he was beaten.

"If you insist on going," he told her, "then take this." Then he slipped his war club from his belt and handed it to her.

"You know how to use it?"

"You taught me," she said, and smiled.

Taylor looked at Danny.

"What do you say?"

He blew a labored breath. "Yeah, I'll go. For you. And for Claudia."

"I knew I could count on you."

"Yeah, well. Summer Court. Winter Court. How much worse could a deranged nunnehi be?"

Chapter 27

The Colors of War

William's dad took him and Jill for a driving lesson on Sunday afternoon. It went pretty well, overall. The parking lot at Riverview High was empty: plenty of room to practice starting, stopping, and steering Mr. Matthews's old Toyota. William couldn't wait to get his learner's permit next fall. His dad just kept mumbling something about insurance rates.

Jill only freaked out once, when she hit the brake a little too hard. William had some choice words to say about his sister's driving. It was probably just a coincidence that the "Check Engine" light flashed on at that exact same time.

On the way home, they picked up pizza for supper. Mr. Matthews pulled into the driveway, and William carried the boxes toward the door.

That was when he heard his sister gasp. He wheeled around. She was staring open-mouthed at a trio of figures walking up the street.

"Taylor?" she said.

Her best friend walked slowly, gingerly, as if she had twisted an ankle or something. Her arm was wrapped in a bandage, and her black leather jacket was draped over her shoulders like a cape. It looked like she had slept in the blue and white dress she was wearing. Or maybe fought a wrestling match, because it looked like she hadn't slept in a week.

Two others walked on either side of her. She was leaning against Danny Underhill. He looked like he'd been through the ringer, too. Half his face was purple and swollen, and his curly hair was a mess. His amber eyes faintly glowed.

William didn't recognize the other person—a girl maybe Taylor's age. Black hair. Medium brown skin. Kind of pretty. Okay, very pretty—but something about the fire in her dark eyes made him want to keep his distance. She was dressed in jeans with tall leather boots and a buckskin jacket. What really got William's attention was the club resting on her shoulders: over three feet long, with a weighted knob at the top.

Mr. Matthews noticed them, too. "W-what the...?"

Taylor saw Jill. She hurried ahead of Danny and the other girl. "Jill," she let the word out like a weary sigh. She was still invisible to William's Second Sight, but it was obvious enough she was tired and scared.

The other two stopped abruptly at the edge of the property. Danny stretched out his foot, then drew it back. He shrugged at the dark-haired girl.

With his Second Sight, William saw the same ghostly cat pacing, stalking toward the newcomers. Daring them to cross into its territory.

"Taylor, what's going on?" Mr. Matthews said.

She looked at him and sighed. "I need to talk to Jill for a minute," she said.

"Come on, son. Let's tell your mom and Maymay that supper's here." He put his hand on William's shoulder and guided him inside. But his body was still turned toward the yard. It didn't take Second Sight to know something weird was going on.

Jill and Taylor sat on the front stoop while Mr. Matthews got out cups and plates and napkins.

William set the pizzas on the counter and hovered in the living room, waiting for Jill to come in. Mrs. Matthews called him to the table.

"I'm coming," he called.

"Don't let your supper get cold," Maymay said. She was waiting for him in the entryway.

"Right," he said. "It's just..."

284

"You've been concerned about your sister."

William nodded. *And Taylor*, he thought. What he said was, "She and Taylor have been friends forever."

Maymay leaned into Willam and set a hand on his shoulder. "But ever since...that time at the mall..."

"It's hard to accept that people aren't always what they seem," Maymay said. "It makes things complicated."

"Maymay?" He paused. He wasn't sure what he needed to say. "Can I ask you something and you promise to tell me the truth?"

"I have never lied to you, William."

"I know...." He took a deep breath. "Maymay, do you think Taylor will turn out like...like the rest of the Good Neighbors?"

Maymay rested on her walking stick. She gazed into William's eyes, and he was fairly sure she was looking at him with her Second Sight.

"The Good Neighbors do as they please," she said. "They're not always predictable. When you think you've got them figured out, that's when they'll do something just to throw you."

"So...is that a yes or a no?"

Maymay shrugged. "Honey, that's a 'how in the world should I know?'"

"Oh."

"But I can tell you this: I've watched Taylor for a while." She started back toward the dining room.

"What does that mean?" William asked.

Maymay stopped. "I don't like what she did at the mall," she said firmly. "She let her feelings get the best of her, and somebody got hurt. A girl like Taylor cannot afford to lose control, William."

William glanced out the living room window. Jill and Taylor were still sitting on the stoop. Danny and the girl were still waiting by the curb, pretending not to notice them.

"I guess not."

"But she did it to protect a friend," Maymay said. And she looked William in the eye. "A *mortal* friend."

285

He swallowed.

"I don't know what she'll be like when she's older," Maymay said. "But right now? There's nothing she wouldn't do for her friends."

The front door swung open. Jill and Taylor came in just as Maymay left the living room. Both of them looked like they'd been crying.

"William," Taylor said. She took a deep breath. "I need to say I'm sorry."

"Okay."

"No, I mean it. I've been a jerk. I haven't been myself. Or maybe I have been myself—but who I am...isn't always a very nice person."

"Taylor, you don't—"

"Will you just shut up and listen?"

Jill put a hand on Taylor's arm. Taylor took a breath and started over.

"I never meant to scare you—or Jill. And I sure never meant to offend your grandmother. I...I've had a lot on my mind lately. That's not an excuse, it's just... There are things you don't understand—not that it matters; I was still a jerk. Not sugar-coating it. Not making excuses... Gah! I suck at apologies!"

"Taylor?"

"Yes?"

"Are you and Jill cool now?"

They traded glances. Taylor nodded.

"Then that's good enough for me."

"William," Jill said. She looked serious. "Taylor explained a little of what's been going on with her. There's trouble."

He looked at Taylor's bandaged arm. He caught a glance of Taylor's friends still waiting outside. The girl with the club was pacing, agitated.

"What kind of trouble?"

Taylor filled him in. Some kind of fae bigwig had been kidnapped, and it was only a matter of time before the woman's people came looking for her. The problem was, the Fair Folk

286

who lived in Macon—it took William a while to process that—looked like they might be responsible. Taylor's people would want revenge. And it all might spill over into the mortal world.

"Taylor thinks she knows where they took her," Jill explained. "She and Danny and the other girl—"

"Ayoka," Taylor added.

"—and Ayoka are going to go look."

William sucked in a breath. "Why Taylor? There aren't any grown-ups who can handle it?"

"They're 'discussing' the matter," Taylor said with obvious scorn.

"But what can you do?"

"Keep an eye on things," Taylor said. "Send word if I find something."

"Just let me get my scrying bowl," Jill said.

Taylor whipped around to face her. "No."

"Right," William agreed. "It sounds dangerous."

"Hush, William," Jill said. Then: "Taylor, you can't do this by yourself."

"I've got Danny and Ayoka."

"Well, you've got me, too. You've got three sets of eyes. Why not four?"

"I'm not putting you in danger," Taylor said. "This is big-league stuff we're talking about."

"Hmm. As big league as your crazy-pants grandma last summer?"

"Yes—and we all know how that turned out."

"William, Jill," Mrs. Matthews called. "Your pizza is getting cold." She turned the corner. "Hello, Taylor."

"Hi, Mrs. Matthews."

"Mom, can I go hang out with Taylor?"

"Well, I suppose, but—"

"Thanks, Mom!" Jill spun around, grabbed Taylor by the arm, and hauled her toward the door.

"Wait a minute!" William called. "If you're going, I'm going!" He'd promised his dad he'd keep Jill safe. It didn't matter how

287

much Taylor said otherwise, this little excursion sounded like the opposite of safe!

Taylor shook her head. "That's not really necessary..."

"Sure it is," William said. "I can help with the...thing."

Mrs. Matthews quirked an eyebrow. "The thing?"

"Yeah. Actually, I should go get some...stuff. I'll be right back."

Taylor hung her head.

"And take some pizza with you," Mrs. Matthews said. "I won't have Taylor's mom put out by unexpected house guests."

"Thanks, Mom!" William called. He grabbed a jacket and a gym bag from his room and then bounded downstairs. He looked over Maymay's shelves—the potions and spells he and Jill had put together under her direction. The wooden scrying bowl Jill had brought back with her from New Orleans. He threw everything he thought might be useful into his bag.

Maymay met him at the foot of the stairs.

"Something tells me you aren't going over to play video games."

William sighed. He couldn't get upstairs without going through Maymay, both literally and figuratively.

"Well..."

She gave him a wistful look. "Did I ever tell you about my great-granddaddy?"

"I...don't think so."

"He was a Houma medicine man," Maymay said. "He's where we...uh...got it."

"You mean magic?"

She smiled. It was the kind of sad, gentle smile she had given him and Jill when Pawpaw died, assuring them everything was going to be okay. "That's right. He wasn't but three years old when he wandered into the bayou. The People of the Forest found him there. They must have thought he had potential, though, because that's when they awakened him."

William didn't know what to say. He stood there, his heart racing, as Maymay continued her story.

288

"Our family's had the gift pretty much ever since. One in every generation until…" She trailed off. As she leaned on her walking stick, she seemed to carry the weight of the world on her shoulders.

"Maymay?"

"Our family's been mixed up with the Good Neighbors since then. Looks like they still are."

"Maymay, Jill wants to help Taylor with something." He paused and looked his grandmother in the eye. "Jill won't go if you tell her not to."

"I can't do that," Maymay said, shaking her head. "Lord knows I want to."

"I don't understand."

She sighed. "You and Jill never asked for this." She spread her arms to indicate the circle of power on the floor, the workbench, the bottles and bags of outlandish ingredients. "But you landed in the middle of it. Jill, bless her heart, got thrown into the deep end last summer. Now you've got to learn it, and you've got to learn it fast—faster than I ever did."

William scrunched his eyebrows. "Do you want us to stay here?"

She ignored the question and asked one of her own. "You want to know the secret to strong magic, William?"

He nodded tentatively.

"Sacrifice."

"Sacrifice."

"That's why I've taught you to meditate. To fast. To do your breathing exercises. But personal discipline can only go so far. There comes a time when a practitioner has got to reach down and find out what he or she is willing to lose. Like Frederick Douglass said, 'If there is no struggle, there is no progress.'"

"You think helping Taylor will be a struggle?"

"Honey, having Taylor in your life in the first place is a struggle!"

William chuckled in spite of himself.

289

"But I also know that you and Jill need to make progress. Before something worse comes along."

William wondered what his grandmother knew—or what she feared.

"So...we can go?"

"Go find out what you're made of." She reached out her arms, and William fell into them.

Maymay sighed. She backed away and held William by the shoulders. She looked at him for the longest time. "If anybody opens a door to the faery world..."

"I'll run the other way," William said. "And if anybody offers me food, I'll just say no."

"That's my grandbaby." Maymay smiled. "Keep your eyes open, you hear?"

"Sure thing, Maymay. Talk to Mom and Dad for us?"

"Of course," she said.

He shouldered his gym bag and ran upstairs, out the door, and into the yard. Taylor introduced him to Ayoka and re-introduced him to Danny. Up close, it was even harder to imagine he ever passed for a thirteen-year-old kid last year.

"Are you sure about this?" Taylor asked. She looked around, not just at Jill and William but at the others as well. "None of you have to do this, you know."

"I think we kinda do," William said.

They all nodded.

"Okay," Taylor said. "I've called for backup." She showed William a smooth, reddish stone before slipping it into her pocket. "But with the ring system shut down, I don't know if they'll make it."

"How are *we* going to make it?" Danny asked.

"The Topside way," Taylor said. She limped toward her house, across the street and two doors up from the Matthewses.

She dug her house key out of her purse and opened the door.

"Dad?" she called.

She went in and gestured for the rest to join her. Danny, Ayoka, William, and Jill crowded in the entryway.

Mr. Smart appeared. His eyes grew wide at the sight of the five of them. Ayoka held her club at her side and angled her body so it wasn't quite as obvious that she was armed with a deadly weapon.

"Uh...?"

"Dad, this is Ayoka...and Danny."

William could pinpoint the exact second Mr. Smart's gaze moved from Danny's bruised face to his pointed ears. That was when his mouth dropped open.

"Pleased to meet you, Mr. Smart," Danny said.

"It is an honor," Ayoka added.

"We were kind of wondering," Taylor said. "Would you drive us to the mall?"

As soon as Taylor changed back into her jeans and tee shirt, everybody piled into Mr. Smart's green minivan. Taylor rode shotgun. Danny and Jill sat in the middle seat. Danny seemed fidgety for some reason. William and Ayoka squeezed into the back. He held his gym bag on his lap and tried not to get any closer to Ayoka than he had to. For one thing, that war club of hers looked dangerous. For another, he was afraid of what that war club might do to him if she thought he was trying to get fresh with her.

"I'm not sure about this," Mr. Smart said for about the hundredth time.

"We're just going to look around," Taylor said. She put her hand on his. "Dad, this is important."

"You really think Athlan is at River Crossing?" Danny said. He shivered and darted his head from side to side.

"Mostly sure," Taylor admitted. "Our Kind are pretty clueless about the Topside world. I bet that's what he's counting on."

"But why the mall?" Jill said.

"I already explained it," Taylor said. "Two things. First, it's completely out in the sticks, magically speaking. Chain stores, money, consumerism. It's like an alien planet to somebody raised in the Wonder."

"You're right about that," Ayoka said. "We have no need for money. And as for these 'chain stores'... I don't even know what you're talking about."

"But Athlan does," Taylor said, twisting around to look at her. "That's the second thing. Athlan told me I should buy cedar-wood oil from a Topside store. He said it once a few months ago, but he said it again yesterday. That's what got me thinking. He's been to a Topside mall. He knows what they're like."

"He knows the cops won't think to look there," William said, "...or whatever you all call the good guys."

"And you're just going to look around?" Mr. Smart said. "You promise?"

"The good guys are on their way," Taylor said. "At least, they will be as soon as Ayoka's grandpa can get them in gear."

"But they'll be lost, won't they?" William said. "They'll miss things you and Jill and I would see right away."

"That's what I'm hoping," Taylor said. She turned back to her dad. "We're not looking for a fight, Dad. Once was enough."

Ayoka leaned into William. "But if there's fighting, I'm glad you'll be there."

"Huh?"

"Your shirt," she whispered. "You wear the colors of a warrior—and the emblem of a powerful magician."

William had look down to remember what shirt he was wearing.

"It's a Spider-Man tee shirt," he said, bewildered.

"Red and black," Ayoka said with approval. "The colors of war."

Nobody else said anything until Mr. Smart pulled into a parking space near the front of the shopping center.

Danny was out of the car in a flash. Jill followed, then Ayoka and William crawled out of the back.

"Call," Mr. Smart said.

"I will," Taylor promised. With that, Mr. Smart pulled away.

292

Chapter 28

The Dark Domain

The parking lot was mostly empty. It was nearly dark, and the mall closed early on Sundays. Taylor gazed from one end of the complex to the other. Everything seemed normal. The only things out of place were Ayoka with her war club and Danny with his pointed ears.

What if she was wrong? What if Athlan and Gwenllian were a hundred miles away? She imagined Athlan laughing at her for thinking she could outwit him, and it made her curse under her breath.

That's when William hissed a curse of his own.

"Of all the..."

"What?" Taylor edged toward him.

"Look, I know we had to be cool around your dad and all, but you realize this could get dangerous, right?"

Taylor bit her lip. "Yeah?"

He spread his arms so his shirt showed beneath his jacket. "So look who showed up in a red shirt!"

"William, this is not a *Star Trek* episode."

"Yeah, but—"

"We need a plan—and Ayoka, you're...attracting attention."

Danny had used glamour to look like an ordinary, dorky teenager, but shoppers on the sidewalks were giving Ayoka wary looks. With that war club on her shoulder, it wouldn't be long before somebody called security.

"I see," she said. The next second, she was gone—completely invisible.

293

Jill let out a gasp. William took the Lord's name in vain.

"Uh…. Well, then," Taylor said. She tried to gather her thoughts. "Okay. Danny, Ayoka, and I have Seeing Stones. Jill, William and I have phones. We need to be in contact if we see anything."

Everyone—at least, everyone visible—nodded.

Taylor pointed. "William and Danny, you go right. Jill and I will go left. We'll circle around and compare notes when we meet by the fountain on the green." She indicated the far side of the complex. She looked where Ayoka might have still been standing. "Ayoka, you go down the center and keep your eyes open. Call in if you see anything. Everybody clear?"

"Clear," Ayoka said from somewhere.

"Let's do this," William sighed.

Taylor and Jill headed out. As they walked past the entrance to an Italian restaurant, Jill nearly bumped into a bronze statue of a boy on his tricycle. For a second, Taylor's eyes met hers. She recognized the distant glaze, the look of barely contained terror.

"No Second Sight," Taylor commanded.

"Shouldn't we be looking for magic?"

"No Second Sight," Taylor repeated, punctuating each word with her index finger. "If you can't shut it down…"

"I can handle it," Jill said. "It's just…so many people."

Taylor looked around. There were maybe three shoppers walking to their cars. She could see a couple of employees in the nearest shop window closing down for the night.

This was looking less and less like a good plan.

She opened up her own magical senses. She wasn't sure if what she did was the same thing as Jill. It definitely didn't freak her out—then again, she didn't have her senses thrown into overdrive by a manipulative fae woman!

Anyway, Taylor didn't think of what she could do in terms of sight. It was more a gut feeling, a sense of when or if magic was being used nearby.

There was something—vague, indefinite. It might have been Jill, or maybe Ayoka lurking invisibly around the corner. Nothing to pin her hopes on.

She wished she had tried some of Athlan's cedar oil.

Hmm.

"Let's pick it up."

"What?"

"I have an idea."

When the sun set, the mall was already closed. Lights in the parking lot blazed cold and white. Employees were either locking up for the night or finishing their closing routines.

She was used to seeing River Crossing full of people. Now it felt empty. Creepy. Sure, the restaurants on the front side of the complex would still be open for a couple of hours, but that seemed too far away to count.

Taylor picked up the pace, rounding the corner and heading back toward the middle of the shopping center.

She wondered why she hadn't seen any security guards.

"Okay," she said. "Let me think."

They had stopped in front of the Yankee Candle. It was dark except for the security lights. Taylor tried to sense anything unusual.

Nothing.

The only sound was the splashing of water in the fountain somewhere behind them.

"You think they could be in *there*?" Jill said.

"That would be too easy," Taylor said. "I was just hoping I'd see something. Find some kind of clue."

Taylor became aware of Danny and William approaching in the dark.

She rested her hands on her hips.

"If I was hiding from the nunnehi, where would I go?" she asked herself.

"Maybe what you said before," Jill said. "Find the most unmagical place you can."

Taylor sighed. "You're right. This isn't it."

"What isn't it?" William asked. He and Danny were jogging toward them.

"I thought..." Taylor suddenly stopped. "Hmm. Maybe."

"What?" Danny said.

"Places like this have a business office, right?"

"Sure," William said. "It's over by the fountain, right? Next to Dairy Queen."

"Let's give it a look."

The grassy space between Yankee Candle and Dairy Queen was called the Village Green Courtyard. In the center was the fountain Taylor had heard earlier. Taylor scryed for Ayoka to meet them there and the rest were on their way.

Danny sidestepped another bronze statue—a boy laying on the grass, reading with his dog at his side.

Taylor felt cool, wet air on her face. A fog was rolling in. Past experience suggested that wasn't a good sign.

The business office was inside an alcove between two stores. There were vending machines, a water fountain, and a maze of offices behind a wall of tinted glass.

Ayoka was standing, visible, outside the doors and looking in.

"Do you see something?" Taylor asked.

She shook her head. "But I *feel* something."

"Let me see," Jill said. She shut her eyes.

Taylor tried to stop her. "Jill, don't—"

"I've got this," she insisted, eyes still closed. She took a few deep breaths before opening them again.

She trembled slightly. Taylor resisted the urge to run to her. Instead, she waved everyone else back.

"Give her some room," William said.

Jill drifted around the alcove as if in a trance. Past the offices, the corridor opened to the left to some kind of loading area. The other side was just a bare brick wall, like the wall at the far end.

"Light," Jill said.

Taylor summoned faery fire and held it aloft. Jill approached the far wall.

296

"Here."

"Are you sure?" Taylor said. "I don't see anything."

"It's there," William said. "Whatever it is." He rummaged through his gym bag and slipped a piece of purple sidewalk chalk into Jill's hand.

She approached the wall. With a trembling hand, she made two long vertical lines, marking out the boundaries of an invisible doorway.

"Ayoka?" Taylor said. "Danny? Any ideas?"

Danny stepped forward. "It's just a really strong glamour, right?" He extended his hand. It passed through the bricks as if they weren't even there. His arm went in as far as the elbow, then stopped.

"There's some kind of knob...," he said. Something clicked, like metal on metal.

"Hold on!" William said. He was looking back toward the courtyard and the fountain.

"What's the matter?" Taylor said.

Ayoka was by William's side in an instant. She raised her club, ready to strike. It burst into crackling orange flame.

"I thought I saw something," William said.

The fog was thicker now, diffusing the glow of the security lights into smudgy blurs. William peered into the silver-gray nothingness.

Taylor leaned in, trying to see what William was looking at. She could barely make out the low, black shape of the fountain in the distance. The splash of the water and the low hum of the lights were the only sounds to be heard.

"Something like what?" Taylor said.

"Something moving."

Taylor held her faery fire aloft once more—and wished she hadn't.

Dark shapes were lumbering silently toward the business office.

A boy with a book under his arm and a dog at his side.

Two little girls.

297

A boy on a tricycle.

All made of bronze.

"The statues," Taylor whispered. She grabbed William by the shoulder. "The statues have come to life!"

Just then, the little dog sprang forward. Ayoka met it with her club and flung it back toward the fountain.

The little girls smiled knowingly at each other.

Taylor blasted the first one on instinct. It had no effect: the girl kept trudging forward. She was in no hurry, it seemed.

Taylor blasted her again—a stupid move, she realized. She hadn't given herself enough time to recharge. Once more, the attack had no effect.

"Danny? A little help here!"

By then, the statue was in striking distance. It kicked Taylor in the gut, and she fell back into Danny as he ran up from behind her.

William stepped in front of the second girl and swept his leg to trip her. She sprawled on the ground.

By then, Ayoka had smashed in the head of the first statue.

William heaved the second one out of the alcove. "They're still coming!" he shouted.

He was right: Taylor gazed across the green and saw other statues on their way. As if that weren't bad enough, the ones they'd dealt with weren't *staying* dealt with. They were shaking themselves off.

Danny cursed. "I must have tripped some kind of alarm!"

Taylor looked forward and back.

"We've got to hold them off!" she said.

"I'm on it!" William called. He had laid his gym bag on the concrete and was busy grabbing things out of it. "Just keep them off me!"

"With pleasure," Ayoka said as she slammed her club into the boy with the book like she was hitting a home run at Turner Field.

The bronze dog bounded toward Danny. He conjured a shield spell in time to deflect it toward Ayoka, who brained it with her club.

Meanwhile, William emptied three bags of grayish powder onto the ground in front of the alcove and tossed two more bags to Jill, who did the same thing at the rear entrance. Taylor had forgotten there was another way in!

A bronze girl, her little sister, and their toddler brother came toward them. Danny tried to blast them, but they kept coming.

"Blasting don't work!" he said.

"No kidding!" Taylor shouted.

There were nearly a dozen of them now converging on the alcove. None of them were taller than about four feet, and all of them wore the smiles the sculptor had cast them with. They looked like they were having the time of their lives.

Taylor spun around to Danny and pointed toward the back wall. "What are the chances that door will get us out of here?"

"Are you nuts?" Danny exclaimed. "That's got to be a shortcut straight to Athlan." He looked nervously at William and Jill. "Your friends are all right, but I don't like the idea of them entering the Wonder."

"Me neither," Taylor sighed.

William shouted, "*Hexiphore!*" Taylor felt a subtle snap, a pulse of magical energy as William's spell took effect.

The three skipping children reached the edge of the powder William had spread out and came to a halt. They pushed as if against an invisible barrier.

"That'll hold them?" Taylor said.

"Maybe," William said. "I'm not going to bet my life on it." He took a piece of sidewalk chalk from his gym bag and began to draw a huge circle that blocked the entire entrance to the alcove. Taylor and Danny moved backward to get out of his way.

The bronze children kept testing the boundaries of William's spell. A little girl with a butterfly on the end of her finger inched closer.

Taylor sighed. She looked at Danny. "Maybe you and I can find the off switch," she said.

Danny scratched his bushy head. "I don't know what spell William put down, but it ain't gonna last all night."

Another statue joined the girl with the butterfly: a boy on stilts. He also crept closer, leaving long scraping tracks through William's powder.

Danny exhaled. "But I ain't got any better ideas."

"Okay guys," Taylor shouted. "New plan! Danny and I are going in. We'll find a way to get rid of these statues. If we can't do that, maybe we can find all of us a way to safety."

"You can't be serious!" Jill called.

The boy with the book flung it just within the boundary of William's spell.

"I don't see any other options, do you?" Taylor said.

"What are we supposed to do?" William said. He rummaged through his gym bag looking for something useful.

"Hold the line," Taylor said. "We don't want to be trapped down there with no way out. Ayoka," she stopped, realizing what she was about to say. She looked the nunnehi girl in the eye. "Protect my friends."

Ayoka's eyes blazed. She gritted her teeth, faced the swarm of statues, and swung her club in a fiery figure-eight.

Taylor hoped they could be threatened by that kind of thing.

Danny reached his hand into the brick wall like he did before. His arm disappeared. Then his entire body vanished at once like it had been sucked through a straw.

Taylor groaned. She had seen something like this before, when she entered her cousin Évastre's place last summer. She groped around inside the wall until she, too, found the knob Danny had talked about. She grabbed it and pulled—and then felt herself being yanked into the Wonder.

It felt a lot like it looked. Her whole body seemed to constrict, twist, and liquefy. It only lasted half a second, though, and then she slammed into Danny's back.

They were in a forest. Above them, the sky was dim orange. No clouds, no stars, no wind. Only a vague emanation of light barely brighter than dusk. The only real light came from an orb of faery fire Danny held in his hand.

Taylor coughed. The air was thick with the smell of pine and sweet, fertile soil.

"Where are we?"

"Deep in the Wonder," Danny said. He had noticed the weird orange sky, too. "Powerful fae'll pinch off a bit, turn it into their own private domain."

"So this is the only way out?"

"As far as I know."

So there wasn't likely a back door. So much for that part of the plan.

They were at the end of a narrow path. Behind them was five-foot outcropping of rock on which a brass knob was set—the only evidence of fae workmanship in sight.

The path led downward at a steep angle. Tangled roots lay exposed, forming a staircase that might almost have been intentional.

"Glamour?" Taylor said.

Danny nodded. They both took a second to cover themselves in magical mist, shielding their presence.

They crept down the path, deeper and deeper into the woods.

At the bottom was a creek. It didn't look deep at all, but Danny frowned even so.

"Water," he whispered. "If we cross it, we'll lose some of our magic."

"You pick the greatest times to tell me these rules, you know that?"

"I just thought you'd want to know."

Taylor sighed. "The path picks up on the other side. See?" She stuck her toe in the water.

"It doesn't look deep," she said, and conjured her own faery fire. Before Danny could stop her, she was halfway across.

The stream was shallow, but the water was icy cold as it splashed against the legs of her jeans. But with each step, Taylor felt her magic draining away. Her fire orb dwindled into nothing. She felt her glamour being stripped away. It left her exposed, an easy target for any homicidal, renegade nunnehi out there looking for some target practice.

Danny caught up with her on the other side. The path led up the bank of the creek, then ended in a T with both arms following the gentle arc of the creek bed. A lazy will-o'-the-wisp wafted through the trees. Just as well—both of them had lost their own fire orbs. Taylor tried to draw magical mist around her, concealing her once more. It didn't work.

Danny looked at Taylor and whispered, "Which way?"

Taylor shrugged and pointed right.

The path rose gently toward a little hill upstream. Taylor tried to use her magic senses with limited success. She stopped and took several deep breaths. She tried to put her natural senses to work, but she couldn't hear or smell or feel anything.

Danny tapped her on the shoulder, and she fought the urge to shout. He pulled her behind the nearest tree. Then she heard it: a gentle thud-thud of something coming down the path.

She scrunched as close to the tree trunk as she could manage.

A deer trotted past. It was big, brown doe, and it came to a halt in front of the tree where they were hiding.

It looked this way and that.

It looked unusually intelligent to Taylor, like it was on a mission. Then she realized it was. It was looking for them: it had to be.

But it didn't see them—or smell them, or whatever sense deer use to detect enemies. In a minute, it trotted along.

A minute after that, Taylor remembered to breathe.

Danny prodded them forward.

"That wasn't an ordinary doe," Taylor said.

302

"Probably somebody faring forth," Danny said. "I bet Athlan noticed us coming through the portal."

"There's a pleasant thought."

The path branched again. To the left, a path ascended perpendicular to the stream. The other branch continued straight ahead.

Danny gestured for Taylor to stay back. He crept to the left passage and, feeling somewhat safe, took two or three steps down the middle of it. He cupped a hand to a pointed ear and stood there for several seconds before hurrying back to Taylor.

He pushed her back into the trees.

First, Taylor heard their heavy footsteps. Then she heard their voices: a series of snorts, hoots, and whistles. She didn't see their huge, lumbering forms until they were nearly on top of them.

Both were over eight feet tall and covered with hair from head to foot. They walked upright, but they reminded Taylor of giant gorillas.

Bigfoots are real? Taylor thought. Then she rolled her eyes and shook her head. *Of course, Bigfoots are real. What was I thinking?*

They entered the crossroads where the three paths converged. The one in front raised a hand, and the other stopped. They peered into the woods all around—they knew something was up. They might have been ape-men, but they weren't idiots.

Taylor tried once more to conjure magical mist. This time, it might have worked; she wasn't sure. At any rate, she and Danny crouched behind a patch of trees and tried to be invisible.

The first Bigfoot sniffed around. It grunted, addressing the trees. A taunt, no doubt. Come out, come out, wherever you are.

The first creature went forward, further up the path that followed the stream. The other went back the way Taylor and Danny had come.

Taylor held her breath as the second Bigfoot crept closer. It couldn't see her, but she could tell by its expression it guessed she was close.

She glanced at Danny. He had figured it out, too. They were about to be caught. Taylor didn't relish the idea of being captured by creatures who were probably working for Athlan.

Danny gestured toward the path from which the Bigfoots had come.

Right, Taylor thought. *Wherever these things came from is where things are happening.*

Of course, that was also where they'd find Athlan Tastanagi.

Somewhere in her gut, Taylor realized Danny was about to give her a distraction.

She had only just realized that when Danny lunged at the nearest creature, transforming into dog form in mid-air.

"Arrgh!" it called. It held up a massive arm to defend itself, but too late. Danny didn't bowl the creature over, but he did force it to back away. Then, like lightning, he was barreling toward the second creature.

Taylor stood stunned for only a second.

She bolted through the trees.

Danny had heard of kolowas, but he'd never had to face one—much less two. He hoped they were no worse than regular ogres. Even with the smell, he'd rather face them than more nunnehi.

The kolowa had sprayed its fear scent: a foul combination of skunk, sweat, dog poo, more skunk, and burning rubber. In his dog form, it was at least a hundred times worse than if Danny had to smell it with his everyday nose.

He feared he would pass out from the stench as the creature took a swipe at his flank, but he was too fast. Danny rolled and darted between the legs of his attacker.

His only hope was speed. It was time to try out the new form he'd been practicing. He still couldn't do any fancy magic, but a pooka who couldn't shape-shift wasn't worthy of the name.

The transformation took no more than a second. Danny's ears grew long and straight. Whiskers sprung out around his upper lip. His body contracted smaller than ever. He felt like he

304

was being smothered, constricted. But the feeling passed in an instant, and before the nunnehi were out of sight, he kicked off on his powerful hind legs.

He was a large, black rabbit.

Nailed it! he thought, twitching his whiskers.

He darted into the woods. In rabbit form, he could lose the beasts in the underbrush. And if he was lucky, they wouldn't even know about Taylor.

They howled and stomped after him, so big and clumsy on their two enormous legs. Danny leaped ahead, waited for them to see him and lunge toward him, then leaped again. The longer he could keep them occupied, the better it would be for Taylor.

He zigged and zagged through the forest with glee. This was his element. Despite the danger, he lived to make mischief and sow confusion.

I can do this all night! he exulted. He waited until the nearest kolowa was almost upon him before he bounded toward it, bolder than any ordinary rabbit, thumped his hind legs against the beast's hairy chest, bounced to the ground, and scampered in a circle around the other one.

He chuckled to himself at their hoots of frustration.

The biggest creature uttered a blood-curdling shriek. The next thing Danny knew, a tree branch was flying over his head.

Danny hopped away as fast as he could. He didn't stop until he was deep in the woods and he could hear no trace of his pursuers.

His tiny rabbit heart beat like crazy. He thought about shifting again, but there was an advantage to being so small.

He thought about Taylor, though. He had drawn the guards away, but now what?

She's smart, Danny told himself. *She'll have all her presence, and the rest of her magic will come back soon enough.*

But if not, there were still three others stuck Topside, trying to hold off an army of pint-sized bronze warriors. No matter how good they were, they couldn't do that all night.

305

He turned his ears around in every direction. The coast was clear.

Danny bolted back toward where he'd left Taylor.

Chapter 29

A Hasty Retreat

"They just keep coming!" Jill shouted.

"I know!" William shouted back. He had done everything he knew to do. The magic was keeping the bronze statues away—for now. But there were so many of them! A boy on stilts. Another with a Frisbee. A little girl in a bathing suit with a floaty around her waist. They weren't especially fast, and they didn't seem to be intelligent.

They were relentless. They pushed against the boundaries of William's banishing spell, and some of them were starting to push through.

Ayoka stood just outside the circle of power in which William and Jill stood. She swung her flaming war club and tossed it from hand to hand. The first statue through the boundary was in for a world of hurt. The seven or eight after that...

William studied the chalk border of the circle he had drawn.

At his feet was his gym bag and all his magical equipment. He didn't see how any of it could help.

But he wasn't going down without a fight. Jill needed him. So did Taylor.

He reached in and pulled out a tapering length of wood, fourteen inches long, carved with intricate knot work around the thickest end.

"You took Maymay's blasting rod?" Jill asked.

"Have you got a better idea?"

"You don't even know how it works!"

"Sure I do. It's all in her spell book."

307

"But you've never even tried—"

"Jill, listen. I know what I'm doing. Just let me be the big brother for once, all right?"

Jill planted her hands on her hips. "Big brother? Give me a break! You're only seventeen minutes older than me!"

CLANG!

Ayoka's club struck metal. William and Jill both whipped around. The little boy with the Frisbee had flung it across the expanse of the banishing spell, but Ayoka deflected it back to the ground. It lay in the no-man's land between the bronze horde and the three kids.

A bronze dog sniffed at the ground five feet away. It wanted to fetch the Frisbee, but it couldn't get any closer.

"If you two have a plan, I'd be happy to hear it!" Ayoka said.

"William's got the plan. *He's* the big brother!"

"Give it a rest, all right?" William nervously slapped the tip of the blasting rod against his thigh.

"Do you have any idea what those things are?"

"Bronze statues?" Ayoka offered.

"Okay, how do you animate a bronze statue?"

Ayoka buried the weighted head of her club in the face of the girl in the bathing suit, then shoved her backward with a kick to the gut. She sprawled on the ground and tried to do the backstroke.

The girl thrashed about as if unsure which way to go. The banishing spell pushed her away, but whatever magic had brought her to life compelled her to inch forward.

She probably looked funny to anyone who wasn't scared for their life.

"I'm going to help Ayoka," William decided. "That means I'm breaking the circle. Jill, you'll have to re-cast it as soon as I leave."

"But—"

"No buts." He stepped outside the chalk line.

"You're impossible, do you know that?"

"I love you, too."

William rushed to Ayoka's side.

"Glad you could join me," Ayoka said.

William clutched the blasting rod. He took a second to concentrate, to feel the flow of his magical aura like when he and Jill had practiced in the basement.

In from the left, out from the right, he told himself.

In his head, he knew how Maymay's tool should work. According to her notes, it worked something like a grounding switch, forcing the target to expel its magical potential.

He lowered the blasting rod at the nearest statue: a little girl with a bronze butterfly fluttering at the end of her hand.

He imagined his own magical reserves building up in his chest.

He extended his hand and uttered the incantation.

"*Bazagra!*"

A finger of silver light shot forth and touched the statue in the middle of the forehead.

It stopped.

William exhaled.

"It worked!" Jill hollered.

"Well done!" Ayoka added, smiling.

The effort left William woozy, but he was eager to try it again on the next statue. With any luck—

"Oh, crud," Jill said.

William's heart sank. The little girl with the butterfly was already on the move again.

"It looks like we can only slow them down," Ayoka said.

He took a breath.

There had to be another way.

"I was asking you how to animate a bronze statue?"

"You can't," Ayoka said with a grunt as she swept the stilts out from under the bronze boy who was walking on them.

"I hate to be disagreeable—*Bazagra!*—but I can think of at least a dozen reasons to question that!"

"Okay, then *I* can't. You can't. We don't have that kind of power. I don't know anyone who does."

309

"So this Athlan guy is either super-powerful..."

"Not encouraging," Jill added.

"...or he's found some kind of hack."

"Some kind of what?" Ayoka said. She crashed her club against the shoulder of a little bronze girl in overalls.

"That's geek-talk for 'He figured out a trick to make it work,'" Jill said.

"Ah."

The statues probed the boundaries of the banishing spell, but came no closer. William reached in his pocket. He had two baggies of banishing powder left, but he didn't want to use them if he didn't have to.

"Jill, your scrying bowl is in my bag," William said. "So's a bottle of water. See if you can zero in on where these statues used to be."

"Where they *used* to be? We know where they used to be!"

"Just humor me, okay? *Bazagra!*" Another statue stuttered to a halt.

"Fine, Mister Seventeen Minutes. Whatever you say!"

He didn't dare turn around to watch. He kept his eyes on the statues. The shopping center was cloaked now in a thick blanket of fog. It was probably keeping any mortals still at the mall from noticing anything.

He knew what was happening, though. Jill would pour out enough water to fill the bowl, then probably sit cross-legged at the center of the circle, gazing into it, opening her Second Sight, using the reflection of the water as a focus.

Second Sight was usually about the here and now. That's all he'd ever managed, anyway. But with a scrying bowl, Jill could sometimes See things at a distance.

He prayed this was one of those times.

Ayoka swung her club in a mighty arc. The boy on stilts fell backward. Again.

"They're still there!" Jill announced.

"Are you sure?"

310

"Of course I'm sure! It's plain as day: those girls cartwheeling, that boy reading his book—they're all still by the fountain."

"Then what's attacking us?"

Jill groaned, and William glanced at her over his shoulder. Her eyes popped with fright.

"Ghosts!" she squeaked.

"Don't look!" William shouted. He didn't want Jill to lose control of her Second Sight. Not now.

He reached in his jeans pocket for his jet amulet. He rubbed his thumb over its jagged surface, took a deep breath, and tried his own Second Sight.

Jill was right. The gathering army wasn't made of bronze at all. If anything, they looked like they were made of smoke. Kind of like the ghostly cat that appeared whenever somebody activated Maymay's wards on their house.

Just then, the boy threw his book at William. He didn't see it coming, and it caught him square in the chest. He stumbled backward, breaking the plane of Jill's magic circle. He felt the magic disappear with a pop, like the air pressure changing on an airplane.

The distraction ruined his concentration, and the approaching forms took on their original appearance.

A little girl with pigtails lunged at Ayoka, coming in under her club and grabbing her around the waist in a crushing bear hug.

Ayoka gasped and dropped her weapon.

William sprang forward. He picked up the club and slammed it into the little girl's back, then pulled Ayoka with him into the circle.

Thankfully, Jill was paying attention. As soon as William and Ayoka were inside, she refreshed the circle with new magic.

"They're wearing us down," Ayoka said. "We're starting to make mistakes."

"But they're not real!" Jill said.

"They're real enough," William said. "They're just not what they seem."

"An illusion," Jill said.

"We are rather good at those," Ayoka said.

"Too good." William paced, careful never to step too close to the circle's edge. The girl with the pigtails lunged forward, but stopped in her tracks at the circle's boundary. *Good*, William thought. With any luck, the circle would keep them safe, at least short-term. Lord knows, they were due for a little luck.

Ayoka was bent over with her hands on her knees. She breathed in harsh, gulping wheezes, an athlete who'd pushed herself to the limit. She needed a breather.

He wasn't much better off, even though she had done most of the physical work.

"Okay," he said. He took another couple of breaths, trying to settle himself down. "Those things aren't just illusions. They're solid."

"Constructs of some kind," Ayoka said. "That makes sense."

"And I'm guessing they're somehow tied to the statues—the real ones."

"Like Maymay's wards," Jill said. "Maymay buried those little statues in the yard…"

"That's what I'm thinking." William nodded.

"So how does any of this help us?" Jill asked.

William paced. The statue-constructs were swarming in front of the alcove now. The banishing spell had nearly worn off. He could only hope the magic circle would hold.

"We know how they work—at least in theory. We just need to…" He stopped himself.

"What?" Jill asked.

"Theory!" He returned to the center of the circle. "I've got an idea, Jill, but I'm going to need your help."

She glanced nervously at the approaching swarm.

"What do you need?"

"Everything you've got."

Taylor hid deep in the woods until she could feel her magic returning. She kept low and still, with her ears open for any hint the Bigfoots (Bigfeet?) were coming close.

When she thought it was safe, she found the path leading away from the stream. Danny thought this was the way to go. She suspected he was right, so off she went. Rather than risk faery fire, she let her eyes adjust to the dark.

Eventually she spied light ahead: a campfire.

She crept forward, keeping to the shadows.

The path opened into a clearing. Taylor climbed back into the woods and approached through the trees.

The clearing was about as big as a baseball infield. Near the center was a small wattle-and-daub house like many she'd seen at Ichisi: white plaster walls, thatched roof.

The campfire was burning outside, and between the fire and the open front door were two other Bigfoots.

They were sitting on stools made from sections of tree trunk. Between them was a table of similar make, and on the table was a checkerboard: the focus of the Bigfoots' attention.

Strewn at their feet were bones: the remains of a recent meal, no doubt. Taylor didn't want to know what they'd had for supper. Or who.

Athlan Tastanagi paced outside the door. He was ready for combat, with a bow and arrows slung across his back and his war club in his belt.

Taylor shrunk further into the trees.

He strode toward the fire, but he kept his eyes on the path.

"Your friends must have found something," he said at last.

The Bigfoots kept playing checkers.

"Hey!" he called. They looked up. "I'm going to see who's coming. Attend to my...guest." He cast his eyes toward the doorway and scowled.

Gwenllian, Taylor thought.

The Bigfoots rumbled and nodded.

Athlan pulled his war club from his belt and jogged away.

As soon as their master left, the Bigfoots hunched back over the checkerboard. One of them moved a checker. It grunted and snorted in what might have been a laugh: "I've got you now, sucker!"

The other Bigfoot emitted a low, rumbling growl. Then he looked at his opponent with a gleam in his eye and double-jumped his checker to his opponent's king row. He let out a gleeful hoot as if to say, "Crown me!"

The game went on for maybe ten minutes while Taylor watched and waited. A light was on inside the house: the only sign of civilization Taylor'd seen.

Gwenllian Birdsong was in there—and Athlan was gone, at least for the moment. Taylor didn't know if she was up for a rescue mission. She definitely didn't want to go up against Athlan again. But what choice did she have? Sure, the nunnehi might be on their way. Maybe by now they'd finally gotten around to checking out her theory. They'd see she was right and send in the cavalry.

Unless, of course, the daoine sídhe were already heading south across the border. In that case, the nunnehi would need every warrior they could muster to defend Ichisi.

She thought about her friends Topside. They were still busy fighting for their lives. She had hoped to find a safe escape route, or at least a way to call off the statues. It didn't look like either was likely.

Her eyes remained fixed on the house. What was going on in there? Could something in there deal with Athlan's Topside defenses?

The Bigfoots went back to their game. She decided to name them Hoot and Grunt after their respective favorite sounds. Hoot was a little bigger than Grunt. Taylor guessed he was about eight and a half feet tall (though it was hard to tell with them hunched over like they were), with Hoot closer to eight feet even.

A shadow crossed in front of the door. Taylor was right: it was Gwenllian. In the glow of the light inside, she looked

314

haggard. Her golden hair was mussed and tangled, but at least she was able to stand. That surprised Taylor after the beating Athlan had given her.

She stood in the doorway. One of the Bigfoots drew himself up to his full height, threw out his chest, and barked a challenge.

"I only want my coffee," Gwenllian said.

The Bigfoot hooted. He ambled toward the fire, snatched an old-fashioned coffee pot off the coals, and poured syrupy black liquid into a matching tin cup.

Gwenllian received the cup from the Bigfoot's massive paw. She didn't look pleased. No Starbucks in the Wonder, Taylor guessed.

Taylor wondered what to do. Was Gwenllian worth risking her life? Not even close. But getting her to safety might be the only way to keep the wrath of the daoine sídhe from falling.

Gwenllian wasn't worth it, but Ayoka and Tsisgwa were. And Danny and Wasko and Haggler and Pete. Not to mention Jill and William and any other Topsiders unlucky enough to get caught in the crossfire.

She didn't relish the idea of taking on either Bigfoot, much less both at the same time.

Then she heard something deeper in the woods. It was moving fast and light—too fast and light to be the other Bigfoots, or even Athlan.

Taylor settled her breathing and tried to sense what was coming.

She didn't get the chance. The next second, a pair of pale yellow eyes bounded toward her. A big, black rabbit poked its head out from the underbrush.

Taylor stifled a gasp.

The rabbit's body morphed and twisted and grew—and grew!—until it was Danny. He held up a finger to shush Taylor, but it wasn't necessary.

Taylor backed away from her hiding place to give Danny a hug. "A rabbit? You picked a rabbit for your new form?"

"Cool, huh?" he whispered. "What's the story?"

315

"Gwenllian's inside," she answered. "Those two things are the only guards I've seen. Athlan is somewhere in the woods."

Danny craned his neck to see the layout of the clearing better.

"I ditched their buddies good," he said. Then he grinned. "They're big and strong, but they ain't that smart. But they won't stay ditched forever. If you got a plan..."

Taylor studied the house.

Apparently, Hoot just won the game. Grunt scowled and, well, grunted. Hoot leaned back and crossed his arms in a satisfied, insufferable kind of way.

She glanced at the Bigfoots. "We could use a diversion."

Danny grinned. "I was hoping you'd say that."

Taylor skirted around the edge of the clearing, magic mist swirling around her like a cloak. When Danny set off his diversion, she wouldn't have much time. As she crept, she counted to herself—one Mississippi, two Mississippi—for a full two minutes.

Another minute.

Taylor stepped into the clearing. Even though she was invisible, she felt exposed. Another few steps, and there was no way she could run for cover if anything went wrong.

She approached the side of the house. Grunt and Hoot had started another game. They were grousing about something, at least that's what it sounded like.

As best Taylor could tell, her glamour was holding up.

So far, at least.

Then a sound pierced the night: a mournful baying howl that seemed to come from everywhere and nowhere.

Grunt and Hoot sprung to their feet, overturning their checker game. They backed into each other, spun around, and barked at each other.

The howling continued.

It was weird enough that faery dogs sounded louder the farther away they were. Knowing that Danny could pull off the same trick was a little unsettling.

But the pooka kept on barking and howling, and the sound got louder or softer seemingly at random as he loped through the woods.

Grunt pointed the direction he thought the sound was coming from.

Hoot disagreed and pointed in a different direction.

Any time now.

Danny barked, loud and angry.

Hoot hooted.

Grunt grunted.

Hoot slapped Grunt on the shoulder and pulled him off into the woods.

Taylor whipped around the side of the building. The door was still open. Inside, Gwenllian was already heading for the door to see what the commotion was all about.

Taylor stepped inside. She let her glamour fall away. Gwenllian looked up with a start.

"What are you doing here?"

"Trying to stop a war. Can you move?"

She breezed past into the open air. "I can do anything."

Taylor wanted to say something about that, but they had to get moving. "What do you know about Athlan's defenses?"

"Apart from the ape-men?" she shrugged.

"There are some bronze statues guarding the place Topside. I've got some friends who'd appreciate it if we could find a way to turn them off."

A Bigfoot shrieked in the woods. It didn't sound like either Hoot or Grunt, which meant the first two creatures were in on the hunt now, too. The odds were getting longer and longer.

"I don't know anything about that," Gwenllian said. "If you want to help your friends, I suggest we get moving." She spun around and charged toward the path.

Taylor muttered, "Right."

317

Neither of them dared conjure faery fire. Taylor led Gwenllian down the path as quickly as she dared in the dark.

She kept her ears open for the sounds of Grunt, Hoot, or the other Bigfoots stomping through the woods.

They made it back to the creek bank. The path was broader here, but more exposed. Taylor made sure Gwenllian kept up. She seemed to be holding her own.

Somewhere around there was the the path up the other bank that led to the exit.

But something wasn't right. Ahead, Taylor saw lumbering shapes in the darkness.

"This way!" she whispered. She slipped off the path and into the woods with Gwenllian just a step behind.

Someone hissed and scrambled out of Taylor's way.

Danny! He had staked out the same patch of woods.

"You're late," he whispered.

"Thanks for waiting."

All four Bigfoots had congregated where the path crossed the creek. They gestured and grunted and growled at each other.

Taylor studied them. They weren't exactly standing guard, but there was no way past them. "Any ideas?"

"I take it that's the way out?" Gwenllian said.

Taylor nodded.

"Then let's not dawdle."

Before Taylor could stop her, Gwenllian emerged from their cover. She spread her arms.

The Bigfoots turned to gape at her.

She spat an incantation: "*Ha nesegi sua!*"

The bank erupted in flames. Taylor shielded her eyes from a blaze as bright as the sun.

Danny cursed.

Bigfoots howled and shrieked and scattered in every direction, some with their fur on fire. One of them tumbled into the creek. Burning embers flitted everywhere.

A spark landed on Taylor's leather jacket. She brushed it away.

"It would seem the coast is clear," Gwenllian said.

Another spark had kindled a smoky fire in the underbrush. Taylor moved to stomp it out.

"Taylor, we ain't got time for that," Danny said.

"But—"

"Taylor, the kolowas are coming."

"The what? Oh." The Bigfoots had, indeed, gotten over the first shock of Gwenllian's fire ball. One still lay in the creek, dazed, and another was nowhere to be seen.

Two of them lumbered cautiously forward.

"All right," Taylor said.

They crossed the stream. Once more, she felt her magic dwindling away.

She led the way. Gwenllian followed her, and Danny took up the rear. Behind them, the woods were starting to burn.

The ape-men were gaining on them. The first one splashed into the creek as Danny scrambled up the opposite bank.

Taylor trudged up the path as fast as she could, avoiding exposed roots and low-lying branches.

She made it to the outcropping of rock and stretched her hand toward the brass knob.

There was a sudden rustling in the trees. Someone else had arrived, and Taylor had a good idea who.

"Not so fast!"

They spun around. Athlan stood there, his face dusted with ash, his war club at the ready, and flanked by two of his Bigfoots. A third—Hoot—still smoldering where Gwenllian's fire struck his back, was rushing to join the others.

"Goodbye, Athlan Tastanagi," Gwenllian said. She pushed forward, though Taylor didn't need the hint.

"After them!" Athlan shouted.

Taylor grabbed the brass knob and felt her body being sucked out of Athlan's domain.

Chapter 30

Everybody Piles On

William watched his sister with growing concern.

She was doing her best, throwing everything she had into the wind spell she'd used against the three-headed vulture at Halloween. But after five minutes of conjuring, William wasn't sure it would be enough.

"You're doing fine, sis," he said.

She nodded, but didn't break off the incantation.

The statues moved about, probing William and Jill's defenses.

Now that the banishing spell had run its course, they could only rely on the magic circle to hold them back.

That and the miniature hurricane Jill was whipping around the green. The statues weren't ever fast, but walking against a gale-force wind slowed them down even more.

More than once, one of them simply toppled over, or even rolled a time or two—only to regain its footing and rejoin the assault.

Jill just kept chanting:

Amou aneme phthaneme pneuma ventibus thoou.
Amou aneme phthaneme pneuma ventibus thoou.
Amou aneme phthaneme pneuma ventibus thoou.
Amou aneme phthaneme pneuma ventibus thoou.

"She can't keep this up!" Ayoka called. She swung her war club nervously. "I'm rested; I can fight them again."

321

"Another minute," William said. He looked up. The moon and stars were hidden behind dark and angry clouds.

"Up!" he shouted. "Push the wind up!"

Jill gave him a look that said, "What do you think I've been doing?" But she extended her arms and gestured upwards, like she was lifting the whirlwind into the sky.

It was working. It just wasn't working fast enough—and Jill was about to give out. She might not make it another minute.

William edged over to Ayoka. "We need a backup plan," he whispered. He hoped Jill didn't hear him.

And he wished to heaven he wasn't the one wearing the red shirt.

Jill kept chanting. There was no mistaking the strain in her voice.

Ayoka looked at him. There was defiance in her eyes, but also desperation. "I don't—"

There was a commotion on the green—shouting in the darkness.

"Outta my way!" a man's voice called.

Ayoka raised her war club like a torch. Its light grew brighter, and William saw what was happening.

Somebody was wailing on a statue with his walking stick. He wore a bowler hat with a long turkey feather in the brim, with a single braid of long, black hair whipping across his back and falling almost to his ankles.

Oh, and he was maybe three and a half feet tall.

"Whoa!"

Another man, no taller than the first and with skin literally as white as snow, dodged and ducked and ran among the statues. It seemed to confuse them; he'd get close enough to slap them in the face or kick them in the gut, then he'd run off, and they'd follow him.

A third man, maybe a little bigger than the other two and definitely fatter, just plowed into statues and knocked them over.

"Are you folks friends of Miss Hellebore?" the little man in the bowler hat shouted. He slammed his walking stick into the shoulder of the little girl in the bathing suit.

"That's right!" Ayoka called. "I take it you're the backup she told us about?"

"You got it!" the fat little person said. A bronze dog statue barreled into him, pushing him backward with an "oof!"

"Sorry we're late!" the albino little person added.

"That's...not what I was expecting," William said.

Lightning flashed—and it was close. The thunderclap came before the sky had even returned to dark.

William looked skyward and smiled.

"Way to go, Jill. We're almost there."

Ayoka gasped. "She's making it rain."

"Not technically," William said. "Air cools as it rises. And cool air can't hold as much moisture as warm. Force enough of this foggy air upward, let it cool..."

"It's brilliant," Ayoka said, her eyes widening. She smiled. William blushed.

The first drop of rain kissed William's cheek.

He turned to Ayoka. She was holding out her hand.

The rain began as a gentle drizzle. It wouldn't be long now.

Running water would collapse a witch's aura faster than anything, Maymay had said. That's why William showered after every lesson; it got the magic off him.

And if William was right, running water would also break the connection between the magical constructs and the focus objects that gave them form.

"It's all right, sis. I think you can stop n—"

Jill slumped over. William was at her side in a heartbeat.

"I'm okay," she mumbled. "Just...tired..."

"You did great! Look!"

On the green, half of the constructs had already disappeared. The ones tied to statues close by held on the longest. When they vanished, William fell to his knees and laughed. He was getting drenched in the rain, but it didn't matter.

323

"We did it!" he exulted. The rain was already slowing down, but it had done its work. It washed away the edges of the circle of power. He felt the magical boundary fade away.

The three little folk darted under the shelter of the alcove. The one in the bowler hat looked annoyed. "You wanna give a guy some warning before you pull something like that?"

"You'll live, Wasko," the albino said. "You needed a bath."

He bowed toward William, Ayoka, and Jill as they huddled at the center of the magic circle.

"You'll have to excuse Wasko," the albino said. "He's an ass..."

"Hey!"

"...But he'll draw fresh magic from the Wonder soon enough, and then he'll get over it."

"But he'll still be an ass," the fat little person added, grinning. "By the way, you got anything to eat around here?"

"Couple of snack bars," William said. "In the bag over there."

"Ah! Don't mind if I do!"

"Uh," the albino said. He looked around the alcove with a curious expression. "We came to help Miss Hellebore?"

Ayoka looked toward the back wall, the rough chalk outline that marked the portal into the Wonder.

"She went looking for another way out."

William gritted his teeth. "Do you think we ought to go looking for her?" He knew the answer—of course, they needed to go. She could be in trouble. He just didn't like the idea. He promised Maymay he wouldn't set foot in the faery realm. Jill's experience last summer told him everything he needed to know about the Wonder.

He looked at the chalk marks on the far wall. They might as well have been a sign that said, "Horrible death straight ahead."

Jill said, "I'm up for it if you are."

He bit his lip. "I don't see how we have a ch—"

Taylor suddenly appeared. Wide-eyed and frantic, she took in the situation: the three exhausted kids huddled on the cement, the absence of attacking bronze statues.

"Clear out!" she yelled, barreling on.

As she spoke, a second figure appeared behind her: a blond woman in a white gown, now tattered and dingy with dirt. William figured this had to be Mrs. Birdsong, the woman who'd been kidnapped.

Then came Danny, stumbling forward so fast he almost lost his balance. "Run!" he shouted. "Kolowas!"

William grabbed Jill and pulled her to her feet.

"What about koalas?" Jill said.

"Beats me," William answered.

The portal opened again.

William stared in awe of what came through. It must have been nearly nine feet tall, apelike, but walking perfectly upright. It bellowed in anger and charged at Taylor, Danny, and Mrs. Birdsong.

The foul stench of the creature hit him a second later, and William tried his best not to gag.

Just then, a second creature appeared. A third—and the third one smoked like it had recently been on fire.

"Run!" Danny called again.

William and Jill broke right; Ayoka broke left. The little people had spread into the green.

The three creatures stormed out of the alcove.

"Those are not koalas!" William cried.

One of them took a swipe at Ayoka. She rolled out of its reach, then swung low, catching another one in the shin. It howled and bounced on one foot.

"Not koalas, kolowas!" Ayoka shouted back. "Man-eating ogres!"

"Is that supposed to make me feel better?" William shouted.

Somehow, William's hand had found the bag of banishing powder in his coat pocket. With no other way to defend himself, he flung a handful at the nearest creature and roared, "*Hexiphore!*"

Its eyes crossed. It twitched and danced around like it had either fallen into a patch of poison ivy or had a bad case of diarrhea.

William really hoped it was the first. At any rate, it hopped away, moaning and gurgling.

The ogres had thrown the entire green into chaos. One of them was chasing the three little people, trying to squash them under his enormous feet in a deadly game of Whack-a-Mole.

Danny and Taylor baited another one, bigger than the others. Danny waved his arms to draw the creature away from Taylor. Then Taylor leaped in and yanked at its hair. It roared as it turned on Taylor, but that's when Danny lunged, smacked it on the leg, and bounded away.

The last ogre, still reeling from William's banishing spell, threw everybody into a panic by stomping about, threatening now to crush Mrs. Birdsong's head with his outstretched arm, now to crush Ayoka between its own massive body and the brick wall where she'd positioned herself.

Jill grabbed William's arm. "The portal is opening again!"

"More koalas?"

No. A single man appeared at the far wall. From the way he looked, he had to be Athlan. He was short, muscular Native American, tattooed, decked out in buckskin trousers and a loose-fitting cotton shirt, both trimmed with black and red. He was bald except for a feathered scalplock. A quiver of arrows and a bow were slung across his back, and he held a flaming war club in his hand.

He plowed into William and flung him to the ground without slowing down.

Taylor barely managed a shield spell to deflect the Bigfoot that tried to smash her head in. Instead, the beast's paw glanced away without touching her.

It was bigger than the others—and stinkier, too.

326

"This way, Stinky!" she taunted. She made a move for the wall while throwing the most powerful addlement she could against the foul-smelling brute. It lowered its head and lunged forward until skull met bricks.

Stinky let out a confused yelp as he collapsed on the pavement.

Then, as Taylor glanced toward the alcove, her heart sank. Athlan had just appeared. He threw William to the ground like a rag doll and stormed into the center of the green.

"There he is!" Taylor cried.

She wasn't the only one who'd seen the Great Tastanagi. Far to her right, Taylor saw Gwenllian Birdsong just as she thrust her arm forward. By the light of the shopping center's security lights, she saw the air ripple as the blast arced from Gwenllian to Athlan.

He deflected the attack with no problem—which didn't surprise Taylor.

She looked around. Ayoka had landed a solid blow against Hoot and managed to set his arm on fire. He shrieked and bounded toward the fountain.

Haggler, Pete, and Wasko had somehow succeeded in hog-tying Grunt with a thin, silvery rope.

Danny, now in his goat form, charged toward Athlan, only to be yanked off his hooves by a ghostly fist that moved at the Tastanagi's command.

"Farewell, Selena Hellebore," he said with a courtly bow.

"Not so fast!" Taylor said.

He chuckled. "You have no idea..."

Before he could blink away, Taylor shouted, "Coward!"

That stopped him. Taylor figured an insult to his honor was the only thing that would.

Ayoka appeared at Taylor's side. The three little folk took up positions behind Athlan. Danny, back in his everyday form and with his eyes aglow, held balls of fire—real, burning fire—in each hand.

327

"Coward?" Athlan said. His demeanor said he wasn't afraid. "Because I won't waste my time against..." he did a quick head-count "...the six of you?"

"Make that eight!" William called. He had his grandmother's magic wand trained on Athlan. Jill stood at his side, ready with a fistful of grayish powder.

Athlan scoffed. "You're out of your depth, Taylor Smart. You're simply not strong enough to defeat me. And since I have nothing to prove to any of you..."

He was about to blink. Taylor knew it. He had refreshed his magic after passing through the stream. If he wasn't already back to full power, he was close enough.

She met eyes with Wasko and his buddies. Wasko nodded.

"Code Mabel!" she cried.

The little folk snapped their fingers, and the green was suddenly alive with the loudest, most raucous, out-of-tune Rockabilly opera music imaginable. The sounds of dying cattle would have been a soothing lullaby in comparison.

Athlan doubled over and clasped his ears.

Danny flung his fire balls at the nunnehi, who deflected them with a shield spell and instinctively fired a blast in Danny's direction. Danny leaped out of the way, rolling across the pavement and coming up unhurt.

Taylor grinned.

After all, even a trained nunnehi warrior needed time to recharge after a blast.

"Now!" she shouted above the din.

Danny added to the fireworks with a stunning spell—a spectacle of lights, fire, and crackling explosions.

Jill ran close enough to land her handful of dust in Athlan's face. She shouted "*Hexiphore!*" with a satisfied grin.

Athlan started to weave and twitch. He lurched backward, trying to escape.

William and Ayoka attacked at nearly the same time. William aimed his magic wand and hissed "*Bazagra!*" Athlan fell to his knees at precisely the moment Ayoka swept at him with her club. He raised his arm to defend, but this time the shield spell didn't form—his magic had been zapped, just like Taylor's had been not too far from here a month ago. The club struck his arm with an unsettling crack.

William hauled Athlan up and trapped him in a full Nelson. Ayoka grabbed his discarded war club and flung it out of reach. The Tastanagi squirmed and wriggled and convulsed under the effects of Jill's banishing spell. It really did uncomfortable-looking things when the one being banished wasn't allowed to leave.

Taylor had zero sympathy for him.

Quite the contrary, she wanted him to suffer. Athlan had hurt Danny and Claudia. He was pulling the sídhe and the nunnehi into war. He had betrayed the trust of people she cared about: Chief Tewa, Ayoka. Yes, even Tsisgwa.

And he had had made a fool of her.

"Okay, so I'm not strong enough—yet..."

She noticed her fists clenched. She had gathered magic enough for a blast, and it felt like a big one.

"But at least I know where I stand..." She glanced at Jill. "...and, as you can see, I've got a few tricks up my sleeve."

Her eyes bore into Athlan.

He shivered. The temperature was falling fast. Taylor could see his labored breath escape his mouth and nose like fog and waft away.

He never looked afraid, though. He seemed poised—or at least as poised as you can look when your legs have turned to jelly and your whole body itches.

"The sídhe are not known for mercy," Athlan said.

"Are you daring me?" Taylor said. She raised her right hand. Magical energy swirled and crackled around it.

"Taylor, no," Jill said, her voice measured but concerned. "We've got him. That's what matters."

"But he's right," Taylor said. Her voice dripped venom. "We—my people—do keep score, don't we? We defend our

329

honor. Anybody who challenges us, betrays us, *humiliates* us, will be made to pay. Isn't that right, Athlan Tastanagi?"

She let her presence flow freely, wave after wave, and never broke eye contact.

Beside her, Danny moaned and shuddered.

William called her name—a question or perhaps a prayer she wouldn't do anything she'd regret.

"That's what you believe, isn't it?"

"Do what you must."

"I intend to."

"Taylor," Jill said again, stronger.

Taylor took several deep breaths. She felt the magic tingling, dancing across her fingertips. Athlan glared at her, daring her to take her best shot.

With all her heart, she wanted to.

"Taylor, no," Jill said.

She clenched her fists. The swirl of magic was almost too much to contain.

Then she glanced at Jill and thought about the kind of person she wanted to be.

"Hold!" a voice called.

All eyes turned upon Tsisgwa as he sprinted toward the green from the back entrance to the shopping center. Behind him came more than a dozen other warriors, all with war clubs or bows at the ready.

Beside him was Mr. Ramos in his bomber jacket and holding his magic staff.

At the back of the procession thumped Blue the giant.

Taylor lowered her hand.

Jill placed an arm around Taylor's waist.

For the first time, Athlan seemed concerned.

Tsisgwa motioned for two of his warriors to take custody of Athlan. William gladly backed away. He blew out a heavy breath as he stared in wonder at the sight of his social studies teacher

330

rubbing elbows with fae warriors. He skirted the edge of the green, keeping his eyes peeled for any further signs of trouble.

"You get used to it," Taylor said. She wasn't sure William heard her.

Tsisgwa immediately turned to Mrs. Birdsong.

"Matron," he said, bowing reverently. "Tsisgwa Imathla at your service. On behalf of the Chiefs of Ichisi, please accept our humblest and sincerest apologies for this incident. Athlan was most assuredly not acting on orders from his superiors." As he spoke, he glanced sidewise at his former commander. He could barely contain his fury as he continued. "By decree of Chief Coloma, he has already been stripped of his command. We will transport him to Ichisi, where he will face the severest punishment our law will allow."

As Tsisgwa spoke, Mrs. Birdsong listened appreciatively. She nodded and looked at him with genuine admiration.

When he finished his speech, she said, "I am...gratified to hear this, Tsisgwa Imathla. But I would have never believed your people would stoop to such tactics. Despite our past differences, I have never doubted the nunnehi are an honorable people."

Tsisgwa bowed, acknowledging the compliment.

"Of course, I will communicate this to my people straightaway."

"It would be our pleasure to escort you home, Matron."

Mrs. Birdsong nodded. "Then we should go—provided my assistant, Claudia, is well."

"I'm told she's doing fine," Tsisgwa said.

"More encouraging news," Mrs. Birdsong said. "Blue, please attend to Claudia until she has recovered and then help her return with my things."

The giant nodded. He approached Athlan and stooped down until he was nearly walking on all fours.

He looked Athlan in the eye.

"You," he growled. Not loud, but definitely angry. "Hurt."

He bared his teeth and set one massive hand atop Athlan's head. It was all his guards could to do keep him standing.

"Claudia." He emitted a low rumble, something felt as much as heard. He could have crushed Athlan's head like a peanut shell. Instead, he held it still so he could look Athlan in the eye.

Blue stared at him long and hard. He removed his hand, pushing Athlan and his guards backward, and rose to his full height. He made the Bigfoots look as short as fifth-graders. Wasko, Pete, and Haggler gazed up in amazement that anything that huge could exist in the world.

Then Blue lumbered away and stood at the back of Tsisgwa's men with his arms crossed.

Tsisgwa nodded. His men returned the gesture, and Athlan and his guards disappeared in a flash of superheated dust.

Tsisgwa motioned to other warriors, who took custody of the three Bigfoots.

Ayoka ran to her cousin. "I knew you'd come!" she said, beaming.

"I'm sorry it took so long," he said. To Taylor, he added, "The Chiefs finally settled down enough to realize your theory was worth looking into."

Taylor approached him. "I'm glad you could finally make it," she said.

Tsisgwa gestured to another team of warriors to investigate the portal to Athlan's domain. With that done, he answered Taylor. "Chief Efau's seers couldn't find Athlan anywhere. They assumed he was cloaked deep in the Wonder."

"But things were going crazy Topside," Taylor added.

Tsisgwa nodded. "And eventually—based on your note to the Chiefs—they decided to look...here." He looked around with an expression that said he wasn't entirely sure the kind of place he was in. "We owe you greatly, Taylor."

"I'll take you up on that," she said.

A bright light and the sound of a car engine interrupted her thought. Headlights pierced the fog. Then she saw the shape of a familiar green minivan.

"Dad?"

Chapter 31

Something Doesn't Fit

It took William a while to focus on anything other than the twelve-foot-tall giant edging around the back of the band of warriors.

Then he noticed Mr. Ramos. His social studies teacher seemed oddly in place surrounded by faery Native American warriors and three-foot-tall...leprechauns? Dwarves? He was going to have to start making a list to keep everybody straight.

As Tsisgwa, Taylor, and Mrs. Birdsong talked, Ayoka approached him and Jill. Her war club was no longer engulfed in flames, and she was using it like a walking stick.

"I was right," she said.

William knitted his brow.

She pointed at his chest. "Red and black. The colors of a warrior."

"You were pretty awesome yourself," Jill said.

She shook her head. "I'm nunnehi. I fight for what's right; it's what we do. But you two...." She now looked Jill in the eyes. "Strong magic runs in your family."

"Our friend needed us," Jill said. William understood that was all the explanation Jill could offer. It was one of the things he liked about his sister.

"Strong magic and strong loyalty," Ayoka said. "A powerful combination."

She focused once more on William.

"Maybe we'll meet again."

333

"Maybe," William said. "I can't say it's been fun exactly, but—"

He forgot what he was going to say when Ayoka leaned in to kiss him on the cheek.

"Till next time," she said, and walked away, smiling.

"Yeah."

William never knew how long he just stood there lost in his thoughts, but the flash of headlights finally shook him awake. Taylor's dad was pulling into a parking spot near the green.

He heard Taylor say "Dad?" and watched as Tsisgwa motioned for his men to stand down. Three archers had already taken aim at the vehicle.

The first person out of the minivan was Maymay. She was halfway to him and Jill when his dad emerged from the middle seat and Mr. Smart finally opened his door.

"Come here, you two!" Maymay called. She grabbed a grandchild in each arm and hugged them tight. "Are you all right? What happened?"

The two dads stumbled forward in a daze.

As Jill talked with Maymay, William drifted toward his dad.

At the same time, Mr. Ramos approached them.

"Mr. Matthews, Mr. Smart," he said. "It's a pleasure to see you again."

They both stared at him.

"Dad, you remember Mr. Ramos? From school?"

"Uh..." Mr. Matthews said. He offered his hand on autopilot.

"I'm sure this is all quite strange to you," Mr. Ramos continued, his staff gleaming with golden light.

William looked around. Native American warriors milled about. Some were working magical repairs on the dents and scorch marks the battle had left. Others wiped away the last of Jill and William's chalk circle. The giant was hauling the last of the ape-men toward the portal to Athlan's domain. Wasko, Pete, and Haggler stood in front of the fountain, arguing about something. The walls were scorched in several places, and there

334

was a gaping hole where one of the Bigfoots had buried its thick head.

About that time, Taylor slammed into her dad and gave him a fierce hug.

"Taylor, what—? Who—?"

"These are my friends," Taylor said. "And...some other guys I don't know. And the lady in white...she's...uh...."

"I don't care," Mr. Smart said, and hugged her back. "Just tell me my little girl is okay."

"I'm fine Dad," she said.

"You didn't call. We were worried."

"I guess we lost track of time."

"Well...if you're ready, we should go."

"Just let me say goodbye to Danny and Ayoka."

William held back as Maymay, Jill, and the two dads made their way back to the car. There was something he needed to know. She followed after Taylor.

"You...could have hurt that guy, couldn't you? I mean...bad."

She sighed. "Maybe."

"But...you wouldn't."

"You don't know that, William." Taylor's face darkened. She looked defeated.

"Sure I do."

"I'm not what you think I am. Your grandma is right.... I'm dangerous."

"I'd agree with that," William said. Taylor's icy blue eyes flashed. He threw up his hands. "But in a good way! Ayoka just told me her people fight for what's right. Isn't that what we've all just been doing?"

Taylor bit her lip.

"You can't be other than what you are, Taylor. I get that. But aren't you the same as Ayoka? Or Danny? Or even those little guys?" Wasko and the others had finished their argument and were laughing by the side of the fountain. "Don't you think you get to choose?"

She sighed. Then she smiled at him. Her eyes glistened. "You're pretty cool, you know that?" She bumped shoulders with him and then looked toward the minivan.

"We'd better go," she said.

Two weeks later, Taylor sat on her log on the edge of the woods, eyes closed, forcing herself to take slow, shallow breaths. She didn't force her consciousness to expand beyond the confines of her head. She simply let it happen: her awareness of her surroundings drifted gently outward like flotsam on the surf.

The sun kissed the tops of the trees, splashing the turquoise sky with broad fingers of purplish pink.

With her eyes still closed, her consciousness brushed against a tiny, shivering body—a lizard scurrying into its hole for the night.

She centered her thoughts on her true name.

A blackbird passed overhead. For a fleeting second, Taylor imagined herself flitting through the air, seeing the world through its eyes, taking in the view from above the treetops.

And then another presence crept into the edge of her consciousness.

"Mrs. Birdsong," she said. She opened her eyes and found the woman she had named walking slowly and gracefully toward her. The last fleeting embers of the faery ring were dying in the distance as it settled back to its dormant state. The Gentry-woman was dressed, as usual, in a gown of diaphanous white that seemed too filmy for the evening breeze.

The older fae affected a slight bow. "I was under the impression you had a bodyguard."

"I convinced them to leave me alone," Taylor said. "I didn't expect to see you...ever."

"You left before I could say goodbye." She sat down beside Taylor. "Osanda has withdrawn her challenge to my appointment."

336

Taylor raised an eyebrow. "And the houses have voted?" Taylor said.

Gwenllian shook her head. "The Summer Assize is still two months away. But I'm confident they'll now see the wisdom of the Primus's recommendation."

"Congratulations," Taylor said. "I won't lie: I would have preferred Osanda. But I appreciate what you said that night, how you respected the nunnehi and that you weren't looking for revenge after what Athlan did."

"It was merely the truth."

"I know. Our Kind don't lie easily." Taylor straddled the log so she could look at Mrs. Birdsong head-on.

"I don't believe it when they say you're just going to be Wakefire's puppet," Taylor said.

"Of course not."

For several seconds, neither spoke. The night sounds of the frogs and crickets began to encroach upon the silence.

"I neglected to thank you," Mrs. Birdsong said at last. Her smile was broad and bright.

"There's no need," Taylor said. "I take it there won't be a war between the daoine sídhe and the nunnehi?"

Mrs. Birdsong shook her head. "Hotheads on both sides have called for it, but diplomacy will prevail. The Summer Court is seeking satisfaction, and I'm sure the nunnehi will comply with any reasonable demand."

"They'll want everybody to know that Athlan was working alone. The best way to do that is to give the Summers a peace offering."

"Exactly."

Taylor looked Mrs. Birdsong square in the eye. The fae didn't lie easily, but that didn't mean they couldn't be deceptive. And Taylor had a theory she wanted to test, something that had become more and more obvious to her in the past couple of weeks.

"Nope," Taylor said, "he wasn't taking orders from his Chiefs." She sat upright. "Or anyone else. Right?"

Mrs. Birdsong crossed her legs. She dropped her smile and regarded Taylor with concern. "How are your friends?"

"They'll be fine," she said. She thought, *And you're changing the subject.*

"You all risked a great deal on my behalf," Mrs. Birdsong said. "Without your help, there's no telling what Athlan might have done to me."

Taylor stood up. She took a breath and put the slightest impulse of presence into her next words.

"It turned out all right in the end."

"Thanks to you."

Taylor frowned, then met Mrs. Birdsong's gaze. "I'm not so sure I had much to do with it."

The older fae leaned back from Taylor's presence but maintained her easygoing smile.

"I've been thinking about everything that happened," Taylor continued. "Something doesn't add up."

"Oh?"

"The more I think about it, it seems we had a pretty easy time breaking you free. Ridiculously easy, if you think about it."

Now it was Gwenllian's turn to sit silently. Her smile faltered, but only a little.

"I mean, that house where he was keeping you? The door was just standing open the whole time."

"I doubt the guards would have let me leave."

"You could have walked right past them," Taylor said. "I thought there would at least be iron bars in the walls to sap your magic, but no. Nothing. The worst they did to you was serve you lousy coffee."

"You were there when Athlan attacked me, Miss Hellebore. Or should I say, attacked *us.*"

Taylor nodded. "You seemed to recover soon enough. And he gave *me* every chance to escape. And then he went out of his way to remind me about the candle shop in the mall. It was almost like he wanted to leave a clue, to lead me—or somebody—straight to him."

338

"You have a vivid imagination."

"Guilty as charged," Taylor said. "But still, there were a lot of people who favored Osanda, weren't there? Powerful people. Despite the fact that the Fairchilds wanted you. Maybe *because* the Fairchilds wanted you."

"In uncertain times, people hold on to what they know," Mrs. Birdsong said. "When all is said and done, they trust Belas Wakefire."

"Uh-huh," Taylor said. "And when times got even more uncertain—the threat of war with the nunnehi, for example—I guess they decided they trusted him even more."

"Are you accusing me of something, Miss Hellebore?"

"Who? Me?" Taylor scoffed. "I'm just a kid. What do I know about fae politics?" She leaned in. "It's just...people wanted to believe in Osanda. A lot of people. Oh, maybe not all the members of the Gentry, but pisgies, pookas, little folk...she had a lot of people in her corner. This bad blood with the nunnehi has been around for what? A thousand years?"

"More or less."

"Osanda was getting through to people. For the first time, some of them could see a different way, a peaceful way. And some of them really, really liked that idea."

"She is naïve," Mrs. Birdsong said.

"I'd say your abduction proved that pretty convincingly." Taylor crossed her arms.

"Just so."

"In fact, it pretty much sucked the life out of Osanda's whole campaign, didn't it? I bet she doesn't have too many friends these days." She smirked and let her hands fall to her lap. "No, I bet the Gentry have been bending over backwards to get away from her. Nobody is going to back her at Court any time soon. At least, nobody with political ambitions of their own—and I'm thinking that's pretty much everybody."

Mrs. Birdsong answered Taylor's smirk with one of her own.

"But now," she pressed on, "the Summer Court is united—and from what you've told me, they're going to get something out of the nunnehi, too."

"You act as if this were the only possible outcome, Miss Hellebore."

"No, it could have ended differently," Taylor admitted. "Maybe your abduction blows up into an international incident. Both sides push for war. What happens then?"

Mrs. Birdsong started to say something, but Taylor cut her off.

"I'll tell you what happens. For one thing, that would have given Wakefire a built-in excuse for anything he wants to pull—not to mention an argument against anything Winter might be planning. The Chiefdom would need to present a united front. I bet there's a whole section of Eldritch Law about bringing dishonor to a Primus in time of war."

"Your grasp of the Eldritch Law is wanting," Mrs. Birdsong said. She smiled and added, "But not entirely inaccurate."

"So, like my dad says, you don't change horses in midstream. If war breaks out, Belas Wakefire's approval rating goes up—and with it, your chances for a seat on the Triad. And even if both sides find a reason not to fight, everyone has been reminded of the nunnehi threat. Osanda looks stupid—naïve, as you say—for even suggesting peace. And, once again, you look like the better choice for the Triad."

"Well, that is certainly an interesting theory, Miss Hellebore."

"There's just one thing I don't understand," she said.

"Only one?"

"If I'm right, and you staged your own kidnapping, it means Athlan was in on it. And that doesn't make sense."

"Indeed," Mrs. Birdsong said. "Why would Athlan Tastanagi help solidify the power of the Summer Court of Arradherry? Surely he'd have been more pleased to see a reformer like Osanda installed than me."

"Maybe it was a chance he was willing to take. He's a warrior through and through, second in rank only to Chief Coloma. If there is war, he gains power. He gains honor."

Mrs. Birdsong wagged a finger. "But if the diplomats prevail—or worse, if he is exposed—he loses everything."

"That's why I think there's still a piece missing. Athlan took a risk, maybe the biggest risk in the history of ever. Sure, it might have worked out for him, but it was more likely to blow up in his face—and that's exactly what happened."

"Not everyone thinks through their decisions, Miss Hellebore. The fact that you continue to press this line of discussion with me confirms this fact."

"It cost Athlan everything," Taylor said. She was through playing around. "Why did he help you?"

Mrs. Birdsong arched an eyebrow.

"Well?"

She slid up to Taylor. Her smile returned—which didn't do anything for Taylor's state of mind.

She bent down to whisper in Taylor's ear.

"He owed me a favor," she said.

Taylor forgot to breathe for at least five seconds.

"He led a scouting party against Dunhoughkey many years ago. They were captured. He had no choice but to bargain with me for the freedom of his men."

Taylor sat there, stunned.

"He was young and inexperienced then," Mrs. Birdsong said. "And not a very strong negotiator."

Taylor swallowed.

Mrs. Birdsong stood up. "So long, Selena Hellebore," she said. "And I do thank you for all you've done."

She strolled confidently toward the ring from which she had emerged.

When Taylor finally remembered to breathe, it came out as a whispered curse.

The wind picked up, suddenly cold and biting. Taylor took another breath.

341

She started toward home. She didn't know what was going to come next, but she was suddenly, painfully aware that Her Kind kept their promises, no matter the cost.

She owed a favor to Mara. One of these days, her grandmother would call that favor in.

The sun slipped down behind the trees.

Taylor walked home in silence.